MARCIE

Mary Peters

ISBN: 978-1-78003-820-9

Printed and published in the UK

Author Essentials Ltd
4 The Courtyard
South Street
Falmer
BN1 9PQ

A catalogue record of this book is available from
the British Library

Cover design by Jacqueline Abromeit

Acknowledgements

To Deborah Folland, a special thanks for all your help and guidance.

To my dear husband Malcolm for all his help and support and my family in the North-East, especially my sister Joan Bell.

Heartfelt thank yous to my friends Maria Henderson and Zoe Kenny, and David Fenton who had the patience of a saint fixing my computer.

Also by the Author

Autobiography
Neither Use Nor Ornament

Children's fiction
Ollie the Orange Otter

Chapter One

Marcie Thomas lived with her parents in Carmarthen, South Wales, in a pretty little village called Trap, on the banks of the River Cennen four miles north of Llandeilo. The village sits on the western edge of Brecon Beacons National Park. Life was very quiet in this sleepy little village till that awful September morning when Tom and Nellie Thomas left Marcie to look after her eleven year-old brother Jack while they went shopping. Jack was playing outside with his football and ran into the middle of the road to pick it up. Marcie had been daydreaming and taken her eyes off him for just a moment when a lorry came down the road at speed and poor Jack, a sickly child from birth and suffering from a rare heart condition, didn't stand a chance.

Marcie's parents were devastated. Proud and reserved, they had always kept themselves to themselves and believed that showing emotion was a sign of weakness and something definitely not to be displayed in public, so the funeral was a quiet affair with just a few neighbours attending, and there was a good spread afterwards.

Following Jack's death life was never quite the same for Marcie as her parents blamed her for their loss. She always knew Jack was their favourite. Excelling at school, he was an academic child who was always willing to please, never answering back, the centre of their world. But life for her was to become a lot tougher.

She could never seem to concentrate at school and lacked self-confidence although she always put on a cheery face. She had a lovely disposition and to add to that stunning looks – long, black, curly hair, petite features and big brown eyes – she brought a smile to the face of anyone who crossed her path. Everyone in the village loved her and although she was only sixteen thought she had a good head on her shoulders and was a joy to be with, unlike her parents who were like the devil incarnate. They didn't have a good word to say about anyone and criticized everyone they came into contact with. Even the vicar from the local church often gave a sermon with reference to them. 'What you reap you will sew. Be kind to

1

the less fortunate people in life,' and his eyes would be focused on Mr and Mrs Thomas sitting in the front pew.

The family lived in a stone cottage which had three bedrooms, a small kitchen and a sparse lounge. It was quite dilapidated inside and in need of a lot of repairs as money was tight, but the place was kept spotless as Nellie, a proud woman and a force to be reckoned with, liked to keep her standards up. You could say she was above her station pretending to be something she wasn't. The large garden was a joy to behold as she put her heart and soul into it, trying to make a good impression on the neighbours who passed by though never crossed her threshold. She kept herself to herself and they knew it.

Tom on the other hand was a broken man who had endured years of nagging from his wife and went along with anything she said just for an easy life. He loved his job as the local postman as it gave him an escape from the barrage of abuse she inflicted on him with her sharp tongue. Life was tough and they had both had different visions of what they wanted their marriage to be when they first met twenty years earlier. Nellie had been a looker, pleasing to the eye, and there was an instant attraction when they first met at a party held by their neighbours, but their eventual marriage was more a case of two people longing for a better life and wanting to leave their pasts behind. Nellie had never seen eye to eye with her parents who had brought her up ruling her with a rod of iron, and being an only child she felt lonely and rejected, longing to escape the arguments and unhappiness she felt. Tom had also had a far from happy home life as his mother left him and his brother when they were young boys on the family farm and ran off with a musician. His father felt so much bitterness and hatred in his heart that he never let them forget what their mother had done. Work became his escape from all his emotions and he never showed the boys any love and affection, just strict discipline.

Nellie had delusions of grandeur being the determined woman she was, whereas her husband liked his laid back life with less responsibility and had no expectations of anything, choosing to do his day to day chores at the exact time every day. Nellie did some cleaning four days a week for a Mr and Mrs Clements who lived a mile away from their cottage, and that was a completely different environment. They were very well off and ran a beautiful hotel with eight bedrooms and stunning views over the valley, which had a river running through it.

At 45 years-old Nellie and her husband could easily be mistaken for a couple in their fifties. Life had changed for them both and sadly they didn't feel the need to look good for one another any longer. The love had gone and they were just going through the motions, but they were both of the opinion that you had to get on with things; in other words when you made your bed you had to lie in it. Nellie kept herself neat and tidy and wore her hair up in a bun but her clothes were dark and miserable, clinging against her thin body, and she never wore make-up as to her it was a waste of time. Her trust in men had gone; in her opinion dreams and desires were for stupid people, as her heart had hardened and no man would ever get close to her again. The light had gone out in her big brown eyes but her husband sometimes reflected back on the beauty he had first met and was filled with sadness, though he made no effort either as some days he never bothered to shave or change his clothing. A big strong six foot man with rugged good looks and thick, black, curly hair, he always looked like he had the world on his shoulders, and his face was full of lines which aged him. The only time he smiled was when he thought about his beloved son Jack.

Two years had passed since their son had died and Marcie was now eighteen and looking for work, but jobs were scarce in the village so her mum talked to the owners at the hotel she worked at and they agreed to take her on changing beds and helping out in the kitchen occasionally. But there was no escape from the watchful eye of her mother. She had worked for Mr and Mrs Clements for ten years and they thought highly of her work so standards had to be kept up so as not to bring shame on the family.

Ian, Mrs Clements son who was 25 was training to be a solicitor. He was extremely academic and very handsome but Marcie had met him on two occasions at the hotel around Christmas time when the family went for lunch as a thank you to Mrs Thomas for all her hard work during the year, and she had disliked him instantly as she thought he had a creepy look about him and a habit of staring. She was right because he caught her coming out of the upstairs toilet on one visit and tried to force himself on her. She struggled but managed to escape his tight grip. She didn't tell her mother as she knew she would never believe her story - she had always had great admiration and respect for her employers due to their hard work and achievements, and had always put them on a pedestal. On the other hand she never let Marcie forget how useless she was, just like her father, and she often called her the scum of the earth and the lowest of the low when things got really heated. Marcie knew she would always be blamed for the death of her beloved brother Jack, who could do no wrong, but she was grieving too; she loved him and life had been so much more bearable when he was around as he always managed to calm her parents down when they started to bicker.

Jane, who was Ian's sister and a similar age to Marcie, was a gentle soul who would go out of her way to help anyone, and she was so pretty with short blonde hair and an elfin, angelic face. She was training to be a nurse at the local hospital and lived in, but she would spend her day off at the hotel helping out her parents and she and Marcie got on very well, often spending their lunch break together.

It was Saturday morning and Marcie heard her mum shouting up the stairs. 'Come on you lazy bones; get up and come down for breakfast!' She knew when her parents were together at the weekend something was going to kick off; usually with them shouting abuse at each other.

'I'm coming, Mum,' and she went down the stone stairs and sat at the wooden bench. Her dad refused to sit at the table and sat by the coal fire instead, smoking his pipe and drinking his tea. Nellie hated the smell of tobacco in the house but that made her husband do it even more, telling her to shut up and get about her business.

Marcie knew it was now her turn for the insults. 'Look at you; what a mess you look. When did you last wash your hair or clean your bedroom? You're neither use nor ornament!' Her mum was in a filthy mood.

Tom went outside into the garden to get some peace; he got fed up with the arguments and bickering and left Marcie to take the brunt of it all. Eventually things calmed down and he went back inside. 'I sometimes wish we had never bought this property,' he said to his wife. 'We were doing alright renting. More bloody expense, I say.'

'Oh shut up,' she replied. 'If it wasn't for your gambling on the horses years ago we would have had some savings by now.' That wasn't strictly true because although he liked a flutter at the local

4

betting shop, the little a week he was left with after paying the bills also had to pay for this tobacco, so that was a bit exaggerated he thought. Tom never wanted much, just a quiet life with no fuss, but that was seen as weak by his wife who hated this attitude and felt trapped with a longing for something more.

Marcie often wondered why her father never came to her defence, choosing to say nothing, but she knew there were secrets in the family. He had never shown her any fatherly love and affection and she had often wondered if maybe she was adopted.

'Marcie, have you cleaned the bedrooms and done all your chores?' her mother asked.

'Nearly, but I haven't done your room yet. Give me strength,' Marcie muttered under her breath. Her mum's constant nagging was getting on her nerves.

Nellie slept in her son's room after he had died and she was very particular that nothing was to be moved. There were still his toys displayed on the shelves and his clothes were still in the wardrobe. 'Don't touch anything; I will see to that,' she replied. 'Just hoover it.'

When Marcie had finished her chores she decided to phone her friend Elsie who she had known since primary school and ask if she could go over.

'No problem,' she said. 'My mum and dad will do us some dinner.' Marcie loved Elsie's parents Jean and Keith, they were a joy to be with; such a happy family. Elsie was the oldest and she had younger twin brothers.

'I'm off, Mum, see you later.'

'Don't be late back,' Marcie's mother said, 'I won't wait up for you.'

It was a fifteen minute bus ride away and when Marcie arrived the family were so pleased to see her. They had all grown to love her, calling her 'a ray of sunshine', and she was so good with the boys. Jean knew the girls looked out for each other and that Elsie was in good hands having a friend like Marcie. Her daughter was a little on the sensitive side being self-conscious of her chubbiness and the thick framed spectacles she wore, and she was always being bullied at school by the boys who called her 'four eyes' and 'fatty'.

Jean felt sorry for Marcie knowing the kind of parents she had but didn't interfere because she felt nothing good would come of it knowing the loss of a son was more than anyone could bear no matter what the circumstances, and you had to keep your own house in order and mind your own business. In the past Keith had two nasty encounters with Tom in the pub, telling him in no uncertain terms how hard he was on Marcie and that he was lucky to have a daughter like her. He said he should be strung up the way he treated her, and it ended up with Keith sporting a black eye, so she felt it was better to stay clear and let them sort it out.

Jean cooked a lovely meat and veg pie and they all sat around the table to eat. 'What are you up to lately?' Jean asked Marcie. 'Are you still working at the hotel?'

'Yes, but I hate working with my mother. She watches me like a hawk and I can't seem to do anything right.'

'That woman needs to be put in her place; she is wicked treating you the way she does. I wish I had an extra bedroom and you could come and live with us.'

Keith looked at Jean in annoyance and told her to eat her dinner as it was getting cold with all her talking. But he couldn't be angry with her for long. 'That was lovely pet,' he said glancing lovingly at his wife who he loved so much and felt so lucky to have. 'Now I am going for a cigarette in the front room.'

As he sat down in his comfortable rocking chair he felt a sadness come over him as he had a soft spot for Marcie and wished he could help her in some way, but was soon distracted when she walked in.

'Thank you so much for the dinner, Mr Jones.'

'You're welcome, Marcie.'

'Would it be alright if I listened to some records with Elsie upstairs in her bedroom?'

'That's alright pet, but keep the music down and tell Elsie that later she must help her mother do the washing up - she knows the rules - we all must do our bit.' Keith was of the old school with old fashioned ideas, but he was the head of the household like his father was and that was the way he was brought up, but nevertheless he had come from a loving home and felt blessed. Jean was happy with the arrangement and never complained because she knew he was a kind, gentle soul and a good father and husband, very attentive and loving.

There was lots of laughter upstairs. Marcie loved music and *If I'm a Fool for Loving You* was her favourite by Elvis Presley; she played it over and over again. The boys played with their train set downstairs as they thought girls' stuff was mushy and stupid, plus they knew not to enter their sister's bedroom without permission.

The evening drew to a close and it was time for Marcie to go home, so Mr Jones took her to the bus-stop and waited till she got on the bus. 'Bye now pet. Take care of yourself and come and visit us again soon.'

'Thanks for everything,' she replied. 'See you maybe next week.'

The weather was shocking that night, there was a gale force wind and heavy rain and the bus driver was finding it difficult to drive so he took the fifteen minute journey very slowly. Marcie and an elderly lady were the only two on the bus so he chatted a bit to them to keep them calm. 'Alright lass, we will be there soon,' but Marcie didn't answer, she was deep in thought thinking about the miserable atmosphere she would be walking into when she arrived home late and the happy household she had just left behind with Elsie and her family; there was no comparison.

When she finally arrived home her dad had gone to bed and her mum was in a rage. She had barely set foot inside the door when her mother stormed towards her. 'What the hell time do you think this is? Do you think I have nothing better to do than wait up for you?'

'Sorry Mum, but the journey took longer because...' and before she could finish her sentence her mum gave her a sharp slap across the face and told her to get to bed.

Marcie lay in her bed crying; she had never seen her mum react in such a way before. She had always had a vicious tongue on her and had pushed her from time to time with force but had never slapped her around the face so maliciously with such hatred in her eyes. She knew things were getting unbearable now and so that night she came to a decision. She must find a way to leave and start a new life outside the village, perhaps move to London and find a job; the further away the better, but one thing was for sure, she didn't ever want to return back home till she had done something with her life. Her parents had made her feel so unwanted and unloved.

Chapter Two

Autumn had arrived and it was blustery and windy outside. Tom had his post to deliver and was wrapped up in his thick overcoat and wearing a cap. He loved getting out of the house after listening to two women prattling on about nothing. He often thought it would be good to find solace in another woman's arms as life with Nellie was like a life sentence, and Marcie, well she was old enough to look after herself. He had done his best bringing her up and she never gave him any grief, but still, she wasn't his. Tom always seemed to be behind delivering his post and it hadn't gone unnoticed by the shopkeepers. He loved the freedom of the outdoors; he could smoke his pipe in peace and go about his business without listening to the constant nagging of his wife, and that was his escape for now. When he had finished he always stopped for a pint at the Stag pub, chatting to the landlady, Betsy. There was a bit of gossip in the village but he didn't care, she was good company and there was no hurry to rush home.

Marcie went to work that day with her face bright red on one cheek where she had taken the blow from her mother. Mrs Clements noticed it; she had a soft spot for her and asked her to come into her office when she had her lunch break. Marcie knocked on the door and entered.

'Take a seat, my love.' She spoke softly even though she was a hard business woman who was the backbone of the hotel and its success. 'I have never been one to pry but I noticed your face is slightly swollen. Can you tell me why?'

Marcie looked down, as she knew she had to be careful what she said. Her mother was well respected in her employment and Mrs Clements often remarked what a godsend she was. Then to Marcie's surprise she got up from her chair and came over and wrapped her arms around her. 'Look,' she said, 'if ever you need a reference I will give you one, but if I were in your shoes I would think about leaving home and starting afresh... and I don't want any atmosphere here. Your mother has been a loyal, hard working employee and I don't want to lose her.'

'But you won't,' Marcie answered.

'I know, but some of my guests have heard you both bickering and it doesn't look good with the kind of clientele I have here. We run a good establishment so I want you to think about what I've said, dear.'

Marcie walked out of the room and knew she was right. Her mother was getting stressed about her being around and she would never live up to her expectations; she would only ever be an embarrassment to her.

That evening there was a knock at the door and Marcie went and opened it. She didn't recognise who it was at first but when he took off his cap she saw it was her Uncle Sam who she had always likened to the fugitive; he popped up once in a blue moon and never kept in touch that often. He didn't even manage to attend her brother's funeral but sent flowers instead saying he couldn't get away from his job sheep shearing on a farm. Marcie wouldn't forget that, but as always she kept her feelings to herself.

'Hello pet, you must be Marcie,' he said. 'What a pretty girl you are.'

Tom's face dropped. 'What the hell are you doing here Sam? I thought you'd got a farm job abroad in New Zealand the last time I heard from you; that's what you said you wanted to do.'

'No. I was thinking of moving abroad but I didn't fancy it in the end.'

Tom smiled. 'Liar! You mean you couldn't find anyone to pay for the bloody tickets more like.'

Sam laughed. 'You know me too well brother. I moved all around the country as a farm hand milking cows, shearing sheep; you know me, I can't stay in one place for too long. My last job was at a farm in Hexham in the north east for a while but I had sex with the farmer's daughter and he booted me out, the bastard. She was up for it, though.'

'Watch your mouth,' Tom said, 'and what's happened to Dad?'

'He passed away; drunk himself silly. 'He never got over our mother leaving, silly bugger! We never heard a dickie bird from her, the cow.'

Tom knew his brother was a good for nothing womaniser; a trouble maker who was his own worst enemy, but he felt responsible in a way for leaving him on his own with his dad to run the rented farm they lived on, and was fond of him in his own way. He was a few years older than Sam and if he had stayed on maybe he could have made a difference. Nellie was upstairs leaning on the banister listening, but she felt in no hurry to come down as she hated Tom's brother with a vengeance...but there was a thin line between love and hate, and there was history between them.

Marcie went upstairs to her bedroom as she sensed an atmosphere and thought it best to make herself scarce, but her mother put paid to that and told her to go downstairs and start peeling some vegetables in preparation for the evening meal.

Tom looked at his brother and told him he could stay for a few days but that he would have to sleep on the settee. Sam looked aghast. 'I'm not kipping on there! What's wrong with sleeping upstairs?' At which point Nellie walked into the room and told him in no uncertain terms that he could like it or lump it and get on his merry way. Sam had no intentions of answering back as there were secrets between them and he could see she was in no mood to listen to his nonsense.

They all sat down for dinner and very little was said, but Sam stole the odd glance at Nellie, thinking that she wasn't the fine looking woman he remembered. She was looking very bedraggled and so thin, but if she was for the taking he wouldn't mind making a move as he guessed there was tension between her and Tom, and it wouldn't be the first time he had bedded her.

After he had finished his meal he asked Tom if he could have a bath.

'Alright, but don't use all the bloody hot water.'

'I won't' he replied as he climbed the stairs. He looked around before he went to the bathroom and he saw Nellie's belongings in her son's bedroom and her nightie lying on the bed. 'Separate sleeping arrangements; I thought so,' he chuckled to himself.

Marcie got up for work the next morning and went downstairs. Her Uncle Sam was having his cup of tea and smoking a cigarette. 'Where's your dad?' he asked.

'He's gone off to work,' she replied.

'Well I must say, you're a fine looking lass. Come and give your uncle a kiss.' She was reluctant but did as she was asked. She hated the smell of his tobacco breath, and he had disgusting habits putting his cigarette stubs in his tea-cup, and he wasn't too fussed about his appearance either – he looked like a tramp with his holey jeans and worn out jumper, although she thought if he was clean shaven and looked respectable he could be a good looking man. Marcie hurried out the door leaving Sam to pour himself another cup of tea.

It was Nellie's day off and she had an appointment to see the doctor to change her pills as she was going through the change, but she had three hours to kill and dreaded coming downstairs to see Sam. When she eventually did she was furious as there was a cloud of smoke in her living room and he had his feet up on her settee with his dirty boots on. 'You never change,' she said. 'You're still the disrespectful person you ever were and I won't have it,' she said. 'You can smoke outside and get them filthy boots off my settee!'

'Hush woman,' Sam replied. 'You are still the most annoying person I know, you with your fancy ideas, but that didn't stop you sleeping with me on the night of your marriage to my brother, when he got so drunk we both had to put him to bed, did it?'

She blushed. 'I don't have to listen to this,' she said, and walked out into the garden. Sitting there on the bench she reflected back. Yes, it was a mistake, but Tom was so drunk he couldn't stand, which had made her feel so angry at the reception. It had barely started when he chose to ignore her and just stand at the bar with his mates laughing and drinking. Sam took the opportunity to step in and asked Nellie to dance. After that he had flirted all night with her. Yes, they both had a lot to drink, but she still felt he had taken full advantage of the situation.

After the wedding Tom never paid her any compliments and showed her no affection either... he had changed. The good times when they were courting were over and he was like a stranger. He had wed her, the deed was done, and she soon realized he wanted her as the mother figure he'd never had and getting married, to him, was just the 'done thing'. Sex meant nothing to him. He mostly lay in bed like a cold fish, which made her feel unattractive and empty inside.

Nellie thought about having an abortion when she found out she was pregnant because she knew for sure it wasn't Tom's but she also knew she would be frowned upon by the church if word got around. She stupidly thought that maybe by some miracle having the baby would bring her and Tom closer together, but it didn't make any difference; Tom never showed any interest in Marcie whatsoever. Nellie took full charge of her and kept Marcie out of his way as much as she could. When she cried she took her straight upstairs never allowing her to make too much noise playing with her toys or getting in his way of watching the evening news. The situation was impossible to bear, but when she had Jack their beloved son some years later, Tom started showing an interest and all the attention went on him. She felt they had something in common at last and she had finally done something to please him. Tom thought his son was the image of him as he had a mole on his cheek the same as his and a mop of jet black curly hair. He doted on him from the time he was born, and it was true, they looked like two peas in a pod. There was no mistake, Jack was his life and they did everything together. He was the son he had always wanted.

Nellie never had her freedom because there was no way, as Tom put it, he was going to support another man's bastard; one was enough. Tom had some purpose in his life when Jack was alive and she felt life was a bit easier...till that dreadful day when the accident happened, and she knew things would never be the same again.

When she had first met Tom he had big ideas about owning his own dairy farm and that impressed her. Security and a good future with prospects was what she wanted. She knew she would never have that with Sam as all he was interested in was being in the company of women and drinking to his heart's content, so she thought Tom was a good catch, the better of the two brothers.

Tom never suspected anything was going on between them all those years ago and was happy knowing they got on well together. She wanted to keep it that way because she knew that was the worst betrayal ever, having an affair with your husband's brother.

Nellie walked back into the cottage, her eyes puffed up and sore and tears running down her face. At that moment she felt like the loneliest woman on the planet. Sam asked her if she wanted a cup of tea.

'No thank you.'

'Come over here and give me a kiss then.'

'No, I won't; you repulse me and you make my skin crawl.'

He could see she had been crying. Sam got up from the settee and walked over towards her and pulled her body close to his. He started to kiss her neck and face all over and she fought back but all the emotions she had cut off for so long came to the surface and she melted in his arms craving for the next move he would make. He took her hand and led her up to her bedroom, and as he told her to sit on the bed he took the slide out of the bun in her hair. She looked as pretty as a picture as her long black hair covered her shoulders, and her face lit up; that was the woman he remembered years ago. For the next hour Sam explored every part of her body and she didn't put up a fight. All the frustrations she had felt for all those years melted away and for that brief period she became a woman again and didn't want it to end.

'My god,' Sam said, 'I can hear someone knocking at the door,' and told her to get dressed and see who it was.

Nellie quickly put her clothes on and went downstairs to open the door to see Mr Williams, the coalman, standing there. 'Sorry if I disturbed you,' he said, 'were you resting, Mrs Thomas?'

'Mind your own business, and no, I don't need any coal today so be on your way, I'm busy.' It didn't take long for her to get back to her normal self as anger and guilt came over her at the way she had opened herself up to a man she knew would soon be on his way.

Nellie was putting the kettle on when Sam came downstairs with a big grin on his face looking like the cat that got the cream and came over to her and put his arms around her. 'Stop that,' she said. 'Someone may come in.' Pushing him away she went upstairs to have a shower and when she came back down he was fast asleep on the settee.

'Wake up,' she said, 'we need to talk. Look Sam, I really want you to go. This is impossible you staying here; nothing good will come of it.'

Sam looked shocked. 'Did you tell Tom?'

'No, he doesn't know she is yours. Remember when we could barely make ends meet and he worked down south for a few months tarmacking the roads? He knew the dates didn't add up and refused to speak about it but I believe he thought it was an affair I had with Terry an ex of mine who used to phone me sometimes. Whenever he had a belly full of drink and saw Tom in the pub he took the mickey out of him saying, "She should have married me your misses," so when we argued I would bring his name up and it worked to put him off the scent and he thought she was Terry's.

When I approached the subject about Marcie in later years he told me to let sleeping dogs lie as what is done is done. I was tempted to come clean but Tom told me never to speak about it again, so I didn't. You know how he was; he didn't like to be the one who was not in control, but he was no fool, make no mistake, he knew Marcie wasn't his daughter so emotionally he felt nothing for her. He just had to be seen to be doing his duty. I wrote you a letter explaining everything but you didn't reply, and then you have the cheek to keep turning up like a bad penny.'

Sam got up off the settee and said he was going for a walk. 'No you're not,' Nellie said. 'You know she's yours and you did nothing about it. I wanted your support but my being pregnant scared you off, and I knew deep down that you would always be the wanderer and irresponsible person you were. And you didn't even come to Jack's funeral!'

'For god's sake woman, shut up! Toms right, you're a nagging woman that would put any man off. Don't blame me; you married him, didn't you?' Sam was getting annoyed. 'You enjoyed our sex together, didn't you? Listen, I did you a favour. You knew my brother could never satisfy you in that department. And I never told you to have the baby; there were other options and I made that quite plain when you rang me at my lodgings. I was always straight with you from the start. I am my own man and never wanted children, but I am so sorry for your loss, I truly am.'

Nellie cried uncontrollably. All those years she blamed Marcie for stopping her being with the man she truly loved, but now she realised it was lust on his part. She was older and wiser now and could see him for what he truly was. She in many ways was her own worst enemy, becoming a replica of her mother. When she was growing up her mother never expressed any feelings towards her and resented the fact she still lived in a council house and was never contented with her lot. She lived in a fantasy world and Nellie realized that it was all in her head too. Nothing would have ever happened between her and Sam. He never wanted to marry and settle down on any terms; his freedom meant more to him than anything.

That evening when they all sat down for their meal, Sam turned to Tom and said he was off after he had eaten as he had heard of a job coming up on a farm in Derbyshire. Tom knew he was lying but he could feel the tension in the air between him and Nellie so he didn't question him. That was Sam, a drifter who always thought the grass was greener on the other side.

Sam walked out the door that evening knowing in his mind it would be a long time before he saw his brother again. If the truth ever came out he would kill him and some things were best left alone. Nellie cleared the dishes and went straight upstairs to her bedroom. She felt so many mixed emotions and regrets but her heart had hardened and she knew she could never turn back the clock. This would be her punishment for the rest of her life for neglecting her daughter and not being the mother she should have been and having a husband she didn't truly love. Or was it her own insecurities and selfishness because she wasn't taught how it was to be loved when she was growing up and found it hard to be that person? But she did find Tom attractive when they first met although she knew he had a vicious temper in drink and could be quite capable of anything like any man, but he had never once struck her although she wished sometimes he had then things might have got resolved one way or the other.

Marcie felt the tension in the house but had ideas of her own. She was going to work the next morning to ask Mrs Clements for a reference and give her notice in, but was going to ask her politely not to tell her mother, as she wanted to be the one to do that.

The hotel was doing well and it was full but she managed to get a half an hour lunch break so she went straight to the office and knocked on the door.

'Come in!' Marcie was shaking because she knew it was an inconvenient time but was determined to get it over with. Mrs Clements fortunately was smiling. 'What can I do for you, dear girl?'

'Well, I would like to give two weeks' notice, and if possible I'd like a reference please as I want to leave home and look elsewhere for work.'

Mrs Clements told Marcie to take a seat. She knew she had to help her in some way but didn't want to take sides and know the ins and outs. She was a formidable woman but having two children of her own, she wanted to help in some way. 'Look Marcie, I have an idea. I know you are ready to leave home and start afresh, and as I said before, I for one think it would be good for you, so I am going to give my cousin a ring. He and his wife run a small hotel in Kings Cross in London and they are looking for a chambermaid who can live in and more or less do the same sort of work that you are doing here. Do you think you would be interested?'

'Oh, yes, that would be lovely...and I would work hard!'

'Well that's settled then, but the only thing is could be as soon as next week as they are desperate right now.' She scribbled the details on a piece of paper and handed it to Marcie. 'Here you are: Mr and Mrs Brown, 12 Argyle St, Kings Cross, and I've also written down the telephone number for you, dear.'

Marcie was filled with excitement though nervous at the same time as she had never been away from home, but this was her chance and nothing was going to get in her way.

'Just one thing,' Mrs Clements said, 'discuss it with your mother tonight as she ought to know, but I can see you have made your mind up already and I wish you every success in the future.'

That evening they were sitting watching television together and Marcie got her courage up and said she was going to London to be a chambermaid and Mrs Clements had arranged everything. Her parents looked at her and her mother was the first one to speak. 'So you went behind my back! Such gratitude, I must say, but I tell you this, don't come back pregnant as there is no place for you here you ungrateful girl!'

To her surprise her dad butted in. 'For god's sake leave her alone. If that's what she wants, so be it, she is old enough to do what she wants.'

Marcie went upstairs to bed thinking she was not going to feel responsible for their unhappiness. It was her turn to make a life for herself but wished things could have been so different and was worried as to what would become of them both.

The date had been set and Marcie had her belongings packed into one suitcase ready for her departure the next morning. She had planned to visit her best friend that week but unfortunately Elsie and her family were ill with flu so told her not to worry, as they were afraid she might catch it. In the end she rung them to say goodbye and that she was sorry she hadn't seen them for quite a while, but they understood what with her working and things happening so quickly. They sent a parcel round to her place with a friend who was passing that way. Inside was an Elvis Presley record from Elsie, which she loved. As she had played it that many times it wasn't new but it was special to her, and there was also a diary with pretty pictures inside and a note which read: *Always in our thoughts. Be happy, you are a ray of sunshine. Keep in touch, lots of love, the Jones family.*

That evening Nellie phoned the hotel and Mrs Clements answered the phone. 'What's the problem ringing me at this time of night?' she said. Her time in the evenings was her own and she felt annoyed that she was being disturbed.

Nellie explained that it was difficult to get Marcie to the station as the taxi fare would cost so much and asked if she could arrange it. She said she would make it up to her by doing extra hours at the hotel. Mr Clements was put out, he felt sometimes his wife was too pushy, but agreed to take her in the end.

He picked her up the next morning but still thought it was unbelievable that their only daughter was moving away from home and they couldn't see her off. Marcie kissed her mother on both cheeks with not much response and then turned to her dad who gave her £20, which was unexpected, and told her to keep in touch. For the first time in her life she felt some warmth coming from him and felt he probably meant it in his own way but that maybe he had a guilty conscience, but she wanted to feel he cared because at that moment it felt comforting.

Mr Clements was a quiet, soft spoken man who was overshadowed by a wife who was definitely the boss, but she liked him, he was harmless and had been very kind buying her a few magazines for the journey and giving her a packed lunch of ham and cucumber sandwiches. Marcie got on the train after waving goodbye to him and looked for a space where no-one was sitting, but it didn't take long before a mature, good looking man in his forties, smartly dressed and carrying a briefcase came and sat opposite her. Marcie felt uncomfortable as she was shy, and feeling nervous about the new job she was going to didn't feel much like talking, so pretended she was absorbed in her magazine with her head down. The train was packed and two other people sat beside them, an elderly couple who were quite obviously married if the massive diamond ring she had on her left hand which you couldn't help notice was anything to go by. Plus her husband fussed around her like a man who adored her and every five minutes asked her if she was alright. Marcie could see they were quite well off as the mink coat and tweed suit, in her eyes, were only worn by the well to do. Her husband wore a smart suit too, with a dickie bow tie and silk scarf loosely wrapped around his neck.

'My name's Bill, what's yours?' said the smartly dressed man in his forties.

'Marcie,' she said.

'And where are you going?'

'To start my new job as a chambermaid in a hotel in Kings Cross. The lady there is a cousin of my last employer.'

But the elderly couple thought she was a bit too forward letting a stranger know her business and chose to look away pretending they didn't hear anything.

Bill carried on talking. 'You seem a bit young to leave home for the bright lights of London, being a big city and all. How old are you?'

Marcie felt he was too forward and said abruptly that she was old enough.

Two hours into the journey Bill had a snooze and so did the elderly couple but Marcie was wide awake thinking about her destination and hoping Mr and Mrs Brown would like her and she would fit into her knew employment. She knew there was no going back now as she had cut ties and wanted to make a good life for herself, but one day when she achieved her independence then she would visit her parents and let them see *she* was in control, not them, and whatever decisions she made would not be made out of bitterness and anger over past mistakes and regrets like her mother and father. She was the child they never wanted but her feelings for them were hard to ignore, as they were the only family she had ever known.

Marcie got off the train at Kings Cross and was amazed at how big it was, but what surprised her the most was the amount of people around; she had never seen so many in her life coming from a quiet village in South Wales.

'Can I take your suitcase?' a porter asked.

'No, thanks,' Marcie said politely, 'I can carry it myself.' It was only small with a few belongings in. As her mother had pointed out, she would be working in a uniform and there would not be much time for gallivanting as she put it. What did shock Marcie was how the night before her mother had neatly ironed all her clothes and even put in extra underwear and two new nighties, plus a floral dressing gown of hers which she kept for best and the black bible she made her swear on every time she thought she was lying. Unfortunately, the truth was this woman had to keep her standards up. Marcie had a chuckle to herself but was relieved and pleased she had done it anyway.

The taxis were lined up outside and Marcie climbed in the first one, gave the driver the address and sat in the back seat. Jim, had picked up a lot of young girls in the thirty years that he'd been a taxi driver and had heard numerous sad stories of them leaving home and coming to London expecting the streets to be paved with gold and having high expectations of glamour and success, but a lot of them who he repeatedly picked up ended up on the streets and homeless. Jim was a father of three and had a lovely wife and children and felt so blessed as his children were all grown up and happy and settled. Marcie got out of the taxi and went to pay him but he saw there was something different about her. She obviously had come from a good family and wasn't cheeky or rough and ready but well mannered and smart. 'That's alright,' he said, 'have this one on me.'

'Thank you,' Marcie said, 'that's very kind of you.' Jim waited a few minutes till he saw her go in the door. He thought she was a lovely girl and hoped she was one of the lucky ones and had landed on her feet.

Chapter Three

Marcie was shocked when she entered the hallway; it was cluttered with lots of ornaments on shelves and had a nasty smell of cigarettes, which she then saw was coming from the full ashtray sitting by the telephone on top of an old cluttered desk. Mr and Mrs Brown greeted her warmly and lead her into the sitting room which was cosy even though the wallpaper was bold pink stripes and the carpet was a patterned shade of green. This was something she had never seen before, as her mother would think those colours were distasteful and always stuck to dark colours and old fashioned furniture. Marcie was astonished by how many big vases filled with plastic flowers there were all over the room, and the fireplace was covered with large ornaments, everything thick with dust.

Nancy was a small, thin woman in her fifties with long bleached blonde hair and petite features and in a way she was attractive, apart from the thick black mascara she had on which covered her big brown eyes and the red lipstick which looked far too brassy. Malcolm was tall and thin and had thick grey hair, masses of it and looked like someone had put a pair of shears to it somehow, it had a will of its own, no style at all, but he had a friendly face. Marcie liked them both instantly.

Nancy sat staring at Marcie and thought what a beauty she was and wanted to make her feel at ease so brought out her homemade scones with a pot of tea. 'You must be starving pet. Eat up and I will show you around the hotel.'

Mr and Mrs Brown turned out to be a down to earth, no nonsense couple who had been married in their teens. They didn't have any children, as there was a problem with Nancy conceiving. They had tried all different hospitals in London but the diagnosis was always the same, virtually impossible, so were always advised to foster or adopt. But they were a happy couple and thought that as this was the card they had been dealt they should just get on with their lives. They had been married for a good many years, never grew tired of one another and were obviously still very much in love. Malcolm, who came from the North East, took it much harder as he was from a large family of four sisters and three brothers and he would have loved children but kept his feelings to himself. Nancy was the love of his life and he felt lucky to have found someone like her, so in his mind there were no regrets.

As they sat chatting and drinking their tea, Malcolm thought she looked quite tired so he interrupted. 'Nancy, let the bairn have some rest as she must be shattered.' Nancy loved her husband, as he was always considerate and knew best.

Marcie was shown her room at the top of the house, three floors in all, and after climbing the stairs was amazed they had six guest bedrooms in total. This was a large house but the guests had to share the one bathroom on the middle floor.

Malcolm opened her bedroom door and apologised for the teddy bears that were covering the shelves. 'Sorry lass, but I think that was my wife's way of dealing with not having a child; she surrounds herself with things like this.' Marcie said it was lovely and cosy and thanked him and he gave her a peck on the cheek and told her to sleep well.

Marcie tossed and turned and eventually got up in the middle of the night and looked out of the window. The hotel backed onto tall buildings and that was the view she had. At that moment she longed to be back in her beautiful village with open spaces and trees and flowers planted around every cottage she passed. With the hustle and bustle and dirty pavements this place was a far cry from what she was used to but knew this was her chance to make something of herself and she would regret it for the rest of her life if she didn't give it a try. Her parents would always get in the way of her dreams and she would feel suppressed all her life.

The next morning Marcie awoke to the mouth-watering aroma of bacon being cooked by Nancy downstairs. There were only two rooms let at the moment, one by an elderly gentleman, Mr Grimes who preferred to be called Terry. His wife had died ten years ago and he lived alone in a big house in Sutton but was visiting a friend in Kentish Town. He loved the hotel and came back every year as Nancy and Malcolm made him so welcome and he felt this was like home from home.

Staying in the other room was Roy, a different kettle of fish entirely. He was a builder who found lots of work in London and travelled up from his home in Yorkshire and stayed in the hotel for weeks or months at a time, depending how long the job lasted. He was a good looking bloke, well built, with curly blond hair and had a friendly disposition, but loved the pubs and would often arrive back at the hotel worse for wear and Malcolm would put him to bed.

Marcie looked at her watch. It was 9.30 a.m. so quickly rinsed her face and hands, brushed her teeth and combed her hair. Luckily, hers was one of the bedrooms with a hand basin and that saved her from going to the bathroom on the middle floor. She felt nervous going down the stairs as her mother would have been furious with her lying in bed so late and would have called her a lazy good for nothing.

Nancy heard her coming down and went to the bottom of the stairs. 'Hello pet, did you sleep well? I thought it best to leave you, as you looked so tired after the long journey getting here. Sit yourself down and I will bring you some breakfast and then we will have a chat; just give me a minute.'

'That's alright,' Marcie said, 'a cup of tea will be fine, I'm not hungry,' but the truth was she felt a bit shy sitting in the dining room with the guests as this was all new to her.

Nancy was a very intuitive woman so suggested they went into the sitting room as the guests had been served and Malcolm was out doing some errands for her so half an hour was neither here nor there; with Marcie's help she would soon get all her jobs out the way. 'How is Joyce?' she said.

Marcie looked at her and guessed she was talking about Mrs Clements. 'She is fine. The hotel is very busy.'

Nancy smiled. 'She was always a lucky sod; always managed to fall on her feet. I remember when we were teenagers going to the dance halls together all the lads fancied her and she had grand ideas even then, but I knew she would be successful. It's a shame our families moved away from one another. We lost touch for years till I found her telephone number in an old diary of mine and thought on the off chance she might know of someone, being in the same business an all, and thanks to her she saved my bacon and I am so pleased you're here. Listen Marcie, I want you to feel this is your home and if you get worried about anything you can come to Malcolm or me.

Marcie chuckled. 'Well, I'm a bit concerned that cigarette smoke is burning my eyes. Aren't you afraid of burning the hotel down, leaving full ashtrays everywhere?'

Nancy gave her a gentle slap on the arm. 'You cheeky monkey!' But she was so pleased she felt comfortable in her presence and they both smiled at one another and felt they were going to get on fine, just fine.

'Just one thing pet; I can't pay you much after deducting your board and lodgings. As you can see, the hotel is very quiet at the moment with not many rooms let and we are just ticking over meeting our bills, but when things pick up I will always see you get a bit more in your wage packet. Is that alright with you?'

Marcie knew she could trust them both and said that was fine. She could see there was so much potential in this lovely hotel but the décor and clutter of the place left a lot to be desired and she wanted to give it her best shot and work hard.

'I will show you where we keep the cleaning stuff and you can make a start upstairs and I will clear the breakfast dishes and do the kitchen.'

Marcie was amazed how each room was filled with so many ornaments on dusty shelves, and these took her longer to clean than the actual room itself. When she pulled the beds out the floors were also covered in muck and dust. She could see these rooms hadn't been cleaned properly in a long time and after three hours she had only managed to do three rooms and still had the stairs and the bathroom to do as well, but hopefully now it would get easier.

Malcolm was in from doing his errands and shouted up the stairs to her. 'Marcie, come down. I have made you a cup of tea lass!'

'I'm coming,' she called down, but could have done without it as at this rate she wouldn't be finished till supper time.

'How are you getting on pet?'

'I'm fine Mr Brown,' she answered.

'Now, hey lass, you call me Malcolm and my wife Nancy. There are no airs and graces here. Were the rooms very bad?'

'Not too bad,' Marcie said lowering her head.

'Who are you kidding?' he said. 'I know my wife does her best but the standards haven't been kept up for quite some time. But keep that between us as the poor soul has had arthritis in her back, hands and feet for years and it's getting a lot worse. The painkillers don't seem to be working much and she has had lots of blood tests but the hospital is baffled; nothing is showing up in her blood. But she is such a proud woman and doesn't like to complain and won't let me help her as she feels me doing gardening work or other jobs I can get my hands on to bring extra cash in when the hotel s quiet and not so busy is enough for me. So you can see why I'm so glad you're here. Plus she gets a bit lonely and your company is grand.'

Nancy walked in. 'Have you given her some biscuits, Malcolm? The poor bugger must be hungry having had no breakfast this morning.' Marcie loved these two; they said it as it was and were always cuddling and kissing each other, which was a far cry from what she had been used to at home.

When it was 6pm Marcie had finished her work and Nancy and Malcolm were so pleased with her. She had worked non-stop but knew they had given her a mountain to climb as there was a lot to do. They both appreciated it and Malcolm cooked a spaghetti Bolognese for their evening meal and they had a bottle of red wine to go with it.

In time Marcie managed to convince the pair of them to get rid of the clutter in the bedrooms and change the décor making it more subtle, but they were both set in their ways and from time to time Nancy would go to car boot sales and bring back boxes of stuff and convince Marcie they were a bargain and would be worth something later on, but she knew it was replacing something she longed for – the child she could never have - and she understood. They were so happy together and so devoted to one another and neither of them had a bad bone in their bodies. Marcie hoped one day it would happen to her and she would find her soul mate, someone who loved her the way they loved each other.

The postman came with a letter for Marcie that morning and it was from her best friend Elsie who said her father had been made redundant. She also said she now had a boyfriend who her parents disapproved of but she was in love and planned to leave home and share a bedsit with him. Marcie knew that although she was so sweet and eager to please, she was vulnerable and lacking in self confidence and was making a big mistake as she was immature. She went on to say in her letter that she was pregnant and the lad was called Pete Banks. Marcie knew him as he attended the same school as them and had a reputation around the village as a villain who took drugs. She felt sorry for Elsie's parents who had always been good to her, and of course Elsie was a dear friend who was more like a sister so she couldn't help but worry about her. She just hoped she could get time off and pay them all a visit but at the moment her hands were tied. She was also concerned about Nancy who was getting worse and worse with her arthritis. However, she was relieved when the hospital finally diagnosed what was wrong with her. She had rheumatoid arthritis and she finally had to admit defeat and Malcolm bought her a fold up wheelchair as she found it harder and harder to walk about. When it came to the stairs he had to carry her up on the days the illness was very active.

Marcie was on the settee in the sitting room watching TV one evening when Malcolm came in looking so sad. 'What's wrong?' Marcie asked. She knew Nancy was upstairs having a rest which happened more and more frequently as the pain was exhausting her.

'You've been with us for some time now and as you know we've grown very fond of you – in fact we think of you as the daughter we never had, pet,' he said with tears in his eyes, 'but I'm afraid we are going to have to put the hotel up for sale as Nancy is finding it so difficult to cope and it's not fair on you doing all those extra hours and having no social life. You should be around girls your own age. It won't happen right now; as you know, the market is quiet and it could take ages to find a buyer, but that will give you plenty of time to sort yourself out. We want to buy a small property next to the beach as Nancy would love that, and we wanted you to know that you are quite welcome to come and live with us if you want to; we will manage somehow.'

Marcie put her arms around him and kissed him. He had enough on his plate looking after Nancy as the disease she had was so restricting and had the potential to get worse, but she felt grateful to them both for giving her self-confidence and telling her she could achieve anything she wanted to, but she wasn't sure at that moment what that was.

That evening she was going to the pub with Roy who she had become good friends with. She admired the way he would help out with the maintenance of the hotel in his free time because he was so fond of Nancy and Malcolm. In return they always put themselves out and often ironed his shirts or gave him a packed lunch when he went to work on the building site. He was treated like one of the family also.

Marcie came down the stairs and she looked stunning in her black dress and with her hair swept back in a pony tail showing off her beautiful features. Roy took her arm and felt proud to be with this gorgeous girl. Nancy was like a mother hen and told them both not to stay out too late. 'Roy, please look after her,' she said.

'I will, don't worry.'

Malcolm was more concerned about the pub they were going to. It had a reputation for being raided as the owner often served drinks after closing time and the police were often called.

After a ten minute walk around the corner they entered the pub and sat on two stools at the bar. Marcie thought it would be a lot busier but it was early and she was pleased as at least they could hear themselves speak. Roy ordered a dry Martini for her and had his usual pint of lager.

'Have you heard from your mother and father,' he asked.

'Not lately, but Mum doesn't tell me much in her letters anyway, just everything is much the same and she is still working for Mrs Clements and Dad is still working for the postal service and telling me not to phone as it is expensive - as if they care.'

Roy felt sorry for Marcie. His parents were amazing; they always encouraged him when he was growing up and it was the same with his sister, but he knew Marcie didn't have that happy family bond as Malcolm and Nancy had informed him before she arrived. They told him to keep it to himself and not to ask too many questions - if she wanted to tell him she would in her own good time. Roy guessed Nancy's cousin Joyce had told them all about her but he knew everyone had skeletons in their closets and he was no exception. He fancied Marcie but he was convinced she was out of his league, a classy girl, not like the usual girls he had taken out. They were smashing and good fun but they were not too shy to speak their minds and loved too much of a good time.

The band started to play dance music so they both got up and danced together and were having a great time. The pub was getting full so it was a good atmosphere until Rob, a drinking buddy of Roy's walked in looking a bit the worse for wear and sat down at a table. Roy was a bit apprehensive to sit with him but he knew he couldn't ignore him as when sober he was a nice guy, so went over to where he was sitting and introduced Marcie.

'Hell man, you have a good looking bird there! You hid that well, you sly dog,' he said.

Roy was furious as he watched his friend grip Marcie's bum disrespectfully, and told him to piss off. 'Time to go home, Marcie,' he said, and she agreed. He had too much respect for her and felt somehow she was different to anyone else he had ever met. He knew whatever happened they would always be good friends.

They arrived back at the hotel and Roy was tempted to give her a full kiss on the lips but knew he was pushing his luck as he could tell she was not ready for that, and besides, he had enough respect for her to hold back, so kissed her on both cheeks instead and said goodnight. Marcie thanked him for a lovely evening.

The next morning Marcie got out of bed and her first thoughts were of Roy. She liked him but thought he was a bit of a Jack the lad like her Uncle Sam; someone who would never settle down with one woman, although she knew Roy was different in that he was a gent in his own way, and she felt guilty even comparing the two together in the same breath. Actually, he was kind and caring, a different kettle of fish altogether whereas she found her uncle to be devious and sly, always thinking about himself and treating women like objects the way he talked about them whenever she was in his company. She knew he was her uncle and was respectful towards him but there was a dark side to him which always made her feel uneasy. He had secrets, she thought, as she had watched him and her mother whispering between themselves when they thought she wasn't looking. She had never had the courage to ask any questions, as she knew she would have been told to 'mind her own business - children should be seen and not heard'. Roy on the other hand was caring and sensitive towards her feelings and would do anyone a good turn. She felt so lucky to have a friend like him.

When she eventually went downstairs she was surprised to see Nancy in the kitchen with her apron on doing the breakfasts. Marcie had taken that role on for quite some time now as first thing in the morning Nancy's arthritis was more active making her joints very stiff and painful.

'What are you staring at?' Nancy said. 'I *have* done this before.'

Marcie smiled. 'I know, but how are you feeling?'

'Fine lass, you know how it is, I get my good days and bad; you never know when it will play up, but I have taken my painkillers and I like to do what I can. You can put your feet up, you deserve it, and I will cook you some breakfast.'

Marcie thought she was such a brave woman and admired her so much, but she hurried her breakfast because there was a family of three due to come and stay for a fortnight and she had loads to do upstairs.

Malcolm was fixing some tiles in the upstairs bathroom and heard the phone ring and shouted to Marcie to answer it. She ran down the stairs and picked up the phone. 'Hello, can I help you?'

'It's me, Jane...don't you recognise my voice?'

Marcie was surprised; she hadn't heard from her for about a year. 'Jane! How are you?'

'Fine. I just wanted to let you know I am a qualified state enrolled nurse now - I passed all my exams. I want to work in a hospital in London as my mum says the wages are better and there are more opportunities.'

'Oh Jane, that's great news! But where will you live?' Marcie asked.

'I suppose I will have to live in the nurse's residence to start off with till I can afford my own accommodation.'

'I'm so happy for you, but I will have to go, I've loads of work to do. I'll give you a ring next week on my day off, I promise. And please give my regards to your mum and dad.' Marcie put the phone down and was feeling a bit sad. She was pleased for her dear friend who was bright and going places, but her news had made her think and she was now apprehensive about what her own future held.

The bedrooms and bathrooms were all finished and Roy walked in the front door with a big box in his hands.

'Put the kettle on pet and make me a cuppa.'

Marcie asked him what his last servant died of.

Roy laughed. 'Cheeky bugger.'

They both sat down to have their tea at the kitchen table and then Roy began to open the box. Marcie was dying to know what was in it.

'Close your eyes,' he said. When he finally told her to open them there on the table was a beautiful spanking new record player in front of her. He knew she had been saving hard for months for one but had ended up spending most of the money on a set of towels to send home for her mother's birthday – not that she deserved them; she hadn't even had the decency to send a thank you note back.

Marcie could not believe it. 'Is that for me? Roy, you shouldn't have! It must have cost you a fortune, at least a week's wages!'

'Look, I go back home tomorrow and I don't know when I will see you again...the building work has dried up here and I may have to look elsewhere.' Marcie hugged him, tears welling up in her eyes as she knew she would miss him so much but she knew they would always keep in touch and nothing would ever get in the way of their friendship.

That evening Roy ordered a Chinese for the four of them as a special treat and had already bought some beers and two bottles of red wine at the off-licence that morning and had put them in a carrier bag behind the armchair as a surprise. He wanted the evening to be special as he knew he had an early start the next morning and wasn't sure when he would see them all again. They played some records and chatted all night and even Nancy was in good spirits. She was in remission with her illness and feeling much better so she indulged herself by having two glasses of wine. Malcolm joked she was always a lightweight when it came to drinking, and after a few sips she started to doze in the armchair. Marcie helped Malcolm put her to bed and kissed them both goodnight before going back downstairs to Roy.

When she walked in the room he went over to kiss her on the lips. He wanted her to know how he felt; this may be his last chance.

'Please don't Roy;' she blushed, 'why spoil things?'

'I have real feelings for you Marcie. From the first moment I saw you.'

'No you don't, it's the drink talking, and even if you have you're leaving tomorrow. Let's just stay good friends.'

Roy knew she was right but before he could say anything else she walked out of the room and went upstairs to bed.

Marcie tossed and turned that night as she did have feelings for Roy but she wasn't ready for a serious relationship, and anyway, he was now leaving. There was a big wide world out there and she had been suffocated for too long by her parents when she was growing up so she felt she had something to prove. She wanted to be strong

29

and independent relying on no-one.

On the train heading back to Yorkshire Roy and was annoyed that he didn't get the chance to say everything he wanted to. He had intended to tell Marcie about his three-year old daughter, Molly, who lived with her mum Kim, but Malcolm and Nancy didn't know about her either as he knew they would have dearly loved a child themselves and he didn't want to rub salt in the wounds. Besides, it had taken him a long time to come to terms with being a dad. He knew Malcolm's ideas about fatherhood, and he'd always said Roy was too free-spirited for his own good and so thought he would think him to be very irresponsible not marrying Kim, even though they were both agreed that one night of passion was not worth a lifetime of unhappiness; especially as she had her eye on someone else. He was allowed to see Molly whenever he wanted to, just as long as he let Kim know in advance and didn't just call at the house when he felt like it. So the arrangement suited them both and she thought he was a good dad and a good provider. Roy knew in his heart that if she ever met someone else and got married things might all change, but not if he could help it; he loved this beautiful girl with the mop of blonde hair and a face like an angel and was so proud to be her dad. He couldn't wait to get back home to see her. Living back with his parents after sharing a flat with his mate wasn't what he wanted but he had done the right thing moving out, as Sally, his mate's girlfriend, had moved in and three was a crowd. One day, he thought to himself, he would buy his own property, or better still build one and find the girl of his dreams, but he knew he had found that in Marcie and hoped she meant what she said, that she would always keep in touch. That's all he needed to give him hope.

Chapter Four

Back at the hotel there was mayhem. The new guests, Mr and Mrs Haley and their son Tim were a nightmare, so demanding and complaining about everything. Nancy was beside herself. First they didn't like their room, they complained that it was cluttered and the wallpaper was stained brown from cigarette smoke, and then the breakfast was cold, the list was endless. Marcie offered to change their room but Nancy was having none of it and in the end they came to a compromise and she said she would knock some money off their bill. Malcolm was becoming stressed and said that the sooner the place was sold the better.

Not long afterwards Malcolm received a letter from a Brigadier Roberts who had seen the hotel advertised in the local paper and was interested in viewing it. She thought it would be an ideal premises to run as a hostel for problem teenage girls who needed accommodation in London till they had got on their feet. They would be supervised by her and a Captain Davis. She had given a telephone number so Malcolm wasted no time and phoned her right away and arranged for her to come the following day.

The next morning the doorbell rang and Brigadier Roberts was standing there all dressed up in her Salvation Army uniform and with documents in her hand. Malcolm was impressed; 10am on the dot as promised. He was feeling excited but unsure at the same time.

'Pleased to meet you,' he said. 'Come in out of the cold,' and lead her into the sitting room. Nancy wasn't feeling too good and had stayed in bed.

'The first thing I want to ask is what your reason for wanting to sell is? We have been to a lot of viewings but they have always backed out at the last minute and I don't want my time wasted.' Brigadier Roberts never minced her words and was quite a formidable woman, a no nonsense type, and Malcolm had picked up on that straight away.

When an hour had passed and Malcolm had been as honest as he could in explaining about Nancy's illness and his reasons for wanting to sell the hotel, he was surprised that she didn't even venture to look around the upstairs bedrooms, only the first floor.

'Thank you for your time, Mr Brown, I will be in touch,' and he showed her to the front door.

The phone call came in from the head office of the Salvation Army a week later, saying they wanted to purchase the property at the full asking price. Nancy and Malcolm were ecstatic but knew they had to concentrate on Marcie as they had discussed her moving with them many times but she wanted to stay in London and perhaps stay with them on weekends. They understood this but wanted to help her all they could and make sure she found accommodation and a suitable job before they left. This would be no problem for them, as they could always rent somewhere for six months or so until they found another house, and anyway, they wanted to take their time and make sure it was the right one as moving could be so expensive. They had decided a bungalow with perhaps a lovely garden at the front would be ideal and would make life so much easier for Nancy.

None of the guests came down for breakfast, not even Mr Grimes who was staying his usual fortnight so Nancy cooked some bacon sandwiches for Malcolm and her and let Marcie have a lie in, as it was her day off.

'What are we going to do about Marcie?' Malcolm said. 'I would hate to see her in a bedsit pet, all on her own. London is a big city and I would be imaging all sorts of things happening to her; she's so young.'

Nancy agreed.

'Well I know one thing we can do. Give her some money for the first six months rental to tide her over till she gets on her feet.'

Nancy loved this kind man and blessed the day she married him. She nodded her head and Malcolm got up out of his chair. 'That's settled then,' he said looking happier. 'Right, I'll see you later; Mr Bennett wants his lawn mowing so I'm off to do it now.'

Marcie came downstairs feeling great after her lie in and Nancy made her some breakfast and sat down with her to have a cup of tea. Marcie adored these two people and was going to miss them but didn't want to spoil their excitement so kept her feelings to herself. Nancy knew her too well and could see she had been upset lately and reminded her that whatever property they bought she would always be welcome as they thought of her like their own daughter and that would never change.

Nancy felt a bit tired, which wasn't unusual with the type of illness she had, so she went back upstairs for a lie down. Marcie read the newspapers and started to look at the job section and something came to her attention: a job vacancy in a large five-bedroom house in Hampstead, which she knew to be a lovely location, as a housekeeper and nanny to six year-old twin girls, driver preferred but not necessary. Marcie thought it was right up her street as she had reservations about living on her own, the thought of which she found daunting and scary. The position was to work for a Mr Evans, so she scribbled his name and telephone number down on a piece of paper and decided to phone that evening as suggested in his advertisement. She assumed he was working all day and that was more convenient for him.

The evening meal was over and Marcie asked Nancy if she could use the phone. She nervously dialled the number and after a couple of rings a man with a husky voice answered. 'Can I help you?'

Marcie explained she was inquiring about the job vacancy.

'I see,' said Mr Evans, 'well, would it be possible to come for an interview, say Friday evening at 6.30? We will have finished our evening meal and the girls go to their piano lessons then?'

Marcie agreed and wrote his address down and thanked him.

Nancy never missed a trick and heard the last bit of the conversation when walking past to lock the front door for the night. 'What was that all about?' she asked.

Alarm bells started ringing when Marcie told her the time of the interview. 'That's unusual pet, giving you an interview that time of night,' and she called Malcolm who was in the kitchen to ask his opinion.

'Don't be daft,' he said, 'he has two young lasses and works all day; not everyone can take time off work.' Malcolm was being practical but could see there was some truth in what Nancy said. He knew she was astute and more often than not she got it right - that's what he loved about her, but he could also see Marcie looking anxious and quickly changed the subject. 'I know Hampstead is a good area and posh people live there.'

'So what?' Nancy said. 'Are you saying we are as common as muck?' Malcolm kissed her on the cheek; there was nothing snobbish about her. She took people on face value and that was another thing he loved about her.

Marcie told them both she would go for the interview and see what happened but declined Malcolm's offer to go with her and wait outside till she had finished her appointment. 'No,' she said, but took him up on his kind offer to book the taxi there and back as she wasn't used to going out in the evening on her own.

On Friday morning Mr Grimes had taken ill so Nancy called for an ambulance and he was rushed into hospital with suspected pneumonia. Nancy stayed by his side till she knew he was settled and made a call to his friend who lived in Kentish Town who said he would come immediately. When he arrived at the hospital Nancy got a taxi back to the hotel. Marcie had cooked the breakfasts and started on the cleaning. Malcolm gave Jim a ring at the taxi office and booked him to come and pick Marcie up that evening. He said that he'd give Marcie his telephone number and she would call him when the interview was over for him to pick her up and take her home. He'd sort the money out with him when he popped into the office tomorrow. Malcolm trusted Jim as he had used his taxi service many times over the years taking Nancy to A&E when his own car was on the blink.

Marcie was unsure what to wear but decided on a grey tweed suit her mother had bought her years ago and wore a white shirt with it and flat heels. Jim arrived outside and tooted his horn and Marcie collected her belongings and got into the cab.

'I remember you,' Jim said. 'I picked you up from the train station ages ago and I never forget a face.' Marcie immediately relaxed seeing his familiar face.

After a while they came to a long drive with conifer trees either side and in front of them was a magnificent Victorian house in all its splendour with a large fountain in front of it. Marcie stepped out of the taxi and Jim got out and wished her luck before getting back in and driving off.

She rung the bell and the door was opened by a tall, well built man in his forties, wearing a smart suit and with a massive mop of ginger hair and big blue eyes. Marcie thought he was handsome but rather intimidating looking. She went to shake his hand but he kept his by his side.

'Come in out of the cold. You must be Marcie. So pleased to meet you. You can call me John or Mr Evans, whatever suits you best,' and he led her into the sitting room and told her to take a seat. The phone started to ring and he apologised, saying he would be back in a few minutes, as he would take the call in his office. Marcie looked around the room and couldn't believe her eyes: thick pile cream carpets with brown leather settees and a huge fireplace in marble.

When he finally made an appearance he said Biba and Tilly were at their piano lessons and he was so sorry they couldn't be present. Marcie had her references with her and handed them to him. One was from Mrs Clements and the other from Nancy and Malcolm. There was a long silence as Mr Evans browsed through them. When he had finished he raised his head. 'Yes, they are satisfactory, but I notice you haven't had experience working with children.'

'No, Mr Evans.' She preferred to call him that, as it sounded more polite.

He then began firing questions at her as if she was in a courtroom on trial. 'Have you got a boyfriend?'

'No,' she answered sheepishly.

'Well that's good; I don't want you bringing any boys back here to stay the night, it would be inappropriate for my two girls. The last nanny I had turned out to be a nightmare. There are rules which must be adhered to,' but he realized he was raising his voice and started to calm down. He could see by Marcie's face that he had gone too far as she was a shy girl, and he quickly changed the subject. 'I am an Orthopaedic Surgeon and have a busy schedule so I need someone who is adaptable, dependable and good with children. They have a routine and a timetable and they both can be a handful if left unattended.'

It was all getting a bit too much for Marcie who felt the interview was like the Spanish Inquisition and couldn't wait for it to be over.

'Would you like some tea?' he asked, but she declined as she was trembling so much she was sure she would drop the cup.

She was curious as to why this good looking man had not

mentioned his wife but decided it was not her place to ask, as there must be a good reason. It was evident there were no pictures of her around the place, just some of him and the two girls and elderly relatives.

Mr Evans explained what her duties would be. Sometimes taking the girls to school after giving them their breakfast and doing some housework, which included some ironing, but he was most particular about his shirt collars being starched. He said he had a cook who had been with him for many years and he hoped Marcie would learn a thing or two from her so that she could take over when she eventually retired. He saw the anxiety on her face. 'I wouldn't worry about that too much; I am a dab hand at cooking myself when I'm around and we often dine out in restaurants.' He then stood up. 'I have to go and pick the girls up from their lessons now, but as far as I'm concerned the job's yours. You can start in a month's time if you accept, but you have to let me know sooner rather than later as I am taking the girls on holiday next week. I expect you have to give your notice in to your employers at the hotel, but I must tell you now, if it doesn't work within a six month trial period I will have to let you go.'

Mr Evans then phoned Jim at the taxi rank for Marcie and when he arrived showed her to the door. Before she left he suggested that when he came back from holiday perhaps he could give her a ring and they could all go out for lunch and that would be her chance to meet the girls.

Going back home in the taxi Marcie had mixed feelings. She loved the house and found Mr Evans intriguing, but she felt maybe she was out of her depth and wouldn't be good enough.

John poured himself a glass of whisky and was quite impressed with Marcie as he thought she looked so innocent and shy and would fit in very nicely. He was a man who loved to be in control and liked vulnerable people who he could manipulate, which gave him a sense of power. He was full of his own importance.

Marcie arrived back at the hotel and Nancy and Malcolm were waiting to find out all the gossip. 'How was it, pet? Did you like him?' Nancy asked.

Marcie explained everything but Malcolm was quiet. 'What's wrong?' Nancy asked.

'Well I am wondering why his wife wasn't there. Don't you find that a bit strange?'

Marcie said she felt tired and kissed them both goodnight, as she didn't feel like discussing it. She wasn't sure what she thought, it had been a long day. But try as she might she couldn't sleep; her mind was working overtime. She liked Mr Evans but thought he was very reserved and standoffish and wasn't sure of her own capabilities of cleaning a big house and looking after the two children, but she could see that maybe he would be more relaxed as time went on. In hindsight she understood that he held a professional position and it couldn't be easy if there was no wife in the picture.

John Evans had his own thoughts about the interview. There was something different about Marcie. He could see she was naive, young and beautiful but was worried about her lack of education, never having been to college or university. He had been brought up to believe that a good education was paramount, but it was obvious to him that she came from humble beginnings as the suit and shoes she was wearing were clean but well worn. That said, he still thought she had possibilities...and she was a beauty, no mistake, and could be moulded with his guidance into a lovely young lady.

He cast his mind back to when he first met his lovely wife Amy, who was a very classy girl, bright and intelligent. She was a medical student and he thought there was nobody like her. She was stunning with long, auburn hair and big brown eyes that could light up a room. Her petite figure on her small stature was perfect and the first moment he saw her he was instantly attracted to her. Joe was also a medical student at the hospital and they became good friends so he introduced him to Amy. The three of them decided to have a night out at a local pub and they all got on so well that by the end of the evening John suggested it would be a good idea to share a flat together. They all agreed it would be a lot cheaper, and in no time at all they became inseparable.

Amy was a bright student and very popular as she was very understanding with the patients on her ward and would always go that extra mile, whereas John lacked personality and his bedside manner left a lot to be desired, but on the theory side he was top of his class. Joe was the joker of the three, full of fun and never took things too seriously, but had a quick mind and somehow scraped through his exams quite easily. Everyone loved him; he was so easy to get along with. John and Amy got closer and closer as time went by, eventually falling in love and when their studies had finished he planned to marry her.

It was the day of graduation when they had all passed their exams with flying colours that John proposed to Amy and she accepted. The wedding was a lavish affair held at John's parent's house in the Hertfordshire countryside and fifty guests attended. Joe was best man.

Afterwards Joe went on to do private medicine in his home town of Bedfordshire and Amy and John both worked at the Royal Free Hospital and bought a lovely property in Hampstead. John went on to be an orthopaedic surgeon and Amy worked in A&.E. Life was good for the first few years. They had a lovely home and good jobs but Amy started noticing how controlling and possessive John was becoming, which caused arguments. When the twins came along they were both delighted but the arguments continued and that's when Amy took to drinking heavily. John blamed her for everything, as having an addiction in his eyes was a sign of weakness, which would not be tolerated especially in front of his girls. He told her to leave and she begged to take her daughters with her but he refused and she had no choice but to go.

John had a very strict upbringing as a child. His father had a military background and was very regimental in his ways; there was no place for mistakes. When young John did something wrong he had his hands slapped with a leather belt and got sent to his room with no supper and that went on all through his young life till he left home.

Amy had always stayed in close contact with Joe but John had become arrogant and big headed and lost all his old friends. Amy moved back in with her parents and started meeting up with Joe regularly and eventually they were inseparable just like the old days. She had never felt so happy. Joe said he had always had feelings for her but John was his friend and he wouldn't have attempted to come between them. Life was good and they made plans to move in together, eventually buying a beautiful maisonette in East-Finchley. Slowly Joe got her on the road to recovery until all that was left to complete her happiness was to fight to get her daughters back where they belonged, with her. John was full of anger and bitterness when he found out and was determined she would have no part in the children's lives; as far as he was concerned she was a failure who never lived up to his expectations as a wife and mother to love, honour, but most of all to obey.

Marcie was concerned. She had a letter from her mother saying her father had left home and was now living with 'Betsy the whore' as she put it, who owned the Stag pub in the village, and wanted her to come home. Malcolm was a kind hearted man and told Nancy that maybe it was time she had a holiday and paid her mum a visit. He knew she had some problems with her which needed to be addressed and he didn't want her to have any regrets later on. He said that as the hotel was quiet they could manage, and Nancy agreed.

Marcie packed her bags the next morning unsure what reception she would get from her mother, but she knew Malcolm and Nancy were right – she should go as she was needed. It had been a long time since she had seen her and maybe she was lonely and they could build some bridges and put the past behind them.

Malcolm drove Marcie to the station and put her on the train. She hugged him so tightly he couldn't breathe. 'Look hinny,' he said, 'you're not walking into the lion's den; me and Nancy are always here for you but I know you love your mum deep down and you have to face things in life however bad in order to move on. Do you understand what I'm saying?'

Marcie looked at this man with so much love in her heart and she felt stronger than ever and kissed him on the cheek. 'I'll be home soon,' she said.

'And we will be waiting for you.'

The journey seemed to take forever but finally she reached her destination and got a taxi to her address. Nellie was at the door to greet her and Marcie thought she had aged tremendously; her hair was greying in places and she had a kind of stoop, but she gave her a hug and welcomed her. Marcie looked around the place and noticed the pictures on the mantelpiece of Jack and Tom were missing. Also, the place wasn't as spotless as she remembered, there was dust everywhere and that unnerved her as her mum was always meticulous and hated dust and dirt. Nellie had cooked chicken and roast potatoes with veg and told Marcie to take her coat off and sit at the table as the meal was ready and would get cold.

Nellie looked nervous as to what to say as she had been living alone for so long and had lost her self-confidence; no longer the formidable woman she once was. Marcie picked up on that and actually felt sorry for this woman in front of her but she still felt anger inside as this wasn't someone who had treated her like a daughter. She thanked her mum for dinner and said she felt tired after the journey so was going to have a lie down.

'Yes, you do that, and when you wake up I'll make you a nice cup of tea.'

Marcie went and lay on the bed thinking. She could see the loneliness in her mother's eyes but now wasn't the time to talk; there was plenty of time for that. The cottage was dark and dreary, lifeless and uncared for and it made Marcie shudder. So many bad memories...the only happy ones she remembered were when her brother Jack was alive; he could light up any room...

A little later Nellie heard Marcie moving around upstairs and quickly put the kettle on to make a cup of tea. When she came down her mother handed her a cup. 'Did you sleep well?' she asked.

'Not really.' There was an awkward silence. 'Where's Dad?'

'I told you in the letter, he is living in the pub with that whore...and I don't want you to go and see him, he is a disgrace. All the people in the village are talking about him leaving me here on my own.'

Marcie had heard enough and let fly. 'Mum, what does it matter? You and Dad never had a good word to say to one another! My poor brother Jack and me had to live with your abuse and arguments, walking on eggshells and afraid most of the time. You make me feel sick to my stomach! Why the fuck do you want to be together?' Nellie was shocked but knew her daughter was right - this was an unhealthy marriage from the beginning and if she had to be honest she didn't love Tom - it was her pride that was hurt.

Marcie needed to get out of the cottage before she exploded again. 'I'm going to visit Elsie's mum; I'll be back later,' but before her mum could answer she walked out of the door. Gone were the days when she had a say in what she did.

After a short wait the bus arrived and Marcie made the journey to Elsie's house. Jean opened the door and was so pleased to see her. 'My god, I can't believe it! Come in; the boys will be so pleased to see you.'

Keith was smoking a cigarette in the garden and when he walked in he flung his arms around Marcie, but she was in shock. What had happened to this lovely man? He had gone thin and looked like he had lost interest in his appearance.

'I know what you're thinking, lass, I can tell the way you are looking at me, but it isn't easy being made redundant and we have had our struggles with Elsie. This has been a bad time for all of us.'

Marcie felt embarrassed. She never meant to make this wonderful family who had always been so good to her in the past feel uncomfortable in her presence.

Jean cooked a lovely broth and baked fresh bread and they all sat down to dinner. Marcie asked them for Elsie's address so she could visit her but they were a bit reluctant as they explained it was a council flat on a bad estate with drug addicts and dealers. They said that when they themselves had visited her they had been on the receiving end of verbal abuse and threats from the dealers who were suspicious of anyone interfering. In time the police advised them to stay away and let them do their job. Marcie felt she owed her friend something and had to try to get through to her somehow - this wasn't the kind, loving friend she remembered, but she knew anyone could screw up; her parents were a reminder of that.

In the end she managed to convince Elsie's parents to give her the address and ordered a taxi to collect her the next morning. Nellie was annoyed thinking she was spending more time going out than keeping her company but Marcie ignored her snide remarks over breakfast and quickly put her coat on when she heard the taxi pull up. When she handed the address to the cab driver he grimaced.

'This estate you're visiting is rough; loads of druggies hang out there. Are you sure you have the right address?'

Marcie was getting irritated. 'Of course I'm sure.'

'Alright love, just asking,' and after an hour's journey he pulled up outside the block of flats.

Marcie got out of the cab and couldn't believe her eyes. There was filth everywhere she looked. Overfull bins spilling rubbish onto overgrown front gardens, and boarded up windows to replace smashed panes of glass. After paying the cab driver Marcie walked up to the main door and rung the number on the intercom. After a while she realised that no one was going to answer, but followed behind as a young unkempt woman pushing a buggy let herself in.

Each block only had four floors and as Marcie climbed the stairs she realised that each floor was as disgusting as the first. There were used needles and plastic bags everywhere, not to mention the stench of goodness knows what. Elsie was on the top floor in the corner flat and outside was a broken chair and four black sacks full of rubbish. Marcie had reservations when she rung the bell but she had come this far and there was no going back. When Elsie answered the door she couldn't believe her eyes. She was heavily pregnant and looked a mess, with greasy, unkempt hair and filthy clothes.

'Marcie, what the hell are you doing here?' Elsie asked, looking embarrassed. 'You'd better come in.'

Marcie looked around the room and couldn't believe what she was seeing; no furniture except for a dirty settee in the middle of the room, and junk everywhere. The floor was covered with lino and a disgusting rug, and there was a cardboard box in the middle of the room with a TV on top.

'I know what you're thinking,' Elsie said, looking nervous, 'but this is all we could afford for now.'

Marcie looked at her friend who was standing in front of her and was overcome with a feeling of sadness. She had a gaunt face, which made her large spectacles look even bigger. 'What the hell are you doing here? Tell me the truth; are you on drugs?'

'Don't be stupid, I'm pregnant, but to be honest, I did dabble with them for a while.'

'Please come with me,' Marcie pleaded, 'and I will take you back to your parent's house; they are worried sick about you.

Elsie became enraged. 'Who the hell do you think you are with all your fancy ideas? Just because you work in London doesn't make you better than me. I'm happy living here and have found someone who truly loves me. It was alright for you; at school everyone fancied you; me, I was just a laughing stock.'

Marcie got angry. 'I agree, maybe that's true, but I would have given anything to have parents like yours. You know how hard it was for me: mine hated me and they wished I had never been born,' and the tears streamed down her face.

Elsie knew she was telling the truth and remembered how Nellie and Tom had treated her and how it had affected her schooling. She often wrote letters in class planning to run away but didn't have the courage to go through with it. Elsie got up and threw her arms around her. 'Sorry Marcie. I know you are a true friend but our lives have gone in different directions. I am happy with Pete and we are so looking forward to the baby arriving. I wish you every happiness, but as my mum used to say, different strokes for different folks.'

Marcie could see she was getting nowhere but made Elsie promise that if ever she needed her help she would give her a ring and she would be there for her no matter what.

'Give Mum and Dad my love,' Elsie said with a sad look about her, 'and tell them I will let them know when the baby arrives. I think it's best if you go now, as Pete doesn't take kindly to strangers around.

Marcie left feeling she had let her friend down in many ways by moving to London, but knew Elsie was adamant that she wanted to stay with her boyfriend, and she had to respect her wishes. When the baby arrived hopefully things might be different and she would maybe ask for her parent's help at some point, as whatever happened they would never turn their back on her.

Marcie phoned Jean and Keith the next morning. They were upset but thanked Marcie for her help; as they at least knew she was alright and there was some glimmer of hope as their daughter had said she would be in touch when the baby arrived.

Chapter Five

Marcie was sitting at home having an evening meal her mum had prepared. She realized her mother would never move on from her past, she was still complaining about her dad every second. 'He's a waster, a good for nothing - always will be.'

Marcie had heard enough and told her to shut up. 'You're rid of him now so let it go. Anyway Mum, I want to go to the Stag pub and see him before I go back to London.'

Nellie was furious. 'What do you mean? He's not interested in you!'

'I know Mum, but he did give me £20 when I was leaving home and I want to give it back as I don't want anything from him. I also want to give him a piece of my mind and find out why he treated me the way he did; after all, he is my dad, and I'm his only daughter.'

Nellie got out of her chair and lost all control. 'You are wrong! He isn't your father and he made my life hell and I wish....'

'Yes, I know...you wish you never had me. Who is my dad? That's all I want to know.'

Nellie could not bring herself to tell her the truth, that it was her Uncle Sam, so lied and told her it was a one night stand with a man who she met in the pub and had never heard from him again. Marcie could tell she was lying. Her mum was a stickler for detail and lived off her past. Somehow, the way she had been treated all started to make sense.

Nellie tried to put her arms around Marcie but it was too late; this pathetic woman who stood in front of her made her feel sick to her stomach with the lies and pretence of all those years.

'I am going to bed and will be going early in the morning. I can't bear to be in this house one minute longer.'

Marcie went upstairs to pack her case and her mum followed her up. 'Look, this is stupid; a few days are not going to make any difference. I promise I'll stay out of your way. I do get a bit lonely here on my own.' In the end Marcie agreed, but only because she would have to buy another train ticket and she didn't have enough money for that.

Nellie prepared breakfast the next morning and Marcie sat down at the table and glanced at her mum who looked defeated and sad, as if she had given up on life itself. 'Mum, have you ever thought of meeting someone else? You are still young enough to you know.'

Nellie was shocked. 'Who the hell would want me now? Mind you, in my youth I was pretty and I used to turn many a man's head – I had a figure like yours.'

Marcie had never heard her mum associate herself to being remotely like her in any conversation they had ever had while she was growing up, and it would have meant a lot to her then, but now she could see she was isolated and afraid of being on her own and was reaching out to her. 'I have an idea,' she said. 'Why don't we go for a walk down the village to that lovely bakery and have a cake and a cup of tea; I can just about pay for that.' The breakfast her mother had prepared was now cold. Nellie thought it was a good idea as she hadn't left the house for a few days and needed some fresh air.

The sun was gleaming through the clouds but it was quite chilly. As they were approaching the bakery Nellie noticed two women sitting outside drinking tea, and as she got closer one of them turned her head and stared at her and started pointing while talking to her friend. 'There she is, the woman who has been spreading rumours about me in the shops! I can't believe my Tom was married to an old crow like you.' Nellie realized it was the village whore as she called her to anyone who was willing to listen; Betsy, the landlady from the Stag pub who was now living with Tom.

'Right, let's go somewhere else,' said Marcie trying to pull her mum in the opposite direction, but in a split second Nellie bent over Betsy who was still sitting down and gave her a sharp slap across her face. With that her friend quickly stood up and slapped her back.

Nellie was incensed. 'You bitch! You're nothing but a whore and the talk of the village! You're running a brothel not a pub! You can have Tom for all I care, he is a good for nothing, spineless man and you both deserve one another!'

Marcie dragged her mum away from the bakery and she could hear Betsy behind her in the background shouting, 'You will pay for that you slut!' as they both hurried further down the road.

The day had gone from bad to worse and Marcie was pleased to get indoors. Her mum was acting as if nothing had happened and took her coat off and proceeded to put the kettle on and make a cup of tea. What Marcie couldn't get her head round was why her mum reacted in the way she did; after all, it wasn't marital bliss with Tom, it was more a marriage of convenience.

Nellie could see she had to say something or she would never see her daughter again so she tried to explain to her how it was when they were both courting and how differently things could have been.

Marcie had heard enough. 'Mother, you have to move on, you're living off your past. There is no such thing as a perfect world. It's your own insecurities that are holding you back; you are just jealous Dad and Betsy have started a new life together and you're here on your own.' But Nellie said she didn't want to discuss it anymore and Marcie left it like that.

Marcie went to bed that night and knew in her heart it would be a long time before she visited home again; she couldn't wait to return back to London and Nancy and Malcolm. She recalled what Malcolm had said to her before she left: *Some people you can't help, but the good news is you know you tried and you have to look forward to your future and make something of your life.*

The next morning Marcie said her goodbye's to her mum and was just about to get into the taxi when she called her back. 'Look love, I don't suppose you have any spare cash to lend me? I'm running a bit short.' Marcie gave her the £5 Malcolm had given her that was supposed to be for magazines and a sandwich on the train, but she was so glad to be leaving that it somehow didn't matter - a small price to pay for getting back to normality.

The train arrived at the station and Marcie got on. The journey seemed to take forever, but when she finally arrived Malcolm was waiting for her. Her face lit up when she saw him on the platform and she fell into his arms and they hugged one another.

'Did you have a good time pet? We've missed you so much. Nancy has cooked you a lovely meal,' but he could tell from her expression that the holiday hadn't gone well.

Nancy was beside herself when Marcie walked in the door; she had missed her company so much and gave her loads of kisses and hugs. Marcie went straight upstairs and unpacked her suitcase and when she came back down Malcolm and Nancy were relaxing in the sitting room. Nancy was anxious to know all the gossip and Marcie explained everything. Malcolm was upset but not surprised. 'A leopard never changes its spots. You have to think about yourself, and if I were you I would phone Mr Evans; he will be expecting a call from you now if you still intend to take the job.'

Marcie phoned him the next day and he arranged to meet her at a restaurant in Hampstead the following day.

When Marcie arrived at the restaurant the next day she was introduced to Biba and Tilly, Mr Evans' daughters who looked like two little models in their gorgeous outfits and with neat plaits in their hair. They were immaculately turned out. Mr Evans politely shook her hand and so did the girls. Marcie felt underdressed in her grey mohair coat with the big collar which she had purchased in a charity shop two years previously and a handbag that belonged to Nancy but which she insisted she use. Marcie hadn't wanted to offend her, but it was so out of date; black with a big buckle on the front and fringes hanging from it.

They all sat down for lunch and John started the conversation. 'Have you decided what you want to do? Are you going to take the job?' Marcie said she would love to work for him but wanted to know if she had the weekends free. He was quiet for a brief moment before reminding her that he wanted someone flexible, but said he was willing to make exceptions if need be. She asked the girls if they enjoyed school and what their interests were and they both chorused, 'Drama and English'. They weren't very forthcoming but she put it down to shyness - they were very polite and endearing and she liked them both. Marcie agreed to take the job and they agreed that she would start the following week, but afterwards felt she should have asked more questions about wages and the hours she would be working, though was confident it would work out fine.

When she arrived back at the hotel Malcolm and Nancy were both crying in the kitchen. 'What's happened?' she asked, concerned.

Mr Grimes had died peacefully that morning in hospital with his friend at his bedside. Marcie flung her arms around them both and shed a few tears herself. She was very fond of him too, and would always remember him as a kind man who lived life to the full and didn't have a bad word to say about anyone, a true gent.

The completion of the sale of the hotel was to take another three weeks but Marcie was preparing to move out to start her new job the following week. Malcolm and Nancy told her there wasn't a problem they could manage themselves as they were arranging for the removal company to do all the packing and they wouldn't be taking in anymore guests. Southend-on-Sea was their next move and they had made arrangements to stay in a hotel right on the front on a long term basis.

The week had flown by and Marcie had mixed feelings about leaving the next morning to start her new job, but Malcolm and Nancy had cooked her a lovely meal that evening and she didn't want to spoil anything by being miserable and seeming ungrateful to the two people she loved most in the world.

Nancy couldn't finish her meal, she was too upset.

'Come on, love, we must be happy for Marcie. She's a young woman who needs to spread her wings and go to pastures new, and she will always be a part of our lives; it's not as if we'll never see her again,' said Malcolm, and smiling, Nancy agreed.

Malcolm left the room and came back with an envelope in his hand which he gave to Marcie. 'This is for you pet, to give you a kick start for your future.'

Marcie thanked him and opened the envelope. Inside was £200. 'I can't accept that. It's far too much.'

Malcolm saw tears streaming down her face. She was completely overwhelmed. 'Come on pet, you deserve it. The day you came into our lives it was like a gift from God. We both love you and want nothing but the best for you.' Nancy got up from her chair and held her close with her crippled hands and blessed the day she had met this wonderful human being who had so much to offer in life with her caring nature.

The taxi arrived the next morning and Marcie said her goodbyes but it was the hardest thing she had ever done leaving these two people who she had become so fond of and loved unconditionally. Jim the cab driver was pleased to see her again but had a few reservations about the area she was moving to as he knew the people who lived there had money and big houses and letters after their names: doctors, journalists and the like and who he had often found to be rude and arrogant and a general pain in the arse when it came to having them in his cab and paying the fare. He had come to the conclusion that the more money people had the greedier they became; snobs in his eye's who he had no time for.

Marcie got out of the cab and thanked Jim and he wished her luck but had the feeling their paths would cross again. John was standing at the door as he had seen the cab drive up from his office window and carried Marcie's suitcase into the house but was a bit surprised by how small and tatty it was. Yes, it was leather, but it was stained and well worn with the handle barely holding onto the case.

'I would like you to meet Mrs Tucker but we all call her Doris.'

Marcie shook her hand, and Doris could see she was nervous and gave her a cuddle. John disliked displays of affection in public and told them he had to get back to the hospital leaving Doris to settle Marcie in and show her around the house.

'Would you like some tea?' she asked.

'Please; with milk and one sugar,' Marcie replied looking around the large kitchen, which had a huge round oak table and chairs in the middle and a beautifully tiled floor.

'I want to give you a bit of advice, Marcie, as I have worked here a long time. Keep your head down and do your work. John is not easy to get along with at times and can be impatient, but he has an important job to do and he loves the girls.'

'Where is their mum?'

'Amy is now living with John's friend from their student days but it's none of our business. All I can say is Amy was a lovely girl but John's parents told me she was an alcoholic who brought shame on the family and walked out and left her two girls, although personally I never believed that. She was a good mum and would never leave her kids intentionally, but I did see her worse for wear on many occasions, poor soul, and going on information from Charlie the gardener, that particular day she was screaming and shouting at John before she got in the car, pleading to take her daughters with her, but he was having none of it. I often think about her; we got on so well. She was soft natured and I felt guilty turning her away when she came to the house to see the girls, but John warned me I would be fired on the spot if I ever let her in,' and tears welled up in Doris's eyes.

Marcie thought it best not to ask any more questions as she could see how fond she was of Amy and how difficult it must have been.

Doris showed Marcie to her bedroom, a large room with two bay windows; it was light and airy with a double bed in the middle and a large wardrobe and chest of drawers. 'I'm afraid I have a lot to do in the kitchen, so you unpack and come down when you're ready. I'm sure you will settle in nicely, and I for one am so pleased you're here.'

Marcie sat on the bed taking in her surroundings. It was a beautiful room and she liked Doris but felt alone and missed the security of Malcolm and Nancy and wondered if she had made a big mistake by not going with them. The view from the window was beautiful. It was of the approach to the front of the house with the huge garden with its fountain and large conifers and a pond in the middle. There was a young man doing the gardening but she couldn't make out what he looked like as he wore a flat cap, though she deduced that it was someone her own age and so maybe she would have a friend after all.

Marcie unpacked and went downstairs to join Doris in the kitchen. 'What can I do to help you?' she asked.

'Well, I am behind, so if you can peel the vegetables that will be a great help, and I'll make a casserole for you all this evening. The girls normally have a sandwich when they come home from school till they have their evening meal with John.' Doris was very plump and short but had a motherly look about her with a rounded face and her grey hair up in a bun. Marcie could see she must have been a beauty in her youth as she had a lovely smile and soft features.

'I noticed a gardener outside,' Marcie said. 'Is that Charlie?'

'Look,' Doris answered with a worried look on her face, 'don't be foolish chatting to him too much as John will be angry. The other nanny we had here for two months was caught half-naked in the shed with him by a delivery man and he told John. Charlie was lucky he wasn't sacked himself but he managed to talk his way out of it. The nanny had to go in the end with no references.'

'That's a shame; it takes two to tango, but I'm not that silly, so you don't have to worry about me,' but she didn't realize that one day she would have to swallow her words.

It was time to pick up the girls from school which was just a short walk away and Marcie went with her as after today that was to be her job. The girls came out of school looking smart in their blue uniform which consisted of a blazer and white shirt with a pleated skirt. They immediately ran to Doris when she approached the school gates and she hugged them. Anyone could see how fond they were of her and she of them, and they walked either side of her holding her hands tightly making no attempt to acknowledge Marcie.

'I think you ought to say hello to Marcie,' Doris said to the girls as they walked down the path. 'She will be the one looking after you from now on and I know you will have some fun times with her if you give her a chance. What do you say?'

They both looked up and gave Marcie a smile but she knew it would take time for them all to get to know each other and she wanted to gain their trust first so she didn't push it.

Doris said goodbye to the girls and Marcie when she got back to the house and said she would see them all tomorrow. Biba was the least shy of the two and told Marcie that she and Tilly had to go upstairs and take off their uniform. They both had their own rooms and they were neat and tidy but Marcie thought they looked stark with no toys around and their shoes displayed in a neat line up against the wall.

Marcie found the house was run with military precision and was told by Biba that they had homework to do for one hour after they had changed their clothes.

'Can I help in any way?'

'Thank you, but it's only drawing and I will help Tilly if she wants me to.'

John returned home around 6.30pm and he put the casserole in the oven to heat up and they all sat around the table for their evening meal. He told the girls to sit up straight and take their elbows off the table. Marcie looked at their faces and could tell they were annoyed but did as they were told. John asked Marcie if the room was suitable and if she needed anything.

'It's fine, thank you Mr Evans,' she said.

He looked irritated. 'Call me John; I get enough of that at work and I want you to treat this as your home, no formalities.'

After the meal John said he had paperwork to do in his office and asked Marcie to see to the girls' baths before bedtime at 8.30 prompt. Biba asked her father if it would be possible to have

Marcie read a bedtime story to them. He looked reluctant at first but agreed. Marcie saw that as a way of getting to know them a bit better and was delighted.

The book they both chose was *Peter Rabbit* and when Marcie had finished reading it she tucked the girls up in bed and gave them a kiss goodnight. She felt out of her comfort zone and wasn't sure what to do next so she went downstairs to the kitchen to make herself a cup of tea.

John called her into his office. 'Take a seat Marcie. I was wondering what you would think of me buying a puppy for the girls. The reason I'm asking is you will have to take it to the park and be responsible for it.'

Marcie loved animals but thought she had enough to do with the housework during the day. 'That's fine by me, but will Doris be alright with that?'

John looked surprised. 'You are quite outspoken; not the little mouse I thought you were.'

Marcie answered back quickly, 'Yes I'm afraid I can speak my mind if need be.'

'Don't worry about Doris, I'll talk to her. Now, is that settled then?' John told Marcie that Sunday was her day off but she could take the girls to the kennels with him on Saturday for them to choose one. The phone rang and Marcie slipped out of the office so that John had his privacy. There was something about him she admired even though he was a lot older and scary at times; so serious - an 'old fart' as Nancy would say.

The next morning she took the girls to school and they both seemed to open up to her telling her what their rota was for the day: drama, music, English, and who their favourite teachers were. When she arrived back at the house Doris was in the kitchen having tea and toast and made her some.

'Well pet, how did you get on with the girls last night? I hope they behaved.'

'They were very sweet, no bother at all.'

'Will you take a mug of tea out to Charlie? He's mowing the front lawn; and tell him if he wants a bacon sarni he will have to come in. It's bloody freezing out there; we are not here to run around after the likes of him.'

Just at that moment Charlie walked through the door. 'I can feel my ears burning, are you nattering about me?'

Doris chuckled. He was a cheeky chappy, but she liked him all the same. 'This is Marcie who is working for us now; and you can keep your filthy thoughts to yourself! She is too good for the likes of you.' Doris knew he had a succession of girlfriends and didn't mind boasting about them. Marcie took it as good banter; she could see there was affection between them both.

Charlie was twenty-five and lived in a bedsit in Kentish Town. He had been brought up in a succession of foster homes from an early age. He was hard working and had worked for John for about three years and they got on well mainly because Charlie had been institutionalized for so long and had learned to adapt to people like John, knowing when to hold his tongue and say nothing. She liked him with his baby face, cropped hair and cheeky grin and immediately felt they would become friends.

Doris told Charlie to get back to work as she was cooking a pot roast and had loads to do. Marcie began to do the cleaning, starting with the bedrooms. When she came to doing John's bedroom she was amazed to see how masculine it was considering he'd been married. There were no feminine touches at all and it was devoid of photos, as if he had tried to wipe way his past and all memories of Amy, but when she delved in the drawers the photos were all placed there tidily, showing holidays together with the girls and pictures of Amy's pregnancy. They had looked like one big, happy family. Marcie felt sad for John but knew there were always two sides to every story and she mustn't let her heart rule her head.

On Saturday the girls were excited as John drove them to Hertfordshire to buy their new puppy. Marcie sat in the front of the car and had packed them all a cheese and ham sandwich and a bottle of water. When they arrived at the kennels the breeder took them to see three litters of West Highland terriers which they could choose from. Eventually John decided to have a dog and not a bitch of which there was a selection of six. The whole process took a few hours and they finally picked the smallest pup of the litter and the girls called him Rupert after Biba's favourite teddy bear.

When they arrived back at the house John went straight to his office and the girls played downstairs with the puppy, which gave Marcie spare time to write letters to Nancy and Malcolm and Elsie.

The following day it was Marcie's day off. Charlie had

mentioned during the week that he was going to the pub with some friends on Sunday afternoon and she would be welcome to join them but she would have to make her own way to Kentish Town Station and he would be there to meet her. Marcie phoned him to let him know she was coming and put on her favourite black dress, but when she walked down the stairs John looked a bit miserable. 'I must say you look adorable. I hope you enjoy yourself, but don't be back too late.'

Marcie felt a little guilty as she had started to feel attracted to John. She tried to dismiss her feelings knowing nothing would come of it; this wasn't supposed to happen. She said her goodbyes and left the house to catch her train.

When she arrived at Kentish Town Charlie was there to meet her with two of his friends Bobby and Val who looked like hippies. She was a bit disappointed at how scruffy they looked considering how much of an effort she had made but realized that was the company Charlie mixed with and had to be polite as she didn't want to offend anyone.

The pub was old fashioned with dark wallpaper and looked like it needed a revamp, but it was their local and after she had a few dry martinis she felt a lot more relaxed. Charlie put his arm around her but she quickly removed it as she didn't want him to get the wrong idea. Val wore a low cut dress which emphasized her bosoms and was loud and a bit over the top but Marcie liked her, as she was easy to talk to and down to earth. Bobby on the other hand was brutal and straight to the point. 'Charlie you must have thought you had died and gone to heaven; she's a bit of all right; I wouldn't say no to a bit of that. Have you tested the waters yet?' What he didn't know was that Marcie had heard every word and felt uncomfortable and wanted to leave but Val insisted she stay and have another drink.

Eventually the taxi pulled up outside to take her home and she thanked Charlie and his friends but she was pleased to be leaving. They were nice enough but she felt they were quite immature and the only person on her mind was John who gave her a sense of security and stability.

When she arrived back she saw his office light on and was just about to go upstairs when he called out to her, 'Would you care to join me for a night cap?'

'Yes, thank you; that would be lovely.'

They sat in the lounge and he poured her a glass of white wine and himself a whisky. 'I have a present for you Marcie,' he said, and he handed her a velvet box.

Surprised, she opened it and her heart melted when she discovered a beautiful gold necklace and locket inside. John placed it around her neck and told her how lovely she looked. Marcie had butterflies in her stomach; she had never been given anything as special as that before. John was good at turning on the charm then switching it off and abruptly told her to have a good night's sleep as she had an early start in the morning, before kissing her gently on the cheek.

In bed, sleep evaded her and Marcie tossed and turned thinking about John and the events of the evening.

Chapter Six

Doris was making breakfast in the kitchen and getting more and more irritated by the minute. Marcie was late coming down and the girls were in the kitchen annoying her chatting twenty to the dozen and she had so much to do.

Marcie came downstairs and apologised to Doris, but there was a veil of silence as they went about their business. Doris gave the girls their breakfast and when they had finished Marcie took them to school and took Rupert with her for a bit of exercise.

In the now peaceful kitchen Doris put the kettle on and made herself a well-earned cup of tea. She had noticed a change in Marcie in the few months she had known her – and she wasn't altogether sure that it was a change for the better. Still, it was early days yet and she was willing to put it down to the fact that she was finding her feet so to speak...

The doorbell rang interrupting her thoughts and she rushed to open the door. Her heart sank when she saw John's parents standing there in all their refinement. Doris stood there wiping her hands down her apron ready to shake their hands but they walked straight past her. Margaret and George were a force to be reckoned with; so formidable and rude, they never came for a visit, it was more like an inspection. Doris excused herself and went back into the kitchen leaving them to go around the house with a fine tooth comb as usual, looking to see if standards had been maintained.

Marcie came back from taking the girls to school and was surprised to see them there. John had told her they had a place abroad, so often spent the winter there.

'How are my darling grandchildren getting on at school?' Margaret asked.

'Fine,' Marcie said, 'they are both doing well.'

'What the hell is that monstrosity?' Margaret shrieked as Rupert came bounding towards her wagging his tail. 'Please get him out of here! What was John thinking of, buying a dog?'

George agreed. 'Dogs should be outdoors in kennels, not inside spreading germs.' Marcie was shocked by their behaviour but took Rupert into another room out of their sight.

There was tension in the air - they were the most unsociable couple Marcie had ever come across, but knew she had to be polite otherwise John would be disappointed in her, so biting her tongue she offered them a cup of tea. Doris had got used to them over the years and kept out of their way, she had encountered their interference and threatened to leave many times in the past, but John had always managed to calm things down, telling his parents she was here to stay, and they finally got the message.

Margaret told Marcie in no uncertain terms that she was lucky to find employment with her son and expected her to clean the place to a high standard. After her inspection she said it was dusty behind the beds and the cream carpets were dirty; the list was endless. Marcie apologised and said she would see to it. When they finally decided to leave after their tea Marcie gave a sigh of relief but they said they were coming back at the weekend to see the grandchildren and for her to let John know. As Marcie saw them out George noticed a stain on her dress and told her to have it cleaned. That was the final straw.

Doris came out of the kitchen when they had gone and saw Marcie sitting on the settee looking upset. 'Come and have lunch and don't worry about them; John won't sack you. I think you're doing a grand job. They are living in a different world to us and love to think we are the underdog. It's all about money, you see, and status, but I would rather have my life any day.'

Marcie felt guilty. If only Doris knew how attracted she was to John and that she was starting to have feelings for him, but then she dismissed the thought, doubting he would ever feel the same way towards her.

John was in a foul mood when he came home. He'd had a telephone call at the hospital from Amy's solicitors with a date to attend court. They said she was back at work and wanted access to the girls. She intended to marry in the near future after the divorce papers came through. Marcie always put John's mood swings down to the stress of his job. He could quite often be aggressive and rude, sometimes reducing her to tears, and that evening was no exception.

Biba and Tilly kept out of their father's way and played in their bedroom after dinner till it was time to go to bed. Marcie tucked them in and came downstairs. John was having a whisky in the sitting room. 'Help yourself to a Martini,' he told her, 'but at this rate I will have to deduct the money out of your wages.' Marcie ignored him and sat quietly,

John continued having more drinks and firing insults at her. 'What the hell are you staring at you stupid girl? Have you nothing intelligent to say, the wannabe from Wales who came to London to make her fortune?'

Marcie had heard enough and got up from the settee to go upstairs. As she did, John grabbed her and kissed her passionately and she reciprocated loving every minute. John looked at her and was mesmerized by her beauty. He unbuttoned her dress and caressed her breasts. Marcie had never been touched like this before; her whole body was filled with excitement and longing; she didn't want it to end. The doorbell rang and John pulled away and told her to tidy herself up as it could be his parents. When she answered the door it was Charlie asking her if she wanted to go to the pub with him and his mates. Marcie was furious as he had interrupted precious time spent with John, but before she had time to say anything John was behind her telling her to go as he had other things to attend to in his office.

Marcie reluctantly went to the pub with Charlie, but he could see her mind was elsewhere, and when anyone spoke to her she was aloof and looked agitated. It made him feel vexed when his friends had welcomed her and put her at ease by chatting to her and she made no effort whatsoever to join in the conversation.

They had been in the pub an hour when he lost his temper. 'What is wrong with you Marcie? You are fucking rude! You've sat there and my friends have bought you drinks and you haven't even had the decency to join in the conversation, you've just looked at them as if they were shit.'

Marcie got up from her seat. 'Get lost, Charlie. I didn't ask them to buy me drinks and talk to me, did I? I've had enough; I want to go home.'

Charlie phoned a cab and was pleased to put her in it and send her home. What had happened to the lovely girl he had first met? She had definitely changed in his eyes, but deep down he knew something was behind it and was determined to find out.

Marcie arrived home and John was in bed so she quietly went up to her room. Thinking back on the evening she was filled with mixed emotions. She felt sorry for the way she'd treated Charlie and his friends but she would have rather spent the rest of the evening with John who she felt she had so much more in common with. She undressed and got into bed thinking about him and the passion they had shared earlier. Just thinking of the way he had caressed her and what might have been had they not been interrupted sent a tingling sensation through her whole body. She lay there replaying the scene in her mind over and over before eventually falling into a deep sleep.

The following morning she found a note that had been pushed under her door. *Meet me at the park by the coffee bar at 12.30pm. xxxx* Marcie was thrilled. She put her best dress on and decided to tie her long, black, curly hair back in a pony tail. When she was satisfied with how she looked she went downstairs. Doris could sense there was something in the air when she walked into the kitchen with a spring in her step and a smile on her face – She wasn't usually a morning person.

'Why are you so happy this morning? Have you found yourself a boyfriend?'

'No, just in a good mood I suppose. What's wrong with that?' But Doris was no fool; she knew the signs. She was practically glowing, so there had to be a boy on the scene; maybe someone she had met at the pub.

Rupert was a pain that morning refusing to get out of his bed for his walk so Marcie took the girls to school without him. Doris insisted she hurried back and walk him as she didn't want puddles all over her kitchen floor. Marcie said she was meeting a friend at the park for an hour and would take him then as she had a few hours owing her.

The morning went by at a snail's pace with Marcie doing her chores and looking at the clock every five minutes, willing it to go faster. When noon finally came she tidied herself up, put her coat and boots on and ushered Rupert into the kitchen where she put his lead on. She said goodbye to Doris and hurried out of the door making her way excitedly to the park.

As she walked through the park looking for John she spotted Charlie sitting by the entrance to the cafe. Looking up and seeing her he walked over, patted Rupert's head and put his arm around her.

Marcie shrugged him off. 'What are you doing here?'

'Sit down Marcie; I need to talk to you.' Marcie sat down but inside she was furious. 'What is going on with you? Is there something you're not telling me?' Charlie knew she had something to hide and was getting impatient. 'I have come to think of you as a friend and you can tell me anything, but your mood swings are becoming an embarrassment. I cherish the people I am fond of, not having much family of my own, so to speak.'

Marcie hated the intrusion and told him he was being paranoid and ought to get a life. Charlie exploded at that point and told her what a stuck up, selfish bitch she had become. With that, Marcie started to cry. Charlie felt he had gone too far and put his arm around her and apologised. Drying her eyes she explained her feelings for John, saying she was sure he felt the same way about her giving her such a wonderful gift and looking out for her.

Charlie bowed his head, feeling sorry for her. 'Don't be so naive, Marcie. The family are in a different league to us mere mortals; they live in another world. He will never love you; he just wants to have his wicked way with you. After all, you are a beauty, no mistake; I fancy you myself.'

Marcie got up off the bench, infuriated. 'How dare you speak to me like that? You're nothing but a gardener who John let stay out of pity and loyalty - you're lucky to still have employment with him! Doris told me the other nanny was sacked because you were caught in the shed with her!'

'OK, so I made a mistake, but he let me stay because he had no choice. John was going to court to gain custody of the girls at the time and he needed me to keep my mouth shut about all the affairs he'd had during his marriage. Amy visited her parents at weekends and that's when he got up to no good. I should know, I drove the girls home sometimes. Poor sods, they were just being used. Some of them were student nurses younger than you.'

Marcie had heard enough. 'Come on Rupert, we're going back,' she said walking away. This wasn't the person she knew, but was it possible he was telling the truth?

Doris could see the change in Marcie's mood when she came back from her walk. 'What's troubling you girl?'

'Nothing. I just have a headache and need to lie down,' and she headed for her room.

After a short sleep Marcie picked the girls up from school and then helped them with their homework whilst Doris cooked dinner.

The meal that evening was a silent one and the girls hardly ate anything, which made John angry. 'Has Doris been giving you biscuits again?'

'No father, we had a big lunch at school and had our usual sandwich when we got home,' Biba said.

'Tilly has the cat got your tongue? What about you? Speak up girl.' Tilly was nearly in tears; she was a sensitive child and hated it when her father raised his voice, which was more often than not.

Marcie spoke up. 'This is probably my fault. I did buy them both a bag of crisps on the way home from school.'

'Alright, you two can leave the table and go to your rooms. Marcie, you can run them a bath, and I want a word with you afterwards.' John was furious. She knew the rules and he didn't intend to let this go.

A little later Marcie tucked them both up in bed and came downstairs to find John pacing the floor.

'What the hell are you thinking of, feeding my girls rubbish? Marcie couldn't believe he was reacting in such a way.

'Don't you think John you are taking it too seriously? They are only children after all.'

'I will be the judge of that. If you let standards slip they will do as they please. Doris spends a long time in the kitchen preparing a balanced diet. What would you prefer to feed them on, burgers and chips, or pizzas?'

Marcie could see he was in foul mood and asked if she could go upstairs to write some letters and have a shower if he had nothing he needed her to do. She also still felt angry herself about what Charlie had told her but thought that was best left that for another time. She had never felt as lonely as she did at that moment and missed Nancy and Malcolm so much. She now regretted neglecting them by only making the occasional phone call to them and writing only once a month instead of every week. She put on her favourite record *If I'm a Fool for Loving You...* and it brought back memories of her and Elsie and the fun they had together. What was she thinking of letting John take over all her thoughts...and him treating her like a child, messing with her emotions? She wrote letters to Elsie and Nancy and Malcolm, had a shower and went to bed.

John was downstairs having a whisky and had calmed down, but the more he drank the more his thoughts turned to Marcie, the beautiful girl lying in bed upstairs.

Marcie heard a knock on her bedroom door. 'Come in,' she said, surprised. John sat on her bed and apologised for his behaviour, and before she knew what was happening she was in his arms. He gently began caressing her body all over, then lifted her nightie over her head and removed her panties. He then traced her curves with his tongue bringing her body to life with sensations she had never felt before. He kissed her mouth and she reached up pulling him closer and kissing him back passionately. It took his breath away when she then began to kiss his body all over, his breathing becoming quicker and quicker. When she placed her hand on his penis and started to caress it, he wanted her desperately...and she wanted him, but she also wanted him to wait just a little while longer but he became impatient and entered her, satisfying his needs completely. As he lay there, the tensions and stresses of the day now a distant memory, Marcie also lay there silently feeling cheated and unfulfilled. John abruptly got out of bed and got dressed. Marcie was unsure of what had just happened, it was all so quick, and then he kissed her gently on the cheek and said he had to go to his own room before the children awoke. She continued to lay there feeling confused and unsatisfied; she felt empty inside. This wasn't how she had imagined her first time would be. The earth hadn't moved and it had all been so rushed, coming to such an abrupt end and leaving her sore and uncomfortable. She hoped that the next time would be better.

The following morning John knocked on her bedroom door to see if she was alright and gave her a passionate kiss on the lips but Marcie didn't respond as she needed time on her own to collect her thoughts. She had feelings for John but after what Charlie had told her she couldn't be sure he felt the same way.

Doris was in the kitchen, her mind working overtime. Her suspicions were aroused when John had told her that a bouquet of flowers was being delivered for Marcie that afternoon as she needed cheering up, and she was to make sure that she got them. When he left for the hospital he said he wouldn't be home for dinner as he had a heavy schedule so to carry on without him. Marcie looked sheepish as she came down for breakfast and Doris was not in the mood to beat around the bush so she came straight out with it. 'Is there something going on with you and John I don't know about?'

Marcie was annoyed with her remark. 'That's my business; I am old enough to do what I want.'

Doris grabbed her by the arm. 'Listen to me; I know you have no friends here and it can get a bit lonely, but you're barking up the wrong tree. He is a man for god's sake and is fulfilling his needs. He doesn't love you, or anyone for that matter. He is incapable; just a selfish human being thinking about himself.'

Marcie started to cry. 'You've got it all wrong, Doris. He is a kind, gentle man and I love him. I know you think I am not good enough but I know he needs me and we can make a go of it.'

Doris knew from experience that she was banging her head against a brick wall and nothing she could say would make any difference. She knew that Marcie was letting her heart rule her head and would only learn by her mistakes. 'Do whatever you want, but be it on your own head young lady. Just don't come crying to me when it all goes belly up – and mark my words it will.'

Marcie didn't want to argue with Doris as she knew she had her own cross to bear. Her husband had suffered three heart attacks and eventually had to have a heart by-pass and still suffered breathing problems. She was the sole provider but her two grown up children, a girl and a boy in their thirties, still appeared on her doorstep for handouts when they were in dire straits.

Drying her eyes Marcie put Rupert's lead on and called the girls and walked them to school. On her way back she decided to walk Rupert through the park – she knew there would be plenty of other people walking their dogs and she wanted to socialize him. But as she walked through the gates a dog bolted past her followed by a girl of her own age frantically chasing him. Marcie approached her as she finally caught up with the dog and managed to put a lead around his neck. 'Hi, I'm Marcie. I thought you had lost him then.'

'So did I! Hi, my name's Zoe,' she gasped, and shook Marcie's hand. They decided to sit on a bench together so she could catch her breath. 'Tosca is a rescue dog, and she is as stubborn as a mule.' Marcie bent down to give her a stroke and she nearly bit her hand off. 'West Highland terriers have a mind of their own I'm afraid, but she is lovable once she gets to know you. I think she just mistrusts people, but in time I'm sure she will be OK. She was mistreated by her previous owners who kept her in kennels outside and never took her for walks.' Marcie kept Rupert on her lap, afraid she might lunge at him, but Zoe told her she was alright with her own breed it was mostly larger dogs she felt intimidated by. Taking a chance she put Rupert down on the ground and thankfully they seemed to get on well together.

Zoe looked at Marcie and could see she had classy looks and spoke well. Zoe was a hippy with long, tangled, auburn hair that looked like it had never seen a brush, but she had a petite figure, small features and big, blue, smiling eyes. She was a chatterbox by nature and continued to make small talk, eventually telling Marcie a bit about herself. 'I live with my partner, Jerry, in a one bedroom flat just overlooking the park. We've lived together two years. We've both recently dropped out of university studying psychology.'

'Is that where you both met?

'Yes.'

'What about your family?'

'My mother brought me up on her own and worked all the hours god sent doing three jobs a day.'

'What are you doing now?'

'Well, I'm working for the homeless selling *The Big Issue* on the streets and delivering food to families who are on low incomes. My partner does odd jobs when he can find them; he has always been good with his hands...very creative, and he's a good carpenter.'

Marcie was impressed and immediately took a liking to Zoe. They exchanged telephone numbers but said that as they both often went to the park they would probably meet up again after the weekend anyway.

When Marcie arrived home Doris handed her the flowers, keeping her feelings to herself and saying nothing. Marcie was thrilled and immediately put them in a vase and took them up to her room to stand on her dressing table. She felt sad in a way that Doris and Charlie were being so unreasonable lately and felt that life would be a lot more difficult now, but she pushed it out of her mind and went about her business.

Chapter Seven

Marcie had worked for John for almost a year and he had continued to visit her room from time to time. Doris and Charlie felt he was using her but kept their own counsel. When John informed her that evening that it was time she had a break and visited her family in Wales, or 'that couple who run the B&B', as he put it, Marcie was astonished; she had spoken about them enough, saying how she missed Nancy and Malcolm and how much they meant to her, so he knew their names. Perhaps he had forgotten. She wondered whether he took anything in that she spoke to him about, but then thought that maybe she was being childish, after all he had a lot on his plate.

John explained he was taking the girls to their grandparents' villa in Spain for two weeks and said that she too could have a holiday as the place would be empty; only the gardener would be there. Marcie felt a little upset, as if she was surplus to requirements...and what about their feelings for each other? Didn't they count for anything? But maybe it was a good thing. She would dearly love to go and visit the two people she loved most in the world who had become more like parents to her.

Doris had overheard John on the phone that morning talking to someone called Rochelle asking her if she had picked up the timetable for the trip. She felt sorry for Marcie...she was in love, and no mistake, but she knew no good would come of it...but she was getting too old to get involved with other people's problems; she had enough of her own. Her back was killing her and was getting worse each day and now she wasn't sure how long she could keep her job, although the money came in very handy.

Marcie got in touch with Nancy and Malcolm and they were over the moon that she was coming to see them both. Malcolm said he would pick her up from the station, no problem.

John made love to Marcie in her room the night before she left and told her how much he was going to miss her. Feeling pleased, she expressed her feelings to him, saying how she was falling in love with him and that she hoped they would have a future together one day.

John got agitated. 'This is all too soon. Just lay back and relax while I make passionate love to you.'

He was much more forceful than usual and made her go into so many positions she was in a spin, but eventually she orgasmed. When John had satisfied his needs also he quickly dressed and went back to his room. Marcie knew this was too mechanical and felt a bit used but John always knew how to get round her and manipulate her, making her feel like a silly school girl who had read the situation wrongly. But things had gone too far; her period was now three weeks late and she knew she would have to speak to him when she came back from her holiday. At the moment she would have to dismiss it from her mind and hope for the best, though she had felt a bit sick that morning. She didn't want to believe the stories she had been told about him; no one could be that callous, surely.

The doorbell rang and it was the kennel maid who had come to collect Rupert for his stay with them till the family came back from their holidays. Marcie went back upstairs and collected her suitcase and brought it down to the front door where she waited for her taxi to arrive – he was running late. He arrived a few moments later and managed to get her to the station on time and Marcie quickly got on the train and settled herself into a seat. She was so looking forward to seeing Malcolm and Nancy. In their last letter Malcolm had mentioned that they had bought a little bungalow by the sea with a small, low maintenance garden which suited them both just fine. Nancy had stopped smoking on her doctor's advice having developed Emphysema so there was no nasty tobacco smells wafting around the place and she kept it immaculate with the help of a cleaner who came once a week for four hours. It was their pride and joy.

The train drew into the station and Marcie collected her case. Walking along the platform she saw Malcolm in the distance and ran to him. He could see she had put a little weight on but she was still the bonnie lass she always was and looked so smart in her fashionable tweed coat and black leather boots. 'Give me a hug, pet, we have missed you so much,' and she could see he had tears in his eyes. 'Nancy is beside herself and never slept a wink last night;

she can't wait to see you so let's get a move on; we don't want to hit traffic.'

Marcie loved Malcolm; he was like a father figure to her, but she knew how set in his ways he was and she would have to tread carefully when she told him about John. She knew she would have to wait for the right moment, and the same applied to Nancy.

Malcolm pulled up outside the bungalow and found Nancy waiting outside in her wheelchair. Marcie jumped out of the car and ran to her bending down and throwing her arms around her. Nancy started to cry and couldn't stop; she was so pleased to see her. Malcolm had to tell her to calm down and handed her the inhaler she now had to use as she started to breathe heavily with all the excitement, bringing on a fit of coughing. They went inside and Malcolm took the shopping list from the kitchen table and said he would be about an hour. 'I'll go and get this lot and leave you two to catch up and have a girlie chat.'

Nancy made a cup of tea for them both. The kitchen was specially designed for someone in a wheelchair: large with drawers and cupboards which were easily accessible. Marcie was impatient to unpack and get settled but Nancy told her to go and sit in the sitting room and have her tea first - there was plenty of time for that. She wanted to know all the gossip about working in the 'big house' as she put it.

'How is your Mr Evans? Has he been treating you right, paying your wages on time?'

Marcie was a little taken aback. 'Of course he has; why wouldn't he pay me? I'm a good worker!'

'Don't get your knickers in a twist pet, the only reason I mentioned it was because these rich people can take advantage.'

Marcie felt a little tired after the journey and Nancy could see that, so showed her to her room and told her to have a little lie down.

Malcolm came back from shopping and they both went into the kitchen to put the food away and finally sat down for a ham sandwich and a cup of tea.

Malcolm could read Nancy like a book. 'What's wrong lass? You look pensive, deep in thought.'

'Maybe it's just me but I know there is something on that girl's mind and I intend to get to the bottom of it. She's very sensitive when you mention Mr Evans.' But Malcolm knew his beloved Nancy also had a fanciful mind like most women and could read into things which weren't true.

Marcie stirred and opened her eyes, feeling better for forty winks. Looking around the room she was impressed by how cosy it was with pretty curtains and lovely new carpet, but Nancy had left her mark - three shelves filled with teddy bears and small ornaments – she had to smile to herself. The unpacking done, she came out of her room and found Malcolm and Nancy sitting on a bench in the garden.

'Here you are pet, sit here next to Nancy and I'll go and get a chair from the kitchen.' Coming back with the chair he told her he had recently received a letter from Roy. 'He mentioned that he tried to phone you at your work on a couple of occasions and the chap who answered the phone said he'd get a message to you but you never got back to him.'

'Oh, there must be some mistake. If Roy had phoned, John would have told me, surely.'

'I don't know about that hinny, but I know he had a soft spot for you and I think he still has. He always mentions you in his letters. We found out he has a little lassie, but I won't hold that against him. You know my views; when you make your bed you lie in it, but he explained to us that the mother of his child had her heart elsewhere.'

Marcie was only half-listening and that annoyed Malcolm, but he bit his tongue; she had just arrived and Nancy had been so looking forward to it he didn't want to spoil it. He had made plans for the three of them to go out for a few meals, and also to go down to the beach as well as visit the nearby garden centre for some new plants for their lovely garden. Perhaps Marcie could help by giving her ideas on where to place them; after all, one day he planned to leave the place to her - she was the daughter he never had and they both loved her like their own.

Marcie was much more open when they all sat down for the evening meal that Malcolm had cooked - roast pork, roast potatoes, veg and gravy. 'I love the girls, and Doris the cook makes lovely meals. The house is to die for and I have a four-poster double bed and a beautiful room of my own.' Malcolm and Nancy kept quiet while she spoke non-stop of how highly John thought of her, often giving her wonderful gifts to show his appreciation and how he couldn't do enough for her.

Nancy got the picture loud and clear. 'You have fallen for him, haven't you, silly girl?'

Marcie looked at Nancy and told her there was nothing silly about it...she was in love with John.

Malcolm had a fierce Geordie temper and always spoke his mind but at the same time he was fair minded and looked at both sides of the story. 'I don't think you can help who you fall in love with, but this man is taking advantage of you; he should know better at his age and in his position. When I see him I'm going to give him a piece of my mind. I'm coming back with you to collect your belongings and you are coming to stay with us.'

Marcie was furious. 'No, I'm not. You're both not listening to me! I love John and I think he loves me.'

Malcolm had heard enough. 'You stupid girl! He is using you. What are you - his nanny? Cleaner? Bit on the side? Have you no shame?'

'Hush Malcolm!' Nancy tried to calm him down. He was yelling at the top of his voice.

Marcie ran out into the garden and Malcolm took Nancy in the bedroom to lie down - all this stress was not good for her. She took his hand. 'Please don't be too hard on her. Remember, it's probably her first love...and you know she tends to let her heart rule her head, being so soft natured. Just give it time and she will see sense.'

Malcolm went for a long walk down to the beach. He felt so angry with this man and had to cool down. Marcie couldn't stop crying and realized she couldn't possibly talk to Nancy about missing her period now.

Malcolm came back from the beach having done some thinking and calmed down. He told Marcie she must make her own mind up, but while she stayed with them she was not to mention the situation as Nancy would just start fretting, and he wanted them to all have a good time. She was relieved and readily agreed.

That evening they went for a Chinese but no one spoke much so Malcolm brought up some ideas he'd had about what they could do with the bungalow. 'We could extend the back and put in a conservatory.' Marcie thought that was a brilliant idea.

Nancy said she would love a sauna but chuckled when she saw

Malcolm's face. 'Only joking; I always thought they were for posh people anyway.'

It had been a long day and Nancy got tired very easily. Her rheumatoid arthritis had gotten worse and she had also developed other complications: corneal ulcers in her eyes, Emphysema and lung fibrosis. Malcolm was so sad watching the woman who he idolised in so much pain. They finished their food and Malcolm drove them home.

Marcie put Nancy to bed and she told her how much she loved her, saying how sorry she was if she had upset her earlier. Nancy flung her arms around her. 'Don't mind Malcolm, his bark is worse than his bite. It's just that we both want the best for you...always have and always will.'

Malcolm was in the sitting room having made hot chocolate for the both of them as he remembered that's what Marcie always liked before she went to bed at the B&B they used to own.

'What I want to know Marcie is what are you going to do if it doesn't work out with this John bloke? I worry for you.'

'Look Malcolm, I'll be alright; but I have to find out for myself and I know whatever happens you and Nancy will be there for me; as far as I'm concerned you are the closest thing to parents that I will ever have, and I love you both.' Malcolm held Marcie in his arms. She was so innocent, he thought, but felt a little better knowing she would come to them if need be.

The following day the sun was shining and they had their breakfast and set off to visit a few garden centres. The first one was lovely, it had a large selection of outdoor plants and a coffee bar indoors selling cakes and sandwiches, so they sat down and had a coffee and cake before purchasing four conifer trees and four trays of pansies. The next garden centre was quite small but it had a colourful array of wallflowers so they bought a few trays and then headed in the direction of the gift shop that Marcie had spotted. It was only small but sold a selection of cards and some beautiful colouring books and pencils, which she purchased as a gift for Biba and Tilly. She also bought some lovely candles and soaps for Nancy. It had been a fabulous day but Malcolm could see Nancy getting tired so they all headed for home so she could have a rest. Malcolm got out of the car and went to put the plants in the shed for the following day, hoping it would be dry and sunny so they could all plant them, while Marcie put Nancy to bed and gave her painkillers and a glass of water. She was a brave soul and never complained.

The doorbell rang just as Malcolm was closing the shed door and he walked to the front to see Jenny the cleaner standing there. 'Ah, Jenny, come in. I was just about to make a cuppa.'

Thanks, Malcolm, but I can't stop; I just popped round to tell you that my Tommy has the chicken pox so I won't be in tomorrow. I'll see if my cousin can look after him the day after and I'll do your cleaning then.' Malcolm told her that would be fine, said goodbye and wished Tommy better and went indoors. He liked Jenny. Nothing was too much trouble for her and she often helped to dress Nancy on her bad days.

A little later Malcolm cooked home-made chips and grilled some hamburgers for their tea and Marcie woke Nancy and helped her up whilst he dished up. When they had eaten, Malcolm went to the dresser and pulled a present out of the drawer for Marcie.

'What's this?' she said.

'Open it up and see,' said Nancy. Marcie carefully removed the beautiful flowered wrapping paper to reveal an Elvis Presley album, *Let's Be Friends*. 'We know how much you like him. I hope you haven't got this one.' Marcie was over the moon and thanked the pair of them but gave them a ticking off saying they shouldn't be spending their money on her.

By the end of the week the garden was looking magnificent with all the new plants. Everyone had mucked in even Brenda and Jim the elderly couple who lived next door.

Sadly it was time for Marcie to go back to London, but she told Nancy she would be back to see them both soon. Malcolm put her suitcase in the car and took her to the station. 'Don't forget us hinny!' he shouted to her as she got on the train. 'We love you.'

Marcie found a seat next to the window and tears streamed down her face. Why was she such a brat at times? Talking about her and John and boasting about the big house she was living in when she should have been asking them about the move and saying how lovely the bungalow was...she hadn't even asked about Nancy's treatment. The train journey was long and arduous and she was wracked with guilt. She was pleased when she finally arrived at her destination. She hailed a taxi and it was midnight before she finally arrived home. There was not a sound to be heard when she opened the front door so she went quietly to her room hoping not to disturb anyone.

Marcie had a restless night. She had a gut feeling something was not quite right but couldn't put her finger on it. When she got dressed she went downstairs to the kitchen to make a cup of tea and Charlie walked in. 'Where is everyone? I thought Doris would be here by now.' Charlie explained John had given him a ring and said he was staying on for a few more days and to let Doris know. 'So she won't be coming in till Thursday.'

'Did he mention me?'

'Not really. But it's not a problem, is it? It gives you more time to yourself without the kids.'

'Oh shut up, Charlie! You know I'm fond of the children.'

'Yes, I know; *and* their dad, more's the pity.' Marcie ignored that remark and made some tea and a bacon sarni for her and Charlie. Afterwards he went back into the garden to cut some hedges. Marcie didn't know what to do with herself so she put on her coat and scarf and decided to go to the park and maybe she'd find Zoe there walking her dog. After five minutes in the park the heavens opened but not before she saw Zoe walking into the coffee bar. Marcie was so pleased to see her and told her she looked as scruffy as ever but Zoe never took offence because her personal appearance didn't bother her. 'How was your holiday?'

It was great to see them both but I wish they didn't worry about me so much, bless them.' Marcie could see tension on Zoe's face. 'What's up?'

'I was just thinking about my mum. I grew up watching her smoke pot everyday and I didn't mind but sometimes as she acted silly and would forget things like taking me to school or picking me up.'

'That's terrible!'

'In your world maybe, but it was the norm for me - and no, she wasn't a bad mother. She loved me and my brother but that was her thing I suppose, her addiction...and now it's mine.'

Marcie always knew she smoked something, as the smell on her clothing made her feel a bit sick at times but she had a great personality and they got on well together. 'Can I just ask you how long have you been smoking pot?'

'Let's see. I think I started having a puff on Mum's cigs when she first asked me to roll them for her and I must have been about ten or eleven... Anyway, enough about me, what's been happening with you?'

'I think I am in love.'

'Who with?' Zoe asked.

'John, who I work for.'

'Bloody hell! I think I would rather smoke dope than go with a man old enough to be my father.'

Marcie ran out of the coffee bar. How could her friend be so insensitive to her feelings? Zoe ran after her. 'I'm sorry; I had no right to say that. Who am I to judge - a dope addict like me who dropped out of university and lives in a shit hole?'

Zoe took Marcie back to her flat where they both had a sandwich and coffee and Marcie opened up to her telling her she was late with her period. Zoe, never one to let the grass grow under her feet told her she had to pop out and would be back in a bit. Marcie tidied up the flat a bit as there were clothes everywhere and the kitchen looked like it had never had a clean.

An hour had passed and Marcie wondered where Zoe had got to when she walked in with a Boots carrier bag and handed it to Marcie. 'This is for you - a pregnancy test kit. Take it home with you and test your urine in the morning and one way or another it will put your mind at rest, but let me know as soon as possible.' Marcie hugged Zoe; she was a true friend, refusing to take any money for it even though every penny for her was a struggle to find.

When she got back to the house she went up to her room and placed the pregnancy kit under her clothes in the drawer and put her new Elvis Presley album on her record player. But the song that always came to mind was *If I'm a Fool for Loving You* as at that precise moment that's how she felt - mixed up, confused, frightened about the future, and so alone.

Charlie called at the house to see if Marcie wanted to go to the pub as he had finished work and knew she was on her own. 'No thanks. I'll stay in and watch a bit of telly, but maybe next time,' and off he went.

The phone rang and she hurried into the office and picked it up. It was John. 'Hi my sweet, did you enjoy your holiday?'

'Yes,' Marcie said, 'but when are you coming home?'

'The day after tomorrow but I have invited a good friend of mine to stay with us. Her name's Rochelle; she's a sister on one of the wards I work on and is going through a bad time. Her husband, a dear friend of mine, has just recently died.'

'How long will she stay?'

'I don't know,' John said getting irritated by her questioning, 'for as long as she wants I suppose. Is that a problem?'

'No, of course not. I'll see you soon,' and put the phone down quickly.

Doris rang an hour later to tell Marcie that she would be back first thing in the morning as she wanted to give the kitchen a thorough clean and do a bit of cooking. 'I'll cook a nice breakfast for me, you and Charlie, too.' Marcie suspected she was bored at home looking after her disabled husband and needed to get out of the house, but she was pleased, as she didn't much like her own company at the present time.

Doris kept to her word and the lovely aroma of bacon and sausages was coming from the kitchen when Marcie walked down the stairs the next morning. It didn't take long before Charlie appeared and they all sat at the dining room table and had a hearty breakfast. 'Marcie, you can help me clean the kitchen cupboards out and peel some vegetables and I will make a casserole just to heat up for tomorrow when John and the girls get back.' Marcie cleared the breakfast dishes away and Charlie went back into the garden to fix the fence that had come down in the bad weather.

Doris asked Marcie how her holiday was. 'Great,' she said, but I was very sad to leave them. Their bungalow was lovely and they seem very settled in Southend.' Doris could tell she wasn't going to say much more and let her get on with her work.

Marcie was annoyed with herself. She hadn't done the pregnancy test first thing when she woke up but knew it had to be dealt with so she decided that as soon as Doris had finished her work and gone home she would phone Zoe and ask her if it made any difference if she did it then.

Later on that afternoon she managed to get in touch with her on the phone but Zoe was in a mood. She had still been in bed as she had been at a music festival the night before. However when she realised why Marcie was calling she apologised and said her friend's three pregnancies were all tested late at night and they were all accurate so she didn't think there was a problem. They then arranged to meet at the park the next day and Zoe said she would keep her fingers crossed that the test proved negative.

Marcie went upstairs and took the pregnancy kit out of the drawer and went to the bathroom. She did a urine test and waited for a minute after which it had turned blue, which meant it was positive. Her heart was racing and she sat down on the edge of the bath to gather her thoughts. She had mixed feelings about what John would say but she knew that whatever he said and whatever happened she would never have a termination - she didn't believe in them - and she would bring the child up on her own if need be.

The following day John came back with the girls and they were so pleased to see Marcie, giving her loads of hugs and kisses.

'Did you have a good time?' she asked them.

'Yes it was wonderful!'

'Take your cases upstairs girls and Marcie will be up in a moment to help you unpack,' said John. He then told Marcie to come into his office and take a seat. 'Look, my friend is coming to stay this evening and I don't want any unpleasantness. I'm not sure how long she will be staying for; it may well be a few weeks.'

'Are you sleeping with her?' Marcie asked.

John stood up behind his desk and bent forward. 'Are you stupid or what? Rochelle and Tony were friends of mine till Tony had a heart attack and died three weeks ago. What the fuck has it got to do with you anyway? It's none of your business - just because I slept with you doesn't mean we are joined at the hip.'

Marcie stood up and walked to the door, turning back to him as she opened it. 'It has everything to do with me when I am pregnant with your child,' she said looking hurt, and walked out the door.

John slumped into his seat. My god, he had really gone and done it now. He would have to go after her and play it cool till he could give her some money and send her on her merry way, as far away as possible. He had his sights set on Rochelle. She had a good job and was very independent financially as her husband Tony, who was fifteen years her senior, had left her comfortably off.

John found Marcie in the garden in floods of tears. 'Just give me time Marcie to take it all in. You know I am very fond of you, and I don't want you to worry about a thing. I will arrange for you to have a termination, discreetly, and pay for it myself if need be.'

Marcie looked up at him, and in that moment for the first time saw him for what he really was. Slapping him sharply across the face, she could hold her temper no longer. 'How dare you plan my life out like that? I don't think for one second you are thinking about me, and no, I don't need your money, just what is owing to me! I hope Amy takes the children off you because you're nothing but an arrogant, cruel, control freak and I feel sorry for any woman who crosses your path! You will use them in the same way you used me for one reason or another.' And with that Marcie ran upstairs and packed her suitcase.

Charlie had seen what happened in the garden and waited till she came down. John went straight to his office and took £200 out of the safe and handed it to her when she finally came down the stairs with her belongings - a small suitcase and a portable record player. Marcie felt sorry that she didn't say goodbye to the girls but maybe Doris could explain something to them in time. She knew she would see Doris again as they got on so well. As Marcie went out of the front door Charlie pulled up in his car and told her to get in. 'No, Charlie, John will sack you.'

'I don't care. I was thinking of moving on anyway. Right, where to?'

'Just around the corner near the park. I'll show you which flat when we get there.'

Charlie drove for a few minutes before Marcie told him where to pull up.

'Bloody hell, Marcie, are you sure? What a dump! Who the hell lives here?'

'My friend Zoe and her boyfriend Jerry. Come in with me – you'll like them both.'

Marcie rung the bell and Zoe answered the door.

'I can see things went well with John then. Come in and sit down.'

Marcie explained what had happened. Charlie took to Zoe right away but couldn't understand how she could live in such a hovel.

'Where is Jerry?'

'We had a row. We're having a lot of them lately; he keeps coming home late and I can't seem to get the truth out of him, but smoking dope can get you like that. We have never been jealous of one another as we are both free-spirited people but I want children and security - I'm ready for that now, but he wants everything to be the same as it was.'

Zoe showed Charlie to the door as he needed to get back to work but he asked her if it was alright to pop in sometimes to make sure Marcie was alright. Zoe was delighted; she had taken a shine to him immediately.

Marcie knew she would have to sleep on the settee but intended to find a bed-sit as soon as she got another job, and she didn't care what that was as long as she could pay for her keep.

A little later Jerry came home and was surprised to see Marcie there with her suitcase. 'Are you staying with us?'

'If you don't mind Jerry, but it won't be for long, just till I get on my feet.'

'No problem at all Marcie.' She liked Jerry; he had always treated her with respect, but she could understand where Zoe was coming from also.

Charlie got back to the house and John called him into the office.

'Who told you that you could leave your job just like that?'

Charlie explained that Marcie needed a lift and he had thought it best to help out, as there would have been a screaming match outside in the garden. He also said that he'd seen Biba and Tilly looking out of the window. John thought that was quite a sensible thing to do and told him to get on with his work but that he would knock money off his wages all the same. Charlie grinned. He was lying through his teeth; he never saw the girls at the window but he had the gift of the gab, as his friends always told him.

Charlie was just about to open his shed when John walked over to him. 'Look, I forgot to ask; where did you drop Marcie off?'

'I took her to the station but she never told me where she was going; none of my business - we weren't that close.'

'OK, get on with your work.'

When John went into the kitchen he saw Doris was upset.

'She's left hasn't she?'

John put his arms around her. 'It's all for the best. She wasn't suitable for the job anyway - quite a feisty girl and no patience with the girls.'

Doris knew that was untrue, and hoped she would hear from her again. She was pleased she had her phone number.

The kennel maid brought Rupert back from the kennels so the

girls were distracted and hadn't noticed Marcie wasn't about, but John was secretly hoping Rochelle would be a big part of their lives now and eventually he would persuade her to move in permanently and sell her own property. She was unable to have children of her own but the girls had taken to her quite well when she joined them for the last few days of their holiday in Spain.

Chapter Eight

Marcie left her clothes in the suitcase, as there was nowhere to put anything, but moved it out of the way into a corner. Zoe was making a pan of vegetable soup for them all but Jerry said not to worry about him as he had a few jobs to do and promptly went out.

'Are you two alright? Marcie asked. 'You seem distant towards each other...maybe I shouldn't have come.'

'Don't be silly; I told you, we are just growing apart, wanting different things out of life, but we will always love each other. I know the day will come when he will just be off without saying a word.'

'My god, Zoe, that's terrible.'

'No it's not Marcie, you just don't understand him. He's like a gypsy - loves moving around the country never staying in one place for too long and living off the land like I did, but he respects my feelings and I respect his. We want different things, but he will always be my friend and I will love him always.'

Marcie couldn't get her head around it; she found rejection so painful as a child. 'Why did you give up your course at university?'

'I suppose I was too busy having a good time and got a bit complacent. Then I met Jerry, and we both wanted to travel...'

'I was just thinking Zoe, why don't you go back to your studies and become a psychologist?'

'Maybe one day. I must admit, that was the only thing I was ever really interested in, but if I did I would have to get help to wean me off the pot. I don't think my mother would be much help though, she tells me she is only having one cig a day but I don't believe that.'

'I'll help you all I can, Zoe, you know that,' and they hugged each other.

Marcie wondered how her own mother was getting on, but if she only knew the truth...

Nellie was quite happy for a change. Sam, her brother-in law, had reappeared and was staying with her. There were all sorts of rumours going around the village, but Nellie didn't care - Tom had his Betsy – and Sam was only staying for a few weeks anyway. Sam had called in to the Stag one evening to see his brother but he had got a bad reception from him. 'What the hell are you staying with her for? Why don't you stay here with us, we have the room?' Betsy agreed.

'Thanks Tom, but Nellie is lonely and she wanted some jobs doing around the place.'

Betsy had heard from the neighbours that the pair of them had been playing music till the early hours of the morning and something was definitely going on between them. They had been seen kissing and hugging each other in the front garden, and also screaming at each other hell for leather. She hadn't said anything to Tom though, as she knew he was fond of his brother, and anyway, as far as she was concerned Nellie was none of his business any longer.

The next few weeks were eventful to say the least for Marcie and her friend. It was just the two of them now – Zoe's instincts had been right, and Jerry had moved out shortly after Marcie had moved in, feeling happier that he wasn't leaving Zoe on her own. Initially Zoe was upset but after a while started looking after her appearance a bit more. Gone were the tangled curls and the hippy clothes and she started to look tidy and pretty. The flat was kept immaculate, though that was more down to Marcie, and they both ate healthily. Marcie's major concern for her friend was the pot smoking, but once Zoe had decided to try to give it up, with Marcie's support and some counselling she was now completely off it. Her mother, who was still on it, was told in no uncertain terms that she was banned from smoking it in the flat when she visited, and on the one occasion that she came to see her daughter she was made to go outside when she started to roll a joint.

One morning Marcie was looking in the papers for a job when she saw an advert for a shop assistant in Bella's Boutique on Hampstead High Road.

'Look Zoe, I'm going to give them a ring.'

'Yes, but what about a reference? John won't give you one.'

'Don't be too sure about that. I'm going to the house to tell him he has to otherwise he will be pestered by the courts to pay maintenance when the baby arrives. Anyway that's the least he can do.'

'Good luck with that one, Marcie, but I wouldn't hold your breath,' Zoe remarked.

The following day Marcie went round John's house and Doris answered the door. She was surprised to see her but pleased at the same time. Her face broke into a smile. 'Come in love; John's at the hospital and the girls are at school.'

Doris put the kettle on and made tea and they both sat down at the kitchen table. 'What's brought you round here?' Doris asked.

'I need a reference from John.'

'Listen pet, I honestly don't think he will give you one, but I'll ask for you and if he agrees I will give you a ring to let you know. I still don't understand what happened with you two.'

'Didn't he tell you? I'm carrying his child.'

'Oh, my Lord!' The bastard! To be honest, I had my suspicions but I prayed I was wrong...and now you've confirmed it... I tried to get info out of Charlie but he didn't say too much.'

They heard the front door open. 'That'll be Charlie wanting a brew,' said Doris, and got up to boil the kettle again. As she did, John came through the kitchen door and stopped in his tracks when he saw Marcie sitting there.

'What do you want?'

'I've come for a reference.'

'Come into my office...and Doris, don't you think you ought to get on with your work? That's what I'm paying you for.'

Marcie walked into his office full of self-confidence but John didn't notice the signs and told her he had no intention of giving her a reference, and as far as he was concerned the matter was closed. John hated any woman telling him what to do - he always liked to be the one in control.

'Yes, John, there *will* be a reference. I'll collect it from Doris tomorrow or there will be hell to pay and everyone at the hospital will know that I'm carrying your child and you wanted me to get rid of it. I may also have to ask for maintenance when the baby arrives and if you are not forthcoming I will get the greatest pleasure taking you to court.'

John agreed, reluctantly, before telling her to leave.

'With pleasure,' and she walked out of the office and then went back and put her head round the door to let him know that it had better be a good one...or else.

Marcie said goodbye to Doris in the kitchen and said she would call in tomorrow morning to collect her reference when the girls were at school.

Back in his office John had a grin on his face. No woman had ever got the better of him - that was a first. Maybe she had more courage than he had given her credit for. He opened the desk drawer, took out paper and pen and began writing.

John had written a wonderful reference saying that not only was she extremely hard-working but she was also adaptable as well as honest and reliable. When she went for an interview at the boutique the owner liked her instantly saying what an exceptional reference she had and offered her the job there and then. She was to start work the following Monday at 9am. Marcie was over the moon and couldn't wait to get home and tell Zoe. Zoe was a bit envious but pleased at the same time; money would no longer be such an issue.

It was Sunday evening and Marcie was dreading going to work the following day. The interview with Bella had gone well, but she was a little apprehensive of working so closely with her. She looked to be in her late fifties and she seemed quite serious and business-like in her smart grey suit. Mind you it showed off her lovely slim figure and the black high-heeled shoes she had worn complimented her slim, shapely legs. She had cropped silver hair backcombed off her pretty, round face and perfectly formed white teeth – a very attractive, smart woman all in all. Marcie knew one of the requirements of the job was to look clean and smart and decided to go through her clothes and sort out what she was going to wear for her first day at Bella's.

In the end she settled on a dark brown suit and black high heels and decided she would wear her hair in a bun. As far as Zoe was concerned she could put a black sack over her head and still look good as she had an amazing figure and stunning good looks. She never wore much make-up either which infuriated her as she always felt she had to work hard at looking good, though Marcie could see the natural beauty in her and always gave her praise.

On the Monday morning when Marcie started work there was only one other member of staff and that was Penny, a young girl of eighteen who Bella thought had a flair for clothes and was good with the customers. Bella popped in the shop from time to time to keep an eye on things but her business always did well as it was the only boutique on the high road selling the latest outfits. She was young at heart and knew the buyer's market, catering for the young people and also women aged between thirty and forty. She also did a big line in accessories: bracelets, necklaces, and bags.

The first day went well and Marcie gave everyone who came into the shop her full and undivided attention, making each customer feel important, even if it meant listening to their personal stories and problems. She liked Penny who was grateful to have someone nearer her own age to talk to and didn't mind making the teas and coffees for them both - she was definitely a people pleaser, but Marcie found her endearing and likable. She also filled Marcie in on Bella. She told her she was married to Jim who had sadly passed away four years earlier with prostate cancer. They had a wonderful marriage and had one daughter who emigrated to Australia with her husband and two children for a better life. Bella encouraged them to go, as she believed children should fly the nest and find their own dreams, but she did get to see them twice a year.

Life had not always been so good for Bella when she was growing up. Her parents were Jewish and owned a jewellery shop in Golders Green. Being fairly well off they sent Bella and her brother to boarding school and when Bella left she started working at a coffee bar on Saturday mornings till she figured out what she wanted to do with her life. That's when she met Jim, who was also born and bred in London, but not Jewish, and they started dating. Her parents forbade it but she ignored them and continued seeing him and they eventually threw her out of the house and she ended up living with Jim's parents. He went on to become a taxi driver while she got her dream job working in a wedding gown shop. Life was tough but they eventually married and saved enough money for a deposit to buy their first home. The years passed by without her parents ever speaking to her again and she eventually heard through the grapevine that her mother had sadly died. Her brother had gone on to be a dentist and he had a Jewish wife but they never spoke to Bella either. She never got over the loss of her family but she knew she had a good man in her beloved Jim and they spent many gloriously happy years together, although there was an emptiness she could never quite fill.

Zoe was finding it a bit difficult trying to get back to her studies in psychology but she eventually made an appointment with a Mr Giles at the job centre who explained to her that it would be a good idea if she did a home course called "Home Learning Psychology" which would still give her the qualifications she needed. He said that in his experience, people who opted out of university never went back. The only problem would be that she would have to finance it, but he said he would send her all the necessary information.

Zoe drove back to her flat in her red mini feeling deflated. Where the hell was she supposed to find that kind of money?

Marcie came home from work on a high as she had such a good day, but Zoe looked miserable.

'What's up Zoe? Did you have a bad day?'

Zoe explained to Marcie what had happened. 'Don't worry,' Marcie said, 'I'll find it for you somehow, even if I had to beg, steal or borrow.'

The doorbell rang and it was Zoe's mum.

'What are you doing here Mother? You should have rung first.'

'My god, can't I visit my own daughter without an inquisition? What's wrong with you - I only came to see how you got on at the job centre?'

Zoe loved her mum and felt awful that she'd snapped at her like that. She apologised to her and explained what had been said.

'Well is that all that's worrying you? Don't be silly, you should have come to me; I'll lend you the money. No, on second thoughts, you can have it - and you will need a new typewriter too.'

Zoe couldn't believe her ears. 'Where did you get that kind of money? I know you have few jobs but still...'

'Look, do you want it or not? It's just money I've put away for a rainy day, so you may as well have it.'

'Thank you so much, Mum; you are the best mother in the world.'

'Well, if that's true I can sit down and smoke my pot.' Marcie looked at her in shock. 'Only joking! That made you both sit up, didn't it? Anyway, I'm off now; things to do and people to see.'

Zoe saw her mum to the door and gave her a big hug and a kiss. As far as she was concerned she did have the best mum in the world, and Marcie had to agree.

Life was looking good, but Marcie knew she would soon be starting to show; she'd been lucky so far, what with being small, but soon Bella would notice, and then what? But for the time being she would say nothing.

Charlie popped round to see them both. He was a regular visitor now and Marcie knew the reason for that - he had his eye on Zoe. They got on so well, even though they were from different worlds. Zoe was academic whilst Charlie could just about read a newspaper. Leaving school with no qualifications and no idea of what he wanted to do, the headmaster and teachers had said he would probably end up in borstal with his attitude to life.

Zoe and Charlie went to the pub while Marcie stayed in on her own watching TV. The phone rang and it was her mum. She sounded beside herself. 'Slow down, Mum, and tell me what's happened?'

'Your Uncle Sam is staying here and I want you to tell him to leave. I'll put him on the phone.'

But he was far too drunk for Marcie to understand a word he was saying, plus there was loud music in the background. When he put the phone down on her Marcie didn't ring back, she felt tired and wanted a lay down.

The next morning she woke up and the flat was empty. She had just made herself a cup of tea when Zoe strolled in.

'Sorry, I should have phoned you but me and Charlie had a belly full of drink with his friends and I slept at his place.' Marcie was annoyed but let it go and got ready for work as Bella was strict about good time keeping and she didn't want to lose her job.

The shop was very busy and Marcie was pleased when she had five minutes to spare to pop to the local bakery and get herself a sandwich. Penny had phoned in to say she had a dental appointment, so she was on her own.

Marcie went to the back of the shop and made herself some tea and thought about the strange phone call she had last night from her mum and immediately felt guilty - maybe she should have rung back. What was bugging her was why her Uncle Sam, who she now knew wasn't really her uncle, was staying with her mum. After all, Tom was living with Betsy now so she was under no obligation to put his brother up. Finding out her dad wasn't her real dad was a blow to her, but one day she wanted to know who her real father was and suspected her mum knew all along but was hiding the truth from her for one reason or another. Just then her thoughts were interrupted by the phone ringing. She picked it up immediately and it was Zoe calling to see if she wanted to go to the pub for a meal that evening with her and Charlie. Marcie said yes, she wouldn't mind as she was getting fed up staying in every night.

Bella called at the shop just before closing time to cash up for banking the next day and told Marcie how pleased she was with her work. She was also pleased that she had kept the shop so tidy and loved the window display she had done.

Zoe was pleased when Marcie arrived home that evening. 'Come on, get ready. Charlie will be here soon.'

'Give me a break, my feet are killing me.'

'OK, I'll make you a tea and run you a bath.'

'Thanks Zoe. You're in a good mood.'

'I am. Mum took me shopping and bought me that portable typewriter over there on the sideboard. Don't you think it's wicked?' Marcie agreed and went to have her bath.

There was a knock at the door and it was Charlie with a bunch of flowers in his hand. 'Are they for me?' Zoe asked.

'Well for both of you really, but mostly for you,' and he gave her a kiss on the lips.

The pub they were going to was a fifteen minute walk down the road so Charlie left the car parked outside the flat and they all made their way on foot. During the week it was quite quiet, it was mostly weekends when it got busy, as that's when they had a band and karaoke. The three of them walked in the pub and it was like a cemetery there was only one person sitting on the bar stool having a pint. Zoe remarked that it was still a bit early so it might get busier later on. Charlie whispered to her that he didn't care so long as he was with her, and Marcie overheard. 'I don't want to play gooseberry all night. I'll stay an hour and leave you both to it.'

'No you won't,' Zoe said, 'we are all going home together. Anyway, I'm starving - who wants the hotpot?' It was a definite yes from Charlie and Marcie, so she ordered three.

Marcie noticed the guy sitting on the bar stool at the bar and said she thought he looked familiar.

'He's probably been into the shop you work in,' said Charlie.

'No, I don't think so, but it's bugging me – I know him from somewhere.'

Bill the landlord served their meal, and she pushed it to the back of her mind until Zoe happened to mention what a good looking guy he was but when she looked at Charlie's face he didn't look too happy.

The meal finished, they were having coffee when the guy at the bar came over to where they were sitting and introduced himself to Marcie. 'Hello, I'm Tony; I work in the high road at my Dad's estate agents, just along from Bella's.'

'Oh right. I could see you were staring at me.'

'No I wasn't...well, just a little. I knew I'd seen you somewhere before,' and they both laughed.

'Sit down and have a drink with us if you like, but I don't intend to stay long myself; I'm shattered.'

Tony declined saying he had a lot of paperwork to do but maybe next time, and left the pub.

Zoe noticed Marcie shifting uncomfortably in her chair and was just about to ask if she was alright when she doubled over in pain, gripping her stomach.

'Oh my god, what's wrong Marcie?'

'I feel like I can't breathe and I'm in a lot of pain.'

Charlie asked the landlord to phone an ambulance when Marcie started to cry and panic - she could see spots of blood coming through her pink dress.

The ambulance was there in no time at all and Zoe went in it with Marcie. Charlie told them he would see them at the hospital when he had picked up the car from Zoe's.

When they arrived at the hospital Marcie was taken into A&E where a female doctor and two nurses were in attendance. They made Marcie comfortable on the bed and pulled the curtain round and Zoe took a seat outside in the corridor and waited. By the time the doctor appeared Charlie had arrived and was sitting with Zoe. 'I think you both may as well go home and come back in the morning. There is nothing you can do I'm afraid; Marcie has lost the baby and we will be keeping her in for observation.'

Zoe thought the doctor quite harsh and uncaring - she wanted to stay with her friend, but Charlie reminded her she needed all the rest she could get to keep her strength up, and that made sense to Zoe so they left the hospital and went home.

The next morning the doctor did her rounds and went to speak to Marcie who had been moved to a cubicle of her own on the wards. 'Hello, my dear. 'How are you feeling today or is that a stupid question?'

At that precise moment she wasn't sure how she was feeling – it hadn't quite sunk in that she had lost her baby; it had all happened so fast.

'We are going to keep you in for a few days at least to run some tests, but unfortunately we don't always have answers as to why this happens to a perfectly healthy person like yourself.'

'Does this mean I can't conceive anymore?' she asked, tearfully.

'No, not necessarily. I have known women to go on and have lots of children after miscarriage without any problems.'

Charlie and Zoe walked on to the ward, but were told they could only stay for ten minutes as it was outside of visiting hours. Zoe handed Marcie a carrier bag containing her dressing gown, pyjamas, slippers and toiletry bag. Charlie said he would make himself scarce after giving Marcie a hug, and left the two girls to have a chat. Zoe pulled a chair up and held Marcie's hand. 'I'm so sorry, Marcie...'

And with that, Marcie let go and cried uncontrollably. 'I really wanted this baby you know. Why has this happened?'

Oh, Marcie, only God knows the answer to that. This pregnancy just wasn't meant to be...but you'll go on to have more babies, you'll see.' Zoe was quite a spiritual person and Marcie always knew that and admired her beliefs, but she wished she could feel like that at this moment; anything to take the pain away.

When breakfast arrived Zoe was told to leave. The ward sister handed her a note with visiting hours on and Zoe told Marcie she would be back to see her later. Marcie asked Zoe to phone Bella and let her know what had happened. She didn't intend lying, as what would be the point? She wasn't sure how long she would be in the hospital anyway.

Zoe and Charlie arrived home and Zoe got straight on the phone to Bella explaining everything. Bella was upset and angry as

Marcie had not been honest with her, but she understood why, as who would employ a young girl who was pregnant knowing she may leave her employment when the baby arrived? 'I'll pop in and see her later on but god knows what will happen to the shop leaving Penny in charge. She's a good worker but a bit of a scatterbrain.'

'Is there anything I can do to help?'

'Thank you, but no, I'm sure she'll be OK for an hour or two.'

Marcie was asked by the sister on the ward if she needed to speak to a councillor. She explained that sometimes it helped as a lot of women suffered with depression after having a miscarriage, but Marcie said no, as she had good friends around her that she could talk to, and that she just wanted to go home.

That afternoon Bella went to visit and Marcie broke down and cried, apologising for giving her so much trouble and not being truthful from the beginning. Bella said she had to put it behind her and that she understood her dilemma. She wanted her to take two weeks off work and said that her job was quite safe - where was she going to find someone to replace her? She was doing a grand job and all the customers loved her. Marcie leant forward and hugged her and thanked her for being so understanding.

'I will pay you for the time you're off, but when you return to work I want your full attention; after all, I am running a business.'

Marcie readily agreed.

'Well, I have to go now as I've left Penny in charge. Take good care of yourself and give me a ring if you need anything.'

Marcie was relieved that she still had a job to go back to. She now had to try to come to terms with her loss and realise that everything happens for a reason – it was just not meant to be. She wiped the tears from her eyes and tried to ignore the feeling of overwhelming sadness.

Charlie and Zoe visited her later on and brought some flowers and grapes.

How long do you think you'll be in here?' Zoe asked

'Not sure, but Bella came in to visit me and said my job will still be there for me when I come out, and she wants me to take two weeks off to make sure I am fully recovered.'

'Great,' Charlie said, 'and don't worry, we'll look after you.'

'I was thinking of visiting my mum actually. Before all this happened I had a strange phone call from her. My Uncle Sam was staying there and she seemed upset.'

'Don't be stupid Marcie, your health comes first. She is quite capable of looking after herself,' said Zoe.

Marcie had to agree. 'Perhaps when I'm feeling stronger then.'

The doctor did his rounds the next morning and said he was pleased as the tests had come back OK and she was well enough to go home on the condition she took it easy for a few weeks. He said he wanted to see her in a week's time for a check-up. When he left she phoned Zoe to see if she could come and collect her.

Zoe arrived to collect her an hour later and Marcie said her goodbyes and thanked the staff.

In the car driving home Zoe noticed Marcie was very quiet.

'Are you alright, Marcie?'

'Yes, I'm fine thanks, just feeling a bit weak.'

'Don't worry, we're nearly home and when we get there you can sleep in my bed; I'm not having you sleep on the settee.'

'No, Zoe, I'll be alright, honestly.'

'No, you won't, and anyway, Charlie said I can always stay at his bedsit if I want to.'

Zoe went out that evening to the homeless shelter to serve some meals and help out in the kitchen, leaving Marcie on her own. She was going to see if she could get someone to cover for her but Marcie insisted as she felt she wouldn't be good company and needed more rest.

Two hours later the doorbell rang and Marcie put her dressing gown on and went to see who it was. When she opened the door she was shocked to see that it was Tony who she last saw at the pub when she was with Charlie and Zoe.

'Who gave you my address?'

'Oh, it was Bella. I met her yesterday on the high road and told her we were friends. I hope you don't mind. I asked after you and was worried when she said you were in hospital.'

'Well she had no right to tell you my business, and I'm surprised she did. I'll be having a word with her.'

'Please don't. It was my fault - I persuaded her to spill the beans – I can be quite a charmer...I'm sorry if I've upset you in any way; that wasn't my intention.'

Marcie was feeling a bit dizzy and Tony noticed, so helped her back on the settee before going back into the passage to close the door.

Marcie was grateful for his help and asked Tony if he wanted something to drink.

'I'd love a cup of tea. You stay there and I'll make us both one.'

When he returned with their tea, Marcie apologised for being rude.

'Can I ask what you were in hospital for? Bella never told me.'

'I had a miscarriage.'

'I'm sorry to hear that. Who is the father?'

'I don't want to talk about him, Tony, and anyway, I don't see him anymore.'

'Do you want me to leave, Marcie? You must be tired.'

'No, you can stay a little longer – at least finish your tea. And thanks for coming to see me, it was good of you.'

Zoe arrived home and was surprised to see Tony there, but before she could get a chance to speak to him he said he had to go as his dad was dropping some files off at his flat. 'I'll ring you tomorrow Marcie.'

Zoe went into the bedroom to put her pyjamas on but was suspicious about Tony. She thought he was creepy turning up like that, but kept her feelings to herself, as she didn't want to upset Marcie.

The next morning Zoe made Marcie a bacon sandwich and a cup of tea and went off to work selling *The Big Issue*. She was running late so Marcie told her to get going and that she would tidy the flat up and see her later.

Just as Zoe left the phone rang and it was Tony. 'How are you feeling?'

'How did you get my phone number?' she asked; she was pretty sure she hadn't given it to him.

'I must have got it from Bella; that isn't a problem is it?'

Marcie was still feeling a bit woozy so let it go.

'Do you want me to get you anything and bring it round?'

'No, I'm fine, honestly.'

'Write my number down and if you need anything just let me know. I have to get to work now.' Marcie scribbled the number down on an old newspaper on the coffee table and said goodbye.

Tony had a lot of clients who wanted to look at properties that day, but his father noticed his mind was elsewhere. 'Your mum and I haven't seen much of you lately. Are you seeing someone?'

'Yes, her name is Marcie and we're great together – she's stunning.'

'How long have you been seeing her?'

'Quite a long time, actually.'

'Bloody hell, you kept that quiet. Why don't you bring her for dinner some time; your mum would love that.'

'Not just yet; give it time – she's very shy.'

Tony's dad knew when to hold back and not push his son too hard as he was very highly strung. He could lose his temper very quickly, so he left it at that.

Tony was an only child and his parents doted on him, but from a very young boy they had problems with him lying and making up stories. He was always getting into trouble at school for losing his temper and hitting other children and generally being very disruptive. He nearly got expelled on two occasions but his mum was on the Parents and Teachers Association and did a lot of fund raising for the school so she managed to get their support. But not everyone agreed, and two of the mum's refused to have anything to do with the PTA after that.

Brenda was a gentle, shy, reserved woman who wanted the best for her son Tony and longed for him to marry and settle down and give her grandchildren. She truly believed if he had someone who loved him his temper would be kept in check, but Ted, his father, was of a different opinion. He believed that a leopard never changes his spots, and that was the card they were dealt with.

Tony had girlfriends in the past but they were all short lived. They didn't hang around for too long. He was possessive and controlling, as one of them pointed out to his mum, but she stood by her son no matter what, sweeping all his bad behaviour under the carpet. His dad on the other hand knew exactly what he was like and would stand up to him, though most of the time he did his best to keep the peace as he could be very aggressive and it was all getting too much for his wife to cope with. She had been on the verge of a breakdown when it all got too much for her before. Ted had to admit though that Tony was good at his job, a real charmer and very persuasive and popular with the people he dealt with - in fact an asset to the company.

Marcie was feeling a little better and was tidying the flat when the doorbell rang. Opening the door she was greeted by a woman with a huge bouquet of flowers. She recognised her from the local florist in the high road.

'Hi Millie. Are they for me?'

'Yes, you must have an admirer.'

Marcie read the note. *To Marcie, get well soon. Tony. xxxx*

She thanked Millie and went inside to find a vase to put them in. She thought he was getting a bit ahead of himself but felt so vulnerable; she had so many mixed emotions. Still, it was a nice gesture, and when she'd arranged them in the vase and put them on the coffee table she stood back to admire them.

When Zoe arrived home and saw the flowers she frowned. 'Where did they come from?'

'Tony sent them; isn't that lovely?'

Zoe wasn't impressed and made her feelings known. 'Look Marcie, you hardly know him...doesn't that bother you? He seems a bit of a creep to me.'

'You're so negative, Zoe. He's just being kind - there are some good people out there you know!'

Zoe could see she was banging her head on a brick wall and changed the subject. 'How are you feeling today? Can I get you anything?'

'No, but you can lighten up a bit and stop worrying about me.'

Chapter Nine

When the two weeks had passed and Marcie went back to work at the shop Bella and Penny were so pleased to have her back. It meant Bella could take a back seat and leave the shop in Marcie's capable hands. Tony often spent his lunch hour with Marcie and they became close and started dating, much to the disapproval of Zoe and Charlie who had their doubts about him but kept their feelings to themselves as she looked so happy.

Marcie was busy in the shop as some new clothes had just arrived and she began to put them on hangers while Penny made a cup of tea out the back for George, the young chap who had delivered them.

'Marcie, you're looking gorgeous today - loving the dress.' It was very short and showed off her long legs.

'Thanks George, you're not so bad yourself,' and they started laughing.

Just at that moment Tony came into the shop and saw them both chatting away and his blood boiled. Marcie could see he was displeased and so could George - Tony was giving him daggers, so he said he had to head off as he had loads more deliveries to do.

'But you haven't finished your tea,' Marcie pointed out.

'That's OK, but thanks anyway,' and he quickly made an exit out the door.

Penny wasn't hanging around either and said she was going to the bakery down the road to buy some croissants. She was no sooner out of the door when Tony grabbed Marcie's wrist. 'What's going on?'

'For goodness sake, what's wrong with you? He's our delivery chap; I was only being friendly and now you're being stupid.' She walked away from him and went around the counter.

Tony was good at talking his way out of situations he'd created and told Marcie he'd had a bad morning. 'One of my clients has pulled out of a sale; I'm really sorry.'

'If there's no trust Tony, this isn't going to work.'

He bent over the counter and kissed her on the lips and she reciprocated. 'Let's forget about it and get back to work - I have all these boxes to unpack.'

Penny arrived back in the shop a few minutes later. 'Has he gone?'

'Don't make mountains out of molehills Penny; he just had a bad morning, that's all.' But Penny knew different. From what she had seen of him he was possessive and jealous, and she didn't like him.

Later on that day Tony phoned and asked Marcie if she would like to come to his flat when she finished work and he would cook a meal for her. His father had recently bought the flat above the estate agents for him. It was a light and spacious two bedroom accommodation, very modern with a balcony leading off the open-plan lounge and kitchen, and it had all mod cons. Marcie said she would let Zoe know she wouldn't be straight home after work, but she doubted she'd be there anyway as she was staying at Charlie's bed-sit in Kentish Town more and more lately.

That evening, just before she closed the shop she gave Zoe a ring. She sounded annoyed as Marcie had arranged to go to the pub with her but had forgotten. She apologised and said she'd see her later.

Marcie had been to the flat once before but only stayed for ten minutes and was looking forward to seeing it again. She rung the bell and Tony opened the door immediately.

'Come in and let me take your coat.'

There was a dining table at the far end of the lounge with a white linen tablecloth on it and a small vase of flowers and some candles.

'This looks lovely,' Marcie said, and Tony poured them both a glass of white wine. He busied himself in the kitchen while Marcie drank her wine and looked round the flat admiring it.

Tony served the meal and they sat down. She was impressed. Beautifully cooked fillet steak and salad was put before her and she tucked in.

'Did you let your friend know you were coming?'

'Yes, but she sounded a bit upset as she wanted me to go to the pub with her.'

'How selfish is that? She knows you're going out with me.'

'Come off it...I can still go out with my best friend, can't I?'

'Course you can, but she has Charlie; it's not as if she has no one to go out with. You're too soft for your own good.'

Marcie didn't want to get into a confrontation; she had been on her feet all day and wanted to relax.

When they had finished the meal they sat on the settee watching TV then went to bed. Tony made love to Marcie, exploring every part of her body. She started to laugh. 'Ooh, that tickles!'

Tony was furious and jumped out of bed. 'You're making fun of me.'

'No I'm not; you're so sensitive, Tony...I'm sorry,' and he got back into bed and tenderly caressed her body and made passionate love to her. When it was all over, they snuggled down under the duvet in each other's arms.

Marcie was the first to wake up the next morning and had a shower and got ready for work. Tony woke up wondering where she was and found her on the balcony drinking tea.

'Did you make me one?' He asked.

'No, you were asleep and I didn't want to disturb you.'

'What about some breakfast?'

'No, I'm off to work,' she said going inside and picking up her bag. 'I want to get in early as Bella's coming into the shop this morning. Sorry.'

Tony kissed Marcie goodbye and said he'd see her later.

Bella was checking the new garments that had arrived in the shop the day before when Marcie walked in.

'Hello pet! How are you?'

'I'm fine, thanks. I stayed at Tony's place last night and he cooked me a gorgeous meal. Things are pretty good between us.'

'Glad to hear it. Just make sure you use protection.'

Marcie blushed and said that they did. Bella never minced her words.

Zoe was waiting at the flat for Marcie when she got home that evening, and couldn't wait to tell her the good news. She was moving into the bed-sit in Kentish Town with Charlie.

Marcie was upset. 'But why? I can move out - you were here before me.'

'Look, I'm happy with Charlie. We've become inseparable, and it makes sense - we just want to live together.'

Marcie wasn't sure what to say. 'Is it because you don't like

Tony being around?'

'Don't be silly, it's nothing to do with him, and anyway we are still best friends and we will see each other all the time and still go out to the pub on the weekends.'

A week later Zoe moved out, and when Marcie told Tony he was happy - he could have her all to himself now, though he didn't say as much to her.

On Marcie's day off she decided it was high time she gave her mum a ring. Her mother answered the phone but sounded strange.

'Have you been drinking, Mum?' Marcie asked.

'Don't be daft, I'm just in a good mood,' she slurred.

'Is Sam still living there?' She didn't want to use the term 'uncle' anymore since she found out her dad wasn't her real dad, and she didn't care too much for him anyway.

'Yes, he is still here; there's not much work about. It would be nice if you came for a holiday, Marcie, I miss you.'

Marcie couldn't believe her ears; there was definitely something amiss. 'I'll try to come up for a weekend if I can. But I must go now; I've got a lot to do. Speak soon. Bye,' and she put the phone down.

Nellie was lying through her teeth. She was drinking on a daily basis and so was Sam. This made for a volatile situation and the police had been called on a number of occasions and told them to keep the noise down. One of the officers had spotted bruising on Nellie's arms and legs, but she told the policewoman she was on anti-depressants, which gave her dizzy spells and that was why she kept knocking herself on things. She said she had made an appointment with the doctor to see about changing her tablets. They weren't convinced, but there was nothing they could do unless she made a formal complaint. Sam had his arm around her tightly when she was being questioned and he kept giving her evil looks, which didn't go unnoticed by the police officers either. There was no doubt in their minds that she was lying – probably because she was scared of him.

Nellie didn't work for Mrs Clements at the hotel anymore, she had to let her go as she was coming into work the worse for wear, but she got an evening job cleaning offices and that suited her as nobody took any notice of what she looked like. Sam did odd gardening jobs around the village though longed to go back and work on the farms but had a bad reputation for getting into fights so his old employers who had given him a chance in the past refused to take him on again. He felt depressed living with Nellie. They were like a time-bomb waiting to go off and he couldn't wait to see the back of her. He thought at one point that his brother Tom would let him stay at the pub as there was plenty of room, but Betsy was having none of it and eventually told Tom what the village gossip was - that Nellie had been having an affair with Sam when she was first married to him and that Marcie wasn't his. That's when everything erupted and Tom told him he was barred.

'Why? Has your bitch of a girlfriend been spreading rumours?'

'You're not my brother, you bastard; I know you've been having an affair with Nellie for years and Marcie is yours. I don't want anything to do with you - don't you ever show your face in here again!'

Sam left the pub and knew their paths would never cross again and he was livid. Nellie was only a bit on the side but he had lost the respect of his brother, which hurt him inside; that was the only family he had.

The weeks had flown by and as time went on Marcie was having doubts about her relationship with Tony, as he was getting more and more possessive and controlling. She decided to end it but she was going out with him one last time to explain things, as he deserved that, she thought, whatever the circumstances.

The shop was busy the next day, full of customers and Tony walked in to tell Marcie he had booked a table at the Indian restaurant on the high road for that evening and would pick her up around eight-thirty. Marcie told him that would be great, but was nervous about ending the relationship.

Bella cashed up and was pleased the shop was doing well and the profits had gone up. Marcie was a godsend. In many ways she was disappointed her daughter had not taken an interest in the shop and her visions, but she had to accept that was not to be.

Marcie had finished work and went home to get ready. Tony was punctual as usual and tooted the horn outside to let her know he had arrived. He sensed she was quiet in the car and asked if anything was troubling her, but she said no as she was still planning in her mind the best way to break the news to him gently. She didn't like his controlling ways but she was still fond of him.

They arrived at the restaurant and were shown to their table by the waiter. They both ordered the same meal, tandoori chicken, tikka masala and boiled rice. Tony ordered a bottle of white wine and when the waiter had left looked at Marcie enquiringly. 'You're quiet?'

Marcie decided to take the bull by the horns and get straight to the point. 'Tony, you know how fond I am of you...but I think we are so different in many ways...and would be better off as friends. I love your company, but I'm sorry Tony, I don't want it to go any further.'

Tony was in shock. 'Do you think you can dismiss me just like that after all I've given you?'

Marcie was furious. 'Who the hell do you think you are? You don't own me; I am not your prize possession!'

Marcie got up from her seat and left the restaurant. Tony followed her out but she told him to get lost and leave her alone. This was not what Marcie wanted; she never intended to hurt him but she felt a little worried as to how he had taken the news, and she couldn't wait to get home.

The following week Tony came into the shop every day pleading with her, saying how much he would change and how much he loved her...and that she was making the biggest mistake of her life. Bella had noticed how stressed Marcie was about the situation and offered to have a word with him.

'Don't bother,' she said. 'Thank you, but it's my problem and he won't listen anyway.'

As time went by he started following her from work, calling out to her. Worryingly, he was also phoning her sometimes four or five times a day and peering into her window at night. When she ignored him he would put notes through her letter box saying things like 'I love you' and 'you will always be mine, you belong to me'.

Things came to a head when she woke up one morning to find him lying in bed beside her with his arms around her caressing her breasts. He had managed to get in through the bathroom window. She screamed at the top of her voice which alerted the neighbours who banged on the door and he managed to escape back out through the window. Marcie called the police and they went to his flat, but he denied everything, saying it was the other way round and she was obsessed by him. Marcie eventually managed to get one of her neighbours to give evidence – they had seen him sitting in his car outside the flat staring in the window through binoculars. Tony was taken to the police station and charged. Not surprisingly his parents stood by him, but he was ordered not to go near the flat or her place of work otherwise he would be looking at a custodial sentence.

Tony's parents loved their son, but enough was enough and they told him in no uncertain terms that he wouldn't be associated with the business if he continued to harass Marcie and they would wash their hands of him. They knew he needed help - it wasn't the first time this had happened. His over possessiveness with girlfriends put the fear of God in them and he needed to learn how to deal with rejection and move forward. His mother suggested he took a break from work to sort himself out, maybe have a holiday, but Tony just nodded his head and left the room; he had no intention of going anywhere.

Marcie woke up one morning to the phone ringing. She picked it up relieved it was Roy on the other end and broke down in tears.

'Are you alright, Marcie? What on earth's the matter?'

'I just thought you were someone else; and after a few minutes she explained everything to him. Roy still had feelings for Marcie and was shocked and annoyed by what she had told him.

'Look, I haven't seen you for ages. Why don't I drive down this weekend and we can have a good old catch-up. Maybe I can cheer you up.'

Marcie was a bit reluctant at first but agreed and gave him the address. 'How did you get my phone number?'

'Nancy and Malcolm gave it to me. I'd tried to phone you when you were working for that Mr Evans and I left messages with him but you never got back to me.'

Marcie understood and apologised.

'Don't worry about it; I'll see you soon enough anyway.'

She was pleased in a way as she was a bit nervous of being on her own now and it would be a relief to have someone in the flat with her. Zoe and Charlie were busy with their own lives as Zoe was studying hard and Charlie had given in his notice to Mr Evans and had a new job lined up at a garden centre in Crews Hill in Enfield. She hadn't told them what had happened with Tony in case they said I told you so. They had never liked Tony, not from day one.

Marcie had a busy day in the shop and was pleased Bella had stayed to help because she normally took a back seat and left her in charge. There was good reason for her being there though - when she cashed up a few times there was some money short in the till. She didn't want to accuse Penny or Marcie till she observed a bit more of what was going on, as she knew it could be just a simple mistake. Tony peered in the window when he passed the shop but noticed Bella was there and quickly hurried up the road.

'I am doing a stock check today and I need you to help, Marcie. Penny can serve the customers and look after the shop.'

The day seemed to go on forever and Marcie was pleased when it was over. She had worked all day with just a fifteen minute break. Bella wasn't happy; she noticed from the stock sheets that there were a lot of items of clothing on them that were not on the rails and she knew they hadn't sold yet, but there wasn't time to discuss it that evening as her friend Beatrice was coming to pick her up and take her to dinner.

'You can go now girls; see you tomorrow,' she finally said, but Marcie could tell there was something wrong - she wasn't her cheery self and had been in a mood all day.

Bella went to dinner with her friend and confided in her, saying she could not believe either one of her girls was capable of stealing; it had to be someone else.

'Do you know much about their backgrounds?'

'Well, I know Penny's mother has multiple sclerosis and is confined to a wheelchair. She has two older sisters that have been in trouble before, but from what Penny says they've grown out of all that. Her father, Colin, is a hard working man; he works as a security guard at a warehouse. As far as I can make out they are a bit rough and ready, but well looked after and seem to be a close knit family.'

'What about Marcie?'

'She's a different kettle of fish entirely. She is independent, proud, and I admire her loyalty to her parents who have never supported her. I would say she is honest as the day is long, and she has such a good heart.'

Beatrice was flummoxed as to what to say. 'Look, the only

suggestion I can make is maybe employ a friend to work in the shop just for a short while. I know you don't like to be tied to the shop with all your charity work at the hospice. I'd do it myself, but you know Fred, he likes me at home and believes that's my place. He is the provider and I am the wife who cooks meals, looks after the children, and see's everything is running smoothly.'

Bella had a lot to think about, but that wasn't such a bad idea. She had someone in mind already – Carol, a retired care worker who had time on her hands.

Beatrice and Bella left the restaurant and said their good-byes and went their separate ways.

Marcie was walking down the road in the pouring rain, her step quickening as she felt there was someone following her. As she approached her gate she turned around, and with a sigh of relief realised it was Roy.

'My god Marcie, you're shaking. I had to park up the road and I've been trying to catch up with you.'

'I am a bit,' she said, 'I thought it was Tony. I'm so glad you're here Roy. Come on, let's go inside.'

Marcie had bought some steak and she had some salad and beers and wine in the fridge that she had bought the day before. Whilst she cooked the meal Roy looked around the flat, which he thought was dismal. She deserved so much more, but he kept his opinions to himself not wanting to offend her.

Marcie loved Roy's company; he was easy to get on with and let her be herself. It was so uncomplicated; a breath of fresh air, but at the same time she knew he had feelings for her and hoped he would keep them to himself. She had just come out of a horrible experience and wanted to be on her own - she didn't intend to have any relationships for a long time.

'Nancy told me you have a daughter, Molly. Why didn't you ever tell me?'

'It never seemed the right time; anyway I hadn't exactly come to terms with it myself, but now I can't imagine not having her in my life - she means everything to me.'

'I lost a child - I had a miscarriage recently.'

'I'm so sorry, Marcie. Nancy and Malcolm never told me. How come? Don't they know?'

'No, I didn't tell them. I didn't want to upset them. As you know, Nancy is very frail and worries about me and they have enough on their plate.'

Roy was upset to hear that this woman who he adored had gone through this experience on her own and went over to her and put his arms around her wishing he never had to let her go.

Marcie removed them as she didn't want to give him false hope and changed the subject. 'Have you got a girlfriend?'

'I did have - her name was Valerie. We went out together for nine months but I finished with her.'

'Why?' Marcie asked.

'I didn't feel the same way as her and couldn't see a future together, but she was great with Molly. I feel a bit guilty about that, but we have stayed good friends.'

Marcie liked that in Roy; he was a gent and hoped one day she could meet someone who was as caring as him. They chatted for a while longer but Marcie was shattered and made Roy a bed up on the settee before giving him a goodnight kiss on the cheek and going to bed.

The next morning Marcie was delighted to see that Roy had cooked bacon, eggs and toast and made a pot of tea for them both before she went to work. 'What are you going to do today? I hate leaving you but Saturday is a busy day at the shop.'

'Have you any jobs you want doing? I can't stand being idle.'

'Well, I have a leaking tap in the bathroom, and my toilet seat is coming off, but you don't have to do anything; just relax. How about I phone up two of my friends Zoe and Charlie and we all go to the pub tonight and eat there?' Roy thought that would be great and gave her a kiss on the cheek and she went off to work.

Marcie arrived at work to see Bella behind the counter with an older woman and instantly thought she had been replaced or was going to be. Bella introduced her friend Carol to Marcie, telling her that she was thinking of buying a boutique in Crouch End for her daughter who was interested in fashion. At the moment she worked as a full time accountant in Surrey but wanted a career change. Carol was going to help out in the shop for a couple of weeks to get some experience so she could help her daughter out from time to time, and wanted to get a feel for it before she committed herself to the idea of buying.

Marcie could see that she was a well-dressed woman, but

thought she had a hard face - maybe it was the tight perm she had and the large glasses on the end of her nose that gave that impression. She felt a little put out by what she saw as an intrusion, but Bella insisted she help Carol in any way she could and told Penny the same, before leaving the shop as she had things to do. She would be back at closing time.

Carol said the shop needed a good sweep and the toilet and small kitchen area at the back needed cleaning. Marcie pulled a face and Carol noticed. 'Do you think it's beneath you? Well let me tell you something young lady, where there's muck there's brass. I have been cleaning all my life and it didn't hurt me; now get a move on.'

'What about Penny?'

'She can make me a cup of tea and then start sweeping the front of shop – there's dirt everywhere.'

It was the first time Marcie had disliked her job and was dreading the next two weeks working with this woman, but knew she had no choice but to do as she was told as Carol was quite formidable and obviously a force to be reckoned with.

The shop was really busy and Penny's two sisters popped in and were surprised to see Carol there.

'Have you two come in to buy something or just look?' She had seen them in the corner of the shop chatting and giggling.

'We're just looking; that's not a crime is it?'

Penny told them to leave, and they did but on the way out one of them shouted, 'Who does she think she is - fat cow!' Penny apologised to Carol for her sister's remarks and Carol said it wasn't her fault and put it to the back of her mind.

Marcie was very quiet and Carol thought she may have been a bit harsh with her and got off on the wrong foot, so told her to have a tea break as she had worked hard and deserved it. She had noticed how good she was with the customers and they all seemed to like her. Carol went into the kitchen and made some cheese and ham sandwiches for them all, passing one to Marcie to have with her tea. Penny looked on. 'Don't worry, I have one for you but I want you to finish hanging those dresses up first.' Marcie thought her bark was worse than her bite and warmed to her a little. Maybe she wasn't so bad after all.

At closing time Bella arrived. 'Is everything alright Carol?'

'Yes, they have both worked hard so they can go now, but the cashing up still needs doing.'

'Don't worry; leave that to me, and thanks a lot.'

Carol left and said she would see them tomorrow.

Bella was worried. Although the till had tallied and everything was in order it only went to prove that Carol's being there was stopping whoever it was that was taking the money. Still, at least she could get a better night's sleep then she had of late knowing the shop was in Carol's capable hands.

Marcie arrived back at her flat and Roy put the kettle on and made her a cup of tea. He could see she looked tired.

'Bad day, pet?'

'Not really; just my feet are killing me.'

'I did those jobs for you and got a bit of shopping in.'

'You're a star Roy, thanks so much. Bloody hell, I just remembered; I forgot to ring Zoe and Charlie to see if they want to join us at the pub for something to eat. Never mind, I'll do it now.'

She got hold of Zoe and she said they'd love to join them. 'We might be a bit late though – Charlie doesn't get in from work till eight o'clock. We'll see you there though.'

'Great. Can't wait to see you both. Bye.'

Roy ran Marcie a bath and opened a bottle of wine. They had plenty of time as the pub was only round the corner.

'I hope you like my friends – they're a lovely couple; very easy to get on with and besotted with each other.' Marcie went on to explain how she had met Zoe in the park and eventually introduced her to Charlie. 'You'd never put them together though, Roy. Zoe was like a hippy when I first met her. She's ever so intelligent, too - she's doing a psychology course at the moment.'

'I'm sure they're lovely if they're friends of yours. I'm looking forward to meeting them. What does Charlie do?'

'He's in charge of a garden centre now, but when I first met him at my other job he was the gardener, and to be honest, a bit of a Jack the lad; loads of girlfriends and always down the pub, but he has settled down now with Zoe and they are so good together.'

Roy wished in his own mind that he could have that with Marcie, but she had just come out of a bad relationship and wasn't interested in having a boyfriend, he knew that. But he was pleased they were good friends, it was better than nothing, he thought, and had no intentions of spoiling that.

Roy looked very smart in his black leather jacket and white shirt and Marcie even remarked how handsome he looked. Marcie wore a simple short, black dress with beads and looked stunning. Roy was taken aback by her beauty, and told her that any man would be a fool to let her go.

'Stop it! Looks aren't everything. Let's face it, I pick arseholes, so that doesn't mean a damn thing. I'm just happy to have friends to support me like Charlie and Zoe, and not forgetting you. It's been lovely having you here.'

When they arrived at the pub it was buzzing; packed full of people with a band playing in the background, but they still managed to find a table in the corner.

'What do you want to drink Marcie?'

'A glass of white wine please. Here, take this,' and she handed him £5.

'Don't be daft! I'll get them in, but what about your friends?'

'Don't worry, they'll get their own when they arrive.'

Charlie and Zoe came an hour later and Marcie introduced them to Roy. 'I'd better get some more drinks in,' Roy said getting to his feet.

'I'll come with you and give you a hand,' said Charlie.

'You kept him a secret - he's bloody gorgeous!'

'Zoe, you have your Charlie.'

'I know that, I'm just being honest. Actually, I think you and him would make a lovely couple.'

'Shut up! He's a friend, that's all. Now don't you say anything.'

'I won't. Anyway, where's Tony?'

Marcie explained that she had finished with him and how he had been giving her trouble.

'Why the hell didn't you ring me and Charlie and tell us?'

'I didn't think he would take the break up so badly...'

'Come on, Marcie, he's a nutter! Creepy and devious - I don't know what you saw in him.'

'I knew you would say that that, that's why I said nothing.'

'You're right, who am I to judge? But what a bastard! I know my Charlie would have punched his lights out!'

'Did I hear my name mentioned?' Charlie said putting the drinks down on the table.

Marcie gave Zoe a look and she told him he must be mistaken.

She then turned back to Marcie and lowering her voice said, 'Right, where were we?'

'Shush,' Marcie said, 'leave it – let's have a good night, OK?'

'OK, but tomorrow I want you to phone me and tell me everything.'

'I will, I promise you, just not now.' Marcie looked upset so Zoe knew to back off.

'I'm starving,' Charlie said, 'but they've stopped doing food.'

'There's a chippie over the road,' said Marcie, 'let's go over there. We can eat it in there; they have a few tables.'

They finished their drinks and walked over to the chippie where they sat down at a table after ordering at the counter. As Zoe removed her coat and placed it on the back of the chair she noticed Tony sitting in the corner. 'Marcie! Look who's over there!' she whispered.

Roy overheard, saw the look on Marcie's face and put two and two together. 'I'm going over to give him a piece of my mind,' he said.

'Please leave it Roy, I don't want any trouble.'

'What's going on?' asked a puzzled Charlie, and Roy explained to him. With that there was no stopping them both and they went over to where Tony was sitting.

Charlie got him by the throat and pinned him to the wall. 'You ever go near Marcie again and I will find you and make your life a misery. Do you understand?' Tony was shaking. 'Not such a big man now, are you?'

Marcie went over and told them to let him go. 'He's not worth it,' she said with a look of distaste, but Roy was furious and punched him in the stomach. Tony doubled over and when they let him go he ran out of the chippie.

Marcie said she wanted to go home and Roy offered to take her. 'No, on my own. Have your fish and chips and I'll see you there.' She said goodbye to Charlie and Zoe and told Zoe she would give her a ring in the morning.

Marcie had only been home about ten minutes when Roy came in.

'What the hell were you thinking of Roy? You've just made things worse! I can't see Tony letting that go, and now I'm scared to be here on my own and you're leaving tomorrow, remember?'

107

Roy didn't know what to say. '...I was only sticking up for you - he needed to be taught a lesson. He makes my blood boil.'

'I know you care for me, but he has issues.'

'Rubbish, he's a stalker and thinks you're his property...or do you still fancy him?'

Marcie had heard enough and said she was going to bed.

Roy tossed and turned that night. The last thing he wanted was to upset Marcie and in the morning he would make it up to her.

It was Sunday and Marcie's day off so Roy got up early, laid the table and cooked a big fry up. Marcie could see he had made an effort and thanked him.

'I am so sorry about last night, Marcie.'

'That's alright. I know you were only thinking of me but I can look after myself. Violence doesn't get you anywhere.'

They sat down for breakfast and decided to spend the day at Hampstead Heath and stop for lunch at a pub nearby. While they sat on a park bench Marcie asked Roy about his work.

'What are you doing now; still doing building work?'

'Yes, but now I have four men I employ and I have three properties I own which I've renovated to a good standard. They were cheap to buy and I get a good income renting them out.'

'My god, you have done well - I am so proud of you. My friend the property developer!' she laughed as she hugged him.

'Not quite, but I'm getting there,' he said, secretly chuffed by her remarks; it meant so much to him. Roy hadn't mentioned his daughter much. He wanted to but was a bit worried that Marcie would get upset as it was still early days after her miscarriage.

They both had a lovely day out but Roy wanted to set off early as it was a long drive back home, so when they arrived back at the flat he put his few belongings in a bag and told Marcie he would ring her first thing the next morning, and in a few weeks time come back and see her, or if she wanted to she could come and stay with him. He kissed her on the cheek goodbye and they hugged each other and Marcie was sad to see him go. Roy had a heavy heart. This was the woman he wanted to marry and spend the rest of his life with. From the moment he first saw her he fancied her and knew she was the woman for him - no other girlfriend had even come close to making him feel like that.

It had started to rain and the wind had whipped up as Roy set off home. The further into his journey he got the worse the weather became, with gale force wind and torrential rain. I really should have got some new windscreen wipers, he thought to himself as he struggled to see clearly. It was now getting late and he just wanted to get home as he had an early start in the morning. He was picking his daughter Molly up and having her to stay with him for the week as her mum and her boyfriend were having a holiday abroad. The next thing he knew he lost control of the car; he couldn't see a thing and swerved off the road straight into a tree, his head hitting the windscreen and taking the full impact. The driver of the car some distance behind witnessed the whole awful scene. Pulling over he immediately dialled 999 and explained what had happened.

In no time at all an ambulance and a fire engine arrived at the scene. A police car also arrived soon after. The fire crew had to dismantle the door of the car to get Roy out and he was carefully put on a stretcher to go to Leicester Infirmary. Although the front of the car was completely crushed and he had what looked like severe head injuries, Roy was still breathing but unconscious. The police were handed his wallet which had a telephone number for his parents in it and they immediately informed them what had happened. After a thorough examination and some stitching and cleaning up of wounds Roy was taken for a head scan. Through all of this he remained unconscious.

A while later his anxious parents arrived at the hospital and the doctor immediately went to see them.

'I'm afraid your son is still unconscious, but we've done a head scan and it didn't show up anything untoward.'

Mr and Mrs Hawthorn heaved a sigh of relief.

'But, as I say, he is still unconscious and so it is early days. You can see him, but be prepared – he has some pretty awful cuts and bruises, though, of course, given time they will heal. Follow me.' The doctor led the way to a private room just off of the ward. 'I'll leave you with him for a few minutes. Please feel free to talk to him, the chances are that he can hear you.'

'Thank you, doctor,' said a rather tearful Mrs Hawthorn. Their wonderful, devoted son was the apple of their eye; someone who always put others first, and to see him like this was devastating, however they were mystified as to what he was doing in Leicester - he normally told them of his whereabouts and hadn't mentioned he was going anywhere that weekend. They had just assumed he was working on one of his flats; Roy was a grafter and often worked all hours to get the job finished. Until he came round it would remain a mystery.

Chapter Ten

Marcie went to work Monday morning wondering why Roy hadn't phoned her like he said he would, but quickly put it to the back of her mind – she'd give him a ring when she got home this evening, she thought.

Carol was in a good mood and the day was going well, but Marcie got the surprise of her life when Jane, her friend from home walked into the shop looking like something out of a magazine in her expensive designer outfit.

'Jane! What are you doing here? Are you working in one of the local hospitals?'

'Yes, remember I told you I was applying for a job in London? Well, I'm at the Whittington Hospital in Highgate!'

'How did you know where to find me?'

'I didn't, it's pure coincidence! My friend told me about Bella's Boutique and I thought I'd check it out.'

'I'm sorry I didn't keep in touch,' Marcie said, 'but how are your mum and dad?'

'You know them, the hotel is their life, but it's still doing well.'

'How is my mum? Is she still working for yours?'

'Good god, no! My mum had to let her go - she was always turning up for work a mess and her breath constantly stank of drink. Didn't she tell you?'

Marcie was embarrassed. 'I'm sorry Jane, no, I didn't know.'

After Jane had browsed round the shop she said her goodbyes and they exchanged telephone numbers saying they would meet up some time.

Carol couldn't help but overhear the conversation about her mum and felt sorry for Marcie. She took her to one side. 'Look, Marcie, I know it's none of my business, but I can see this news has come as a bit of a shock to you. Do you want to have your break now?'

'I'm alright, thanks Carol. I knew my mother was drinking but she never told me she'd been sacked. She loved her job at the hotel but I am a bit worried as to what is happening to her... especially with Sam there.'

'Who is Sam?'

'He's my uncle, or so I thought till I was told my dad isn't my real dad... it's a bit complicated. Not being rude, but I don't really want to talk about it if you don't mind.'

'That's alright, love, but I'm here if you need me,' and she left it at that. She could tell that this was a proud, independent girl who was stubborn, and she knew she had been through a lot as a child. Bella had filled her in on the details, and she knew it was best to hold back and respect her wishes - there was no point in pushing her.

The day had gone well and the shop was as busy as ever. Carol was beginning to think Bella may have made a mistake with her cashing up; after all she could get a bit forgetful at times. Her feet were killing her; this is one job I wouldn't like to do permanently, she thought. Penny and Marcie were lovely girls who seemed very honest and she felt she was wasting her time.

Roy's parents had now been joined by their daughter, Kate, and Kim, Molly's mum at Roy's bedside. Kim had remained friends with the family and Roy's mum had called her from the hospital.

'Where was he coming from?' Kim asked.

'Not sure, I just thought he was working on his house the weekend,' his mum said. 'He would always let us know if he was going elsewhere. But it doesn't matter where the hell he went, he's with us here and I hate to see my son lying in a coma like that. Speak to him - the doctor said he may be able to hear us.'

Marcie finished work and as soon as she got home she phoned Roy but got no reply. Perhaps he was avoiding her. The only reason she could think of was that as she hadn't responded to his advances, he had decided to move on. It was a shame as she was so fond of him, and had hoped they would always stay friends.

Jane phoned that evening and they decided to meet up in the Crown Inn in Highgate. Marcie was a bit nervous about travelling on a tube at night so ordered a taxi. Jane was pleased to see her when she walked in the pub but Marcie was surprised to see that she had two friends with her.

'This is Val and Ruth.'

Marcie thought they looked like hookers in their skimpy outfits and high heeled shoes. Jane went to the bar to buy them all drinks while Marcie started chatting to the two girls.

'What job do you do, Val?'

Val laughed. 'Well this may shock you, but we're pole dancers in a club in Soho.'

Marcie didn't know what to say after that but it wasn't long before Jane came back with the drinks. 'How long have you been working in the boutique?' Jane asked.

'Quite a while now – I love it. Bella's a good boss and looks after us.'

'I bet the money is crap,' said Jane.

'Not really; it pays my rent and I manage somehow. Do you enjoy working at the hospital?' Marcie asked, and the two girls started giggling.

Jane explained that she had lied - she wasn't working there any longer because the sister on the ward had taken a disliking to her and she had left and was working in the West End at a pole dancing club with Ruth and Val.

'Does your mum know?'

Don't be stupid! I write letters and as far as she is concerned I am working at the hospital - and don't you dare tell her otherwise - I will tell her when I'm ready.'

'Don't worry, of course I won't; it's none of my business, but I don't understand why you chose to do that after all the exams and hard work you put into getting there.'

'She can do what the hell she wants to, you stuck up prat,' sneered Val. Jane told her to shut up as Marcie was a good friend of hers and Val said nothing.

Marcie stayed in the pub chatting but was relieved when Jane called a taxi for her at the end of the evening. As she got in it she told Jane she would keep in touch.

Alone in the back of the taxi with her thoughts, Marcie felt sad that someone as bright and academic as Jane had wasted her talents. She thought back to what she had told her about her mum losing her job and decided that tomorrow when Bella came in to cash up she would ask her for a week's leave to visit her in Wales as she was now quite concerned about her.

The news didn't go down too well with Bella, and in the heat of the moment she told Marcie about the money missing from the till and that her stock was down.

'You surely don't think for one minute that I would do that when you have shown me nothing but kindness!' Marcie cried.

'Look, I'm not blaming you, I have no proof, but I had no choice but to ask you. Anyway, let's leave it for now, and yes, you can take a week off, and then hopefully we can sort it out one way or another.'

But Marcie felt she was being accused and was so angry she told Bella to stuff her job, she was leaving. 'I'll come in the morning for my wages.'

That evening when Zoe rang, Marcie told her what had happened and couldn't control her emotions crying hysterically on the phone.

'Calm down, Marcie. Bella is a good woman and the truth will come out. Just concentrate on yourself for now; things will work out, I promise you. Do you want me and Charlie to come over?'

'No, it's OK, I'll be alright. I'm collecting my wages in the morning and catching a train to visit Mum.'

'Phone us when you get there, and Charlie will pick you up from the station when you come back. Love you, hun.'

'Love you too, and thanks; I'll give you a bell.'

That night Marcie gave her mum a ring to let her know that she was coming and what time she would arrive.

The next morning Bella was waiting in the shop to give Marcie her wages and when she walked in she asked her to go through to the back so they could have a chat. 'I am sorry if you thought I was accusing you and regret the way I said it, but I am running a business I have worked hard for and it would be unfair to ask Penny and not you. I do trust you, Marcie, and when you have visited your mum in Wales your job as manageress will still be here for you when you get back.'

'What about Carol?'

'She's not interested in the job, believe me.'

Marcie gave Bella a hug and knew she meant every word and said she would be back next week. 'I know you worry about your mum, Marcie, but please don't let her manipulate you and take advantage - and look after yourself. I care about you like my own daughter,' she said, and kissed her on the cheek.

Marcie got a taxi to the station and got on the train feeling less stressed knowing she had her job to come back to.

Nellie told Sam he had to leave as Marcie was coming and she didn't want him there.

'I'm not going anywhere,' he replied.

'Please, just till she leaves - I don't want any trouble.'

'Alright, I'll stay at Jack Bevan's place, his misses won't mind.'

Nellie didn't like Jack; she had known him for years and he was a drunken wife beater. She had suffered years of abuse at his hands, and his three children hated the sight of him, two of them choosing to leave home and work away in Scotland.

Sam packed a few belongings in a bag and told Nellie he was off but would be back after her precious Marcie had gone back to London. 'I may well hang about till she arrives and tell her I'm her dad,' he said threateningly.

'Leave it alone, what good would it do? If you open your big trap I may never see her again!'

'That got you scared, didn't it?' he sneered. 'Have you any money on you, I'm broke?'

'Well, there's a surprise. Here, take this tenner, that's all I can give you, and get lost.'

When Sam finally left, Nellie set about giving the place a good clean from top to bottom. What with one thing and another she had let her standards drop and the place was like a pig sty with beer cans under the bed and empty whisky bottles everywhere, not to mention that her bedding hadn't been changed for weeks or maybe longer...she couldn't remember. She was shaking now and her body ached - her and Sam usually had a few beers in the morning.

By mid afternoon the house was looking more like a home and Nellie made a beef and ale stew. When she had it simmering away she decided one little drink wouldn't hurt and opened a can of beer. One became four and she took the stew off the stove and had a lay down on the settee.

Marcie was banging on her mum's door but could get no answer so went next door to ask if she had gone out. Fred, the elderly neighbour who had known Marcie for most of her life came to the door. 'Hello Fred. I was wondering if you know where my mum is. I'm getting no answer.'

'She's probably there pet, but out for the count.'

'What do you mean?'

'You're not going to like this, but I have called the police many times with the racket going on in there, and that Sam gives me and my wife a load of abuse. I have always been fond of you, lass, but I want nothing to do with them two. I know Tom was a miserable bugger but I curse the day he moved out.'

Marcie apologised and Fred closed the door.

Nellie had woken up just as her daughter had knocked next door, and she'd heard every word that was said through her open window. She quickly got up and went to the door.

'What the hell is going on Mum? I felt so embarrassed talking to Fred – he's a frail old man and doesn't need all that aggro!'

'He's a pain in the arse - always complaining - and that wife of his is no better!'

'Mum, what has happened to you? I remember when you worked for Mrs Clements - she was so proud of your work.'

'Oh, her, Lady Muck! Too good for the likes of us. All those years I slogged my guts out for her and she told me to leave!'

'Because you were stinking of booze, Mother, and looked a mess. Jane told me!'

Nellie went upstairs to lie down – her way of coping when things got heated. Marcie could see she had been drinking by the empty beer cans on the side in the kitchen, and she collected them up and threw them in the bin. She then set to and washed the kitchen floor – it was sticky where beer had been spilt. When she had finished, she took her small case with her few belongings up to her room and putting the case down looked around her. Her mum had always been such a meticulous woman but there was dust everywhere and it was a mess. Marcie put her clothes in the drawer and went downstairs. She felt shivers run up her spine...this was such an unhappy home in her childhood and thoughts went back to her brother when he was alive. Oh, how she missed him... Her eyes filled with tears – she would never get over the loss.

When Nellie woke a short while later she went downstairs and started to peel some potatoes and put the stew back on to warm.

Marcie went to talk to her. 'Where's Sam?'

'He is staying with some friends.'

'I don't know why you have him here, Mum.'

'I suppose I get lonely at times.'

'You're sleeping with him, aren't you?'

'That's my business, Marcie.'

'What are you thinking of? He's gross...*and* he's your brother-in-law!'

Nellie ignored that remark and started to set the table.

'I want to visit Elsie tomorrow and see her baby. Why don't we take a walk to the village in the morning before I go and you can get your hair done, Mum, it looks a mess. You may not need an appointment at Jasmine's Salon if it's just a cut and blow dry.'

'I don't feel like it and it costs money, which I don't have.'

'I'll pay' it's no problem.'

Nellie was not in the mood and went to the fridge to get a can of beer. Marcie grabbed it out of her hand. 'You don't need that; it's still early, what's wrong with you? Don't you think you have had enough?'

There was a knock at the door and Marcie answered it to see Sam standing there.

'I just thought I would pop in to see my niece.'

Nellie was furious. 'I told you to stay away!'

'Don't be like that. No harm done is there? How are you Marcie?'

'Get lost! You're nothing but trouble...and stay away from my mum; you're taking advantage of her being on her own!'

Sam started to laugh. 'You stupid girl; she can't get enough of me and it's been like that from the first time I met her; isn't that right, Nellie?'

'Please get out, Sam.'

'I'm going, don't worry, but I will be back,' and he walked out the door.

Marcie was in shock and asked her mum just what he meant.

'Nothing, he is winding you up.'

'Liar! You know more than you're letting on. When I was younger I remember you two used to whisper to each other all the time and flirt with one another. I want the truth or I will leave right now.'

Nellie walked over to the settee and sat down, her hands over her face. 'Sam is telling the truth. We did have an affair...but Tom wasn't interested in me. As soon as he put the ring on my finger he didn't pay me any attention.'

'Why didn't you leave him?'

'In those days you just got on with it I suppose and where was I supposed to go with no money? He was a worker and the bills were paid.'

'Who is my dad? I want to know!'

'Sorry Marcie, but Sam is your dad...'

Marcie couldn't believe what she was hearing. This man that she couldn't stand the sight of was her father. 'Why did you never tell me?'

'What was the point? Tom would have left me. He used to be close to his brother when they were growing up and I let him think it was someone else.'

Marcie ran out of the house into the garden. All those years of lies and deceit! No wonder she felt so rejected growing up. The tears ran down her face and she sobbed.

Her mum came out into the garden and put her arms around her. 'Get off me! I hate you!' Nellie started to cry too, and she realized for the first time how much her past mistakes had such an impact on her daughter and truly wished she could turn back the clock and start again.

Marcie went upstairs and packed her bag; she needed to get away. Nellie knew there was no stopping her, she had to let her go, but made her promise she would keep in touch and maybe one day find it in her heart to forgive her.

Marcie walked to the taxi rank and climbed in a taxi. The nearest place was Elsie's parents and she decided to get the taxi driver to drop her there, hoping that maybe she could stay with them till she'd arranged to see Elsie and sorted out another train ticket back to London.

Marcie knocked on the door and when Jean answered it she was shocked to see her standing there with her suitcase.

'Marcie, how lovely to see you! What's happened? Aren't you staying at your mum's?'

'Hello Jean. I was at mum's house but I can't stay there.'

'Why ever not? Come in, come in. It's freezing out there.'

'I wouldn't normally ask, but can I stay here for a few days?'

Just then Elsie appeared and couldn't believe it was Marcie. 'You never told me you were coming home.'

'Sorry, it was all a bit spur of the moment. I was coming to see you tomorrow but had a row with Mum.'

'What about?'

'Elsie, go and put the kettle on love, and let Marcie take her coat off. Give her some space, poor bugger.'

It didn't take long before Marcie was in floods of tears telling Jean what had happened.

'I always had my suspicions as to why he was staying with your mum. When Tom moved out there was gossip in the village but I never knew the affair had been going on so long. Shameful I say, but you have to think about yourself and let her get on with her life – she's her own worst enemy.'

Elsie came out of the kitchen and put her arms around her telling her she could sleep in her room with her and the baby, Eddy.

'No, knowing you two you'll keep my grandson awake. The boys are off camping with their dad – you can have their room, Marcie,' said Jean.

Marcie couldn't believe Elsie was a new mum - she looked radiant, really well. 'I can't wait to see him, where is he? And what about Pete – you're obviously living back here now?'

'Eddy's sleeping; he's so good, never any bother and is always smiling. My mum and dad spoil him rotten. I don't see Pete anymore – good riddance, I say; we're better off without him,' and Jean nodded her head in agreement.

They chatted for hours but Marcie felt drained with all the upset and Jean told her to go upstairs to bed. 'Things will look better in the morning, pet.'

Marcie tossed and turned for hours, her mind working overtime, until she fell into an exhausted sleep.

She woke up the next morning to Eddy screaming for his feed, and she got dressed and went downstairs.

'Good morning, did you sleep well, pet?' Jean could tell she hadn't, her eyes were all puffy and she looked pale. Elsie came out of the kitchen with Eddy in her arms, a beautiful chubby baby who looked just like his mum with big brown eyes and a round face.

'He's gorgeous, Elsie!' and she handed him to Marcie who rocked him back and forth and made a fuss of him.

'It suits you,' said Jean smiling. 'I'll have to do some shopping today but its pouring down with rain so I won't ask you both to come with me as Eddy's had a bit of a cold. He's better off staying in the warm. Do you need me to get you anything Marcie?'

'No, I'm fine thanks, but I want to give you some money towards my keep.'

'Don't be silly, you're not planning to move in for good are you? I'm sure we can manage to feed you for a day or two,' said Jean smiling as she went to get her coat.

When Jean had left Elsie made them both a sandwich and wanted to know all about Marcie's job. 'It sounds glamorous working in a boutique - are the people snobby?'

'Not really; a bit reserved but Bella is easy to get on with. I've made a few friends, Zoe and Charlie who are living together now. I think you would like them...oh, and guess who came into the shop? Jane whose mum owns the hotel I worked at. I think you met her once or twice.'

'I remember. What's she doing down in London?'

'She's a nurse.' Marcie didn't want to say otherwise as it was her business and Elsie had a habit of putting her foot in it and might tell someone - she never could keep a secret. They used to joke about that.

Jean came home from shopping and said she saw Nellie on the high street with Sam. 'They didn't see me though, they were across the road, but they looked like two homeless people. They were a real mess and I'd say they'd been drinking – your mum was very unsteady on her feet.'

'It didn't take her long to get Sam back, did it?' murmured Marcie bitterly.

'Maybe I shouldn't have told you, Marcie, I'm sorry.'

'I don't care; they are welcome to each other,' she said, but Jean could tell she was a bit upset. Marcie put all thoughts of her mum and Sam to the back of her mind determined to make the most of the short time she had to spend with this wonderful family. She spent the rest of the day catching up with Elsie and making a fuss of little Eddy. They were such a close family and she found herself wishing she had one just like them. Elsie was a good mum and she envied what she had. She knew it would be a long time before she would return to Wales - the only good memories she had of growing up there were of her brother and of the times she'd spent with Elsie and her parents, but now she wanted to get as far away from her mother and all the gossips in the village as soon as possible. It was the only way she could move on with her life, and now she couldn't wait to get back to London.

Marcie sorted her ticket out and was leaving the following morning, but Jean tried to persuade her to stay longer as she had just arrived, but she knew it was probably for the best. If she got back to work it would take her mind off things.

Jean cooked a lovely roast dinner that evening and put a bottle of red wine on the table. 'It's been lovely having you here, Marcie,' she smiled as she poured three glasses out and took a sip herself. 'Cheers! I hope you won't forget us.'

'I won't and I hope you will come and stay with me, too, and I'll show you the sights of London.'

'I don't think so pet, it's too posh for me, I would be way out of my comfort zone.'

'Speak for yourself, Mum! I wouldn't mind coming to see you, Marcie.'

'Any time; you know you'll be welcome, and bring Eddy with you.'

The next morning Marcie said her goodbyes when the taxi arrived to take her to the station. As they waved her off she felt sad not knowing when their paths would cross again.

The train was packed and she just managed to get a seat, but the carrier bag that had her boiled egg sandwiches in that Jean had kindly made for her was squashed to pieces. The journey seemed to take forever but she finally arrived at her destination and got a taxi to take her to her flat.

When she walked in it seemed the loneliest place in the world after leaving Elsie's house with the baby there and Jean. She went into the kitchen to put the kettle on and made herself a cup of tea. After an hour of busying herself unpacking her things and putting her dirty laundry in the washing machine, she sat down. Her thoughts went to Roy and she couldn't understand why he hadn't returned her phone call. That's it, she thought, I'm going to call him again and ask him what the matter is. They would have to clear the air, this was silly. Yes, it was a shame that she didn't feel the same about him as he did for her, but nevertheless she valued his friendship and she missed him. She dialled the number, but again there was no reply.

Marcie was bored and gave Jane a ring. 'Hi Jane, it's me,

Marcie.'

'Hi Marcie. What are you up to? Are you doing anything tonight?'

'No, I don't have any plans. What did you have in mind?'

'Well, it's my night off. Why don't we meet up and we could have a meal at my favourite restaurant in Soho. Just get a taxi and I'll meet you there.'

'Are your friends going to be there?' Marcie asked.

'No, they are working tonight.'

'OK. What should I wear?'

'It's casual, but something smart.' Jane gave Marcie directions and they arranged to see each other there at 7.30.

When Marcie arrived at the restaurant she was appalled – it was so grotty looking. As she walked in she could see Jane sipping a glass of wine sitting at a table near the kitchen waiting for her.

'Hi Marcie. Let's eat straight away, I'm starving. Here's the menu - what do you fancy? There's cheeseburgers, pizza, or their special, pork and mashed potato and veg with a bolognaise sauce.' Marcie and Jane ordered the pork but when it arrived it was like slop on a plate.

'I'm sorry Jane, but this is horrible.'

'I agree,' said Jane after picking at her meal. 'It's usually much nicer than this. Let's pay the bill and go to a bar I know down the road in Berwick Street.'

Walking along, Marcie felt uncomfortable dressed in her smart tweed suit and high heels next to Jane. She looked tarty with her short skirt and thick make-up, not to mention her back-combed hair stiff with lacquer. Jane stopped at the entrance to an open doorway on the main street and Marcie looked in to see a flight of steps going down into the darkness.

'What is this place? It's not a pub.'

'No, it's like a club, but you can have drinks. My friend Jessie who often comes to watch me pole dancing works here – you'll like her.'

Marcie walked down the steps and when she got to the bottom she was baffled – there were at least a dozen scantily clad girls sitting at mirrored dressing tables who looked like they were getting ready to do a show. There were clothes and make-up everywhere. Jane went to get Marcie a drink at the other side of the room and introduced her to Jessie as she was coming out of another room at the back.

'Hi, Jess. This is my friend Marcie.'

'Bloody hell! You look like you're going to work at an office. What a geeky outfit.'

'Don't be fucking rude, Jessie!'

'Sorry! Pleased to meet you Marcie,' and she shook her hand, but Marcie felt so uncomfortable and just wanted to get out of there.

'Come on Jane, let's go.'

'Why are you being so boring, Marcie? Let's stick around.'

'What do these girls do?'

'It's a clip joint - easy money. They stand upstairs talking to punters at the door and arrange to meet them at a certain address. They take money up front but then don't actually go with them. They have to sound convincing though.'

Marcie had heard enough and walked upstairs telling Jane she was hailing a taxi and going home. Jane followed her and they started to have words at the door when a handsome passer-by caught Jane's eye. 'Hi gorgeous. Fancy a bit of fun with me?' and he stopped in his tracks and turned to her.

'How much do you charge?'

'£40 for two hours of my undivided attention, but not here – I'll give you my address and meet you there, but I want half the money up front.'

With that he reached inside his jacket and pulled out a badge. 'You're nicked, love.' He read Jane her rights and walked her down the road to a waiting police car. Once she was safely in the car with one of his colleagues to keep an eye on her he walked back to have a word with an open-mouthed Marcie.

'Do yourself a favour, miss, and go home and think yourself lucky you're not in the police car with your friend being charged with soliciting.'

'But...honestly...I never knew...'

'Look, we've had complaints about this place and we've been watching it for a while. I can see you're not dressed like the rest of them and you seem a nice girl. Don't get lured into this way of life like a lot of girls your age that leave home for the bright lights of London. I'm taking your friend to Bow Street Police Station and she'll go up in front of the magistrate in the morning. Go on, go home love, and if I ever see you here again you'll be nicked, too,' and with that he turned and headed for the police car.

Marcie hailed a taxi to take her back home and was in tears. What had become of her friend? This was too much; she just wanted to go to bed and crawl under her duvet and forget about the whole horrible thing.

The next morning Jane appeared in front of Bow Street Magistrates Court after spending the night in a cell. As it turned out she was lucky, the judge let her off on a conditional discharge as it was her first offence.

Marcie woke up the next morning with Jane on her mind and wondering what to do. She just couldn't believe what had happened last night. Later on that day, she decided to give her a call.

'Oh, Jane, thank god you're home! Are you alright?'

'Yes, No thanks to you. Why didn't you say something?'

'Jane it had nothing to do with me. By rights *I* should be angry! What the hell are you doing associating yourself with people like that and taking me to that place? We were only supposed to be going out for a nice meal and a drink together. Anyway, what happened?'

Jane explained that she appeared in court and got a conditional discharge.

'What is happening to you, Jane? I remember you were always the one with your head screwed on and I used to envy you!'

'You don't know anything about me Marcie.'

'Well, tell me.'

'Can I come to your place tonight and I'll bring a bottle of wine?'

'I don't mind, but don't bring any of your friends with you, I don't want them knowing where I live.'

'No problem.'

Marcie gave Jane her address and they said their goodbyes before putting the phone down. She cared about Jane who had always shown her nothing but kindness when she worked for her mother, but knew there must be something she was hiding - she came from a loving family and had the best start in life. She just couldn't understand it.

Marcie went to the market to get some shopping and bought pasta and tuna to make a pasta bake for them both, some salad and bread and fresh fruit for a fruit salad for dessert. Whatever she cooked was going to be better than the rubbish they ate last night at the restaurant, but eating out and getting a taxi home had left her a bit short. The rest of the day she spent happily cleaning the flat but she couldn't shake off thoughts of Roy and the possibility of him being upset with her. She dialled his number but again got no reply.

At eight o clock the doorbell rang and it was Jane.

'Ah, you're right on time. You found it OK then? Here, give me your coat and come on in.'

Jane thought the flat was cosy - much better than her accommodation as sharing with other girls it was always messy. Marcie poured them both a glass of wine and they sat down on the settee.

'I spent the night in a police cell; it was bloody awful.'

'Why did you go to that place? Have you worked there yourself?'

'Hell, no! When you work in a club everyone knows everyone around Soho; I just started chatting to Jessie and she was thinking of taking up pole dancing herself.'

'Don't you miss nursing, that's what you always wanted to do?'

'I do, believe me, but I made the biggest mistake ever and started having an affair with Dr Rea who did the rounds on our ward. I fell madly in love with him, and his wife, Trish, who was the sister on the ward found out and made my life a misery.'

'What did he do? Did he leave her?'

'No, he told me it would be better for all concerned if I gave my notice in and had nothing more to do with me.'

'I don't know what to say. The bastard...but Jane you should never have got involved knowing he was married.'

'I know, but he told me he wanted a divorce because the marriage hadn't worked for a long time and he loved me. To be honest, after I left the hospital I didn't care about anything...I felt my whole life was over and went out drinking every night. That's where I met my friend in Soho who told me about the pole dancing club, and I applied and got the job straight away.'

Changing the subject Marcie said, 'Let's eat,' as the drink had taken an affect and she hadn't eaten all day.

Marcie dished up the pasta bake with a green side salad and fresh crusty bread. 'This is lovely Marcie, a bit of a change from the shit we ate last night, eh?'

'Oh god, yes, that meal was awful!'

'It's lovely here, really cosy.'

'Yes, I like it here but I may have to look for cheaper accommodation - I can just about afford the rent, which doesn't leave me much to live on and now I'm struggling a bit to be honest.'

'That would be such a shame... I've had a thought though! How about if I moved in with you? I can always look for a job locally and that would give me a fresh start!' she said excitedly.

Marcie was silent for a moment but thought that actually it wasn't such a bad idea. 'The only thing is I have some house rules, Jane. For starters, you have to forget about your so-called friends in Soho - you're much better than that - and we share everything, the rent, bills, cooking and cleaning. And I can't afford to eat out all the time at fancy restaurants.'

Jane laughed. 'I'm sure we will make a good team, and I promise I won't let you down. Thank you so much!'

At the end of a lovely evening Jane got a taxi home having made arrangements to move in at the weekend.

The next day Zoe rang for a chat and Marcie told her the news about Jane moving in.

'Are you sure your doing the right thing? You don't want her friends from the West-End turning up.'

'No, I told her that, but she needs support and her helping with the rent money will come in handy.'

'Well, as long as you've got that straight with her you shouldn't have a problem. How did you get on at your mum's?'

Marcie told Zoe all about her mother's drinking, and how she'd told her that her Uncle Sam is her real father.

'Oh Marcie, I'm so sorry. You were brought up with a lot of secrets and lies you must feel so angry.'

'I do...but I'm moving on and I won't be paying her a visit for a long time. She can get on with it. Sam and the drinking's her problem, not mine – I refuse to take responsibility for her well-being just because she's my mother. If she won't try to help herself and listen to reason, I give up!'

'We'll have to get together, Marcie, I haven't seen you for a while.'

'Well, Jane's moving in on Saturday, why don't you and Charlie come over at about 7 o'clock and I'll cook a meal for us all?'

'That'll be lovely. We can chat more then.'

'Great. Look forward to seeing you.'

'OK, see you then, pet. Bye.'

Chapter Eleven

Marcie was wondering how Bella and Penny were getting on at the shop without her and if Carol was still there. She liked her but enjoyed the freedom of being manageress and being left to her own devices. But Marcie was in for a shock...

Unbeknown to her, Penny had been sacked and Carol had been asked to stay on for a few more weeks till she found someone else to replace her. On the first morning that Marcie was away the shop had been busy, but when there was a quiet few minutes Carol said she was going to make her and Penny a cup of tea and went in the back leaving her on her own. As she came back with a tray in her hands she saw Penny putting some clothes in a carrier bag that her sister was holding. 'What's in the bag?' asked Carol, immediately suspicious by the look on Penny's face - she had guilt written all over it. Carol quickly locked the shop and looked in her bag, which contained two dresses and a necklace. 'What do you think you are doing? And don't try to tell me she's paid for these – I'd have heard the till.'

Penny didn't know what to say and knew she had been caught red handed. Carol called Bella and she immediately came down to the shop. 'You stupid girl! Didn't you think we would catch you eventually? Is it really worth risking your job for?'

Penny's sister stepped in insisting she was going to pay for the goods, but when nobody would believe her she told them all to fuck off. Bella knew the family had a few problems what with their mother having multiple sclerosis and their father Colin being the main provider. 'You're fired, Penny. You've got off lightly because I'm not going to call the police, but let this be a warning to you and don't you or your sisters ever step foot in my shop again. I've been lenient because of your dear parents who I'm sure have done their best for you under the circumstances. But before you go, a word of advice, don't be influenced by your sisters – they most certainly do not have your best interests at heart or you wouldn't be in this mess now. You disappoint me, Penny. Now, please get out of my shop.'

'Can I have a reference?' Penny asked.

'You most certainly cannot. Now go.'

Bella was distraught. She had become fond of Penny but knew she had no choice but to fire her.

Carol stood there aghast. 'Why didn't you call the police Bella?'

'I think they all have their cross to bear as a family, but I have my business to think of and it will hurt them much more knowing they have lost Penny's wages coming into the household.'

'You're too soft for your own good Bella!'

'I know, but I've been fortunate in my life and I don't think Penny deserves any more grief. She hasn't had it easy and I can see she has a tough road ahead of her.'

Carol conceded that perhaps she was right, and realised how lucky she was to have such a kind and compassionate friend as Bella.

Marcie was having a lie in the next morning when the doorbell rang and woke her up. She got up and went to the door wrapping her dressing gown around her and was surprised to see it was her next door neighbour - they had never spoken before, other than a quick hello in passing.

'Sorry to bother you, but have you any milk you can spare?'

'Erm...yes, come in and I'll get you some.'

Iris was a thin, scruffy looking girl in her twenties with a gaunt face and greasy long blonde hair. Marcie knew she had three young children and was a one parent family. The only people she had visit her was an older couple who Marcie presumed were her parents.

Opening the fridge Marcie got out a bottle of milk and handed it to her. 'Would you like a cup of tea?'

Iris thanked her. 'Yes, please.'

Marcie could tell she was shy and very immature. When they both sat down to have their tea Marcie asked her about her children and she looked sheepish.

'The social worker wants to take them away. They're saying I'm an unfit mother...but I do my best.'

'Who is looking after them now?'

'My parents are there - they come once a week so I can do my shopping. Actually, I had better get back. Thanks for the tea.'

'That's OK. Listen, any time you need help I am always here,' and as soon as the words were out of her mouth Marcie regretted saying them. She had guessed they were a problem family with the shouting and noise she could hear coming from next door late into the night from time to time.

The next day Marcie was just leaving her flat to do a bit of shopping as she had Jane moving in and Zoe and Charlie coming for dinner, when Iris caught her unawares and asked if she wanted to come in for a coffee.

'Well, I must go and do my shopping but I have ten minutes to spare - thank you.'

As Marcie walked into the flat the stench of the place hit her right away, and looking round she had never seen so much filth. There were clothes everywhere, it was a complete hovel and the children were running around with no nappies on and treading in their own excrement. A Yorkshire terrier pup lay in a basket in the corner – maybe he was the culprit, she thought. She followed Iris into the kitchen, which wasn't any cleaner than the lounge with at least eight black sacks of rubbish piled up next to the sink. Iris made them both a coffee and Marcie asked about her parents.

'What do they do?'

'My mother's a cleaner but my stepfather hasn't worked for years. He reckons he has a bad back, but I think he's just a lazy sod.'

'Why are the social workers involved?'

'They say I'm not coping and have given me a few months to sort myself out or they will put my children into care.'

'What about their father?'

'He buggered off ages ago - he never had a job either.'

'Your mum and dad must worry about you.'

'No, not really. My mum's alright but my stepfather can't keep his hands to himself and keeps touching me; he's a real dirty bugger.'

'Why haven't you told anyone? That's disgusting!'

'I did but no one believes me.'

Marcie had heard enough and told Iris she had loads to do and she must get going.

'You didn't drink your coffee,' Iris remarked, 'it's gone cold.'

'That's alright, but thanks anyway. Bye.' Marcie was relieved to get outside into the fresh air. As much as she felt sorry for Iris she must keep her distance and not get involved - she needed much more help than just the odd pint of milk and maybe the social workers were the best people to help her.

She walked down the high road and called into Greggs the bakers and bought four homemade mince pies and then called next door at the greengrocers to buy some carrots and potatoes. That will have to do, she thought to herself as she looked in her purse and realised she had very little money left.

Later on that afternoon Jane arrived with her suitcase. Marcie was shocked when she picked it up; it weighed a ton. 'Where do you think I am going to put all these clothes?'

'My books are in there as well.'

'I'll have to buy you a cheap rail down the market and put it in my bedroom as my single wardrobe is full. You do know you're sleeping on the sofa bed in the sitting room?'

'No problem,' Jane said, 'I can sleep on a clothes line! I've brought a bottle of wine with me – shall I open it now?'

'No, leave it for us all tonight. Zoe and Charlie are coming for dinner.'

'Alright, bossy boots,' and they both laughed.

Zoe arrived that evening on her own. 'No Charlie?' asked Marcie when she opened the door.

'No, he decided to go to the pub with his mates. I think three women prattling on frightened him off,' she laughed.

Marcie introduced the two girls to each other and went into the kitchen. Jane poured them all a drink.

'Love your leather boots, Jane,' remarked Zoe.

'Aw, thanks, I bought them in the West-End.'

'What job are you going to look for? Marcie told me you were a qualified nurse.'

'You mean before I did pole dancing?' and they both chuckled. 'I would love to do nursing again; maybe work in a private nursing home. Are there any round here?'

'There's one in Highgate, try that.'

'Come on, girls, food's ready, come and get it,' and they sat at the small dining table in the corner of her sitting room.

'Oh, I nearly forgot,' said Zoe, and went to her haversack and pulled out a bottle of wine.

Marcie started talking about Iris next door and what she had told her about her stepfather. Zoe wasn't surprised. 'I thought he looked a real creep when I saw him, but Iris only moved in two weeks before I left so I didn't really know her that well. The last tenant was a lovely elderly man called Bill. He went for his pint of beer at the local pub every day and was a real gent, but he moved away to be near his brother in Bolton I believe.'

Jane liked Zoe; she was down to earth and quite friendly and Marcie was pleased they seemed to be getting on well.

'Phew! I'm stuffed - that was lovely grub, Marcie,' said Zoe, wiping her mouth on a napkin, 'but you two must come to my place and I will cook next time.'

'You mean get a takeaway; there's hardly room to swing a cat in your bedsit!'

Alright Marcie, don't rub it in, but seriously, we have put our names down on the council list for a flat.'

'I think you have to have children, don't you, otherwise you don't stand a chance?' said Jane.

'Well...I'm pregnant and Charlie's over the moon!'

'Congratulations! You sly dog, you kept that a secret! How far on are you?' said Marcie.

'Three months.'

'Why didn't you let me know earlier? I thought friends didn't keep secrets.'

'Sorry Marcie, but I didn't know how to tell you with you not long having had a miscarriage...'

'Don't be daft. I'm really happy for you both! Anyway, that means more wine for us - you can't drink too much in your condition,' and they all laughed.

Jane and Marcie finished off the bottle of wine and Zoe had a coffee instead. 'I am getting off now, I feel tired, but we must all meet up for a drink sometime - no alcohol for me - my Charlie only lets me drink orange juice in the pub, so don't let on I had a glass of wine tonight.'

'Your secret is safe with us!' and Marcie showed her to the door. 'Goodnight pet, drive home safely.'

'I will. Thanks for a lovely evening. Night.'

'I'll wash the dishes,' Jane said yawning.

'No, don't bother, leave them till the morning. I'm off to bed, goodnight.'

Sunday morning Jane and Marcie had breakfast and chilled out listening to records. They had intended to go to Hampstead Heath and have some lunch at a pub but the weather was shocking. The heavens had opened and it was a freezing cold day.

'Life is strange,' said Marcie, 'who would have thought we would share a flat together in Hampstead when we come from such different backgrounds?'

'What does it matter? Different strokes for different folks, that's what my mum used to say.'

They spent the rest of the day watching TV and generally lazing about.

On Monday morning Marcie was getting ready for work and told Jane to buy the local papers and look for work. She felt guilty leaving her on her own.

'I will,' Jane said, 'don't worry about me - I will occupy myself. Now you get going.'

'See you later pet. Phone me if you need anything.'

Bella was in the shop when she arrived, which she thought unusual, and Penny was nowhere to be seen. Carol came through from the back with a tray of teas. 'Ah, Marcie, just in time for a cuppa.'

'Thanks Carol. I didn't expect to see you here. Where's Penny – running late?'

Bella told Marcie what had happened and she couldn't believe what she was hearing. She liked Penny and felt sad as they had got on so well working together. Bella had her committee meetings to deal with for her charity and had to go and said she would pop back later to cash up the takings.

Jane felt bored on her own and walked down the shops and bought a few newspapers, stopping at a cafe to have a coffee and look up the job sections. One advertisement caught her eye - a qualified nurse was needed for the night shift at a private nursing home in East Finchley and applicants needed to have experience of working with the elderly, in particular the terminally ill. She finished her coffee and wandered home to make a telephone call.

She spoke to the staff nurse on duty who arranged an appointment for the following day for her to come and see her. Jane felt elated as she had worked on a geriatric ward at the hospital and loved it.

Marcie had finished work and was walking down the road when she bumped into Tony. 'How's life treating you? I miss you, Marcie.'

'Piss off! I certainly don't miss you! Now let me pass you creep.'

Tony grabbed her arm. 'Who the fuck do you think you are?'

'Much better than you, now get lost,' and she ran down the road shaking.

When she arrived home Jane was there. 'How was your day?'

'Not bad. I have an appointment at 1 o'clock tomorrow at a nursing home in East Finchley. Wish me luck.'

Marcie wasn't feeling in a jolly mood and it showed on her face.

'Is there something wrong? You don't look too happy.'

'You know I told you about Tony? Well I have just bumped into him in the street and he grabbed my arm and said he missed me, the creep.'

'Do you think he is going to hassle you again?'

'He had better not otherwise I'll call the police,' but Jane could see she was upset and worried.

The following day Jane went for her appointment and was greeted by Staff Nurse Miller who showed her into her office for the interview.

'I normally wait till I have some form of reference but we have had an influx of new patients and we need help straight away. Are you free to start next week?'

'Yes, I am.'

'Well, what I will do is make a few phone calls. What hospital did you say you worked at?'

'I was working at the Whittington Hospital in Highgate for a year.'

'Can I ask what made you leave?'

Jane felt awkward and wasn't sure what to say. 'I had personal problems.'

Staff Nurse Miller prompted Jane again, but still didn't get a satisfactory answer, with Jane saying she didn't want to talk about it. From that point on it became a very uncomfortable interview, ending with Staff Nurse Miller saying that she had other applicants still to see and would be in touch shortly with her decision. When she walked out of the nursing home Jane knew she had blown it. She knew she should have been more cooperative and taken her chances and told the truth.

Marcie felt sorry for Jane and decided to take her out that evening for a meal to cheer her up. 'You can't afford that, Marcie.'

'No, I can't really but I have a bit of savings put away and this is an emergency; you are getting on my nerves moping around the flat.'

'To be honest Marcie I would like to work in a hospital environment, I think that would suit me better.'

'Well, go for it. There are plenty of hospitals round here. Come on, think positive.'

Over the next few weeks things started looking up, especially when Jane was accepted at the Royal Free Hospital as a nurse working on the Geriatric Ward. To her surprise they had received excellent references from the Whittington Hospital and Jane was actually relieved that she never got the job at the nursing home in East Finchley. She received a letter from them saying the post had been filled and wishing her all the best for the future. Marcie was so happy for Jane but she had mixed feelings as John worked there and it left a bitter taste in her mouth. She chided herself, she was becoming paranoid - it didn't mean they would come in contact. Jane knew her thoughts and told her to stop worrying.

Chapter Twelve

Malcolm phoned Marcie as she was getting ready for work one morning to say Nancy had been taken into hospital with pneumonia. Marcie knew how serious this was as Nancy had it once before and her lungs had deteriorated even further - having emphysema and fibrosis didn't help. Marcie didn't hesitate and contacted Bella immediately, saying how worried she was and that she wanted to be with them.

'Of course you must go, Marcie. Don't worry about the shop, Carol is here and it's not busy at the moment, we can cope. But let me know what happens; ring me when you get there.'

Marcie left Jane a note on the coffee table and threw a few items in a bag and phoned for a taxi, which came straight away to take her to the station and she caught the train dreading what she may find when she arrived. She loved Nancy like the mother she had always wanted and was worried about Malcolm. She couldn't imagine how he would cope without her - she meant everything to him. Nancy was his whole world. When she finally arrived at her destination after what seemed an age, she got a taxi to the house. She hadn't wanted Malcolm to pick her up, as he was so distraught.

When Malcolm answered the door he broke down and Marcie held him in her arms and didn't want to let go. After a few minutes he took her coat - he was always the gent - and they both sat in the sitting room.

'This is the worst I have seen her pet, she looks like all the fight has gone out of her and she keeps looking into space. I can't seem to get through to her.'

Marcie leaned across to hold his hand; this man who she had so much love and respect for was hurting so much inside. 'Be strong for her, she needs that more than ever, but you know she is a fighter and if anyone can pull through, she will.' Malcolm had never left her bedside, but the staff nurse on the ward insisted he went home, as there was nothing he could do and he needed some sleep. 'I'll make some tea and sandwiches and after we've eaten we will go to the hospital.'

'Thanks for coming, Marcie, Nancy will love seeing you.'

When they arrived at the hospital the sister in charge took them both aside in a small room. 'Your wife had a good night and has slept well. We have put her on a course of antibiotics; the doctor thinks she may have had the pneumonia for quite some time. 'You can go and see her now but don't stay too long as she needs plenty of rest.'

As they walked onto the ward Marcie saw Nancy sitting up in bed but on a drip and with a mask over her face.

'My Lord! I didn't expect to see you here, Marcie!' and she gave her a hug.

'How are you feeling?'

'Very weak but the doctor says my temperature has gone down and I've no fever now.'

Malcolm was thrilled. 'I told you hinny - you can beat this.'

'What about your job, Marcie?'

'Don't worry, Bella is looking after the shop, and anyway I wanted to be here with you.'

'My goodness, you look grand. I hope my Malcolm has given you some breakfast.'

'Stop worrying about me and just get yourself better,' Marcie said taking her thin hand. She was shocked to see how much weight she had lost since her last visit.

The nurse came over to give Nancy a bed bath so they told her they would go and have a cuppa in the canteen and come back shortly. Malcolm asked her if she needed anything. 'Not really, but I wouldn't mind a ciggie.'

'No you don't,' he said, and turned to Marcie. 'She gave up months ago, I'm so proud of her.'

'Only joking, you silly bugger. Now let this kind nurse do her job and off with you both,' she laughed reaching out to kiss them.

Sitting at a table with a cup of tea each, Malcolm asked after Marcie's mum. Marcie explained about her visit and told him about her uncle being her real dad.

'That woman has issues...and I have told you before, move on and think about yourself for a change.'

'That's exactly what I'm doing now.'

'I had a phone call from Roy's mum. It's a sad affair him being in a coma, but me and Nancy haven't been able to get to see him.'

'Coma? Roy? What do you mean! I've tried to ring him several times but got no reply!'

'Sorry pet, but with Nancy being so ill these past few months I didn't give it a thought...just assumed you knew...'

'What happened? He was fine the last time I saw him!'

'Apparently he drove into a tree in bad weather and is in a coma at Leicester Hospital - has been for months.'

'My god! That's why I never heard from him!'

'His mum used to ring me to thank me for looking after him when he stayed with us at the hotel and she's always kept in touch. As you know, he was like a son to us.'

Marcie was crying. 'Now I know why he never answered my calls...this is awful!'

'Kim, the mother of his child is there at his bedside every day, apparently, and of course, his mum and dad. I think I will have to go and see him, and Nancy wants to come too, bless her. If she improves and the doctors allow it maybe we can all visit him together. Come on now, stop crying. I know you have a soft spot for him – more so than you let on.'

Marcie was devastated. Her heart sank – she hadn't realised just how much he actually meant to her and she vowed to herself that as soon as she was no longer needed by Malcolm she would go straight to his bedside; this man who had always looked out for her and treated her with nothing but respect. Life was cruel, she thought. People like Roy who were the salt of the earth went through things like this and the likes of John and Tony who didn't have a decent bone in their body just sailed through life.

As the week went on Nancy improved and was now ready to come home. The doctor had ordered her to take it easy and rest and had told Malcolm that the antibiotics were doing their job and she had improved considerably. Malcolm made a lovely meal of roast lamb and veg and potatoes and was over the moon that he had her home. Over dinner Nancy told Marcie she had made a will and that she was the full beneficiary – everything was being left to her.

Marcie couldn't believe it. 'You don't have to do that for me. I love you both unconditionally.'

'We know that pet,' said Malcolm, 'but we never were able to have children and you're like a daughter to us. Maybe when we are long gone you can buy a shop of your own and make us proud. The only thing is you would name it after my Nancy. Maybe something like Nancy's Naughty Negligees!' he said laughing.

'I will do my best,' she said blinking away the tears. She had so much sadness in her heart and couldn't even think about life without these two dear people who meant the world to her.

Malcolm drove her to the station and kissed her goodbye and told her to take good care of herself and ring him when she got home.

When she arrived home Jane was pleased to see her and told her she'd had a gentleman caller.

'Did he leave his name?' asked Marcie puzzled.

'Yes, he was called Lee and said he was a friend of yours and Zoe and Charlie's.'

'What did he look like?'

'Very handsome. I invited him in and he was great company. I opened up a bottle of wine and he said he worked as an estate agent on the high street. He said he was single, I hope you don't mind...'

'Fucking hell, Jane that is Tony, the one I was telling you about! Now please don't tell me you slept with him!'

Jane was shocked. 'Bloody hell, Marcie! I wouldn't have let him in if I'd known...but I promise you nothing happened, though I *was* tempted!'

'That's not funny, Jane. He is stalking me and the thought of him being in my flat makes me feel sick!'

'He was a real charmer...and I'm sorry. What are you going to do?'

Marcie knew she had to call the police as he had already had a warning not to go near her.

A little later the police arrived and took all the details, saying they would pay him a visit and get back to her.

When they had left, Jane poured them both a glass of wine.

'Look, tell me exactly what he said,' said Marcie, taking a large sip of her drink.

'Like I told the police, I opened the door and he asked where you were. I said you were in Southend seeing friends of yours and he said he was a friend of Charlie and his girlfriend and hasn't seen you all for while as he has been so busy. He was very convincing, and as it was pouring with rain I felt sorry for him and asked him in. I must admit, he did ask a lot of questions about you.'

'Such as?

'Have you got a boyfriend; do you go out much, that sort of thing. I thought that was a bit strange but I just thought he was asking after you as he hadn't seen you in a while and you were a good friend of his. My god Marcie, what are you going to do?'

'I'm going to get him charged - I can't live in fear; you never know what else he will do. I must give Malcolm and Nancy a ring to let them know I arrived home safely otherwise they both won't sleep tonight worrying about me.'

Marcie dialled the number and Malcolm answered. 'Hello hinny, are you home now?'

'Yes, a little while ago. Is Nancy OK?'

'Yes pet, she's resting so I won't disturb her. I'll get her to phone you tomorrow.'

'OK. Malcolm, can you give me Roy's mum's number and I will try and get in touch with her?'

'Don't worry, when I speak to her next time I will ask her if it's possible for her to give you a ring, but write this number down anyway,' and Marcie scribbled it down. 'I haven't heard anything from them for a while but I don't want to pester them both too much as they have a lot on their plate.'

'I understand. Love you both.'

'Likewise pet,' and they both put the phone down.

'Jane, I feel so tired. If you don't mind I'm off to bed.'

That's alright. I'll watch a bit of telly. Goodnight, God bless.'

'You too.'

Marcie couldn't sleep thinking about Roy. She tossed and turned. If only she had known she would have been there with him and never left his bedside. It must have happened around the time he left her after spending the weekend at her flat. She had always felt there had to be a good reason as to why he hadn't kept in touch but never envisaged anything like this.

Jane got up early the next morning and got ready not wanting to be late on her first day at the hospital. Marcie wished her the best of luck as she walked out the door and said she would see her later.

When Marcie got to work Bella was pleased to see her. 'How is Nancy?'

'Much better thanks. She's out of hospital and recovering at

140

home. Where's Carol?'

'She won't be coming back - her heart wasn't in it and she felt guilty leaving her husband on his own all day. It was only ever a temporary arrangement but I thought she might have stayed on after Penny went. Still, I understood, and between you and me I don't think she was aware of the market trends; not like you. I have a new girl starting today. You may know her, she worked at Stella's the clothes shop up the high road, but I have told her you are manageress.'

'Why did she leave?' Marcie asked.

'The wages were low, but I'm not paying her much more...still, that's her business. I took her on because she has worked in retail for many years.'

Ten minutes later a tall, voluptuous woman with a pretty face and short dark hair walked in. 'Marcie, this is Pat,' introduced Bella.

'I know you, I have been in your shop quite a few times,' Marcie said.

Pat smiled. 'Yes, I recognise you too. You bought a black dress but returned it as the hem came down and it had a hole in it.'

'That's enough chatter, you two, you're here to work.' Bella was getting agitated as there was new stock in and she wanted them to start pricing it up.

Marcie apologised, but Pat was a bit surprised, as she had taken Bella to be a bit of a pussy cat. Bella had a lot on her mind as she was trying to raise money for the hospice and had a meeting to go to. Eventually she left them both to it and said her goodbyes.

'Bella seems a hard task master.'

'Not really, she has always been good to me and I'm quite fond of her; she just takes a bit of getting used to.' Marcie left it like that and showed Pat the stock at the back of the shop that needed pricing up. She busied herself sorting the clothes on the rails and generally tidying the shop, but it was very quiet so she made them both a cup of coffee and told Pat to come and join her at the front of the shop where they both sat down to have a break.

'Where do you live?' Marcie asked.

'East Finchley, but I have a car so it doesn't take me long to get here. I live with my son Dexter who is ten, but my mum lives around the corner and she's a great help. What about you?'

'I live with my friend Jane who is a nurse. We've known each other for years and are best of friends.'

'That's nice. My husband buggered off with a twenty year-old he met in the pub when Dexter was only two.'

'How old are you then?'

'Thirty-nine, but I know what you're going to say, I look much older.'

Marcie did think that but felt a bit sorry for her so she disagreed and said she thought she looked about thirty-six. 'Have you got a boyfriend?'

'Yes, but he's a married man.' Marcie was shocked and Pat could see that by the look on her face so quickly asked, 'What about you?'

'No, I'm not interested at the moment.'

A customer walked in so Pat went out the back to finish what she was doing while Marcie served her.

The rest of the day went quickly and Pat asked Marcie if she wanted to go for a drink at her local pub as Dexter was staying at his nan's for the night. 'I can drive you back home after,' she said.

'Yes, why not,' said Marcie. She wanted to get to know her a bit more as they would be working together and Jane was meeting a friend in Oxford Street after work.

Bella came to cash up and told them both to get off home, as she wanted them in bright and breezy in the morning.

Pat drove Marcie to her place first and she was impressed. It was a lovely two bedroom council house with a beautiful front garden and facing a small park which was well maintained. The whole area was lovely with lots of trees on either side of the road and very quiet. Pat got changed and Marcie felt a bit underdressed even though Pat said she looked fine in what she was wearing. 'What about a glass of wine now before we hit the pub?'

Marcie said OK, but in situations like this she was a bit hesitant as she wasn't a big drinker and had a feeling Pat would throw caution to the wind as she seemed a bubbly, outgoing and very outspoken person, and that made her feel a bit nervous. They had one glass of wine but Marcie then insisted on going to the pub, saying she couldn't stay out late, using the excuse that Jane would be wondering where she had got to.

They arrived at the Red Lion pub around the corner and it was empty but the person behind the bar informed them that it would get a lot busier later on. An hour later people started to come in and Pat noticed a couple sitting in the corner that she knew. 'That's Amy and Joe; let's go over and join them, they are friends of mine.'

When she had introduced Marcie they sat down and Pat was telling them how she worked with Marcie at Bella's shop in Hampstead and it was her first day but she loved it. Amy was very friendly and Marcie took to her right away and thought how attractive she was.

'Where do you live Amy?'

'Behind Pat, in a cul-de-sac.'

'Have you any children?'

'Yes, twin girls from my first marriage.'

'That's lovely. What are their names?'

'Biba and Tilly. They live with their father.' Marcie put two and two together and realised who she was speaking to. She couldn't believe the coincidence but thought it best not to let on that she used to be their nanny.

Pat went to the bar to order more drinks and Joe got up to help her. When she turned and saw them chatting at the bar she could have sworn they were flirting. Perhaps Joe is the married man she's carrying on with, she thought, and then tried to dismiss the feeling of unease that was creeping up on her. Amy was very open in her conversation and told her she had battled in the courts to get her daughters back and had won custody of them once a fortnight. She said the judge thought it was in the girls' best interests to stay with their father because of their schooling.

'Do you and Joe have any children of your own?'

'Sadly we lost a child. She had severe heart problems and only lived a day...but she will never be forgotten. I'm reluctant to try again. Joe loves my girls like his own, so I am happy and contented that I have two wonderful, healthy girls and I think I am so fortunate, at least I get to see them, even if it is not on a full time basis.

Pat and Joe came back to the table with a tray of drinks. Marcie could see the looks they were giving each other and felt sorry for the woman that was sitting in front of her who was being taken for a fool.

After a while Marcie told Pat she wanted to go home but said she would order a taxi if she wanted to stay with her friends. 'If it's OK with you. Don't you mind?'

'No, I need to get back. Jane will wonder where I am.'

The taxi came and Amy gave Marcie her number; they had got on like a house on fire and Amy said she would love for them both to meet up. Marcie got in the taxi and felt sad. She had loved the twins when they had been in her care and still missed them, but to meet up with their mother and having her suspicions about Pat and Joe would be so awkward. But they had got along famously and she had liked Amy immediately. She decided she would play it by ear, hoping she had read the situation wrong.

The months passed and Marcie loved working with Pat - she had really grown to like her. She was good in the shop, so adaptable working with the customers with all their complaints, plus she was funny and likeable. However, she held back from socialising with her, telling a white lie that she now had a boyfriend. The downside was that Pat constantly went on about her boyfriend, and Marcie didn't want to get involved.

Bella was pleased with Pat. She was a hard worker, the only thing that irritated her was that she could talk the hind legs off a donkey and she occasionally had to tell her to give her tongue a rest.

Amy kept her word and gave Marcie a ring to ask if she wanted to go to her place for a meal. She apologised for not getting in touch sooner but said she had been looking for a job so had been busy.

'Great,' Marcie said, 'when did you have in mind?'

'How about tomorrow after work?'

Marcie was looking forward to meeting Amy again but knew she had to come clean and dreaded it - especially knowing she had once fallen in love with her ex-husband, the man who she truly hated.

She went into work the next day but didn't mention to Pat that she was seeing Amy in case she wanted to go with her. Marcie got the impression Pat had exaggerated her friendship with Amy - they were like chalk and cheese, and thought it more likely they were just acquaintances who went to the same pub.

In her lunch hour Marcie gave Mrs Hawthorn a ring to ask about Roy but she was not very forthcoming. 'I am just trying to remember who you are. I have heard your name mentioned,' she said, 'but I can't place you.'

'We've never met but I worked at the hotel in Kings Cross where Roy used to stay and we were good friends. Malcolm told me what

144

happened. Is he still in a coma?'

'I'm so sorry; yes I'm afraid he is.'

'I was thinking of paying him a visit.'

'No that won't be necessary. His father, sister and I are there every day and of course Kim who has been marvellous. They have a beautiful daughter together called Molly. I must dash, we are going to the hospital now, but thank you for your best wishes,' and before Marcie could say another word she had put the phone down.

What Marcie didn't know was Kim and Roy's mum had become very close and she was now a big part of their family, which suited her as she saw her granddaughter most days. Kim hoped that if Roy recovered he may still have feelings for her as the other guys she had met since him didn't want commitment. Roy had worked hard to build up a business and own a few properties. She knew he could give her and Molly stability, and for that he went up in her estimation as a good catch.

Marcie was upset but she hoped and prayed he would recover and eventually get in touch with her so she could have the opportunity one day to tell him how she really felt. She got through the rest of the afternoon and waited for Pat to leave first because if she knew she was going her way she would have offered to give her a lift. She ordered a taxi and ten minutes later she was on her way. When she arrived at the maisonette in East Finchley she thought how small it looked but the front gardens were immaculate and the cul-de-sac was lovely. She rung the bell and Amy opened the door.

'Marcie, come on in,' and she followed Amy up a flight of stairs. At the top in front of her was the bathroom and to the left was a cosy sitting room with an archway leading to the kitchen and dining area. It was lovely.

'I bet you're shattered after being on your feet all day. Let me take your coat and scarf and I'll make us a cup of tea.'

'Thanks,' Marcie said and sat down on the sofa. 'How long have you known Pat for?'

'I'm not sure,' Amy remarked, 'but she makes me laugh. She tells everyone I'm her best friend, which isn't true. Between you and me I think she's a bit lonely. If I see her on the high road we have a coffee together though. I think she's harmless enough - my Joe feels sorry for her being on her own with Dexter.' Amy sat down to have her tea with Marcie but could see she had gone a bit quiet.

'What's wrong, Marcie? You look a bit upset.'

'I am dreading telling you this, but I think you ought to know I worked for your husband John as a nanny for a year and looked after the twins.'

'Why didn't you mention it to me in the pub?'

'I felt awkward having just met you, but when you mentioned you had twin girls called Biba and Tilly I knew it was you.'

'Bloody hell, you must know all about me.'

'Not really. John didn't talk about you that much.' Marcie wished the ground would open up and swallow her. 'I felt a bit guilty because I never got to say my proper goodbyes to the girls because I left abruptly.'

'Why was that?' There was silence as Marcie looked at the floor. 'Come on, you're holding something back; tell me.'

I stupidly fell in love with John and thought he felt the same about me...and then I got pregnant...and he didn't want to know...'

'Good god! That man wants hanging! He took advantage of you; I can see that. He was a manipulative, controlling bastard but at the same time he could be such a charmer...and to the outside world he was a gent and a good husband and father. So you have a child...'

'No, I had a miscarriage...' and she started to cry.

Amy went to her and held her. 'We all make mistakes, believe me, but you have to put it all behind you and move on – I have. You're better off without him.'

Marcie dried her eyes. 'How are the girls? I bet you miss them.'

'Yes, I do, but I have them every other weekend. When I went to court to get full custody we had a counselling meeting and the girls got upset, saying they loved their school. They were both doing so well that John and I decided it was in their best interests to leave the girls with him as uprooting them would do more harm than good. As much as I wanted full custody I knew that was the right decision. They love Rochelle - apparently she spoils them rotten - and when I met her at court I have to say she seemed really nice. I think it took me a long time to come to terms with it and it put a wedge between me and Joe. He would have loved children of his own so losing the baby and then having two miscarriages...well, it was tough for both of us.'

'You could still try now.'

'No, to be honest Marcie, I am over forty now and I don't want to try again – we've been through so much already. I have my job working for an agency doing private nursing and Joe is a GP around the corner at the medical centre. I'm quite happy with my lot and hopefully when the girls leave school they may want to come and live with me, who knows?'

'Something's burning in the kitchen,' Marcie said.

Amy quickly got up from her chair and ran through to the kitchen to see smoke bellowing out of the oven. 'Oh dear! The chicken and roast potatoes are ruined! How about a takeaway? I'm so sorry!'

'No, that's alright, I'm happy to have a sandwich, thanks.'

Amy made Marcie a cheese and cucumber sandwich and a coffee and remarked that she wasn't having one herself. 'Joe is at the pub and he is famished when he comes home so I will have to order food for us both when he gets in.'

Amy ordered a taxi for Marcie as it was getting late and she was tired after being on her feet all day. 'You must come and visit when the girls are here; I'm sure they would love to see you. Anyway, give me a ring – you're welcome anytime.'

Marcie thanked her and was a bit relieved to hear the tooting of the car downstairs. It had been an emotional evening but Amy had left a good impression on her, she really liked her and wanted to meet up with her again.

Marcie arrived home shattered and couldn't wait to get into bed. She could see Jane fast asleep on the sofa with her clothes still on but didn't want to disturb her. She must have had a good night, she thought chuckling to herself.

The next morning she made some scrambled eggs on toast for the two of them and woke Jane up who wasn't too pleased as it was her day off, but she got up anyway. 'What are you going to do with yourself today?'

'Not sure, but I have a load of washing to do and I might clean the flat.'

'My god, what's come over you? Have you got a fever or something?'

'Cheeky bugger! I won't do it then!' and they both laughed.

'Who was that friend you met in Oxford Street?'

'Justin, a student doctor in his third year - he's bloody gorgeous. Would it be alright if I bring him here so I can cook him a meal sometime?'

'I don't see why not, it's your home too.'

'Thanks. I know you'll like him, he's dead easy going and it's good to have a man around. Maybe we can give him some jobs to do.'

'What are you like? Ever the opportunist!'

'I'm only joking, Marcie, I really like him.'

'Good for you, but I must get ready for work otherwise Bella will be giving me the sack.'

Marcie walked to work, reflecting back on last night and hoped she was wrong and Pat wasn't having an affair with Joe. She knew Pat lived in a bit of a fantasy world sometimes and went over the top with all her stories.

When she arrived at work Bella was doing the window display and was in a right mood. 'Who did this?'

'I let Pat do it, why?'

'I'm paying you as manageress to see to this; it's awful! Who the hell mixes pink with orange?'

Pat came out from the back and had heard every word. 'What's wrong?'

'I don't want you to do the window display in future. I think you must be bloody colour blind, it's disgraceful!'

Pat held her tongue for once; she knew not to answer back – she could see Bella was angry. Marcie had never known Bella to lose her temper and wondered if she was ill or something was troubling her.

An hour later Bella left the shop and there was a sigh of relief. Pat was furious. 'What is wrong with that woman?' Marcie ignored the remark and went in the back to make them both a cup of tea but she could still hear her prattling on about it so came out to the front of the shop and told her to shut it as she was getting on her nerves. Pat never held grudges and started telling Marcie how she had a great night last night with her boyfriend.

'What's his name?'

'I just call him by his nickname, Jed.'

Marcie knew she was lying; her face went red. 'What's his real name?'

'I'm not telling you, the less you know the better.'

'Fair enough, but how often do you see him?'

'He sees me when he can and hopefully we will be together when he gets his divorce. You're a prude Marcie, aren't you?'

'Look, I'm not a prude but nothing good will come of this...anyway, it's your business not mine.'

Pat felt a little awkward and told Marcie she was going to the bakery and asked if she wanted anything.

'No, but hurry back because it's not really your lunch hour yet and if Bella pops back she'll go mad.'

'OK. Won't be long.'

Marcie couldn't work Pat out. She had a good heart and was very attractive - she could have any guy, what the hell was she messing around with a married man for?

The day seemed to go on forever and Marcie was going home to put her feet up and have a nice hot soak in the bath. Bella was worrying her and she promised herself she would have a chat with her tomorrow and make sure she was alright, but in the meantime all she wanted to do was get home.

Jane had cleaned the flat and done all the washing and cooked a shepherd's pie for the two of them.

'Hi! Have you had a good day?'

'Not really; that Pat talks nonstop and to top it all I think she is having an affair with my friend Amy's husband.'

'Do you know for sure?'

'Not really, but if I find out she is I will wring her bloody neck. Amy is such a lovely person. She's had her fair share of shit and doesn't deserve it.'

Marcie went for a bath whilst Jane heated up the shepherd's pie.

'It's ready!'

'I'm coming,' answered Marcie, and went and sat at the table. 'Thanks Jane, you're a star; this is really tasty - I was starving. Are you going out tonight?'

'No, I thought I'd stay in and watch the telly as I'm back at work tomorrow.'

'How's your job going?'

'I'm loving it. The staff nurse is really cool, not stuffy at all, and the patients are a great bunch, but I forgot what hard work it is. If I never see another bed pan it'll suit me, but I love listening to the stories of the olden days. Poor buggers, that's all some of the really elderly patients have, their memories. I got a ticking off the other day for spending too much time chatting to them, but I can't help it.'

'You're a soft sod deep down, and that's why you make a good nurse - full of empathy.'

'There's no more shepherd's pie if that's what you're after,' Jane laughed.

'I'm stuffed. Have you heard from your mum and dad, Jane?'

'Yes, they are both fine, and my mum said she is so proud of me but I'm missing them. When I get my holidays I'm going to see them, and my brother.' Marcie disliked Jane's brother immensely but never let on. Sometimes you had to let sleeping dogs lie.

The phone rang and it was Malcolm. 'Anything wrong?' Marcie asked.

'No lass; can I not give you a ring to ask how you are?'

'How is Nancy?'

'She's fine and sends her love, but she gets tired easily and is resting. I got a phone call from Roy's mum, she told me he has come out of his coma but will be in hospital quite some time as he needs to get his strength back.'

'Malcolm, that's the best news you could have given me. I'm so happy! I phoned his mum and asked her if I could visit him but she was a bit offish with me.'

'Listen, pet, give him a chance to recover. He needs his family around him - just think how they are feeling. You'll get your chance later on, but it's great he has come out of the coma, that's the most important thing, and my Nancy is over the moon. I must go now; Nancy's calling me.'

'Please give her my love. You know how much I love you both.'

'I know that, and she does too. Take good care of yourself. Bye, pet,' and Malcolm put the phone down.

Marcie went into the sitting room and broke down. All the emotions she had been feeling for Roy had come to the surface.

'What's up, Marcie, bad news?' Jane was worried – her friend had been so chirpy a few minutes ago.

'No, quite the opposite - Roy has come out of his coma!'

'How wonderful! Now you can stop worrying; I am really happy for you. Let's get a bottle of wine from the off licence to celebrate!'

Yes, let's!' and Marcie offered to go; it was the least she could do after the meal Jane had cooked.

Chapter Thirteen

The following day Marcie went to work full of the joys of spring, but it was short-lived as when she arrived Bella was still in a bad mood. 'You're ten minutes late...and Pat's not here yet either,' she said pacing up and down.

Marcie felt she had to say something; this was so unlike her. 'Bella, what's wrong? You're always in a bad mood lately. Have I done something to upset you?'

Bella sat down on a stool. 'Sorry, love, but I can't discuss it now. Why don't we go and have a drink after work?'

'I'd love that. Where shall we go?'

'How about Jack Straws Castle? It's a lovely pub, and maybe we can have a bite to eat.'

Pat showed up an hour late but luckily Bella had gone off to a meeting by then. 'Bella is going to have your guts for garters; you're really late.'

'I know but Dexter has a fever so I had to wait till Mum came round to look after him. Sorry!'

'Just get to work. You can mop out back, it's filthy.'

'Why doesn't she get a cleaner to do that? It shouldn't be my job.'

'Stop moaning will you. She has a lot on her mind at the moment, and besides, it won't take you that long, it's a small area to mop.' Marcie thought Pat was selfish at times, acting like a spoilt brat.

The day was busier than usual, which would please Bella, and it made the time go quickly.

Bella came to cash up later that evening but Pat had shot out the door early trying to avoid a good telling off.

'Right, that's done. Are you ready, pet? Let's go.'

Marcie put her coat on and they took a slow walk up to the pub. When they arrived they found a table next to a lovely log fire. The waiter came and took their order of steak, chips and salad and a bottle of red wine.

'This is a lovely pub. Jim and I spent a lot of happy hours in here. I do miss him...'

'Is that why you've been a bit stressed lately?' Marcie remarked.

'I've been seeing Barry, a retired policeman for the last six weeks, but I've called it off.'

'Why? I'd have thought it would have been good for you.'

'I feel I'm betraying Jim's memory. He is the only man I ever had and I know you'll think I'm an old fool but no one can ever replace him.'

'Where does Barry live?'

'He has a house in Barnet and lives on his own. His son has flown the nest and works in Scotland, and his poor wife Cathy died four years ago.'

'I don't see why there's a problem. Surely it's good that you have companionship?'

'True, but I have my work and friends, though they have partners...and I must admit I get a bit lonely in my big house. Barry stayed with me a few times - in my spare bedroom, you understand, but he drove me to distraction leaving the toilet seat up and his socks on the bathroom floor. When he cooks the kitchen looks like a bomb has hit it. My Jim was meticulous - everything had its place. I suppose I'm set in my ways.'

'Look Bella, tell me the positives about Barry.'

'Well, he is funny, a good sense of humour, and very kind - a real gentleman. He's a bit rough round the edges but very knowledgeable about so many things and so interesting to talk to.'

Marcie laughed. 'So he is not all bad! You should give him a ring.'

'I don't know if he will speak to me. I told him he was a dirty old man when he tried to get fresh with me...but I do miss his company. He made me realise after Jim died that life goes on, but I only wish I knew what to do because I don't want to lead him on - I know how keen he was on me.'

'My advice would be to ring him up and arrange to see him and explain how you feel. Tell him you miss him but you want to take things slowly and I'm sure he'll understand.'

'Who put an old head on your young shoulders? Thank you so much for listening, Marcie, my friends wouldn't understand.'

Bella insisted on paying the bill and they went their separate ways.

Marcie arrived indoors and there was no sign of Jane. She must have met up with her friend Justin, she thought, so went and ran herself a bath. It's funny, she thought, lying in the hot soapy water, she had always seen Bella as having everything she could wish for but realized anybody could get lonely, and that's how she felt at that moment wishing Roy was there with her. At times like this the flat seemed so empty.

Jane gave Marcie a ring to say she was staying at Justin's place and she would be home the following evening when maybe they both could go out to the pub. 'That would be great. Have a nice evening you two,' and Marcie put the phone down.

Bella wasted no time when she arrived home and phoned Barry.

'Bella! How are you?'

'Fine thanks. I just wondered if you want to go for a meal some time.'

'You've changed your tune.'

'Isn't that a woman's prerogative?'

'I'd love to...how about Saturday? I will pick you up at your place about eight-thirty?'

'See you then,' and Bella was relieved that was over; she had been dreading ringing him.

The next morning she arrived at the shop with a big box full of Christmas decorations that she had brought from home. It was only four weeks away and she wanted to put on a good display as it was usually a busy time of year and profits always went up. Marcie got to work on time and so did Pat but Bella was in a good mood and didn't look at her watch like she usually did.

'Hello pet. Lots to do today. Could you dress the window and use these decorations? But don't go over the top - I like things simple.' Marcie was excited; dressing the window was her favourite job. 'And you Pat,' Bella said, 'can start by putting the kettle on. It's freezing in here; I think we should all have a hot drink.' Pat looked bemused; she hadn't seen Bella in such good spirits for a long time and quickly went out the back to make the tea.

By the afternoon the shop looked very seasonal and it was filled with customers. Bella stayed on to help, as there were no meetings for her to go to. The day went well and Bella bought them sandwiches from the bakery down the road as they had both worked so hard. Marcie asked about Barry but Bella waited till Pat went in the back to make coffee to explain that she had been in touch with him last night and they were meeting up on Saturday for a meal.

'Fantastic!' Marcie said. 'I am so pleased for you! Did I tell you Roy is out of his coma and making good progress?'

'Things are looking up pet, we can only hope and pray but I believe good things happen to good people, and you know I want the best for you.' Bella was fond of Marcie and knew she had her head screwed on and in time would make good decisions if she was given the chance. 'What about your mum? Have you given her a ring?'

'No, she drains the life out of me. Although I feel sorry for her I am angry at the same time, if you know what I mean.'

'Listen honey, she is the only mum you have when all is said and done. All I know is you have to learn to forgive; you don't want to carry bitterness to your grave. You are a lot stronger than her. Christmas is coming up, so why don't you give her a ring?'

'I understand what you're saying, but I can't see how I can help her - she is her own worst enemy and doesn't seem to know how to move on.'

'Maybe she feels in many ways she has screwed up and is filled with insecurities, but she could have given you away, so that's in her favour.'

When Marcie was walking home she reflected on what Bella had said and she decided she was right, whatever the circumstances. She was doing what she wanted to do and she would never feel responsible for her, but she did bring her up so she felt strong enough to talk to her and not allow her to put feelings of guilt on her.

Jane was dressed to the nines and waiting for her when she got home. 'Come on Marcie, get ready. Justin is meeting us at the pub; I hope you don't mind.'

'Bloody hell I thought it was just me and you - a girl's night out?'

'I want you to meet him.'

Marcie was annoyed but didn't show it, though she was not in the mood to play gooseberry. 'I think I'll give Zoe and Charlie a ring and see if they want to join us. We can meet them at the pub,' she said picking up the phone.

'Good idea. I like those two...but they have to pay for their own drinks.'

'Shut up! They usually do anyway!'

'Just joking, Marcie. Who rattled your cage?'

'They're not answering - I'll give them a ring from the pub.'

Half an hour later Marcie was ready. 'Let's go.'

When they arrived at the pub it was packed with customers and decorated for Christmas.

'I can't see Justin anywhere; I hope he understood my directions on how to get here.'

'Don't worry,' Marcie said, 'he'll be here.'

Justin came fifteen minutes later and Jane introduced him.

'Pleased to meet you,' he said giving Marcie a kiss on the cheek. 'You two find a seat and I'll get the drinks in. What are you both having?'

'Two white wines, please,' and they found a table to sit down at.

'What do you think?'

'I think he is very polite and handsome...he seems nice.'

Jane's face lit up. 'I knew you would like him.'

Justin came with the drinks and sat down.

'Jane tells me you're in your third year. What would you like to specialize in?'

'I would love to work on a children's ward. I did six months there in my training and I loved it.'

'Are you going to work in London when you are qualified?'

'Not sure yet; maybe.'

Jane was getting bored. 'Marcie let's put work aside - I'm fed up talking about the bloody hospital.'

'Leave her alone; at least she's interested in what I'm doing.'

'What do you mean by that remark?'

'Hey you two! Don't start arguing or I will go home.'

They both started to laugh. 'Take no notice. We like a good argument! But I wouldn't change Jane for the world.'

'Glad to hear it,' laughed Marcie. 'Now, let me get the next round,' and she walked off to the bar. She put in her order and was waiting for the drinks when she felt a tap on her shoulder. Turning round she came face to face with Tony.

'Marcie, hi.'

156

'Oh no. You're back then? The police were looking for you...they want to ask you some questions.'

'Drop the charges Marcie, please. I have a new girlfriend now and I won't bother you again. Come on; let me buy you a drink.'

'You bastard! You put me through hell and back. I feel sorry for the girl, whoever she is. Go away and leave me alone.'

Marcie paid for the drinks and took them back to the table shaking. 'That shit Tony has just approached me at the bar. What a cheek - he wants me to drop the charges!'

'I hope you told him to take a running jump? You should inform the police you have seen him,' said Jane, furious.

'I don't think he'll bother me now, but anyway it's not up to me, the police can still charge him for stalking me. I hate him! Look, if you don't mind you two, I am going to go home. Seeing him has ruined my evening and I feel tired anyway. You stay and enjoy yourselves.'

'No, no, we'll come with you, no problem,' insisted Jane.

They all put their coats on and headed back to the flat and Jane stopped at the off licence to get a bottle of wine. When they got indoors Marcie said she was going to have an early night. 'You're welcome to stay with Jane, Justin. I'll leave you two to it – I'm off to bed.'

Marcie felt envious; she had no partner in her life and had watched all her friends pair up: Zoe and Charlie, Jane and Justin, even Bella had someone. She wished she could have Roy in her life – that would make it complete...she missed him so much.

The next morning she woke up early feeling low and went into the kitchen to cook breakfast for everyone but Jane and Justin had already gone. They must have had an early start at work, she thought, but decided to make the effort and cooked herself scrambled egg on toast. When she'd eaten she decided to give Zoe a ring.

'Hi Zoe. How are you?'

'Fine; the antenatal clinic are pleased with me. How are you?'

'Feeling a bit sorry for myself this morning... I miss Roy but there's nothing I can do about it, he needs time to recuperate so I have to respect that.'

Zoe felt sorry for Marcie. She deserved to be happy but knew that if there was to be any chance with Roy she would need to be patient, as he needed time to recover after coming out of the coma. 'Listen, how about we meet up tomorrow night at your place and order a takeaway?'

'That would be nice.'

'Say about seven?'

'OK, you're on. I'll see you both then,' and Marcie put the phone down.

Elsie rang half an hour later to tell her she had seen her mum in a terrible state in the shopping mall, falling all over the place drunk and someone had called the cops who came and took her off in a police car. Marcie was upset but did her best to hide it. 'Well, that's her problem. She doesn't want my help, so she can get on with it. Anyway, how are you?'

'Great, but I was wondering if I can come and visit you. I have a new boyfriend, Ray, who I'd like you to meet. Can I bring him as well? Mum said she'll look after Eddy for me.'

'Yes, I don't have a problem with that, but can I get back to you as it would be better if I have time off to spend with you?'

'Fantastic, but let me know; I'm missing you!'

'Me too. Speak to you soon.' Good god, she thought, even Elsie has a boyfriend, and it made her even more depressed. But bless her, she was a good friend with a good heart and she was pleased for her but she knew she had no expectations of life – she was easily pleased. So long as he was better than the last boyfriend and treated her well, did it matter, she thought?

Her mind went back to Tony. She would never feel comfortable knowing he was around and decided to phone the desk sergeant at the police station.

'This is Marcie Thomas. I'm just ringing to let you know my ex-boyfriend Tony Jenkins was in the Wheatsheaf pub in Doyle Street last night and you have a warrant for his arrest.'

'Hold on one moment,' he said, and went to get the file.

Marcie waited patiently.

'Hello? Right, he has already appeared in court and was charged?'

'Yes, he was, and I am afraid he is still stalking me.'

'Are you at your residence now?'

'Yes, but I have to go to work soon.'

'I suggest you stay where you are and I will send one of my

officers round to see you.'

'Alright, I'll be here.'

Marcie put the phone down wishing she hadn't rung them. The shop was busy this time of year and Bella needed her there. She quickly gave Bella a ring but she was understanding and said not to worry, she would cope; it was more important she got things sorted, and she wished her luck.

Marcie waited for an hour and finally she saw the police car outside her flat so she went to the door and let the young officer in.

'We have a Tony Jenkins in our custody now, Miss.'

'Where did you find him?'

'At his flat. Did he say anything to you in the pub?'

He wanted me to have a drink with him and drop the charges.'

'Leave it with us and we will be in touch. He will probably appear in court again and may have to attend as a witness but I think he is most likely looking at a prison sentence this time. We take these charges very seriously, but he won't bother you now.' Marcie showed the policeman to the door and thanked him but was too upset to go into work and took the rest of the day off. She needed to speak to Malcolm and tell him what had happened - she wanted reassurance that she had done the right thing, as she felt sorry for Tony's parents with what they must be going through.

She dialled the number and Malcolm answered straight away. After explaining everything to him he said, 'You did the right thing hinny, but you never told us how bad the situation was.'

'I didn't want to worry you both.'

'I know lass, but you know we are always here for you. I hope they lock him up and throw away the key!'

'Is Nancy well?'

'Not really pet, she has another chest infection and I have the nurse with her right now.'

'Oh Malcolm, I'm so sorry, and here's me telling you *my* problems.'

'That's OK. I'm pleased you let me know. Marcie, I'm sorry but the nurse is calling me so I have to go.'

'No worries. Give Nancy big hugs and kisses from me.'

'I will. Love you,' and he put the phone down.

Marcie made herself a cup of tea. How she wished she was with the two of them right now. They always made her feel safe and secure. Malcolm was having a hard time of it recently with Nancy. Her immune system was low so she was forever getting colds and flu and it weakened her lungs, but she was a fighter and had battled with illnesses all her life so he tried to keep her positive, but Marcie knew as well as he did that the outlook was grim.

She spent the rest of the day cleaning the flat and that helped keep her mind off things but she was pleased when Jane arrived home from work.

'Have you had a good day?'

'My feet are killing me. One of my elderly patients died today, she was ninety but I was so fond of her. She never complained and always had a smile on her face.'

'That's sad, but she had a long life, bless her,' Marcie remarked.

'What was your day like? You're home early.'

'I didn't go into work,' and she explained why.

'My god, Marcie, how are you feeling now?'

'Mixed feelings, but I know the bastard is not getting away with it.'

'Good for you. Do they want to speak to me as I was the one in the flat when he came here pretending to be someone else?'

'I'm not sure, but is that a problem?'

'Hell no. He's a menace. They can speak to me anytime. Anyway, I'm starving. What are we going to eat?'

'Beans on toast, I can't be bothered to cook.'

Jane had an idea. Let's get a taxi, my treat, and hit the shops in Oxford Street to do some Christmas shopping; it'll cheer you up!'

'That's not a bad idea but I haven't got much money. I can probably afford a few things though.'

Marcie got ready and they ordered a taxi. When they arrived Oxford Street was buzzing with Christmas shoppers. Their first port of call was Marks and Spencer's and Marcie bought Bella a lovely colourful scarf. Jane wanted to get something for Justin but he was hard to buy for, as he had no interest in clothes. After a while she settled for some nice after shave. They spent two hours walking around and when their feet began to hurt and they'd had enough they stopped for a bite to eat at a hamburger bar. The Algerian waiter made a beeline for Marcie and flirted outrageously with her but she was irritated and was pleased when they got a taxi home.

Sitting with their feet up enjoying a well-earned glass of wine, Marcie remarked to Jane, 'I wonder how Bella is getting on with Barry, her date tonight?'

'Good god, she's getting on a bit to be going on dates!'

Marcie was annoyed. 'What are you trying to say – she's past her sell by date?'

'Not really, but she is getting on in years.'

'I do think you are stupid at times Jane, we all have feelings, and I say good for her.'

'Blimey, Marcie, you do take things seriously at times.'

'I like Bella, and I care about her, you know that.'

Jane knew when to get out of her way and went to run herself a bath before an argument erupted.

Marcie had Bella on her mind but she need not have worried. She was in the restaurant with Barry and they were having a wonderful time. Barry had arrived with beautiful flowers and told her how much he had missed her. She explained how she had been scared to open up to him because she had only had one partner in her life and that was Jim, but said she wanted to take things slowly and hoped they would eventually have a future together. Barry agreed and they enjoyed each other's company.

When Jane got out of the bath Marcie made her favourite hot chocolate - her way of saying sorry for snapping - and they sat and watched telly for the rest of the evening.

On Monday morning Marcie went into work and Bella was in full work mode. 'Right, we have so much to do today. I have decided to give an extra ten percent discount off all goods and I am expecting the shop to be busy...' At that moment Pat walked in sporting a painful looking black eye. '...What the hell has happened to you?' asked Bella.

'I had a row last night with a girl in the pub and she punched me in the eye.'

Marcie was having none of it. She was almost sure she was having an affair with her friend's husband and there was more to the story than she was letting on. Two customers had just walked in so she let it go for now but decided she would give Amy a ring in her break without letting on.

Bella was furious with Pat. 'This really doesn't look good

serving customers with that black eye. I suggest you go out the back and cover it up somehow.'

Marcie had brought her make-up bag with her and handed Pat some foundation cream. 'See if this helps.'

'Thanks, but I don't know what all the fuss is about; it doesn't bother me.'

'You silly girl! What impression do you think you are giving my customers? This is a respectable boutique and appearances count!' Bella hated her couldn't care less attitude.

The shop was busy just as Bella had predicted and even Pat worked hard and was polite to everyone, but come closing time she was in such a hurry to get off she forgot to take her umbrella and the cakes she had bought from the bakery in her lunch hour - as it was raining buckets outside Marcie suspected she was hiding something.

When Marcie arrived home she took off her coat and phoned Amy. 'How are you?'

'Are you joking? You know full well how I am.'

'What do you mean?'

'That slut who is working with you has been seeing my husband - and don't tell me you didn't know!'

'I didn't, honestly! I had my suspicions, yes, but I didn't actually know for sure...'

'Why the hell didn't you tell me Marcie?'

'Look Amy, she is someone I work with, but I don't really class her as a friend. She was the one who introduced me to *you* as her close friend. I promise you I didn't know. I thought I saw Joe flirt with her a bit in the Red Lion when they went to the bar to get the drinks in, and she had told me she was having an affair with a married man when she first started to work at Bella's shop, but I couldn't be sure it was Joe, and I didn't want to cause any trouble as I wasn't positive.'

In the end Amy believed Marcie was an honest person and had no reason to lie. 'Sorry Marcie, I'm a bit uptight at the moment as you can imagine. Look, can I come to your place tonight and we can talk? I don't want to be here when Joe gets home.'

'No problem. Let's say about eight and I'll cook us both a meal.'

'I 'm not worried about that; don't go to any trouble, we can get a takeaway if need be.'

Marcie felt sorry for Amy; she had been through so much.

162

When she finished work she rushed home and made sure everything was looking neat and tidy.

The doorbell rang and it was Amy. 'Come in and let me take your coat. Bloody hell, you're soaking wet.' When Marcie looked at Amy's face she could tell she had been crying.

Amy thought the flat was lovely and cosy and she sat down on the armchair and made herself comfortable. 'You have to excuse me for the way I spoke to you on the phone - my head is all over the place.'

'It's OK, don't worry about it. I have to ask you...did you give Pat that black eye?'

'No, I didn't.'

'I thought not – I just couldn't imagine you doing that. But someone did!'

'I wanted to, don't get me wrong, but it was her friend in the pub who gave it to her.'

I'll make us a coffee and you can tell me all about it.'

A short while later Marcie came back with two steaming mugs of coffee and put them down on the table. 'Are you hungry? Can I get you anything?'

'Thank you, but I couldn't eat a thing.'

'OK, perhaps a bit later. Right, tell me what happened.'

'Well, it was Joe's birthday and he'd been busy all day at work and was shattered so he was happy for us to just go across the road to our local for a few drinks and something to eat. He was never one for too much fuss anyway. When we arrived we sat at a table for two as we wanted to be on our own - I hate sitting at a large table with other people you don't know sitting beside you. We ordered steak and chips with salad and two beers and were talking about selling our property and getting something bigger because the girls have to share a room when they come and stay. As far I was concerned we were doing OK. Then Pat walked in with her friend and a guy who I had never seen before. They sat at the far end of the pub and during the evening they all got quite loud - I reckon they were all a bit pissed - and her girlfriend started shouting at her calling her a fucking bitch, and then punched her! Joe told me to keep out of it but I felt sorry for Pat as the bloke joined in and started pushing her.'

'Christ! What did the owner do?'

'He told them to leave but they wouldn't so I went over to talk to Pat as there was a crowd gathering around them. Her girlfriend told me to piss off and get back to my own table. I said she was acting like an idiot and should calm down. "You're the fucking idiot," she said. "Your bloke is having sex with her behind your back."'

Marcie saw the tears well up in Amy's eyes. 'What did you do then?'

'I ran out the pub and went straight home. An hour later Joe walked in. He was adamant it only happened once when he went over to fix a leaking sink. He said she brought some beers out of the fridge and one thing led to another and they had sex. He said he had regretted it ever since.'

'Well, for what it's worth, I believe him. Pat lives in a fantasy world. She can be very manipulative, and knowing Joe he probably felt sorry for her.'

'Does that make it any better? He screwed her! How can I ever trust him again?' Amy was angry. 'I would never dream of doing that to him!'

'I really don't know what to say, but I do know Pat is a compulsive liar. She often comes into the shop telling me how she has been out with loads of guys in the past: a policeman, a celebrity, and even a millionaire. I know it's all made up, so I'm inclined to believe Joe; it probably was just the once.'

Amy knew Marcie was probably right but it didn't detract from the fact he had slept with another woman. They chatted for a while longer and had another coffee. 'I have to make a move now; my mum's coming to stay with us for a few days. It was planned ages ago and I have told Joe to keep out of my way and stay with friends. I can't throw him out as he has his job around the corner at the medical centre.'

Marcie got her coat and showed her to the door.

'Come to mine next weekend – Biba and Tilly are going to be there and I know they'd love to see you again.'

Marcie hoped they would both work it out as she was fond of Amy and liked Joe but could never imagine what she would do in her situation and how she would feel. Men, she thought, and immediately her mum sprang to mind and the way she was being used and exploited by Sam. She decided to take Bella's advice and give her a ring to see how she was.

Nellie answered the phone.

'Hi Mum, it's me. How are you?' Although Marcie knew her mum was in a bad way she was still shocked when she heard her voice. She was rambling on, not making any sense at all and then ended the conversation rather abruptly by saying something about things she had to do, before hanging up on her.

Nellie put the phone down and collapsed into her armchair. What had she done! Her eyes travelled across the floor to where Sam lay motionless, his head on the hearth with blood seeping from a gaping wound. She slowly rose to her feet and dialled 999...

It had all started kicking off that morning when Sam said he was leaving right there and then, and she had pleaded with him to stay, but they drank all day and continued to argue till they were at screaming pitch. Their elderly neighbours knocked on the door concerned but got no answer. Sam became abusive telling Nellie she looked a disgrace and that he had never loved her, she was just a convenience and he wanted to move on as he'd had a belly full of her nagging. Nellie jumped up out of her seat and flew at him punching and kicking. Sam was laughing in her face. 'You stupid cow! Sit down,' but she wouldn't and that's when Sam put his hands around Nellie's throat and squeezed tightly. She was struggling to breathe and instinctively pushed him back with all her might. As she did, he tripped and fell backwards on the stone hearth and hit his head. There was blood everywhere. As drunk as she was, Nellie panicked and shouted at him hysterically over and over again to get up, but he didn't move. And now here she was waiting for the emergency services...not knowing whether Sam was alive or dead.

As the police pulled up outside and Nellie struggled to her feet to go to the front door an ambulance could be heard coming down the street. As she opened the door to the two police officers she collapsed, crying hysterically. They helped her inside and sat her down trying to make sense of the situation. Sergeant Ross immediately went to the motionless Sam and tried to find a pulse. He was still breathing but his pulse was very weak – he knew he was in a critical condition. At that moment the paramedics came bursting in and Sergeant Ross got out of their way, shaking his head at his fellow officer intimating that there was very little hope for him.

Nellie was in a terrible state, shaking all over and muttering that she 'didn't mean for this to happen'. The other police officer, a young woman, made her a cup of sweet tea hoping it would calm her nerves so that they could begin to interview her. She knew this couple of old, and had been called here on a number of occasions recently when they were drunk and causing a disturbance.

Interviewing Nellie was hard work, as she was so distraught, screaming and shouting and not co-operating at all. The paramedics now had Sam on a stretcher and took him out to the ambulance to rush him to the hospital. Sergeant Ross decided that the best thing to do was get Nellie down to the station and take it from there as they were getting nowhere with her at the moment.

When they arrived at the station the duty doctor examined Nellie and was shocked at the amount of bruises covering her body. He immediately gave her a sedative to calm her down, as she was so distraught and told the sergeant that in the best interest of his patient it would be better if she had some rest before she was interviewed. Photographs of the bruising were then taken to be kept for evidence and Nellie was put into a cell to get some sleep as the sedative was beginning to take effect.

The following morning the hospital phoned to tell the desk sergeant that Sam had died – he had a large blood clot on his brain due to the fall. The call was immediately put through to Sergeant Ross who was asked if Sam had any relatives they needed to contact. He told them that once he had interviewed Mrs Thomas he would get back to them with any information they needed.

When the sergeant took Nellie out of her cell that morning she appeared to be much calmer. He took her into a small room ready to start the interview.

'Do you want a duty solicitor present?'

'No, not really.'

'I would advise you to, Mrs Thomas.'

Nellie insisted she didn't need one but due to the seriousness of the case he finally convinced her otherwise, and brought him into the interview room.

'How is Sam?'

'I am sorry to tell you he has passed away.'

Nellie looked numb but was ready to make a statement. She relayed to the officer as much as she could about Sam and their life

166

together. She told him Sam had rages of anger when he was drinking and on that particular evening he put his hands around her neck and she had pushed him away and he fell backwards onto the hearth, and that's when she saw the blood coming from his head and phoned the police.

'Why didn't you immediately phone an ambulance?'

'I don't know - I just panicked I suppose; I wasn't thinking straight.'

Sergeant Ross asked Nellie if she wanted to make a phone call to anyone as she was allowed just one. She immediately phoned Marcie.

When Marcie heard the news she was dumbfounded. 'What's going to happen now?'

'The judge may send me to jail,' she said.

'For god sakes, Mother, you have really gone and done it now...but it was accidental...you were defending yourself. Look whatever happens, I hope you will get some help now. You're screwed up and I won't shed any tears for Sam or attend the funeral I'm afraid. I blame you in many ways; why didn't you chuck him out when he became so abusive towards you?'

Nellie started to cry and put the phone down. She knew in the cold light of day her daughter was right - there were choices in life and she had made bad ones.

For the time being Nellie would be kept on remand until a trial date was set. Her solicitor had warned her that there was a possibility she would be tried for manslaughter but that he would do his utmost to prove that it was accidental death.

Chapter Fourteen

Marcie confided in Bella who kept her busy for the next few weeks to take her mind off things. She was quick to advise her that her mother was not her responsibility. 'She's a grown woman and should have known better; after all, she was the adult and your protector and yet was emotionally blackmailing you. She will have to move on and concentrate on her own future, but in time who knows what will happen when she gets the help she needs? You may have a relationship in the future when all this is sorted out, but only time will tell.'

Marcie took her advice and was working hard in the shop but Pat was getting on her nerves. She said she had a new boyfriend on the scene - a bouncer at a night club who had a pad in Chelsea. Marcie wanted to say something about Joe and give her a piece of her mind but had promised Amy she wouldn't say anything, as she didn't want to put her job in jeopardy. Bella had enough on her plate and besides, Pat wasn't worth it.

The shop was so busy Bella had decided to bring in a new assistant, a 16 year-old school leaver, for the Christmas period. It was her neighbour's niece, Ella, who had a delightful bubbly personality and was very friendly. Marcie showed her the ropes and they got on well, but being older than Ella, Pat thought she could give her orders, though Marcie as manageress soon put her in her place.

It was Christmas Eve and the shop had been a success. Bella couldn't have been more pleased and was so looking forward to having two days off with Barry and returning back to organise the January sale.

'What are you doing for Christmas, Marcie?' Bella asked.

'Zoe, her mum and Charlie are coming.'

'Has Zoe got her council flat yet?'

'No, she has viewed a few places but they weren't suitable.'

'Beggars can't be choosers,' Bella said, 'otherwise the council will take them off their list.'

'I know, but the flats that were offered were disgusting, so I can't blame them.'

Bella left the shop early as she was meeting Barry for lunch - things were going well between them and they had made arrangements to spend Christmas together at Bella's house. She couldn't have been happier.

It was a long day and the takings had never been so good. When Bella came back to cash up she gave them all a £20 bonus and a special gift for Marcie, a lovely necklace she had admired for a long time. 'I'm closing up now so off you all go, but I want you all back here prompt after Boxing Day.' Cards were exchanged and Pat and Marcie gave Bella a small gift and she wished them all a merry Christmas.

Zoe's mum, Irene had phoned and insisted she would cook Christmas dinner for all of them as that was the least she could do, so Marcie had agreed and on Christmas morning was up bright and early and prepared the turkey ready for the oven and had drinks chilling in the fridge. They were arriving at 10 am.

The doorbell rang and Marcie opened the door to the three of them who stood there smiling with gifts in their hands. Charlie had also brought a case of beer. 'Merry Christmas!' they chorused.

'And Merry Christmas to you too! Come on in out of the cold and I'll get us all a drink. I'm afraid it's only fresh orange juice for you, Zoe, but I have freshly squeezed it, none of the concentrated stuff for you!'

'Bloody hell it's Christmas and I can't have one glass of wine?'

'Not in your condition, pet,' Charlie piped up, 'so stop moaning.'

Zoe's mum went straight into the kitchen and Marcie showed her where everything was. 'Are you sure I can't help you?'

'Don't be daft; leave it to me.'

The meal seemed to take forever and they were starving by 5 o'clock when Zoe's mum eventually put dinner on the table. Unfortunately it was a complete disaster, maybe due to the fact she kept going outside to smoke her pot. The turkey was dry and she had left the giblets in the plastic bag inside. The stuffing was sloppy and looked like cat food, the roast potatoes were slightly burned and the veg was overcooked. 'Mum you have ruined the dinner,' Zoe remarked.

Charlie and Marcie were being polite and trying to eat it, but eventually, Marcie, who was not one to make a fuss, said she would cook a fry up or do turkey sandwiches later.

'Sorry about that, I feel guilty as hell.'

'You should Mum; I can't understand why you offered to cook in the first place - I was brought up with beans on toast or scrambled egg! What were you thinking of...?'

Marcie interrupted, 'Come on Zoe, no big deal, she tried her best.'

The rest of the day was spent with Zoe laying in Marcie's bed as she felt tired nearing the end of her pregnancy and Zoe's mum left after dinner as she didn't like sitting around for too long; she had always been a free spirit and had people to see and places to go.

Charlie sat in the sitting room talking to Marcie. 'Have you seen Mrs Evans lately?'

'You mean Amy?'

'Sorry, that's what I called her at the big house when I worked there - old habits die hard.'

'That's alright,' Marcie laughed. 'She's having a few problems at the moment. Joe, her partner, has had a one night stand with Pat the girl I'm working with. Pat's making out it was an affair, but I hope they work out their differences. Amy is lovely person, and she was always so nice to me and a real lady on the few occasions that I saw her when I was working for John. Now, him, he's a different kettle of fish, a real bastard. Have you heard from Doris?'

'Yes, I got a Christmas card from her. She doesn't work anymore; she looks after her disabled husband, as he is much worse. She's his full time carer now.'

'I feel guilty because we lost touch and I really liked her. I must give her a ring soon. What about Biba and Tilly? I had arranged to see them but had to cancel that weekend, so I've been invited up to Amy's for a meal tomorrow, but I don't know what to expect if Joe is there. I only hope there isn't a bad atmosphere, it will be so uncomfortable.'

Zoe came out of the bedroom. 'Sorry I slept so long, I felt shattered. My mouth's ever so dry; I'm as thirsty as hell.'

Marcie made them all a cup of tea. 'Are you both hungry?'

'No, not me,' Zoe said, 'my mum's cooking's put me off food for life. She was never good at cooking Christmas dinners. In my house when I was younger it was fish fingers and chips or chicken nuggets! I can't ever remember having a proper Christmas dinner; she was always stoned out of her mind.'

'Not much change there then,' Charlie said, and they all laughed. 'If you don't mind we'll be off now. When will Jane be back?'

'Not sure, she never tells me exactly what her shifts are at the hospital but she said she would be back tonight and to save her some food.'

'Don't bother,' Zoe said, 'otherwise she will be back at the hospital - as a patient, not staff!'

Marcie fetched their coats. 'Zoe, you make me laugh,' she said as she showed them both to the door. 'Drive safely; it's getting icy out there now.'

They said their goodbyes and when Marcie closed the front door she realised how hungry she was and went and made some turkey sandwiches and poured herself a glass of wine before sitting down to relax for the evening. Food aside, it had been a lovely day. She loved the quilt Zoe and Charlie had given her but felt a bit guilty, as she had only given Zoe and her mum a simple scarf each and Charlie a pair of gloves. The quilt was beautiful and must have cost a pretty penny.

A couple of hours later Jane arrived home hungry and exhausted. It had been a long shift and Justin was still working so they had made no arrangements to meet up.

'Are you hungry?' Marcie asked, but one look at the plate of food Marcie had saved for her and she decided that all of a sudden she wasn't.

'Bloody hell! Who cooked this? It's as dry as hell – yuk!'

'I know, it was Zoe's mum, she overcooked it, but I have a tin of ham I can open if you like and some salad in the fridge.'

'That's fine,' Jane said, and poured herself a glass of wine. 'I've just thought - where's my pressie?' Marcie handed her some perfume she had bought her. 'Thanks a lot! I have just run out of mine,' and she went in the bedroom and came out with a large box of chocolates. 'Here, these are for you.'

Marcie thanked her and opened them up. They were delicious, and she stuffed herself till she felt sick.

'When are you seeing Justin?'

'Tomorrow morning. I'm going to his parent's place for dinner. Have you heard from Roy?'

'No, I thought I might get a Christmas card at least, but nothing,' and she started to get upset.

Jane put her arms around her. 'These things take time - he will get in touch, I'm sure.'

'I'm not so sure; I wish I could have your positivity but I think he has forgotten about me and moved on.'

'Don't give up, Marcie. I'm a nurse and I know he will have to have physiotherapy and get used to his surroundings again. Being in a coma for so long...it's psychological as well as medical. The road to recovery is usually a long one.'

Marcie knew Jane was telling the truth and she had to be patient.

'Have you heard from your mum?'

'No.'

'Well my mum phoned to wish me a merry Christmas and she said that the gossip in the village is that your mum has been taken to Swansea on remand until the trial.'

'Yes, I had gathered that. It's a psychiatrist she needs; I think she has deep emotional problems. You probably think me very hard but whilst she's in custody at least she can't drink, and hopefully she'll have time to think about how she's treated people in the past, especially me.'

Jane changed the subject. She could never imagine not having the parents she had who were there for her no matter what. She yawned. 'I think I'll turn in for the night – it's been a long day. Goodnight.'

'Night Jane.'

Marcie stayed in the sitting room wondering if she had become like her mother, a hard cow, and just as bitter and twisted; god forbid!

The next morning Marcie got dressed and went in the kitchen. There was no sign of Jane but then she saw a note by the kettle. *Have a good day, catch you later. xxx.*

She decided to give Malcolm a ring. He answered immediately. 'Malcolm, it's Marcie. Did you have a good Christmas? Sorry I didn't call yesterday, it was mayhem here.'

'Hello pet. Nancy was disappointed but I know when you young girls get together you forget about us oldies.'

Marcie felt terrible. 'I'm truly sorry; I wouldn't hurt you and Nancy for the world! Did you get my presents?'

Yes, lass, they were lovely. Nancy especially liked the cat ornaments - you know she likes her knick-knacks, and I loved my pullover - very thoughtful of you, thank you.'

'How is Nancy?'

'Well you can have a word with her, I'll hand you over.'

'Hi, my precious, how are you doing?'

'I miss you so much, Nancy,' and Marcie began to cry.

'Hush now, I'm fine. How about you?'

'I haven't heard from Roy...'

'I know you have feelings for him pet, but if things are meant to be they will, and by my reckoning last time I spoke to him he thinks the world of you, so chin up.' Nancy couldn't speak for too long as she got out of breath so easily, so handed the phone back to Malcolm.

'When are you coming up to visit us? We would love that.'

'As soon as I get time off I promise I will.'

'OK pet. I have to go now; Nancy wants to go to the loo. Love you.'

'Me too,' and they put the phone down.

Marcie felt awful – she really should have given them a ring on Christmas day. How selfish of her - things were getting on top of her and at times she just couldn't cope, but she had to go and visit Amy and get herself ready, there was no way she was letting her down. When she had showered and put her make-up on she got dressed and phoned a taxi.

When she arrived Biba and Tilly were so excited they were waiting on the doorstep with Amy as the taxi pulled up. As soon as Marcie got out they ran to her cuddling her with all their might.

'My goodness,' Amy said, surprised at their response, 'they certainly didn't forget you. Come on girls, give Marcie a break and go inside. Come in Marcie, and make yourself comfortable.'

The sitting room was lovely, with a gorgeous tree in the corner and the mantelpiece filled with Christmas ornaments and candles. The girls couldn't hide their delight, showing Marcie all their presents. Marcie handed them her gifts - a haversack each, with loads of stickers on and they loved them. She gave Amy a large tin of biscuits and a bottle of mulled wine.

'Girls, now go and play in your room till I get dinner sorted and let me and Marcie talk.'

'Alright, Mum,' Biba said, but they both went off reluctantly in a huff.

'No Joe today?' Marcie asked.

'He's across the road with his mates in the pub. I told him to keep out of my way because you were here and I wanted a girlie chat.'

'How are you getting on?'

'I can't get my head around what he did and it's hard to trust someone after that, but I believe him when he says she meant nothing to him. I see her shopping in the village and it makes me feel so angry thinking she is laughing at me the cow, and you know how people gossip...'

'I think you have to move on, and I don't honestly believe he would choose her over you, but I can understand how you feel.'

'Why the hell did he do it, I want to know? We have both been through so much.' At that point she heard him walk up the stairs and they both changed the subject.

'Hi Marcie, lovely to see you,' he said as he walked into the room looking sheepish. 'God, I'm starving.'

'Dinner is ready now. Call the girls.'

Amy dished up and they all sat round the table to a meal of gammon and pineapple accompanied by new potatoes and roasted vegetables.

'This is delicious, Amy,' Marcie remarked, and went on to tell them in detail about the disastrous Christmas dinner they'd had.

'Bloody hell,' Joe said, 'it's a wonder you're still sitting there.' Marcie felt embarrassed and wished she had kept her mouth shut; she sounded ungrateful. After all, Zoe's mum had tried her best.

When the meal was finished Joe brought the drinks out. 'There's vodka and coke or Bacardi or whisky - your choice Marcie,' he said. She ended up having two Bacardi and cokes and felt rather tipsy. Joe was very attentive and a real gent and they were all having a wonderful time.

'I can't believe how fond the girls are of you, 'Amy remarked. I think you did a marvellous job when they were in your care, and I hope we will always stay friends.' Marcie hugged Amy; she was a good mum and she adored her children.

'I have to go now, I feel paralytic!'

'Don't worry, I've phoned a taxi and it'll be here in a moment,'

Amy laughed as she helped her put on her coat.

'Thank you both for a great day,' and she kissed the girls and promised them both she would see them soon.

'Wait one moment,' said Amy going into the kitchen, and brought out a present for her - a cookery book by Mrs Beaton wrapped up in tissue paper. 'Every girl needs one of these,' she said handing it to Marcie who ripped it open.

'Aw, thank you!' she said hugging Amy close. Joe followed her down the stairs and helped her in the taxi and kissed her on the cheek and thanked her for coming. Marcie had the best time ever, especially seeing the girls, but couldn't wait to get to her bed.

When she arrived home the place was empty, Jane was nowhere to be seen, so she got undressed and went straight to bed and slept like a log.

The following morning she went into work and Bella was there waiting for her. 'Did you have a nice Christmas?'

'Not bad, thanks, but I'm pleased to be back. How about you?'

'Wonderful! Me and Barry had a great time, he really is a sweetheart. I wonder where Pat is.'

'I don't know, but she should be here by now.'

'If she thinks I'm putting up with this she is sadly mistaken,' Bella said, annoyed.

'Ella isn't here either,' Marcie pointed out.

'That's alright, she phoned me to say she had rung for a taxi but it hadn't turned up so I can excuse her. She was only supposed to be here for the Christmas period but I quite like her so I have offered her a permanent position and she has accepted.'

Ella walked in half an hour later. Marcie was pleased she was staying as she liked her also and found her easy to get along with.

'I don't really expect it to be busy today; people have their families and are taking it easy not going out of the house or doing much shopping, so we need to get items priced for the forthcoming January sale.'

Bella was right, the day was slow and hardly any customers came into the shop. Once they had got everything priced for the sale Bella told the girls they could go home early. Pat hadn't bothered to show up, so when they had gone she gave her a ring to tell her not to bother to turn up tomorrow either, as she was too unreliable and didn't require her services anymore. Pat gave her a load of abuse on the phone and Bella hung up on her.

That evening Marcie cooked a meal for Jane. She had phoned earlier to say she was on her way home. Justin was doing some overtime at the hospital and she was delighted to be able to have a good catch up. She walked in the door an hour later.

'My god, something smells good!'

'I've done us a stew and dumplings and there's some wine in the fridge.'

'What have I done to deserve this?'

'Be quiet and sit down, you cheeky bugger!' Jane took off her coat and sat down while Marcie put the meal on the table and poured two glasses of wine.

'Don't you get fed up not having a boyfriend, Marcie? Roy hasn't been in touch at all and I was thinking...Justin has a lovely single friend called Peppi, he's Italian and a student nurse, we could go out the four of us for a meal some time.'

'I must admit, I'm beginning to think Roy has forgotten all about me and moved on.'

'Look, you don't have to stay in every night. It will do you good to get out – it's just a bit of fun - and you never know, you might enjoy yourself.'

'On one condition. Tell him it's as a friend and nothing more.'

'Bloody hell, Marcie, you're a killjoy...but alright, I will put him straight; you're not looking for a relationship.'

'How's your love life anyway?'

'Justin is caring, loving and very passionate in the love making department - he can't get enough of me.'

'Stop it! Too much information. But I think you both make a lovely couple and he is so laid back. I am so happy for you both.'

'I forgot to tell you, my mum phoned and she sends her love by the way. She said there was a funeral for Sam but there were only a handful of people who turned up so not much of a send off. Tom went but not Betsy and the vicar gave a small speech, but I don't know who paid for it all.'

'How did your mum find out?'

'The gossips in the village I expect, they don't miss a thing. Apparently the trial is next week. I asked her to let me know the outcome.'

'Oh dear; poor Mum. I know she's telling the truth about what

176

happened – I just hope the jury sees it that way. To be honest I never liked Sam. Growing up he gave me the creeps, a real slime-ball but he was my uncle, or so I thought, so I had to be polite to him but he had a mouth like a sewer. I don't know what Mum saw in him...and to think he was my real dad makes my skin crawl... I know I shouldn't speak ill of the dead but Mum is better off without him.'

'Perhaps you should go and visit her.'

'Jane shut up, please, I'm not ready and I'm not sure if I ever will be.'

Jane knew she was talking about a touchy subject and soon changed it. 'What's for pudding?'

'There's ice-cream in the freezer if you want some.'

'No I don't fancy it, but you can pour me another glass of wine.'

'Pour it yourself! What did your last servant die of? I got a letter from the courts today. Tony is on trial next Tuesday; they want me to attend at 10am.'

'Shit! I'll come with you, don't worry.'

'What about your work?'

'I'm on nights next week so I can come.'

'That will be great; I could really do with your support.'

'Do you think he will get a prison sentence?'

Marcie had a worried look on her face. I'm not sure, but I feel like shit because his parents will be there and god knows what they will say to me if he does. I was thinking of dropping the charges.'

'Don't be bloody stupid, you will have to pay a fine for wasting police time, not forgetting the court case.'

'I know Jane, but he hasn't bothered me since seeing him in the pub has he?'

'Hardly, he was in custody. He was warned to stay away from you and didn't,' Jane said. 'And just think, if he gets off scot free he may stalk someone else! He's a menace and you can't trust him. Don't forget he sent you to hell and back.'

'You're right Jane, he doesn't deserve to get away with it.'

The day of the court case came round all too soon. When Marcie and Jane arrived and went into the reception area waiting to be called, sitting just across from them was Tony who was talking to his barrister, and his parents were sitting next to him. Marcie had eye to eye contact with his parents who looked at her in disgust, but this didn't go unnoticed by the barrister who reminded them not to say anything to Marcie, as it wasn't in their best interests.

A few minutes later Marcie's barrister came rushing up the corridor apologising as he had been dealing with another client and was running late. He then quietly told her that Tony was pleading guilty, which made his job much easier. 'The judge may not call you to the witness stand but may just give a verdict with all the evidence put in front of him,' he said. Marcie was relieved.

They went into the courtroom and the judge put Tony on the stand. He pleaded guilty and the judge asked him if he had anything to say.

'No, Your Honour.'

'I have no choice but to take this matter seriously. I understand you have been cautioned once more since the last time you appeared in front of me, so I am sentencing you to six months in custody at HM Prison Swansea. Stalking someone is an offence and I hope this will be a lesson to you and you will have time to reflect in prison on the seriousness of this offence. The court is dismissed.' Tony put his hands over his face and started to cry and tremble in the dock. He was then taken downstairs in handcuffs to a cell.

Marcie quickly came out of the courtroom with Jane behind her, afraid she might bump into Tony's parents who she noticed were crying in the courtroom. 'Bloody hell, let's get out of here,' she said to Jane, glad that it was all over at last.

As they left the courtroom her barrister was waiting outside in the corridor. 'Good result!'

'Thank you so much,' Marcie said, 'but I thought he would get three months?'

'He probably will only serve three if he behaves himself and is a model prisoner, but in my experience people like him carry on offending. I think his sentence was rather light.'

'Well, I need a stiff drink right now,' she said and shook his hand. 'Thank you for everything.'

'A pleasure,' he said and walked off down the corridor.

'Right, let's get out of here and go to the pub across the road,' said Jane looking at Marcie's pale face, and gripped her hand tightly. 'I think we could both do with a drink.'

Once in the pub Jane told Marcie to sit down and she went to the bar and ordered two glasses of white wine.

'You're starting early, I've not long opened. We serve tea and coffee as well if you'd prefer,' said the elderly publican.

'No thanks, this is an emergency. My friend over there is in shock,' replied Jane.

'Whatever you say, miss,' he replied pouring the wine.

Jane paid him and carried the two drinks over to the table. 'My god! Some people are so nosy!'

'Why? What did he say?'

'Never mind; drink up.'

'Thanks so much for coming with me Jane; you'll be shattered tonight working nightshift. I reckon we should head for home after this drink.'

'How are you feeling, Marcie?'

'How do you think I'm feeling? It's awful for his family, but I got fed up with looking over my shoulder whenever I walked up the high street and I never felt safe in my flat when I was on my own. Let's go home, Jane; this has drained me. I just want to put it all behind me.'

When they arrived back home Jane went to lie down and Marcie gave Bella a ring.

'Are you alright pet? How did it go?'

'Tony got sent down for six months.'

'Serves him right, stupid man, but it's his parents I feel sorry for.'

'I know, Marcie said, I feel sad about that.'

'Look you did what you had to do and if I was in your shoes I would have done the same thing so don't reproach yourself, just try to forget about him.'

'Thanks Bella, but do you want me to come into work?'

'No, you're alright, we are managing me and Ella and Barry is popping in to take me for lunch at one o'clock. No, don't worry, I will see you bright and early tomorrow morning, but I may want you to do some overtime on Saturday.'

'No problem,' Marcie said, 'see you tomorrow.'

Marcie opened her post and there was a letter from her mum which read …

My dear daughter, Marcie,

I hope you are well. I am writing to tell you that a court date has been set for two weeks time and I am just hoping and praying that the outcome is the right one. Sam and I had our squabbles but I would never have harmed him – just a shame I can't say the same for him. I just hope the jury see it that way. I have been put in a rehab wing and am doing well and have put on a bit of weight – I haven't had a drink in weeks. The staff here have been very kind to me in fact. We are allowed visitors and I would love you to come and see me if you have the time.

Lots of love, Mum.

Marcie thought the letter was short but she felt a bit happier knowing she was being treated well. She knew in her heart she wasn't quite ready to see her yet, so she put the letter away safely in a drawer and hoped that maybe in time she would forgive her for not being the mother she was supposed to be.

Marcie decided to give the flat a good clean and do some shopping later that afternoon. It took two hours to clean the place through but it looked immaculate. She couldn't help but reflect on how her mum would have been like that in the early days - nothing out of place and everything spic and span; at least she taught her something, though never in her wildest dreams would she have thought her mother would have let her standards drop as far as they had.

Jane was still sleeping so she got some carrier bags from the kitchen and put on her coat and scarf and walked down the high road to do her shopping. The weather had changed dramatically, and the heavens opened so she quickly headed for cover to the local coffee bar. Once inside, she realised that others had had the same idea – it was packed. She peered around for a table but they were all taken apart from one with just an elderly lady at it. 'Do you mind if I join you?' Marcie asked.

'Not at all, my dear. You're drenched; you will catch your death.'

'I'm alright,' Marcie replied slipping off her wet jacket and putting it on the back of the chair before ordering a coffee.

The elderly lady was looking at her so Marcie thought it polite to make conversation. 'Do you live around here?'

'Just by the park. I have lived in my flat for fifty years; I wouldn't live anywhere else. My husband loved Hampstead, bless him, but sadly he passed away ten years ago.'

'I am so sorry, Marcie said, 'you must get awfully lonely.'

'Me? No, I have my memories...and we had two wonderful daughters together who are now living in different parts of the world. My Gemma is in Australia and is married and has two boys and my Patsy is doing volunteer work as a nurse in Africa. She devotes her life to her work so has never married or had children.'

'You must feel so proud of them both.'

'I am. As long as they're both happy, when my time comes I can rest in peace.'

The waitress brought Marcie her coffee and she sat chatting to the elderly lady for a while. Glancing out of the window she saw the rain had stopped. Marcie loved talking to this lovely woman but she had shopping to do and it had stopped raining outside so she told her it was lovely to have met her and left the coffee bar.

As Marcie headed for the supermarket she saw Mr and Mrs Jenkins walking towards her. Great! she thought. Feeling nervous and awkward she put her head down hoping they would walk straight past but they both came face to face with her.

'I hope you are satisfied with what you have done, you stupid girl. You have ruined my son's life!'

Tony's dad told his wife to be quiet. 'We have warned him many times and you can't blame the poor girl for that.'

'Mrs Jenkins, I'm sorry I have caused you so much pain but he frightened me. You have no idea what he put me through.'

'Bullshit! My son has his faults but you have wrecked his life.'

'Let's go, love,' said Mr Jenkins grabbing his wife's arm and pulling her away. He looked back at Marcie apologetically and continued to walk away.

Marcie did her shopping but her mind wasn't on it, she just kept thinking back to her encounter with Mrs Jenkins. What a horrible day I've had, she thought to herself, and was pleased when she eventually arrived home.

Jane had been out of bed an hour and wondered where Marcie had gone but was delighted when she walked in the door with shopping in her hands, as the fridge was bare. 'I'm starving,' she said.

'Well, there is bacon, sausages and eggs and fresh bread. Do you fancy that?'

'You don't need to ask - I could eat a horse!'

Marcie busied herself in the kitchen putting away the shopping and making the meal. When they sat down at the table Jane could see Marcie looked pensive.

'You OK? What's up?'

'Nothing really, just Tony's parents having a go at me on the high road today.'

'No! How dare they!'

'His dad was much more understanding, I really like him – it was his mum who was horrible...'

Jane hugged her. 'Don't worry, it's their problem, not yours. Now, let's talk about Sunday when you meet Peppi.'

'What? Have you made arrangements already?'

'No time like the present! He is looking forward to meeting you and I promise you he will meet all your expectations.'

'I haven't got any. What the hell are you talking about?'

'I know, but you don't want to be seen with an ugly sod.'

Marcie was unsure what she was letting herself into but the way she was feeling she didn't give a damn. 'What does he look like then?'

'Tall, slim, and he normally wears tight jeans and t-shirts and has olive skin with black curly hair and gorgeous features - big brown eyes and a lovely smile.

'Fucking hell, Jane, you are very observant! You don't fancy him yourself, do you?'

'No chance. Justin is everything I want in a man.'

'Thank god for that. Now what time are we meeting up?'

'Say about seven-thirty; Justin is coming here and we are getting a taxi to an Indian restaurant in Soho and meeting Peppi there.'

Marcie felt a little excited after the morning she had at court but wasn't letting on to Jane, as she would have read the situation wrong. She wasn't looking for a partner but thought a change of scenery and good friends around her would do her the world of good.

The week flew by and Sunday evening soon arrived but Marcie wasn't sure whether to dress up or down, she didn't want to give Peppi the wrong impression on her night out. Jane was dressed in a short mini skirt and high heels and was shocked to see Marcie looking like a frump. It was as if she purposely wanted to put him off. She wore a long black dress with long beads and her hair was up in a bun.

'Blimey Marcie, that ages you by about ten years - you always look classy and fashionable; what the hell is that all about?'

'I don't want Peppi to think he has any chances with me.'

'Fucking hell, he'll run for the hills seeing you in that outfit, no worries about that.' Jane couldn't believe it. 'What you're wearing is what my grandmother wears and it would put any man off of even talking to you, but I would like him to stay for the meal at least!'

Marcie chuckled. 'I'll get changed. I take it this is a definite no then?'

She went into the bedroom and put a beautiful flowing pink floral dress on and let her lovely curly hair down - she looked amazing. 'Will I do now?'

Jane was overcome. 'You look stunning; now you put me to shame.'

'Hardly,' Marcie said. In her eyes Jane had the most beautiful face; small featured but stunning good looks.

Justin arrived wearing casual jeans and a short-sleeved black shirt and a leather jacket. Jane thought he looked so handsome and so did Marcie. The taxi arrived and took them to the restaurant and when they walked in Marcie was impressed by the sheer size of it - it was enormous and very colourful inside with lots of beautiful pictures on the walls and a massive fish tank placed in the middle of the room. The waiter showed them to their table and they sat down.

'Where is Peppi then, I thought he was meeting us here?' asked Jane.

'He'll be here,' Justin said, 'no worries,' and ten minutes later he arrived.

Jane introduced Peppi to Marcie and he kissed her hand. Jane had not exaggerated, he was handsome and well-dressed in casual clothing; Marcie was impressed.

The waiter took their orders and Peppi remarked how beautiful Marcie was and asked why he hadn't been introduced to her before.

Justin smiled. 'She's too classy for you mate.'

'Stop it,' Marcie said, 'you're making me feel embarrassed.'

Peppi asked Marcie about herself, but she was holding back and he found it a bit uncomfortable so started chatting to Justin about work.

'Are you alright?' Jane asked.

'I'm fine, but I just need a few more drinks and I will feel a bit more relaxed.'

As the evening went on she relaxed more and opened up to Peppi, telling him all about her life, and he mentioned his family who lived in Naples. 'I have two sisters younger than me and my grandmother lives with my mum and dad as my granddad passed away five years ago. We are all very close.'

'Who are you living with here in London?'

'I share a flat with Peter, near the hospital; he is also a student nurse.'

'Have you got a girlfriend?'

'You're asking a lot of questions.'

'Sorry,' Marcie said, 'it's not like me at all - just tell me to shut up!'

'I'm only kidding; I love your company, but I can't understand you not having a boyfriend for such a long time.'

'Who told you that?'

'Jane mentioned it.'

'Well she should mind her own business...'

At that point Jane overheard the conversation and butted in. 'For god's sake Marcie, I didn't mean anything by it, but you haven't been seeing Roy or anyone, have you?'

'I know, Jane, but you know how I feel about him.'

Peppi was shocked. 'I apologise, Marcie, I didn't mean to upset you.'

'You didn't, don't worry.'

'Who wants another drink?' interrupted Justin. 'We came here to enjoy ourselves,' and everyone calmed down.

After a couple of hours Jane said she was tired and Justin had an early shift at the hospital in the morning so when they had paid the bill they went outside. 'Marcie, you don't mind if I stay with Justin at his flat tonight, do you?'

'No, not at all.'

Jane turned to Peppi. 'Will you do me a favour and see Marcie gets home safely?'

'It would be my pleasure,' he replied, and Justin and Jane kissed them both goodnight and walked off. Peppi walked down the road with Marcie and asked her if she fancied a coffee so they stopped at a little Italian coffee bar. Peppi was intrigued with Marcie - she was intelligent but had a life which was far removed from his. His childhood was bliss, with loving, hardworking parents. His family owned a lot of land and grew vegetables which they sold at the market as well as supplying them to local restaurants. They weren't rich but were happy with their life and were devoted to their children.

'My birthday is next week and I am having a party at the flat. Would you like to come, Marcie?'

'I'm not sure...'

'Why not? I cook lovely pasta dishes, which my mother taught me to make and there will be a lot of my friends there. I think you should start enjoying yourself. You take life far too seriously from what I can see.'

Marcie looked annoyed. 'You hardly know me.'

'I think I do. You have been through a lot. Jane told me all about you, and before you say anything, she has your best interests at heart. Life is too short to sit back and wait for this bloke Roy to ring. My mother always taught me that if two people are meant to be together they will be, but in the meantime have some fun and enjoy yourself. I am a nurse and believe me I have watched young people die from all sorts of problems - their life cut short at such a young age.'

Marcie knew he was right - she was acting selfish, feeling sorry for herself, but she did feel lonely in many ways and missed male company...and Peppi *was* interesting to be with and not bad to look at either. She chuckled to herself. 'Alright! You win. I can't see why we can't be good friends and have some fun, but I warn you...step out of line and you're for it!'

Peppi bent over and gave her a kiss on the cheek. He was spellbound by her beauty - he definitely fancied her. Marcie hailed a passing taxi and they both got in and he dropped her off at her flat. He got out and escorted her to the front door before giving her a gentle kiss on the cheek and saying he would call her. He then climbed back into the taxi and waved goodbye.

Going indoors Marcie thought what a lovely evening she'd had, but she was tired now and decided to go straight to bed.

Chapter Fifteen

The next morning Marcie had a spring in her step and arrived at work a little early, but Bella looked very serious and wasted no time telling her that they needed to have a little chat.

'Why? What's up?' Marcie asked frowning.

'Marcie there's no easy way to say this, so I'll come straight out with it: I've put the shop on the market.'

Marcie's face dropped. 'But why?'

'Look love, I have been having a lot of problems with my health lately, put it down to old age, but my joints are killing me, especially my back, and I have always wanted to do a bit of travelling and spend more time with my family in New Zealand. Barry is up for that too, and we're not getting any younger so now's the time. But don't worry, the market is slow at the moment and property is not selling so it could take a while.' Marcie was pleased for Bella but the news was a shock and Bella could see it on her face. 'I would love to leave the shop in your hands, and I know how much you love it and would make a great success of it, but the value of my house has gone down and I have my family to consider - my grandchildren's education - and I need to put some money away in case they decide to go to university. There is so much more I want to do in life and I want to retire before it's too late to retire, if you know what I mean.'

'I understand, but I can't imagine working for anyone else...and I do love working here.'

'Well, whatever happens I will see you are alright and give you a glowing reference, but you're young and I know you will make something of your life, so let that be the end of it for now, we have work to do.'

The shop was busy but Marcie's head was all over the place. She felt upset - her world was turning upside down and she hated the thought of moving on. The shop had given her a sense of stability and security and she was worried what the future held for her.

Come lunchtime Ella went to the bakery to get some cheese rolls.

She was a happy teenager, very adaptable and always willing to please. When Marcie sat down for lunch with her in the back of the shop she asked her if she had a boyfriend.

'Me? No, I hate boys; I like girls. I disappointed my parents, they always wanted to dress me up like a girlie girl but I was a tomboy and played with trains and trucks rather than dolls.'

'I'm surprised you chose to work in a dress shop.'

'I don't mind working anywhere so long as I have some money. My parents are great but encourage me to work and earn my own money. My mum's a cleaner and does two other little jobs and my dad is a road sweeper and works for the council, but they have always worked hard and they have never been out of work. I've always had good clothes on my back and decent food and lived in a comfortable home.'

'Have you any brothers or sisters?'

'I have a brother who buggered off a year ago with his girlfriend and we haven't heard from him since.'

'You must miss him.'

'I do, but I know he'll turn up one day.'

'How old is he?'

'Twenty-one.'

'He should know better than to put your parents through that.'

Marcie could hear Bella shouting from the front of the shop: 'Back to work you two, I need to get going.'

'Coming,' Marcie called, and told Ella to drink her tea fast as Bella was on the warpath.

It was closing time and when Bella had left earlier she told Marcie to cash up, and after locking up to take the takings to the bank down the high street, which she did before walking home.

Jane was working so Marcie took off her coat and made herself a sandwich. She couldn't be bothered to cook for herself and decided to have a good soak in the bath and watch a bit of telly. Just as she was on her way to the bathroom the phone rang. It was Peppi.

'What are you doing tonight?'

'Relaxing, why?'

'Can I come over?'

'You don't waste any time – I've only just met you.'

'Don't be silly; I'm sitting here on my own and I would love your company - no strings attached. I'll bring a bottle of wine with me?'

'Well, alright...but I want an early night. I'd better give you my address.'

'No need, I remember it from when I dropped you off last night.'

'What time are you coming?'

'I can be there in half an hour?'

'OK, I'll see you then.'

Marcie quickly went into the bathroom to have a quick wash and put some lipstick on. When she had done that she ran a brush through her hair and changed her clothes and the doorbell rang. Peppi stood there with a bunch of flowers and a carrier bag.

'Come in,' she said, curious to know what he had in the bag.

'I've brought a homemade pizza, I made it myself yesterday, and a bottle of red wine for us,' he said. 'I take it you haven't eaten? Now, where is the kitchen? Let's get the oven on.'

Marcie heated up the oven and put his coat and scarf in the bedroom. They both sat down with a glass of wine.

'You look so tense, Marcie, let me massage your shoulders.'

'I'm fine, really,' she said, but Peppi put his glass on the table and did it anyway.

'What a cosy flat. But it's a bit small. How many bedrooms do you have?'

'Oh, just the one.'

'How the hell do you cope - the two of you having one bedroom?'

'It works OK. Jane sometimes works nights and we swap over sometimes, me sleeping on the sofa and her sleeping in my bed. I think the pizza can be put in the oven now,' said Marcie getting up and going into the kitchen.

'Justin has been looking to rent a flat with Jane, hasn't he?'

'News to me,' Marcie said, going back into the sitting room having put the pizza in the oven. 'She could have mentioned it to me.'

'Whoops, I've put my foot in it, haven't I?'

'That's alright; to be honest I thought it would happen at some point.'

Marcie made a salad to accompany the pizza and they both sat down and had another glass of wine and chatted while they waited for the pizza to cook.

'You know you really are beautiful,' said Peppi becoming serious and staring into her eyes.

'Stop, you're making me blush,' she replied looking away. Just then Peppi put his finger under Marcie's chin and turned her face to his. They looked into each other's eyes and he gently kissed her on the lips. Her initial reaction was to pull away, but his kiss was so gentle that before she could react she melted into his arms. They kissed passionately for a long time, Peppi saying how beautiful she was and how he wished he'd met her sooner.

'The pizza can wait,' he said standing up and going into the kitchen to turn the oven off. All of Marcie's senses had come alive and when they progressed into the bedroom and Peppi gently removed her clothes she just knew she had to have him. She lay in bed whilst he stripped naked. It had been a long time since a man had touched her and while she waited for him her body tingled in anticipation of what she knew was about to happen. Peppi climbed into bed beside her and gently drew her to him, exploring her body slowly and tenderly covering her in kisses before entering her and bringing her to orgasm. They came in unison and afterwards he covered her naked body with the sheet and hugged her to him. Nothing was spoken between them for a while - this was a moment to be remembered. Peppi said it was amazing, but whilst Marcie agreed, she knew it was just sexual frustration and hoped Peppi wouldn't read too much into it. But she didn't want to say anything to hurt his feelings, as he had been a wonderful lover - gentle and giving in his love making - so told him how wonderful it was.

When they eventually got out of bed they were starving, so heated the oven up again and sat on the settee to eat the pizza.

'It's getting late, Peppi; I don't want to throw you out but it's time to go.'

'My god woman, you've used me and now you're throwing me out!'

'No, it's not like that, honestly.'

'Hush, I'm joking. You're right, it's late, so I'm going right now, if you'll phone me a taxi, please?'

Fifteen minutes later a horn sounded outside and Marcie showed Peppi to the door. He took her in his arms and gave her a passionate kiss. 'I'll give you a ring tomorrow, OK?'

'That's great,' she said and went inside and closed the door, wondering if she made another bad decision. She had mixed feelings about the evening. Peppi was keen on her though, no doubt about that.

Jane walked in ten minutes later. 'I have a flu virus coming on, I feel like shit. The staff nurse took my temperature and it's high...' Marcie went straight into the bedroom to put a clean sheet on the bed. 'What are you doing?' Jane asked.

'Just changing the bed linen. Put the kettle on and I will be with you in a minute.'

Jane made them both a tea and Marcie told her to get into bed. Jane was shivering and felt sick. She got undressed and put her nighty on and was just about to get into bed when she noticed a man's watch on the rug. Picking it up, she called Marcie in. 'Who does this belong to?'

'Oh, Peppi came round - it must be his. Give it to me, and I'll make sure he gets it back.'

Jane was annoyed. 'You mean to tell me you gave me so much grief in the restaurant about Roy and yet you have slept with Peppi?'

'None of your business.'

'For fuck's sake Marcie, what is going on?'

'OK, OK, You're right! But I never intended for that to happen...'

'I don't give a shit who you sleep with, and I do understand how you feel, I just want you be honest with me and not make me feel I'm the bad one for wanting you to enjoy yourself and have some fun.'

'Look, I do find Peppi attractive and interesting but I'm scared of getting hurt...and now I am having doubts as to whether Roy even remembers me. I get envious at times - you have Justin and Zoe has Charlie and even Bella in her latter years has found companionship with Barry. I get a bit frustrated wishing for a future with Roy...and wondering if it'll ever happen...'

Jane put her arms around Marcie. 'I don't care what you do so long as you're happy. I'm not judging you, we are good friends...but what I really want to know is...was he good in bed?'

'Piss off Jane, you really take the biscuit! But in answer to your question...yes, yes he was!'

Jane slept soundly and Marcie tidied up the sitting room and did the washing up before settling down to sleep on the sofa.

The next morning Marcie got up and went into the bedroom to check on Jane. 'How are you feeling this morning?'

'A bit better, but weak.'

'Look, I'll make you some scrambled eggs on toast and tea but then I'll have to get ready for work, I'm running late.'

She quickly got washed and dressed and gave Jane her breakfast. 'I'll pop back at lunch time to bring some fresh bread from the bakery, and there's some tomato or lentil soup in the cupboard you can have with it.'

'Thanks Marcie. I'll eat what I can of this and then I'm going to have a doze – try and sleep it off.'

Marcie grabbed her bag and rushed out the door to work and when she arrived Bella was in good spirits so didn't notice she was actually ten minutes late. Ella went out the back to make some tea but Bella shouted at her to bring the blue bucket out, as quickly as she could.

'Christ! That's all I need. There's water dripping from the ceiling!' It wasn't the first time it had happened. Bella's tenant, the old lady who lived upstairs, was getting very forgetful and she suspected she had forgotten she had left the bath running again. 'Pass me my keys, Marcie and I'll go up to her.'

Bella let herself into the upstairs flat and walked into the sitting room where she found the old lady fast asleep in the armchair. 'Daisy, wake up!' and she ran into the bathroom to turn the taps off. When she returned to the sitting room she gave Daisy a telling off. 'Why don't you wait till the home-help comes to give you a bath? It's overflowing and the water is coming through into my shop again.'

'Stop fussing, woman,' Daisy said, 'I'll pay for the damage.' She had once been a strong, independent woman – a headmistress in her youth - but was now frail with arthritis and poor eyesight and needed help to get around, though she was as stubborn as a mule. The home-help came in three times a week but she didn't hang around. She did what she had to do and couldn't wait to get away from the cantankerous old dear.

'Look, I'm going downstairs to phone my builder and see what he can do. Would you like a cup of tea before I go?' Bella asked, beginning to feel sorry for her.

'If it's not too much trouble...and a slice of toast wouldn't go amiss.'

Marcie and Ella were mopping the shop floor when Bella eventually came back down. Going straight to the phone she called Lester, a hard working self-employed builder who had done plenty of jobs for her in the past.

'Hi Bella. What's up?'

'I have bloody water coming through my ceiling into the shop. Daisy's let the bath overflow again; can you come and see to it?'

'No problem. You're lucky; work is slow at the moment. I'll be there in half an hour.'

'Thanks so much – you're an angel.'

Lester was true to his word and arrived on time. Marcie and Ella had thrown some sheets over all the garments to stop them getting ruined but fortunately nothing was damaged too much except for a few scarves and small items.

'There isn't a lot we can do now, but time is money so Ella you can go to the shops for me and get me some food shopping and Marcie you can go the bakery and get some cheese rolls and maybe some cakes. What I want you to do later on, not now, is go upstairs and keep Daisy company for a few hours and take her some lunch. She must be finding this ordeal a bit harrowing at her time of life. I know it isn't your job but if I am going to pay you for today I may as well get my money's worth out of you two.'

'I don't mind,' but I promised to take Jane some fresh bread in my lunch hour as she is at home in bed with a flu virus.'

'You can do that,' Bella said, 'but don't take too long.'

After working hard all morning to put the stock in the front of the shop into the store room at the back, Bella told Marcie she could go home and see to Jane, so she quickly put on her coat and dashed to the bakers. When she arrived at the flat she quickly heated some soup up for Jane and gave her some fresh crusty bread on a plate to go with it.

'How are you feeling? Any better?'

'Yes, much better thanks, and Marcie, thanks for taking care of me.'

'No worries, but I have to go back to work now. The old girl in the flat above the shop let her bath overflow this morning and Bella's had to get a bloke in to fix the ceiling where the water's come through into the shop...it's been manic.'

'Oh dear! You'd best hurry then.'

'Yes, I'm heading back right now. See you later.'

'See you later.'

There was dust everywhere in the shop when she returned and she could see Bella getting more and more stressed. 'Do you want me to make you some tea?'

'No thanks, not for me, but you can make Lester one and then go upstairs and keep Daisy company. Here's the key to the flat.'

Marcie made Lester his tea and then went up to the flat to see Daisy sitting in her armchair. 'Hello, I'm Marcie. Bella told me to come up and keep you company for a while.'

'My eyesight is fading so come sit on the settee here where I can see you. You're a little beauty my dear, you remind me of myself in my younger days. Do you see the chest of drawers over there in the corner? There are some photos in there. Pass them to me and I'll show you.'

Marcie went over and opened the drawer to find a loose pile of photos sitting on the top. She took them out and passed them to the old lady.

'Ah, now this is me with my mum and dad and brother at the seaside,' she said smiling and handing the photo to Marcie.

'My god, you were stunning!'

'I was; I took after my mother who sadly died from a heart attack when I was twelve. My father was strict and Victorian in his ways. To him education was everything and what we didn't learn at school he taught us at home. My brother and I were well versed having been encouraged to read books on history, politics, geography...all subjects really.'

'What did you do?'

'I studied English mostly, as I loved reading about great writers such as John Byron or Samuel Johnson. My head was always in a book. I was fascinated by the history of these people so I went on to be a teacher, and eventually became a headmistress in a small infant school in Surrey for many years. My brother ended up doing what he loved best too, working in art galleries. His passion was abstract art.'

As Marcie listened to Daisy reminiscing she found her admiration for her and what she had achieved in her life growing.

They had chatted for quite some time and Marcie could have listened to Daisy's interesting stories all day, but time was getting on and she thought it best she went to see if she could lend a hand in the shop.

'Well, it's been lovely chatting to you Daisy. I had best make a move now but can I come and see you again some time?'

'I would love that. Anytime, my dear; it has been a pleasure meeting you,' and she held out her hand for Marcie to shake. The 'old school' attitude had never left Daisy.

Marcie took her hand. 'Oh, I nearly forgot - I brought you two cheese rolls,' and she took them out of her bag and put them on the small table beside her.

'You're very kind, my dear. Now off you go, I'm feeling tired now.'

'Do you want me to help you into bed?'

'No, no, I think I can manage. Can you see yourself out?'

'Yes, of course.' Marcie couldn't help giving this elderly lady a hug and a kiss, but she could tell she found this show of emotion a little awkward, being the reserved person she was.

Marcie walked down the stairs and went into the shop.

'I hope Daisy didn't give you a hard time - she's a darling but can be a bugger at times.'

'No, I really liked her. I noticed there were books everywhere on the shelves, but I don't think she reads them now as her eyesight is pretty bad.'

'Yes, a lot of them are quite old and some are rare. She was a real literary person in her day and did a lot of travelling all around the world. Her social worker told me she is highly intelligent and versed in most subjects coming from good stock. But she's getting increasingly frail now. Three years ago she had a nasty fall and ended up in the Royal Free Hospital with a broken arm. I try to look in on her every week, bless her. I'm afraid old age comes to all of us – I'm having pains in my joints as well my back now. Actually my back's really playing me up at the moment.'

'Bella sit down,' Marcie said, 'and let me make you some tea.'

'Yes, I think I will. I wouldn't mind a cuppa. Would you pass me my bag and I'll get my painkillers out?' Marcie had never known Bella complain much about her health and felt sorry for her. She forgot she was getting on in years herself and maybe that was the real reason she wanted to sell the boutique.

Lester came over to them and told Bella he had fixed the damage to the ceiling. 'It has to dry out mind, which will take a few days and then I'll come back and paint it.'

'Thanks Lester. What do I owe you?'

'Don't worry, you can pay me when I come back next time.'

'Where's Ella?' Marcie asked.

'I sent her home; she couldn't do much here and the shopping she brought back for me from the supermarket earlier was completely the opposite of what I asked for. She can be a bit of a divvy sometimes. Look, forget the tea and you get off now, too. I'll close up – I've had enough for one day.'

When she arrived home Jane was up watching telly.

'You're back early?'

'We couldn't do much because of the ceiling. I went and kept Daisy company upstairs for a while – she's lovely.'

'You mean Bella's tenant?'

'Yes, that's her; she's a real sweetie. Has anyone rung me?'

'Peppi has, and he told me to tell you to give him a ring back.'

'Did you tell him he left his watch here?'

'No, I forgot, sorry.'

'Are you hungry?'

'Not really. I'll eat something later; the soup and bread you gave me earlier has filled me up. I reckon I'll be back to work soon, I'm feeling a lot better and I get so bored sitting around.'

Marcie gave Peppi a ring. 'Jane said you called. You left your watch here.'

'I'll get it tonight when I call round to see you.'

'Cheeky monkey! I don't think so; Jane isn't well and I didn't say I wanted to see you again, did I?'

'Playing hard to get, are we? I see, well I don't give up that easily. Are you coming to my birthday party tomorrow?'

'Sorry I can't I'm keeping Jane company, but happy birthday for tomorrow anyway.'

'What about Sunday? We could go out for a meal somewhere?'

'Alright. What time were you thinking of?'

'Say I pick you up at your place around seven. I have to go, someone's calling me. See you Sunday.' and he hung up.

Jane heard the conversation and had a big grin on her face. 'You do really fancy him, don't you?'

'Jane, you infuriate me! Of course I find Peppi attractive, but you're reading too much into it. I am just having a casual relationship and it's early days.'

'You make me laugh, Marcie; you don't know a good thing when it's hitting you in the face. Peppi is a real nice bloke.'

'Now you're annoying me! I've been hurt enough. I'm just having fun, so back off.'

Jane walked into the bedroom. She didn't mean to upset Marcie but she was getting on her nerves lately. Perhaps Justin was right and they should rent a flat together. With them both working they could afford to rent a two bedroom place...and she would have more space and eventually they could save up to buy a property together...

Marcie felt guilty that she had been so sharp with Jane and walked into the bedroom. 'I'm sorry Jane. I didn't mean to snap at you – I don't know what came over me.'

'Forget it. I've been meaning to talk to you anyway about me and Justin. We're looking for a rented flat together around this area, but it means you'll be on your own...and I do worry about you.'

'Well don't! I knew this would happen one day, and I'm pleased for you both, though I will have to find another lodger as it will be difficult for me to pay the rent on my own.' Marcie pretended to take the news happily but she knew it would be a struggle. Living in London wasn't cheap and the landlord kept putting the rent up.

Jane had said she felt well enough to go back to work and so phoned into the hospital to say she was returning. They were short staffed so were pleased she was coming back so soon but put her on the rota system on night shifts, starting tomorrow, which didn't make her too happy.

Marcie had a phone call late that evening from Malcolm. Nancy was in hospital with pneumonia again but this was serious and they didn't think she could survive it. Marcie wept as Malcolm struggled to tell her what the doctor had said: that she's a fighter but it would be a miracle if she lasts the night. Malcolm broke down.

'I'm coming,' Marcie said, 'I'll get a taxi to take me there.'

'Don't be silly, hinny, it will cost you a fortune and I doubt whether you will get here on time.'

'Oh Malcolm... OK, well I am going to catch the first train

tomorrow morning and go straight to the hospital. You don't need to pick me up from the train station, I'll get a taxi.'

'Alright love, I'll see you then. I must go and sit by her bedside now.'

'I understand. Tell her how much I love her...'

'I will,' and he put the phone down.

Marcie hadn't felt so much pain in her heart since her brother died and cried uncontrollably. Jane held her tightly and cried with her, as she knew how much Marcie loved the two of them. Jane went into the kitchen and made them a cup of tea.

'I must phone Bella to let her know I'm not coming in tomorrow.'

'Here, drink your tea and try to calm down a bit before you phone her.'

She did as she was told and then put in a call to Bella's home number.

'What's up pet? It's not like you to phone me at this hour.' Marcie could hardly contain herself and burst into tears again. 'Calm down, Marcie, and tell me slowly. I can hardly hear you...what's wrong?'

'Malcolm phoned. Nancy's in hospital again. She has pneumonia and it's doubtful she'll make it through the night. Oh Bella, I can't bear the thought of him all alone at the hospital!'

'What do you want to do love?'

'I want to get a taxi and go up there, but Malcolm has told me not to.'

'Look, Barry's here. How about he picks you up and drives you to the hospital? I don't like the idea of you going such a long way on your own in a taxi – it'll take at least an hour and a half. I want you to put a few clothes in a bag and be ready for Barry when he gets there – he's a stickler for time – he'll be about twenty minutes. And Marcie, I think you should phone Malcolm back to let him know you are coming.'

'No, I think it's best if I just turn up – he'll tell me to wait until tomorrow otherwise, but I think that'll be too late... Thank you so much Bella. The only thing is, I don't know how long I'll need to be away.'

'Don't worry about that girl, just be strong and take good care of yourself.'

'I will, and I'll phone you tomorrow. Thanks again.'

Bella said goodbye and put the phone down.

'What have you roped me into now?' asked Barry although he had heard parts of the conversation and worked it out for himself, more or less. 'You want me to pick Marcie up at her place and drive her where?'

'Southend, to the General Hospital.'

'Who's in hospital?'

'Nancy, Malcolm's wife, and from the sound of it she won't last the night.'

'Where am I staying when I get there? I don't want to sit around the hospital, they need to be together and have their own personal space.'

'Just go and stay in a bed and breakfast for the night and you can drive back in the morning. Marcie will be staying at Malcolm's bungalow with him for a while.'

Barry put on his coat and scarf and Bella took two small bottles of water out the fridge to take with him for the journey. 'I hope Marcie is ready for me, I hate hanging around.'

Bella was getting cross. 'Sometimes you fuss too much about nothing Barry. Just think of that poor woman in hospital fighting for her life.'

'Sorry, you're right. I'm just getting old and cantankerous.' He gave Bella a kiss on the cheek and she told him to drive carefully as he walked out the door.

Marcie was waiting in the sitting room with a haversack with a few clothes in and Jane had done two rounds of cheese and ham sandwiches and put in a few bags of crisps in case they got hungry on the journey; it was her way of showing she cared as she didn't know what else to do. There was a knock on the door.

'Are you ready pet? We should get going.'

'Thanks so much for this Barry,' Marcie said, and turned to Jane who was standing behind her and gave her a big hug and a kiss. 'I'll phone you tomorrow. Will you be alright?'

'Don't worry about me; I've got my job to keep me busy. Now, get going.'

They got in the car and Barry drove off, relieved to see that he had nearly a full tank of petrol so wouldn't have to waste time stopping on the way. Fortunately, because it was late there was very little traffic on the road so they would make good time hopefully. Barry didn't know Marcie that well and didn't know what to say in case he put his foot in it. Marcie thanked him again for taking her but she wasn't in the mood to make conversation as her head was all over the place and all she could think of was Malcolm and Nancy.

Eventually Barry broke the silence. 'There is some bottled water under the seat if you're thirsty, love.'

'I'm alright, thanks, but do you want me to get you one?'

'Yes please, I'm parched.'

'I have some sandwiches in my bag if you're hungry?'

'That's OK; I had a big meal at Bella's. Keep them for yourself, you might need them later on and I'm sure Malcolm won't have eaten anything. When we arrive at the hospital I will take you to the ward and then shoot off if you don't mind. I'm sure you and Malcolm will have a lot to talk about. Did you tell him you were coming?'

'No, I didn't because he would have told me not to, but he will be OK when I tell him you gave me a lift. I am so grateful to you Barry.'

They arrived at the hospital and went straight to reception. 'I've come to see Mrs Brown; she's in intensive care.'

'Are you relatives?'

'No but I'm a very dear friend. She is like a mother to me.'

Just one moment; take a seat over there while I make a phone call.'

Malcolm was informed and came downstairs looking exhausted. It was the first time Marcie had seen him unshaven.

'What are you doing here, lass? I told you not to come.'

Barry explained that he was a friend of Bella's and had given her a lift. Malcolm thanked him and shook his hand. 'It's nice to meet you,' Barry said, 'but I'm so sorry it had to be under difficult circumstances.'

Marcie held Malcolm's hand tightly. 'How is she?'

'I am happy you're here but I need to get back to her.'

'I'll be off,' Barry said, and Marcie kissed him on the cheek and thanked him once again.

'Yes, thank you, Barry. I wonder if it'll be alright to take Marcie back up to the ward with me. Nancy's in a room just off of the main ward anyway,' said Malcolm, 'so we won't be disturbing anyone.'

'I don't see why not. Ask the sister on the ward to make you both a cup of tea,' he could tell they were both numb and in shock. I'll leave you both to it.' '

Malcolm took Marcie to Nancy's room and as they walked in and Marcie saw her lying in the bed looking like all the life had gone out of her and barely breathing, she stifled a sob. Malcolm reached for another chair and put it next to his. 'Come and sit down love.'

'Can she hear me?'

'Yes, but hold her hand to let her know you're there. She has mentioned your name since she's been here.'

'Nancy? Oh Nancy, I love you so much. You have been like a mum to me...' and the tears streamed down her face. Marcie felt Nancy stroke her hand gently, but she was too weak to speak to her in return. They sat in silence, both holding her hands and every now and then Malcolm would get up and kiss Nancy on the forehead. His Nancy, the love of his life...he could never imagine life without her. He knew the fight had gone out of her and what he wanted to happen now was for her to let go, she had battled enough in life with her illness, now it was time for her to rest in peace.

Nancy was pronounced dead at 2 am.

The staff nurse came into the room and gave her condolences. She told Malcolm that all the nursing staff loved Nancy. 'She was a wonderful lady and very popular with everyone here. She will be sadly missed.'

'Thank you for looking after her so well.' Over the last six months Nancy had been admitted many times for her breathing and they had given her oxygen and put her on a drip of antibiotics. Sadly this time she had not responded to the treatment.

'I think you both need some rest. Go home and come back later. Your wife will be taken down to a private room in the mortuary and you can see her there later.'

Malcolm held Marcie's hand. She was shaking and crying as they left and walked down the corridor. She knelt down on the floor with her hands clasped over her face and wept uncontrollably. Malcolm knelt beside her and held her in his arms. 'Let it all out love,' he whispered, and then broke down, too. He felt anger, sadness, and a sense of loss that he knew in his heart would never leave him - the pain was unbearable. Once he had pulled himself together he calmed Marcie down and dried her eyes. Bringing her to her feet he helped her to reception and a taxi was called to take them home.

Walking slowly back into the bungalow they were both overcome with grief once more. Seeing Nancy's wheelchair next to the settee and her favourite slippers beside it Malcolm was taken back to a couple of days ago when Nancy had ticked him off for forgetting to bring them in the ambulance with them. He slumped down into an armchair and put his head in his hands.

'I have some sandwiches and crisps in my bag, should I put them on a plate and make us a cup of tea, Malcolm?' said Marcie, unsure what to do next.

Clearing his throat, he replied, 'That will be grand lass; we need to keep our strength up. I promised my Nancy to be strong and always be there for you... I know she loved you dearly Marcie, and she often said to me that if she had a daughter she would have wanted her to be exactly like you.'

'I can't believe she has gone...'

'Well, you know she was very spiritual. She believed she would never leave me. Her body might have gone, but her spirit will live on all around me all the time. She said that when I got upset to talk to her and she would hear me. She also said she wanted me to be happy and if I met someone else that would be fine by her just so long as she treats me right otherwise she'll haunt her for the rest of her life. Silly bugger she was. But there's not much chance of that - Nancy was my life and there is no one out there to match her.'

Marcie was deep in thought.

'What are you thinking about pet?'

'Do you think Nancy heard me when I told her how much I love her?'

'Of course she did. She knew that anyway and she always wanted nothing but happiness for you. I think she felt you had a bad start in life and deserved better...but she was proud of the woman you had become.'

'I'll get the sandwiches and make some tea.'

'No, forget that. Come on, let's get back up the hospital to see my Nancy. Put your coat on.'

'Malcolm, I really think you should try to get some rest and we'll go back in the morning. Nancy wouldn't want you driving like this and it's the middle of the night. Let's have that cup of tea and then try to get our heads down for a bit.'

'Yes, I know you're right Marcie. OK love, get the kettle on and then we can hopefully get a bit of shut eye.'

'I will. And Malcolm, if there's anyone you need to inform we can do that in the morning before we go to the hospital.'

The next morning after he had made a few phone calls Malcolm drove them back to the hospital. By the time they arrived it had started to rain. 'Let's get inside quick; my Nancy hated the rain, it brought on her arthritis.'

'What did you say?'

'Nothing Marcie, just muttering on to myself.'

When they both arrived on the ward staff nurse Watson who Malcolm recognised greeted them both and took them into a small waiting area. 'Wait here and I will get your wife's belongings, Mr Brown, and then I will take you down to the mortuary.'

'Thank you nurse,' and Malcolm turned to Marcie and put his arms around her.

The staff nurse came back with a small carrier bag and handed it to Malcolm. 'Come with me downstairs and I will show you where the mortuary is.'

When they got to the bottom of the stairs there was a reception desk and the staff nurse spoke to the receptionist who was sitting behind it. A few minutes later she told Malcolm to take a seat. 'I think you will have to wait a few moments till she calls you. When you have finished here come up to the ward Mr Brown, but take your time,' she said gently squeezing his hand.

Eventually Malcolm and Marcie were shown into the room where Nancy was laid to rest. She looked so peaceful and beautiful.

'No more pain and suffering, my darling. I hope him upstairs looks after you, my angel,' and the tears ran down Malcolm's face.

Marcie held Nancy's hand and kissed her cheek trying to swallow down the enormous sob in her throat that was threatening to escape. Malcolm drew Marcie to him enveloping her in his arms and then the floodgates opened and she cried until she could cry no more. They said their goodbyes and slowly went back upstairs to the ward. Staff nurse Watson saw them coming and approached them.

'This is your wife's death certificate, and I have given you details of a number to phone for the funeral arrangements.' Malcolm thanked her and the staff and now couldn't wait to get out of the hospital. He wanted to get out of there and collect his thoughts and grieve in his own surroundings, his and Nancy's surroundings.

As they let themselves in to the bungalow the phone was ringing. Malcolm answered it.

'Malcolm, it's me, Roy. Mum's just told me the sad news...I'm so sorry for your loss. Nancy was a lovely woman...someone I respected and loved...'

'I know that lad. Will you be coming to the funeral? Nancy would have wanted you there.'

'Yes, I'll be there; just let me know the details and I'll be there. Do you want me to come over now? Are you OK?'

'No, no, that's alright. I will let you know when I've sorted things out. My head's all over the place right now.'

When Malcolm had put the phone down Marcie asked, 'Who was that?'

'Roy; he's coming to the funeral.'

'Oh, I'm pleased. Is he coming on his own?'

'For god's sake Marcie, I couldn't care less who he brings! Does it really matter?'

'I didn't mean to upset you. I'm sorry, Malcolm.'

'No, no, it's me that should be sorry. I just feel so angry at times. My precious Nancy was taken away from me and she wouldn't hurt a soul. She had so much goodness in her.'

'I know; life can be so unfair at times.' And she couldn't help but feel a little guilty, as she couldn't stop the feeling of excitement building up inside her at the prospect of seeing Roy after all this time. If anyone was going to help her through this and understand her he would, and she couldn't wait to see him.

Chapter Sixteen

Nancy had already discussed her funeral arrangements with Malcolm for when the time came, and wanted to be buried in the small parish church two miles away, which she often attended on her good days when she felt well enough. She wanted no fuss afterwards, just a simple spread put on and lots to drink. She wanted laughter and a celebration of her life, not doom and gloom. Shelly, who was a good friend and worked at the bakery down the road, offered to do the catering at the bungalow free of charge.

On the day of the funeral there were twenty guests, including Malcolm's family, a few people from the church, neighbours and two nurses from the hospital. Everyone who attended held Nancy in the highest regard. Nancy had also planned the service, including prayers, songs and hymns that were special to her. She adored Frank Sinatra and as the service began, his dulcet tones could be heard singing *My Way* - one of her favourites. Malcolm stood up and said a few words about his brave, beautiful, beloved Nancy, and Marcie read a poem that Nancy particularly liked and had requested. The service ended with the congregation singing *Rock of Ages* – another favourite. There wasn't a dry eye in the church.

Malcolm wasn't religious at all but held on to the belief that there was something, a higher power, and just hoped against hope that one day they would be reunited. Nancy was buried in the church grounds and friends remarked how beautiful it was, with willow trees planted everywhere and a well kept graveyard with a historic church built in the 1830s with so much character and history. Afterwards, everyone made their way to Malcolm's bungalow and Shelly was waiting there for them to arrive having produced a simple but plentiful spread. She had certainly not let Malcolm down.

Marcie had spotted Roy on the way out of the church. He had arrived late and sat at the back so as not to disrupt the service. Now back at the house she was finding it hard not to keep looking over at him as he chatted away to a neighbour. When she next looked over at him he was standing alone so took the opportunity to go over and talk to him.

'Hello Roy. It's lovely to see you – you're looking well.'

'I could say the same thing about you; beautiful as ever,' he said, his heart racing.

Marcie was apprehensive about what to say next as now wasn't the time to talk about her feelings, not at Nancy's funeral. In the end she opted for polite conversation. 'So sorry to hear about your accident. I hope you're fully recovered?'

'I'm on the mend but it's taken a long time.'

'I phoned you a few times; your mum answered the phone. Did you get my messages?'

'No, I didn't...the cow! I'll be having words with her when I get home.'

'Don't be too harsh; she was just worried about you.'

Roy was annoyed. He had just assumed Marcie had moved on, but that hadn't stopped him thinking about her – in fact he never stopped thinking about her.

'I missed you Roy...so much...'

'Oh Marcie, me too. I'm so sorry... This is a sad day for all of us. Nancy was so good to me...' and before either of them could stop themselves they were holding each other tightly. Roy was the first to gently pull away.

'I heard Kim was at your bedside every day...'

'Yes she was...and we are getting married soon...'

Marcie was dumbfounded and just couldn't believe what she was hearing. She felt she had put her life on hold for so long, never really giving herself totally to anyone because Roy was always at the back of her mind. She forced herself to calm down.

'How about you are you seeing anyone at the moment?'

Ye...yes, Peppi; he works as a student nurse at the hospital in Hampstead.'

'I'm so happy for you, Marcie, you deserve the best.'

Thanking him, she kissed him on the cheek. 'Now you must excuse me. I'd better make sure everyone's being looked after,' and she walked away, numb.

Roy wandered into the garden and made his way towards Malcolm. 'I am so sorry for your loss. I always thought Nancy was the salt of the earth and she always looked after me,' he said, tears coming to his eyes.

'Come on mate, hold it together, I've done enough crying for both of us. My Nancy was very fond of you - you were always in her thoughts. You know that whenever you want to visit you are quite welcome here. My home is your home,' he said patting him on the back. 'Have you spoken to Marcie?'

'Yes, I have. She tells me she has a boyfriend.'

'Don't put too much creed on that lad; I reckon she has deeper feelings for you than she is letting on. Mark my words.'

They chatted for a while longer and Roy told Malcolm of his impending marriage to Kim. 'Speaking of which, I should make a move. I've got an early start tomorrow and an appointment to see the priest with Kim for the wedding arrangements,' he said shaking Malcolm's hand.

Seeing this, Marcie made her way over to say goodbye. 'Every happiness for the future, Roy,' and to her surprise he took out his card and scribbled his private phone number down for her, handing it to her and discreetly telling her to keep in touch. 'Don't forget; ring me whenever you need me.' Malcolm stood at the door and waved him off.

Gradually people started leaving, and Malcolm gave a sigh of relief when the last guest said her goodbyes and he closed the front door after her. Marcie made a pot of tea and they sat in the living room reflecting on the day's events.

'Well, my Nancy had a good send off, just as she wanted.' Marcie agreed that it was a beautiful service and a wonderful gathering of friends and family. Malcolm took his last sip of tea. 'Right, I'm off to bed, I'm shattered – it's been a long day. We'll tidy this lot up in the morning. Good night love, and thanks for everything.'

'Night, Malcolm. See you in the morning,' she said standing up and giving him a hug. 'I think I'll do the same.'

The next day Marcie was woken by the sun coming through a gap in the curtains. Stretching, she got out of bed, put on her dressing gown and went to make herself a coffee. The kitchen was spotless. Looking around for Malcolm she suddenly heard the lawnmower starting up and realised he was in the garden. Going outside she was greeted by Malcolm mowing the lawn. 'What on earth are you doing?'

'I know lass, but I needed something to do. I've tidied up the kitchen and sitting room, and if you just give me a minute I'll come and make you some breakfast.'

'I can see that – the bungalow's like a new pin!' she said feeling guilty. She had intended to tidy up before Malcolm woke up. 'My, you have been busy, Malcolm!'

'I know, but being Nancy's carer she kept me on my toes...but I would do it all again if I had to.'

He made them both bacon and eggs and toast with a pot of tea.

'Thanks Malcolm, that was lovely. Is there anything you want me to do?'

'No, you just relax this morning; I have some paperwork to sort out of Nancy's.'

'What are you going to do with all her clothes?'

'They are staying where they are; I'm not ready to deal with that at the moment. Maybe in time, but not now.'

'I understand, Malcolm; that was a stupid thing for me to say.'

'No, not at all! You were only trying to help hinny.'

There was a knock at the door and Marcie opened it to see Shelly standing there.

'Hi love, I've just come to collect some dishes.'

Malcolm heard her from the bedroom and shouted for her to come in. 'They are all washed and in the kitchen, but I was going to deliver them to the shop for you later.'

'That's alright, Malcolm, I was passing so it saves you the bother.'

'Do you want a cup of tea?' Marcie asked.

'I wouldn't say no. Milk with one sugar, please.'

'What about you Malcolm?'

'If you don't mind I will leave the two of you to have a natter; I have a few things I want to do.'

When he had gone, Marcie looked at Shelly, worried. 'He doesn't stay still for five minutes...'

'That's probably his way of coping; just let him be.'

'I worry about him, you know, when I go back to work, leaving him on his own.'

'Don't. I'll pop in to see he's alright, and the neighbours are pretty good.'

'Thanks, I'm sure you have enough to do though. Do you have a family? I mean, are you married?'

'I was but he left three years ago; I threw him out.'

'Why? Sorry...I'm being nosy now, aren't I?'

'No, not at all. I couldn't trust him. I got fed up with going through his pockets and checking his wallet and bank statements. He'd had three affairs in the past and I'd had enough. Actually, I have never been so happy in my life! I'm lucky, I have my daughter who is helping me in the shop and we are very close. She doesn't miss her dad at all; she just says good riddance to bad rubbish. Anyway, I must get back to the shop; my daughter will be having a fit, but it was lovely meeting you. Bye Malcolm!' she shouted, putting her head out of the garden door to call to him in the shed. 'Anything you need just let me know.'

'Thanks Shelly, you're a star!' and she walked out the door and got into her car and drove off.

Malcolm came back into the house. 'Has she gone?'

'Why? I like her.'

'So do I, but she can talk the hind legs off a donkey!'

Marcie laughed. 'True, but she seems a good friend.'

'My Nancy admired her so much. She said she had balls selling her house after the divorce and buying a bakery. She's a canny woman and very independent...and she would do a good turn for anyone. Changing the subject Marcie, I was thinking about going to stay with my brother and his family in the North-East. They spoke to me about it yesterday and I've been giving it some thought this morning. Over the years we haven't kept in touch much, as you know Nancy was always my top priority, but I was thinking about going this weekend – it'll do me good to get away for a bit.'

'Oh, I was hoping to stay with you a bit longer...'

'Look, Marcie, I think you should go back to work - you know you love your job and I don't want you worrying about me. As Nancy would say, life goes on.'

'I can't help it...but if you're sure that's what you want...?'

'I do! Now that's the end of that. I have something for you.'

'What's that?'

'Nancy's jewellery,' and he brought a box out of the chest of drawers in the sitting room. 'I don't think there's much value in it,' he said opening the box. 'Nancy never liked expensive stuff; it was mostly costume jewellery she got from market stalls, but she wanted you to have it.'

'Thanks, Malcolm, I will treasure it always,' she said, accepting the box from him.

'You do know the bungalow is in your name if I snuff it?'

'Malcolm! I don't want to talk about that now. You're making me feel depressed; we've just lost Nancy, I don't want to lose you too...'

'Sorry lass, I didn't mean to upset you,' he said, going to her and hugging her.

Later that day Marcie rang Jane to tell her she was coming home. She packed her bags reluctant to leave Malcolm so soon, but he promised her he would be fine and took her to the station the next morning.

'Ring me as soon as you get home so I know you've arrived there safely.'

'I will Malcolm,' she said, hugging him before getting on the train and settling herself by the window. As the train started down the platform they waved to each other and Marcie was filled with an overwhelming feeling of sadness for him. The journey seemed to take forever and she closed her eyes and recalled all the kindness that Malcolm and Nancy had shown her over the years, not quite believing that she would never see Nancy again.

By the time she finally arrived home she felt physically and mentally drained. Jane greeted her at the door and was pleased to see her.

'I missed you so much, Marcie.'

'Me too.'

'How did the funeral go?'

'Nancy had a wonderful send off but I can't quite believe she has gone.'

'Peppi has been phoning you nonstop, and he wanted your number but I didn't give him it just in case you didn't want me to.'

'Thanks for that; he was the last person I was thinking of,' she said, taking off her coat. 'I must call Malcolm and let him know I'm home.'

'I've got a bottle of wine chilling in the fridge – I'll go and open it.'

'Hi Malcolm. I'm home now.'

'Thanks pet for letting me know. You take good care of yourself and don't worry about me. I'm travelling to the North-East tomorrow, but I don't know how long I'll stay for, I'll play it by ear. I'll give you a ring when I get there. I must go now, I have some soup on the stove. Love you.'

'Me too. Look after yourself, Malcolm. Bye,' and she put the phone down.

Jane brought the wine and two glasses in and put them on the coffee table. 'How is he?'

'Nancy was his life, but he's going to stay for a while with his family. Being with his brothers and sisters will do him the world of good; I hate to think of him in the bungalow all on his own.'

'Ready for a glass of wine?'

'Oh, yes please. I'll just go and get these clothes off and put my pyjamas on.'

Jane got some nibbles out the cupboard and they both sat on the settee chatting and sipping their wine.

'Marcie, now's as good a time as any to give you the news.'

'What news?'

'Your mum's trial was last week. Marcie, the outcome was good. She was found not guilty. Although Sam died from a blow to the head when he fell, there was a verdict of accidental death. Mum said that your mum's gone straight into a proper rehab centre and the house is up for sale.'

'Well thank god for that!'

'Apparently, even a few of her neighbours stood up in court and said that he was violent towards her, and there was evidence of the police being called out to them on a regular basis and they had seen the bruises for themselves, as well of course as the state she was in on the night he died.'

'Well I just hope she doesn't start drinking again.'

'Rehab should sort her out. Mum's given me a forwarding address. She's been to see her and she was at the trial. She said it looks like she's trying to get herself back on track. Here, you'll need it if you're going to visit her.'

'I don't honestly know if I can, Jane,' said Marcie, reluctantly taking the piece of paper with the address on. I still feel bitter towards her for the awful childhood I had – and of course all the lies and deceit. Maybe in time...'

'Well, it's up to you...'

'Anyway, how's Justin?' she asked, changing the subject.

'He's fine. Actually, that's something else I needed to speak to you about. We've been looking at a few flats and have found one in Highgate. It's a two bedroom ground floor flat with loads of parking space.'

'Good god, you're leaving me too.'

'I told you we were moving in together didn't I?'

'Oh, I know, it's just that what with everything else that's happened lately...but I'm happy for you both. Take no notice of me. When are you moving in?'

'Next week. I hate to leave you, especially now, but the rent is cheap and you can come and stay with us anytime you want.'

'I know that; it's just me feeling sorry for myself, losing Nancy and then you leaving...'

'We won't be far away.' Jane put her arms around Marcie as she could see the tears welling up in her eyes. 'We'll always be best friends, you know that. Did you see Roy?'

'Yes, I did. You won't believe this, but he's getting married soon...to Kim.'

'Fucking hell, Marcie, what did you say to him?'

'What was I supposed to say? "No, you're not, it's me you should be marrying, and by the way, you're making a big mistake"?'

'Well, I know it's hard, but I think you will just have to put him out of your mind once and for all. Peppi is dead keen on you; just give him a chance - he's such a lovely bloke.'

'I'm beginning to think you're right. Pour me another drink, I feel like getting pissed.'

They continued to chat and had just finished off the bottle of wine when the phone rang. Feeling a little the worse for wear Marcie answered it.

'Marcie, hi, it's me, Peppi. I've missed you. Jane told me you were coming back today.'

'Did she now? Well, what are you up to?'

'I'm just sitting here on my own watching the telly.'

'Why don't you come round - we have some catching up to do.'

'Great! I'll be there in twenty minutes.'

When Marcie put the phone down and looked at Jane she could see she was annoyed. 'I thought it was just me and you having a catch up. Why the hell did you invite Peppi round at this time of night? I'm knackered.'

'Stop moaning. You're always telling me to enjoy myself and seize the moment.'

'We've both had too much to drink; now is not a good time...you're not thinking straight.'

The bell rang and Marcie got up to answer the door, stumbling over the mat as she did so. Peppi stood on the doorstep with a big grin on his face, holding a bottle of wine.

'Hello gorgeous, have you missed me?' asked Marcie.

Peppi could see she'd been drinking and handed the wine to Jane. 'Peppi, don't give her any more booze, she's had enough for one night.'

Marcie overheard. 'Shut up you. You're not my mother you know!'

'Look, I'm really tired and need to go to sleep.'

'That's OK, you can have the bedroom. We're OK out here, aren't we Peppi?' Marcie said slumping down onto the settee.

'OK, if you're sure, I'll say goodnight then,' and Jane left them to it.

'Are you alright? I've never seen you in this state before. Look, I think it was a bad idea me coming round tonight. Looks like you could do with sleeping it off.'

'Oh, well fuck off then! I don't need you. As a matter of fact you're not all that.'

'I think you're upset Marcie. I'm going to go home I think,' he said picking up the bottle of wine from the table and heading to the door. He didn't dare leave it there looking at the state she was in.

'I think I have had too much to drink, please come back.'

'I'm going to make you a coffee to sober you up,' he said making his way to the kitchen and filling the kettle. When he came back with the coffee she was sprawled on the settee out for the count. Taking her coat from the hook on the back of the door he covered her with it, turned out the light and left.

The next morning Jane got up and went to the kitchen and made a coffee for herself. She could see Marcie stirring on the settee. 'I'm making coffee. Want one?'

'Yes please.'

Jane gave her what for. 'You can be such a bitch sometimes,

Marcie. I overheard you shouting at Peppi last night. If you really don't want him then tell him, don't lead him on. He's a good friend of me and Justin and you're just using him.'

Marcie got up off the sofa bed, angry. 'Who do you think you are? After all, you hadn't known Justin that long before you were besotted by him - maybe I'm a bit choosier!'

'How dare you talk to me like that? We are happy together!' Jane went into the bedroom and got dressed for work. She was disgusted in Marcie. Some friend she'd turned out to be. 'I am off to work. I hope you're in a better frame of mind when I get home,' and she walked out, slamming the door.

Marcie felt terrible and knew she had gone too far. She busied herself getting ready for work, but it was the last thing she wanted to do, and eventually had a coffee and left the house without bothering to put any make-up on.

When she arrived at the shop Bella remarked how awful she looked. 'I'm so sorry for you your loss Marcie. How was the funeral?'

'It was held at a beautiful church and I said a few words and so did Malcolm, but I can't get my head round not ever seeing Nancy again...I feel so empty inside.'

Bella put her arms around her. You will cope in time, but she wouldn't want to see you looking like this.'

'What do you mean?'

'Well, your top has dirty stains on and your hair looks a mess.'

'Sorry, I'm not with it at all today. Me and Jane had a few glasses of wine when I got back yesterday and I'm not feeling too great this morning.'

'That's alright, I'll let you off this time; it's understandable given the circumstances,' and she kissed her on the cheek.

Ella could see Marcie wasn't herself and went and made her a cup of tea.

'Remind me never to drink again - I feel as sick as a dog.'

Thankfully the shop was quiet. Bella went to see her bank manager and Marcie took the opportunity to give Peppi a ring.

'Hi Peppi, it's me, Marcie. I just phoned to apologise for last night, I'm really sorry.'

'No worries. Look, you've caught me at a bad time, I have an exam this afternoon and I'm studying. I'll ring you tonight,' and he put the phone down before she could answer.

The morning was dragging and Marcie was looking forward to lunchtime so that she could get some much needed fresh air. She looked at her watch, willing the hands to go round quicker, still, only half an hour to go. The bell over the shop door rang and she looked up to see Jane coming in.

'Are you OK?'

'I feel like shit. Jane, I'm sorry for what I said, I didn't mean it.'

'I know. We are alright aren't we?'

'I couldn't have managed without your support these last few months.' Marcie felt ashamed.

'Only the last few months?' and they both chuckled.

'How about I buy us a take-away tonight?'

'Sorry, I can't, I'm staying at Justin's flat tonight. But another time, yeah? Must dash otherwise I'm in big trouble, my lunch hour's nearly over,' and she gave Marcie a hug and rushed out of the shop.

It wasn't a profitable day, Bella was disappointed when she cashed up but when she spoke to other retailers on the high road they were down on their profits also. She had been through this recession before but knew this happened from time to time in her line of business. She consoled herself with the thought of Barry coming round for dinner later – that always cheered her up. Marcie was pleased when it was closing time and couldn't wait to get home and soak in a nice hot bath.

'See you tomorrow, Marcie. Let's hope we are a bit busier than today.'

'I do hope so. Yes, see you tomorrow.'

Walking home thinking about what to do for tea and deciding she really couldn't be bothered to cook she called in at the chippie.

'Cod and chips, please.'

To take away?'

'Yes, please,' she said digging into her bag to find her purse.

'You're not your usual cheery self. Hard day?'

'You could say that.' She was well liked around the area and always had a kind word to say to everyone she met but felt lonely knowing she was going back to an empty flat, and with Jane moving out at the weekend it just made her more miserable. She hated the thought of being on her own.

When she arrived home she took off her coat and sat on the settee eating her fish and chips out of the paper. She had just finished eating when Zoe rang.

'How are you? I'm so sorry I didn't phone you sooner.'

'I'm alright; coping, I suppose.'

'You're strong Marcie, if anyone can get through this you can.'

'Thanks for the vote of confidence. How's Charlie?'

'It's been manic here lately. We've moved into our council flat in Lady Margaret Road - it all happened while you were away. But we had loads of help from Charlie's friends at the garden centre. I'm so happy it's sorted before the baby arrives, which is anytime soon. Why don't you come for dinner Sunday? Charlie will be pleased to see you.'

'I will have to let you know. Jane's moving in with Justin at the weekend and may need some help.'

'Is it a rented furnished accommodation?'

'I think it must be.'

'Well there's no excuse then. Come Sunday; she won't need that much help with the move and I'm dying to see you.'

'Give me your new number bossy boots and I'll give you a ring and let you know once I've spoken to Jane.'

Laughing, Zoe gave her the number and they said goodbye.

Marcie had a hot bath, put her nighty on and switched on the telly. She had just started to doze off when she was startled by loud banging on her front door. Panic set in. Since all that business with Tony she hadn't really felt comfortable being home alone. 'Who is it?' she shouted from behind the door?'

'It's me, Mum.'

Marcie opened the door. 'What the hell are you doing here?'

Nellie walked in. 'Don't be cross with me Marcie. I've been doing so well that the board of doctors said I could go and stay with friends or family for a week on the understanding I go back and finish my treatment. I gave them your address and told them it would be alright if I stayed with you. The staff nurse said she didn't think there would be a problem.'

'What a cheek! They should have let me know first. How did you know where I live?'

'You sent me a card once with your address on and I handed it into the office. You're down as my next of kin.'

'Well, I'm going to ring them right now; give me the number.'

Nellie dug deep into her bag and after some time brought out a card with the details of the rehab centre on it and handed it to her daughter. Marcie dialled the number.

'I'm calling regarding Nellie Thomas, one of your patients. Who am I speaking to please?'

'This is Staff Nurse Weatherspoon. Can I help you?'

'Yes, you can. My mother, Nellie Thomas, has arrived on my doorstep and you didn't inform me she was coming. This surely can't be normal procedure?'

'Just one moment, please. I need to make some enquiries. Hold the line; I'll try not to keep you too long.' A few minutes later she came back on the line. 'I'm so sorry; it seems there has been a lack of communication with our office staff. Although we encourage patients of ours to get back into the community by letting them stay with their family and friends for a short period, which helps their recovery, we normally let them know they are coming and have confirmation that this is acceptable. The only thing I can do under the circumstances is ask you to let her stay tonight and put her back on the train tomorrow. Your mother is doing very well with us. She is making great progress and becoming more and more independent. We are extremely pleased with her willingness to work with us through the therapy sessions and she is more or less ready to leave, but her house is up for sale so we are looking for alternative accommodation for her.'

'Well, I'm pleased to hear it, and I *will* let her stay for the week as she's here now, but I suggest that in future your staff communicate better. I have a full time job to hold down and this is really not convenient at the moment.'

'I can only apologise profusely, and please rest assured that the staff concerned will be dealt with accordingly.'

Marcie thanked her and put the phone down. Nellie was sitting on the settee looking nervous. 'Can I stay then?'

'Looks like I have no choice. I also have a flat mate so you will just have to sleep in my bed with me. Frigging hell, Mum, you really take the biscuit!'

'Sorry pet. I know I'm a bloody nuisance...but can I have a cup of tea? I'm ever so thirsty.'

'And no drinking alcohol, mind. If you do you'll be going

straight back where you came from.'

'I don't touch the booze now, honestly.'

'Right. I'll go and make you that tea. Put your holdall in the bedroom with your coat and I'll sort you out later.'

Nellie looked around the room. It's really cosy, Marcie; I knew you would do well for yourself.'

Marcie gave Nellie her tea. Have you eaten anything?'

'No, not since breakfast.'

'Well, I can make you a cheese or ham sandwich - I'm afraid I need to do some food shopping.'

'A cheese one will be nice...with a bit of pickle on if you have some.'

When Marcie finally sat down with her mum and had a good look at her she had to admit to herself that she could see a marked improvement. Her hair was pinned up neatly, she had a bit of make-up on and the plain blue dress she wore looked lovely on her slim figure. 'I must admit, Mum, you're looking the best I've seen you look for a long time.'

'Thank you; I do feel good. The counselling sessions are helping me no end, but I get panic attacks from time to time.'

'Are you on any medication?'

'Yes, I take tablets for depression. The psychiatrist reckons I've suffered with it for many years and asked if my mother or father or any of my family suffered with it.'

'The main thing is you're getting help, but what worries me is where are you going to stay when they discharge you?'

'Don't worry, they will refer me to social services, and I should get a few bob from the sale of the house eventually.'

'I don't think you will get much, Mum, it needs so many repairs doing to it.'

'I know, but it's still a good size with a large garden and that will attract some buyers.'

'I was just thinking, Mum, what are you going to do all day? You do know I work full time at Bella's Boutique on the high road?'

'Don't worry about me, I can do a bit of shopping for you tomorrow and maybe cook you a nice meal when you come home.'

'Thanks Mum. Are you sure you'll be alright?'

'I told you, I'll be fine.'

Marcie went to her purse and got some money out to give to her.

'I don't need any money, I have some. Put that back in your purse. Is there anything special you want me to get you?'

'No just some fresh bread and something for dinner tonight. I'll do a big shop at the weekend.'

'Have you not got a boyfriend in your life, Marcie?'

'Well, I'm seeing Peppi, an Italian guy, but it's early days. I had a miscarriage not long ago...'

'Saints preserve us!' Nellie was shocked. 'I am so sorry Marcie; was it the Italian guy's child?'

'No, someone else. Look Mum, I'm not being funny but I have to get up for work tomorrow morning and I'm shattered. You sleep in my bed and I'll sleep on the settee - my friend Jane is staying at her boyfriend's flat tonight.'

'Are you sure?'

'Yes, no problem.' Nellie got up, said goodnight and kissed Marcie on the cheek.

Chapter Seventeen

The next morning Marcie got up for work but was running a bit late so told her mum to help herself to breakfast. 'There's porridge and other cereals in the cupboard. I have to dash.'

When she arrived at work Bella was already busy sorting through bags of stuff she had bought for the new window display and had some ideas on how to change the shop window. Valentine's Day was coming up and she had an array of items in keeping with the theme – cupids, hearts, flowers and so on.

'What I want you to do is change the window into a Valentine's display and make it very romantic and eye-catching. Marcie was in her element; that was the kind of thing she enjoyed doing.

As she was working she told Bella her mother had turned up and she was staying for a week.

'Glory be to Jesus; that's all you need!'

'I know, but what could I do? I couldn't turn her away.'

'How is she?'

'She seems well and she's actually looking a lot better.'

'What's she doing today? Not knowing the area she must feel strange.'

'Well, she said she was going shopping and cooking for us tonight. That should keep her busy.'

Nellie got washed and dressed and put on her coat and boots and walked down the high road to do some shopping. She hadn't had any breakfast so stopped at a café bar for a tea and a scone. The busier it became the more worked up she got until eventually she had a mild panic attack. Pulling herself together she quickly paid the bill and went out into the fresh air, taking deep breaths like her counsellor had told her to do. Calming down, she walked further down the road to the butchers where she bought stewing steak, sausages, bacon and a chicken. The greengrocer was next door so she bought a variety of veg; now all she needed was a fresh loaf of bread. Wandering along the street she passed Bella's Boutique and decided that once she'd found a bakery she would pop in and say hello to Marcie and let her know she had done the shopping. She eventually came to the bakers and went inside and bought a crusty loaf and some rolls. Heading back she made straight for Bella's.

Bella was behind the counter serving a customer. 'I will be with you in a minute.'

'No, that's alright; I just popped in to see my daughter, Marcie.'

Bella shouted for Marcie who was in the back making tea. When she came out she looked annoyed. 'Mum, you know I'm working. What are you doing here?'

Bella stepped in. 'We're not that busy Marcie, make your mum some tea. Pleased to meet you. I must say, I can see who Marcie gets her looks from.' Nellie smiled and thanked her. She did look good and had made an effort with her make-up and hair today.

Marcie handed a cup of tea to her mum.

'Right, I'm going to have a little break now,' said Bella. 'Nellie, why don't you come to the back of the shop with me and we'll drink our tea; Marcie will look after the shop for ten minutes.' Nellie followed Bella to the back of the shop.

'Marcie has told me so much about you. She does worry about you, but I'm worried about *her* as she has been through so much lately what with Nancy dying.'

'Oh, I didn't know that...'

'She hasn't told you?'

'No!'

'Look I'm going to be frank with you. I am very fond of your daughter and hope you are not here to give her anymore grief.'

Nellie felt awkward. 'I'm on the road to recovery now. Thank you for being so good to Marcie. She's lucky to have a boss like you.'

'Well, she's a lovely girl and we've become friends.'

Marcie was in the front of the shop wondering what they were talking about. She knew Bella didn't mince her words and hoped she didn't upset her mum too much. Just then Nellie came walking through the shop. 'I am going now Marcie, I'll see you when you get home and I will have a nice meal waiting for you.'

'Thanks Mum, see you later.'

'Your mum seems a nice woman,' said Bella. 'I do hope she's turned a corner, for her sake and yours. I believe everyone deserves a second chance,' and she left it at that.

Marcie was pleased the day was going well. The shop was a little busier than it had been lately and as usual she loved serving the customers, especially the ones who asked for her opinion when they tried on an outfit and then went on to purchase the items.

When it came to closing time Bella asked Marcie if she wanted her mum to stay with her, as there couldn't be much room in her small flat. 'No, its fine, we'll manage. Thanks anyway, Bella, it's really good of you to offer.'

When Marcie arrived home she was pleasantly surprised to see her mum had made a huge effort. 'Something smells good.'

'I made your favourite, stew and dumplings with mashed potato – you loved that when you were younger.'

'That's lovely; thanks Mum.' Marcie looked around her tidy flat. 'I see you have been cleaning. Oh, and you've bought some flowers. The flat is tidier than I have seen it in a long time.'

Nellie served the meal and they both sat down to eat. 'Bella was telling me Nancy died - I am so sorry to hear that.'

'Why? You didn't know her. She was like a mum to me...'

'I realize that, but if you keep putting blockages there, Marcie, we can't move on...and I am trying.'

'I know, Mum, but it takes time. But I promise you one thing; I will do my best.'

'That's all I'm asking,' and Nellie's eyes filled with tears. She was so proud of Marcie and the independent woman she had become. She just hoped she would make her proud of her one day.

'I was just thinking, Mum, when you get out of the rehab will you be going back to work?'

'I hope so, pet; I loved working in the hotel. That's where I was happiest the most and I was a good worker.'

'What if I owned my own shop one day? You could come and work with me.'

'I would love that; I just wish I could afford to buy you one.'

'Miracles do happen, Mum. We both have to stay positive,' and she kissed her mum on the cheek. She could really see she was trying. At that moment Jane walked in the door.

'My goodness! I didn't expect to see you here, Mrs Thomas,' and Nellie stood up and gave her a kiss.

'Sorry, Jane, I meant to phone you. My mum is staying for a

week, but don't worry, she can sleep in my bed with me and you can have the sofa bed.'

'That's not necessary, I can stay at Justin's flat - I'm moving out at the weekend anyway.'

'Are you sure?'

'No worries, that's fine. My god, I'm starving. That looks lovely,' she said, looking at the plates of stew and dumplings on the table.

'Sit down,' said Nellie, and she went into the kitchen and dished up a large plate of food for her. She put it in front of Jane.

'Ooh, lovely. Thanks Mrs Thomas.'

'You really must call me Nellie. How is your mum, Jane?'

'She's great. The hotel is doing well.'

'Give her my regards when you next speak to her.'

'I will,' Jane replied, being polite knowing the circumstances and why she left.

When they had finished the meal Jane went into the bedroom and put a few of her clothes in a small case and Marcie followed her in. 'I feel awful, Jane, it's like I'm throwing you out.'

'Don't be silly! It's good for you to spend time with your mum - I understand. And let's face it, sleeping with your mum would surely make you feel awkward after she more or less rejected you when you were growing up. It takes time to put things right.'

'Do you know something Jane Clements? I am so glad you came back into my life - what a good friend you are.'

'Hush! So are you! Listen, I will collect the rest of my clothes at the weekend,' she said, putting her coat on and picking up her case and taking it into the sitting room. 'Lovely meeting you again Mrs Thomas...I mean Nellie. I'm sure I'll see you again soon.'

Marcie went to the front door with her and kissed her on the cheek. 'Thanks again, Jane. See you soon.'

Nellie was impressed. She could see that her daughter was well liked and had good people around her. She went into the kitchen and washed up the dishes and made them both a cup of tea. She handed one to Marcie. 'I think I'll go and have a lie down, I'm feeling a little tired now. My medication has that effect on me sometimes and it's been a busy day.'

'OK, no worries.' Once Nellie had closed the bedroom door Marcie called Zoe to let her know she wasn't coming for dinner

Sunday as her mum was staying with her. Zoe was shocked and worried but once Marcie told her that she was getting her life back on track and had been no trouble she managed to convince her that she was fine.

Nellie cooked and cleaned all week and Marcie had to admit that she had seemed to have turned a corner – she was no bother at all.

Jane and Justin came on Saturday to collect the rest of her things, and when they had left Marcie suggested going to Hampstead Heath for a walk and some lunch, and Nellie loved it.

By Monday Marcie couldn't believe how the week had flown by and it was time to say goodbye to her mum already. For the first time in her life Marcie felt a little sad about parting from her and hoped they would continue with the kind of relationship they now seemed to have. She could only pray that her mother stayed on the right track.

A few days later Marcie was getting ready for work one morning when the phone rang.

'Remember me? It's Peppi. Sorry I never phoned you back.'

'That's OK. I had my mum staying with me anyway. How are you?'

'Busy as usual, but I will know my results soon - if I have passed my exams or not.'

'I'm sure you've done well.'

'I was wondering if you would like to go out for a meal tonight.'

'That would be lovely. I would love to invite Zoe and Charlie to join us if you don't mind; I haven't seen them both for a while.'

'No problem; the more the merrier.'

'Where were you thinking of going?'

'How about the Indian restaurant on the high road?'

'What time?'

'Say eight thirty? I will meet you there.'

'That will be lovely.'

'Looking forward to seeing you,' he said.

Marcie put down the phone thinking she would have to make sure she didn't drink much. She cringed at the thought of the last time she had seen him. She put the thought to the back of her mind and phoned Zoe to make the arrangements.

Marcie was excited to meet up with everyone and when she

arrived Peppi was waiting outside with a bunch of flowers for her. She went up to him and kissed him on both cheeks. 'Are they for me?'

'Who else? You look gorgeous!'

'Thank you. Come on, let's go in and wait for Zoe and Charlie.'

The restaurant was full but the waiter managed to find them a good spot right at the back which was quite cosy.

When Charlie and Zoe arrived Marcie was shocked to see how big she was. 'My god Zoe, I think you're ready to drop that baby!'

'Yeah, I know,' she replied. 'Charlie hasn't stopped moaning - he thought we should have stayed at home. I have never seen a man panic like him.'

'I'm only looking after your best interests you cheeky sod!'

Zoe gave him a filthy look and told him he was stressing her out.

They sat down and Marcie introduced them to Peppi.

'Lovely to meet you Peppi; you two look good together.'

'Don't start, Zoe, you have a vivid imagination. We are enjoying each other's company me and Peppi, that's all.

The waiter came over and took their order.

Charlie asked Peppi what work he did. 'I'm a student nurse but I'm waiting for the results of my exams at the moment. I'd love to get a placement at Great Ormond Street Hospital working with children eventually if I do pass, but I'm not sure if I have. I didn't mind the practical side but the theory was doing my head in - there was so much to learn.'

'I'm sure it'll be worth it in the end. Good on you mate; I take my hat off to you.'

Eventually the meal came and they were half way through when Zoe with a pained expression on her face asked Charlie to phone an ambulance. 'I think my waters have broken.'

'Shit!' Charlie went white. 'Look after her while I go outside and make the call.' Outside, Charlie tried dialling 999 but wasn't getting any reception on his phone. He was just about to go into full panic mode when he tried again and got through immediately. The good news was, the Royal Free Hospital was only ten minutes away and the ambulance arrived in no time.

Zoe told Charlie to ring her mum to let her know. 'I want her there with me at the birth, Charlie.' He did as she asked and she said she was leaving right away.

'Do you want me to come in the ambulance with you Zoe?' asked Marcie.

'No, stay with Peppi. Charlie and my mum will be at the birth and I don't think they like too many people there at one time. But don't worry, I'll get Charlie to phone you when the baby arrives.' Marcie hugged her and watched them go off in the ambulance.

Peppi could tell by Marcie's face that she was disappointed not to be going with them. 'Are you alright?'

I would have loved to be there with her...'

'I know, but they are probably the two most important people in her life - you can understand that.'

Marcie felt embarrassed. 'I'm being a bit silly and insensitive aren't I?'

'I would say just a little naive maybe.'

At that moment the waiter approached them. 'Sorry to interrupt you, sir, but the bill hasn't been paid as yet.'

'No worries, I'll pay it right now.' Peppi went inside and paid. When he came back outside he remarked how expensive the meal was.

'Cheap skate, stop moaning.'

'Where are the flowers I bought you?'

'I hope you don't mind, but I gave them to the ambulance woman to take to hospital for Zoe.'

'It would have been cheaper to have gone to the chippie,' Peppi remarked. 'Come on, I'll walk you home.'

When they arrived at Marcie's flat they stood outside in awkward silence. 'Well, goodnight then. Thanks for the meal.'

'Aren't you going to ask me in for a night cap?'

'You mean can you come in and make mad passionate love to me? Well, the answer is yes.'

'That's where you're wrong. I have an early shift tomorrow morning and I only want a drink, then I'm going home.'

Marcie blushed and unlocked the door feeling stupid. She took his coat and then got some wine out of the fridge and poured him a glass.

'Are you not having one yourself?'

'No, I don't fancy one. I wonder how Zoe is.'

'She'll be fine; it's a good hospital and she'll be well looked after. Look, I have the weekend off, how about I come here Saturday and cook you a meal. I'll bring all the food with me and the wine.'

'That would be lovely; I'll look forward to that.'

'Then that's a date. How about I come early, say about nine-thirtyish so we can spend the day together?'

'OK, why not!'

Peppi finished his drink and left, giving Marcie a passionate kiss on the lips.

The following morning Marcie had just come out of the bathroom when the phone rang.

'We have a baby boy Marcie! He weighs 7 lbs. 6ozs.'

'Congratulations! That's wonderful news...but shouldn't you be in bed?'

Zoe laughed. 'I feel fine! It was the quickest baby they've ever delivered the midwife said. My labour was only six hours.'

'Charlie must be over the moon to have a son. What are you calling him?'

'Josh - what do you think?'

'Sounds good to me.'

'Charlie was useless at the birth, he had to keep going outside because he felt faint and my mother wasn't much better either. She must have been smoking pot outside because every time she came back into the room her coat stank of weed. The nurses kept remarking on the awful smell.'

'I would have died a thousand deaths if it was me!'

'No, not me, I'm used to it. But I have to say, she's been great - she bought the cot and pram and has been a godsend.'

'When I finish work I'll pop up to see you - I'm so excited to see the baby...and tell Charlie congrats!'

'Will do. See you later.'

Marcie couldn't wait to visit Zoe at the hospital. When she told Bella about the baby she insisted she took two hours lunch break. 'Go this afternoon and take her some grapes and magazines.'

'You're very kind Bella; thank you.'

'Don't be daft. Good friends are hard to come by, take it from me - and I was young myself once you know. Ella what do you think you're doing,' Bella shouted, 'standing around doing nothing! Make us a cup of tea,' but Marcie could see she had a cheeky grin on her face.

'Poor bugger; you frightened the life out of her.'

'I think she has girlfriend troubles. I saw her arguing with a girl one evening when I closed the shop up. Young love...bless her, I wish I could go back to my youth,' Bella remarked. 'The years seem to go by so quickly, so make the most of it Marcie, time is precious.'

The sun was shining and customers packed into the shop. Bella had invested in a new line of clothing, dresses with shoulder pads which were selling like hot cakes, but Marcie wasn't impressed, she preferred the miniskirts.

'Can I go now?' Marcie asked Bella. 'It's 1.30 – my lunch break.'

'Yes, you get off now, but don't forget to come back; I need you here.'

'OK, I'll see you in a couple of hours. Thanks again, Bella.'

Marcie headed straight to the supermarket where she bought some grapes and went next door to buy some magazines at the newsagents. When she arrived at the hospital she got the lift and went straight up to the maternity ward and spotted Zoe in a bed in the middle of the ward.

'My god, I didn't expect you here! Why aren't you at work?'

'Bella knows how excited I am to see the baby so has given me an extended lunch hour to come and see you.'

'That was nice of her.'

'So, where's the bonnie lad, as Malcolm would say?'

'Right here, but I think he is sleeping.'

Marcie went round the other side of the bed and bent over to look in the crib. 'Oh, Zoe, he is beautiful! But I'm not sure who he looks like.'

'I think he has Charlie's nose, don't you think?'

'I'm not sure, too early to tell. Where is Charlie anyway?'

'He's taken Mum for something to eat in the canteen downstairs.'

'How was the labour?'

'A nightmare! I kept shouting at Charlie that it was his fault getting me up the duff and never again! I don't know how people have three or four children, it's so bloody painful. Sit down next to me and tell me all the gossip.'

'Nothing much to tell.'

'So sorry about Nancy. How are you coping?'

'I get my good days and bad days but I'm getting there.'

Zoe got out of bed and hugged her. 'You'll get there, but it takes time.'

Marcie noticed her flowers in a vase next to Zoe's bed. 'That was really nice of Peppi, bringing me flowers.'

Zoe laughed. 'It was...and now their mine.'

'That's alright; saves me buying you some, but I have brought you some grapes and magazines,' she said handing over a carrier bag.

'Thanks a lot but I will be going home in a couple of days, they only keep you in here if really necessary - they need the beds. I know what I wanted to ask you. Your mum came to stay with you; did she abscond from the clinic?'

'Zoe I think you have been watching too many movies. She is in a rehab centre for her alcoholism and seeing a psychiatrist as well, that's part of the agreement with the court - that she got help. But they should have let me know she was coming and somehow cocked up the paperwork and I knew nothing about it till she arrived on my doorstep. Still, in the end I told them she could stay with me.'

'How was she?'

'Brilliant, no bother. I never thought I'd see the day when I said that!'

'I'm so glad, Marcie. You never know, there may be hope for her yet. Are you and Peppi an item now? He seems a lovely bloke; not bad on the eye either.'

'I like him a lot and he is fun to be around, but I find him a bit immature. I think he's been spoilt growing up.'

Josh started crying. 'Could you give him to me, Marcie, he probably needs a feed.' Marcie gently picked him up and handed him to Zoe who began to breast feed him. 'This is the part I don't like - I'm never sure whether he is getting enough milk or not.'

Just then Charlie walked up the ward with Zoe's mum. 'Hi Marcie. What do you think of our little man?'

'He's adorable. Congratulation's Charlie, and you too Irene, or should I say Grandma? Look I'm not being funny but I have to get back to work or Bella will be wondering where I am. I'll pop in to see you tomorrow.'

'No, don't worry. I'll be home in a couple of days, so just come up for dinner at our new flat when I get home...and bring Jane with you. I'll give you a bell anyway.'

'OK, if you're sure.' Marcie said her goodbyes and left the hospital.

When she arrived back at work Bella was pleased to see her. 'We've been really busy; I'm shattered. I just need to pop out to the post office and go to the bank - can I leave you in charge and I'll be back later?'

'Yes, of course, that's fine,'

'How is Zoe by the way?'

'They named the baby Josh and he's a real cutie. Zoe looks really well.'

'That's good, but I must dash. See you later,' said Bella as she hurried out the door.

Ella looked in a mood. 'What's up with you misery guts?'

'Nothing.'

'Must be something, you're normally a cheery soul.'

'I finished with my girlfriend last night.'

Oh, why?'

'She was snogging another girl at the back of the pub. She denies it, but I saw her with my own eyes.'

'Well, she is a two timing bitch. I would say move on and meet someone else. She doesn't deserve someone as sweet as you.'

'Thanks Marcie, I will.'

'Now more importantly, how about you go to the bakery and get us both a sausage roll and a currant bun? I didn't get time to eat in my lunch break.'

'Sounds good to me,' Ella said cheering up immediately.

Bella came back just before closing time and told them both to go home and said she would cash up.

Marcie had just arrived home and was taking off her coat when the phone rang.

'Hello, hinny. How are you?'

'Malcolm, hi! I've just got in from work. I'm fine thanks. How are you?'

'I'm OK. I think I'm ready to go back to my bungalow now. It's been great being around the family but they breed kids like rabbits up here - I didn't realize how many relations I had. The kids are driving me mad; I think I'm just set in my ways. I like my routine, but I'm dreading walking into the place knowing my Nancy won't be there.'

'Do you want me to come up the weekend?'

'Hell no, I have to get used to it pet; you worry about yourself.'

'Well, I'll try and visit you soon.'

'That will be nice but I might do a bit of volunteer work for the elderly; that will keep me out of mischief.'

'I'll give you a ring over the weekend.'

'Ok, I should be home by then. Take care. Love you to bits.'

'Me too,' and Marcie put the phone down.

Later on in the evening Amy phoned. 'Can I come up to your place Saturday?'

'What's happened, you sound a bit upset?'

'I am. I went over the bank accounts and found items relating to purchases that Joe has made – things such as jewellery and perfume over a period of a few months. Also there were receipts from restaurants that I know for a fact I never went to with him.'

'My god, Amy he's been lying to you! What did he say?'

'He didn't get a chance, I threw him out.'

'I have Peppi coming Saturday, but don't worry there will be enough food for the three of us; you're quite welcome to come.'

'Are you sure you don't mind?'

'Positive! I would love to see you. Come about one o'clock.'

'Well, if you're sure?'

'Yes, see you then hun, and we'll have a good chat. Don't worry, things have a habit of sorting themselves out.'

Marcie put down the phone. Bloody hell! She wanted a quiet day in with Peppi, but on the other hand she hadn't seen Amy for a while and under the circumstances she would have felt awful putting her off.

On Friday after work Marcie got a little bit of shopping from the supermarket and then stopped at the off licence to buy two bottles of red wine for the next day. Continuing her journey home she suddenly felt dizzy so sat herself down outside a cafe just a few yards away. She ordered a coffee and by the time she had drank it felt able to continue to make her way home. When she arrived back at the flat she put the shopping away and Peppi rang.

'Are you still up for tomorrow?'

'Yes, but my friend Amy is coming; she has a few problems - I hope you don't mind.'

'Christ, I thought it was just going to be me and you.'

'You'll like her, and I could hardly refuse.'

'That's OK, but I hope she likes Italian food.'

'I'm sure she will, Peppi. Look, I'll see you tomorrow. I don't feel so good so I'm going to have a lie down. Is there anything you want me to get?'

'No, I've got it sorted. See you tomorrow.'

The next morning Marcie got up early feeling much better and Peppi arrived on the dot of 9.30 carrying loads of shopping.

'Bloody hell! You'd think you were feeding the five thousand,' Marcie laughed as she let him in. 'Go through to the kitchen. What we having?'

'For starters a lentil soup, and the main course is Italian sausages in red wine with pasta. I'm doing apple torte to follow.'

'Sounds delicious.'

'What time is your friend coming?'

'Oh, not till about one. Come on, let's have a cup of tea and then I'll help you with the food.'

The morning passed quickly and Amy arrived on time bringing a bottle of wine with her.

'Thanks for having me. I hope I haven't put you two out?'

'Don't be silly. Let me take your coat and Peppi will get you a glass of wine.'

'I must say, something smells good.'

'Well, the first course will be ready soon.'

Peppi handed Amy a glass of wine. 'You two sit and have a chat; the food won't be long now.'

A short while later Peppi served the soup accompanied by warm ciabatta bread, and then sat down with them and they started the meal.

'Marcie was saying you come from Naples? I remember going there on holiday with my parents when I was a child – I loved it'

'I am going back there in a few weeks as my grandmother has not been well, but I think one day I will return for good.'

Marcie looked surprised. 'You never told me that!'

'We are a very close family and I can't imagine living in London forever. They need my nursing skills over there as much as here.'

'I agree,' Amy remarked. 'You never forget where you come

from, and family is so important. You're in your third year, aren't you?'

'Yes, just waiting for my results.'

'I remember when I was in my first year. It was long hours and hard work. I thought of giving it up on many occasions but I'm so glad I didn't.'

The two of them continued to talk about nursing for a while and Marcie was feeling left out. These two had a lot in common but she had heard it all from Jane and Justin so she decided to take the bull by the horns and change the subject. 'So, Amy, what's happening with Joe?'

'He's an arsehole. He must have been seeing Pat a lot longer than he was letting on.'

Peppi intervened. 'A good looking woman like you - he must want his head testing.'

'Thanks Peppi, that's nice of you to say.'

They had all cleared their plates. 'Well, that was delicious,' said Marcie. 'I'm full to the brim.'

'It was,' agreed Amy. 'You're quite a cook.'

'Well, you weren't exaggerating, Peppi. Your mum taught you well,' added Marcie topping up their wine glasses.

'Peppi, how old are you?' asked Amy.

'Old enough,' he replied, laughing. What are you trying to say?'

'Nothing, just you have a baby face; but you could be a model with your good looks.'

Marcie could see Amy was flirting with Peppi and was beginning to get annoyed. She got up from the table and started to clear the dirty plates. 'I'll wash up now; I hate dirty dishes hanging about.'

Amy immediately offered to do them but Peppi insisted she stayed where she was. 'Let Marcie do them. You're the guest and I cooked the meal, didn't I?

The dishes done, they all continued to chat and Peppi served the apple torte, which was delicious.

Marcie was relieved when Amy finally said it was time for her to go home and asked Peppi to phone for a taxi. 'Don't be daft, I haven't had much to drink – I'll give you a lift.' Marcie agreed, but told him to be careful just the same.

Amy hugged her and thanked her for a lovely afternoon. 'I'll give you a ring soon.'

'OK, look after yourself and I'll speak to you soon.'

They both got in the car and Marcie went back inside feeling slightly put out that Peppi had paid more attention to Amy than her. But thinking about it, Amy had done her fair share of flirting too. She was older and should have known better – and this thought made Marcie feel disrespected by them both.

When Peppi arrived back at the flat an hour later he could see Marcie wasn't in the best of moods. 'What's up?'

'You! I'm a bit annoyed that I couldn't get a word in edgeways with you two.'

'Come off it, I was just being sociable to your friend. She's lovely; so easy to get along with, and to be honest I felt a bit sorry for her, that's all. You're not jealous are you?'

'No I'm not, but I won't be taken for a fool either.'

'Come and sit on the settee with me, you silly girl. I'm here with you aren't I?' and he gave her a kiss on the cheek.'

Peppi stayed the night and they made love, but there were lingering doubts in the back of Marcie's mind as to whether he was being honest with her and if she could trust him or not.

The next morning they both got up early and Marcie cooked bacon and eggs for breakfast. 'How about we go to the park today?'

'Sorry, I've promised a friend of mine to help him with some revision and then we are going to the pub afterwards.'

'You must be joking! I thought you would spend a few hours with me at least.'

'Come on Marcie, I don't get a lot of free time, and I promised my friend...'

'What am I supposed to do?'

'Go and see Zoe and Charlie and the baby; you said you needed to visit them and see their new flat.'

'Don't worry about me - go if you must.'

Peppi washed the breakfast dishes and kissed Marcie goodbye. How the table has turned, she thought. Now she wanted to spend some time with him, he was less willing. Men!

A little later the telephone rang and Marcie answered it immediately, hoping it was Peppi and he had changed his mind.

'Hi hinny, I just thought I'd call and let you know I'm back home in the bungalow.'

'Hi Malcolm. Are you OK?'

'Yes, peace and quiet at last. My neighbour has brought a Sunday lunch in for me, and apple pie for afters; doesn't look as good as my Nancy's roast dinner, but it was kind of her all the same. Have you got an invite to Roy's wedding?'

'I haven't heard a dickey bird from him since the funeral, but he'll get in touch soon I imagine.'

'How's work, Marcie?'

'It's OK. Bella is itching to sell the shop but no buyers as yet.'

'That's good hinny, otherwise you'll be out of a job.'

'The trouble is I can't see myself working anywhere else.'

'Don't put yourself down pet; anyone with any sense will take you on.'

'I don't mean that, I just love working there.'

'I had better eat this dinner now me bairn, otherwise it will be stone cold. I'll speak to you tomorrow.'

'Love you loads.'

'You too.'

Chapter Eighteen

Over the following weeks Marcie carried on seeing Peppi and he even met her from work a few times but he was now becoming increasingly unreliable and kept making excuses when he let her down or didn't turn up. One morning just after Marcie arrived at work, Bella said she wanted a quiet word with her.

'What's up?' she asked.

'Barry took me to my favourite Italian restaurant on the high road last night and Peppi was sat at a table with a very pretty woman...'

'Really? What did she look like?'

'Older than him but very elegant and well-dressed. She had long, auburn hair and was quite slim.'

'Oh...it could have been a relation of his visiting from Italy, I suppose. Are you sure it was Peppi?'

'Quite sure. I recognised him from when he picked you up from work a couple of times – and I never forget a face.' Bella could see the tension on Marcie's face. 'Are you OK?'

'Yes, I'm fine. If it's not a relation it could be a colleague from the hospital.' But Marcie knew different; she had described Amy to a tee, but wasn't letting on, as it could be something and nothing. She had tried to ring Amy a few times after she had come for the meal at her flat but got no reply, and she thought it was a bit strange that Amy hadn't called her back. She tried to put it to the back of her mind and get on with her work. There would be plenty of time to talk to Peppi later as they were meeting at her local for a drink tonight.

Marcie had been waiting in the pub for a full hour when Peppi eventually turned up and she was furious. 'What the hell time do you call this? I have been propositioned twice; it's so embarrassing sitting here on my own!'

'Sorry, but I finished work late. I'll get the drinks in,' and he walked away and over to the busy bar.

By the time he came back with the drinks and sat down Marcie's blood was boiling. 'Is there something you're not telling me?'

'Don't start, Marcie, I'm tired.'

'Bella saw you in the Italian restaurant with a woman the other night, and by the description she gave me I would say it was Amy.'

'Have you spoken to Amy?'

'What the hell does that matter? I'm asking you!'

'Look, I have taken her out a few times for meals - she's good company, that's all. You're making a mountain out of a mole hill. And anyway, you're always telling me you don't want a serious relationship.'

'That's immaterial, you bastard, she's a friend of mine...and don't tell me you haven't fucked her as well! You're disgusting!'

'Marcie, people are listening; keep your voice down.' Marcie picked up her glass of wine and poured it over his head; she then stood up and walked out of the pub.

When she got indoors she went straight to the phone and dialled Amy's number. She answered immediately.

'You slut!'

'Who the hell do you think you're talking to?'

'Peppi told me about you and him!'

'I'm sorry, but he said you both agreed there was no commitment to each other and that it was just casual. I admit he took me out for dinner as a friend on a few occasions but if he told you anything different he is lying. That's all that's happened and I don't intend to see him again.'

'I don't believe you. What was he to you...your toy boy? After all, you're over the hill compared to him!'

'Look Marcie, I can't talk to you when you're like this - I'll speak to you when you're in a better frame of mind.'

'Don't bother. You're welcome to each other, you bitch!' and she put the phone down. She slumped down onto the settee, tears rolling down her face. She felt so betrayed. She had thought Amy was a trusted friend.

When she calmed down a little she was annoyed with herself for the way she handled the situation. She knew what Nancy would have said: *Rise above it girl. Keep your dignity and self respect and walk away - his loss not yours.* She knew deep down that Peppi and her were totally different in many ways. He had been spoilt by his parents and had a close knit family, so would never really understand who she was and how she felt, but that was no reason for anyone to take advantage of her good nature. So in hindsight she was pleased that she had poured a glass of wine over his head; he deserved it.

Marcie tossed and turned, not sleeping well at all that night, but by the next morning she had made up her mind to be strong and think positive, concentrating on her job and maybe asking Bella if she could do some extra hours in the shop.

When she got to work Bella could see she looked tired. 'You look rough; bad night?'

'You could say that.'

'Oh dear. Why?'

'Well I may as well tell you - I won't be seeing Peppi anymore.'

'Why's that?'

'That girl you saw him with in the Italian restaurant was my friend Amy, and he has been seeing her.'

'You don't half pick 'em girl! I think I would give boys a wide berth for a while if I were you. Put it down to experience. We all make mistakes, but that's OK so long as we learn from them.'

'I was wondering if I can do extra hours - maybe work every Saturday?'

'I wish you could; I hate coming in myself, I much prefer to spend the whole weekend with Barry but I can't afford to pay you any more money. The shop is ticking by nicely but you know that in retail it can be busy one month and not the next.'

Marcie was disappointed but didn't show it. She was finding it difficult paying the rent and all of the bills. She tried to brush it from her mind – she would just have to use what little savings she had to make ends meet. She went in the back to make some tea. 'Ella, do you want a cuppa?'

'Yes please.'

'I just love these dresses with the padded shoulders Ella, don't you?' said Bella holding up a silky emerald green dress.'

'That actress Joan Collins wears them in that American series *Dynasty*.'

'That's right, Ella. I'll make a good shop assistant out of you yet,' and Bella patted her on the back.

After they had drank their tea Marcie asked if she could go to the newsagents. She wanted to get some envelopes so she could write a letter to her mum. 'Yes, you go – it's rather quiet at the moment.'

Marcie grabbed her coat. 'Thanks, Bella. Won't be long.'

When she arrived at the newsagents there was a long queue. She chose a pack of envelopes and waited her turn. She eventually got served and was about to dash back to the shop when she noticed a familiar figure with her back to her. She went up to her and tapped her on the shoulder. 'Doris! Is that you?'

She turned around. 'Marcie! Hello my dear; how are you?'

'I'm fine. What are you doing here?'

'I thought I would stroll around the park and feed the ducks. I have so much time on my hands lately.'

'What about your husband?'

'He died a year ago, God rest his soul. I was his full-time carer when I left the big house working for John. Sadly, in the end he had no quality of life and I think he just lost the will to live. You see, he was always a strong, hard working man, but the heart attacks took their toll on him. He always felt tired and weak, and in the end I did everything for him.'

'I'm so sorry Doris, and I wish I'd been there for you.'

'No worries, I'm sure you had enough on your plate at the time.'

'Listen Doris, I have to go back to work, but why don't you come Sunday to my place, say about midday, and we can have a catch up?'

'I would love that.'

Marcie got a pen out of her bag and scribbled the address on one of the envelopes she had just bought. She gave Doris a hug and said she had better get going and hurried up the road knowing that Bella wasn't going to be too pleased. She should have only been a few minutes and now a full half an hour had passed.

Fortunately the shop was busy so Bella hadn't noticed the time and Marcie quickly took her coat off in the back room and went to the front of the shop. 'Watch the shop and finish serving this customer while I go for some lunch, would you?' Bella called to her from the counter.

'No problem; off you go,' she said walking towards the counter.

'Don't get above your station with me, Marcie Thomas,' Bella said sarcastically, but grinned from ear to ear.

Sunday soon arrived and Marcie was busy preparing a chicken salad for Doris and a trifle to follow. She felt a little unsure of herself as Doris was such a good cook and made hearty meals, but that's all she could afford so she would have to make do.

The doorbell rang and she rushed to answer it. Doris stood there with a lovely bunch of flowers. 'Here, these are for you, my dear.'

'Thank you so much. Come on in and let me take your coat.'

Having given Marcie her coat and settling herself down on the settee, Doris looked around. 'It's rather small, but I must say, Marcie, you've made it quite cosy. Do you live here on your own?'

'I do at the moment. I've had friends living here in the past but they've moved in with their boyfriends. I haven't done much for lunch, but I have a chicken salad for you. Is that alright?'

'Sounds good to me.'

'So, are you hungry? Shall we eat now?'

'Aye lass, but you shouldn't have gone to any trouble,' replied Doris, sitting at the table, but it's very kind of you.'

While they sat chatting and eating their lunch, Marcie couldn't help noticing that Doris had lost that spark she used to have. She always seemed to be so upbeat and full of self-confidence.

'What do you do now to occupy yourself, Doris?'

'To be honest, I am lost not having anything to do or anyone to look after - I find it so depressing. Even though I know people have my best interests at heart when they tell me to take it easy and find a hobby, I know I need to work for the sake of my sanity. I have always been so active... I went to the doctor who put me on anti – depressants because I was getting to the point where I didn't want to get out of bed in the mornings; I just didn't see what I had to get up for.'

'Have you ever thought of doing volunteer work?'

'What sort of volunteer work?'

'Well, maybe working in a charity shop.'

'No Marcie, not being funny but handling all those dirty clothes is not me. You don't know where they've been.'

'What about working at a homeless shelter as a cook?'

'Now you're talking. I would love to do that... anything to keep me busy.'

'I'll tell you what, I'll speak to Bella, my boss at the shop. She works for several charities. I'll see if she knows of anywhere, and if she does I'll go with you when the time comes to give you a bit of moral support.'

Doris flung her arms around Marcie. 'Thank you pet; it would mean so much to me.'

'Do you ever see the Biba and Tilly?'

'Not now; I did when I first left. I visited the house and saw them once but after that when I tried to see them again he told me I had called at an inconvenient time, so I didn't bother after that. You know the old saying, out of sight out of mind, but it was so hurtful at the time as I was very fond of them both.'

Marcie explained how she had seen them and the circumstances of her meeting and becoming friends with Amy, but that they had had a fall out.

'What a shame. I found her to be a lovely girl, but very nervous. If she told you nothing happened with your boyfriend then I must say I believe her. She had her fair share of problems in the past, but for all that, she was honest and caring when I knew her. But I agree with what you're saying; she crossed the line meeting up with your boyfriend behind your back. What a stupid girl, but I expect with all her troubles she was feeling a bit lonely. At the time I knew her she was a very insecure person even though she was brought up by good parents, but who knows what happens behind closed doors. She never talked much about them; maybe they were strict and had high ambitions for her. That's no excuse, I know, but you must remember Marcie, we all do stupid things at times. Life's too short to hold a grudge. Give the lass a ring and let her say her piece.'

'I don't know about that Doris, I'll have to think about that one. Did Charlie tell you I had a miscarriage?'

'Yes, and I was so sad to hear that pet. But you are doing alright for yourself and I don't mean to sound harsh but if you had John's baby your life would have been hell - he would have taken you through the courts like he did Amy and wouldn't have stopped till he got his own way and custody of the baby. I realize now what a bitter, twisted man he was. His parents have got a lot to answer for, bringing up a self-centred, spoilt, arrogant, cruel man. You had a lucky escape leaving him, Marcie, always remember that.'

'Yes, I think you're right, Doris.'

'I feel a bit tired honey. Could you find my coat for me? And I need to get home to feed Giles anyway.'

240

'Giles? Who's he?'

'My cat. Don't be silly; at my time of life you don't honestly think I meant a man?'

Marcie laughed and handed Doris her coat and showed her to the door. 'Will you be OK? Do you want me to phone you a cab?'

'No pet, I don't believe in paying for taxis, they bloody rob you with their prices; I'll catch a bus. It was lovely seeing you again, Marcie. Thank you so much for lunch, and I am definitely interested in doing some volunteer work.'

'Hold on a moment and I'll give you my phone number,' and Marcie scribbled it down and handed it to Doris who kissed her goodbye saying she would be in touch very soon.

Marcie was just about to tidy up when the phone rang. It was Peppi.

'What do you want?'

'I need to see you; can we meet up tonight?'

'Piss off and don't phone my number again,' she shouted and slammed the phone down. Bloody cheek, she thought to herself, he has some nerve.

She cleared the table and washed up deciding to treat herself to a long, hot bath, watch a bit of TV and have an early night. She had another one of her dizzy spells coming on, but this time she also had pains in her arms and legs, which worried her. The sooner she made an appointment to see the doctor the better.

The following morning Marcie made a phone call to the medical centre and managed to get an appointment for 6pm.

When she got to work she could tell Bella was on good form. 'Will it be OK to leave here half an hour early tonight Bella? I've managed to get an appointment with my GP; I think it's time I sorted out these dizzy spells.'

'Of course, love, no problem. I wonder if you have high blood pressure, or maybe it's some kind of vertigo or an an infection occurring in the inner ear – that can make you dizzy. I know it's worrying, but you did the right thing getting an appointment with the doctor.'

'I was thinking I may need glasses - I'm hoping it's something as simple as that.'

Peppi called in the shop that afternoon but Bella, who was aware of the situation and what had happened, gave him what for. 'You don't bother one of my staff while she is working unless you have come to purchase an item of clothing. Now I suggest you leave right now.' Peppi turned around and walked out the shop.

'Thanks Bella. I don't know what he wants – he knows I don't want anything to do with him.'

'That's what he doesn't like; his ego is bruised. Ella make us all a brew, I'm parched...and get that tin of biscuits from the top cupboard out. I need to go on a diet but today is not the day. My Barry says every day I say the same thing, but I always had a bit of meat on me; I would hate to be skinny, so take me or leave me I say!'

'You're funny, Bella,' Marcie remarked, smiling.

'Not really pet, I just like to keep things real.'

The shop was busy for the rest of the morning. Bella had been on the phone for the past half an hour and when she put it down she was beaming.

'Would you believe it? The estate agent is bringing someone round tomorrow to view the shop!' Marcie said she was pleased for her, but her heart sank. The job was like her security blanket, her second home, but she tried not to show her feelings, as Bella had always been good to her.

Bella let her go early and she arrived at the surgery in good time for her appointment. She let the receptionist know she had arrived and settled down in a chair. A few minutes later her name was called and she was directed to the third floor, first door on the left. She knocked on the door and went inside.

'Please take a seat, Miss Thomas. Now, what can I do for you?'

As she sat down she noticed it wasn't the usual doctor she had seen in the past, but a young guy who seemed quite serious in his demeanour. 'Well, I have been having a lot of dizzy spells lately, plus fatigue, and pains in my joints.'

'Any other symptoms?'

'No, nothing else really.'

'How long do these spells last for?'

'A few hours and then I feel alright.'

The doctor took her blood pressure and examined her ears and told her that the nurse down the corridor would take a blood sample from her. 'I also want you to give a urine specimen and we'll go from there. I have been looking at your records but there is no indication you are on any medication at the moment and are in reasonably good health.'

'What do you think it could be, Doctor?'

'I can't be sure until I get all the results back, but I am writing a prescription out for you and you need to take these tablets once a day and make another appointment at the desk to see me on Friday when I should have the results.'

'Thank you.' She then walked along the corridor to see the nurse who was quite a formidable woman. Marcie gave a urine sample and then sat at her desk to have her blood taken.

'Keep your arm still, please. OK, that's you done,' she said hurrying Marcie out through the door. My god, she thought, this woman has no people skills whatsoever. She then went back down to reception and made another appointment but couldn't wait to get home, though at this moment in time she would have given anything not to be going home to an empty flat.

Doris phoned that evening to thank her once again for the lovely meal and ask if she had spoken to Bella.

'I'll speak to her in the morning and give you a ring. Sorry, but I have had a lot on my mind lately.'

'Anything I can do?'

'No, but thank you, and we will have another catch up soon. Take good care of yourself and I will sort something out.'

'You're an angel, Marcie. Speak to you soon,' and Doris put the phone down.

The next morning Marcie went into work and spoke to Bella about Doris during her tea break. 'Leave it with me pet, there is a charity I support for homeless pregnant women in sheltered accommodation, and if she is a cook I am sure I can find her something. The wages will be a pittance, mind you.'

'I don't think she's worried about the money, it will just give her something to do. She's so fed up – it'll be like therapy for her.'

'Give me her telephone number and when I find something I'll give her a ring.'

'Thank you, Bella, I appreciate it. She's on anti-depressants and I worry about her.'

'Yes, I know – your head's in the clouds today.'

'What do you mean?'

'Well, you've not long been in and already you've given the

wrong change to a customer and priced up that last delivery incorrectly.'

'I'm sorry; I've got a lot on my mind lately.'

'How did you get on at the doctor's last night?'

'Well, the nurse took blood and urine samples and I have to wait for the results.'

'When do you get them?'

'I have another appointment to see the doctor Friday.'

'Look, I can see you're worried; I'll come with you.'

'Thanks, Bella, but honestly I'll be fine.' Bella knew how stubborn she could be so decided to leave it at that.

The week flew by and the day of the appointment came. After work Marcie walked to the surgery and didn't have long to wait until the doctor called her into his office.

'Take a seat, Miss Thomas. I have the results of your tests back and unfortunately they are inconclusive and further tests will need to be done, so I'm going to refer you to the hospital to see a neurologist.'

'What's wrong with them?' Marcie asked, frowning.

The doctor could see the concern on her face and said very sympathetically, 'Just some small abnormalities, but there could be a number of reasons for these so I don't want you to be overly concerned at this stage. Let's get you referred to the hospital and we'll go from there. You should receive a letter within the next few weeks with an appointment, and in the meantime keep taking the tablets I gave you; they'll help with the dizzy spells.' Standing up he shook Marcie's hand.

'Thank you, Doctor; I'll wait for the letter then.'

Two weeks later, tired and aching after what had seemed a very long day at the shop, Marcie returned home to find a letter stating that she had an appointment at the hospital with the neurologist the following week.

When the day arrived more blood and urine samples were taken and she was given a CAT scan and an appointment with the specialist for the following week to discuss the results.

Bella was worried about Marcie. As the day of the results loomed nearer she seemed to be becoming more and more withdrawn. When the day finally arrived she offered to go with her for moral support but Marcie wouldn't hear of it, knowing Bella would have to close the shop, as she would never leave Ella in charge.

When she walked into the hospital she was in bits dreading what she was going to hear, and the receptionist called her name twice before she realised it was her turn. Taking a deep breath she stood and walked to room five as directed by the receptionist.

'Please take a seat, Miss Thomas. How are you feeling?'

'Not too bad, thank you.'

'Good. Now, I'll come straight to the point. We have found from your scan that there are signs of nerve damage in the brain, which leads me to believe you have multiple sclerosis. MS is an autoimmune condition - this is where something goes wrong with the immune system, the body's defence against infection. MS affects nerves in the brain and spinal cord, causing a wide range of symptoms, including problems with muscle movement, balance and vision. Each nerve fibre in the brain and spinal cord is surrounded by a layer of protein called myelin, which protects the nerve and helps electrical signals from the brain travel to the rest of the body. In MS, the myelin becomes damaged. This disrupts the transfer of these nerve signals, causing a wide range of potential symptoms, such as: loss of vision – usually only in one eye; spasticity – muscle stiffness that can lead to uncontrolled muscle movements; ataxia– difficulties with balance and co-ordination and fatigue – feeling very tired through the day. Do you have anything you wish to ask me?'

'How will it affect me? Can it be cured? Marcie asked trembling.

'There is no known cure as yet, and some of my patients find it a frustrating and challenging condition to live with at first, but new treatments have considerably improved their quality of life. I know it's a lot to take in, but I have a booklet here for you to read to give you a better understanding of the condition.'

Marcie burst into tears and the doctor handed her the box of tissues on his desk. 'I will be monitoring you in the future and will forward a report on to your GP. I will see you again in three months time, but in the meantime if you have any concerns, please phone the hospital and speak to the receptionist who will book an earlier appointment for you to see me. Take these tablets four times a day, they will help with the pains in your joints,' he said, handing her a prescription.

'Thank you,' she said shaking his hand, and timidly walked out the door.

On the journey home her head was spinning. This wasn't supposed to happen to her - she had ambitions one day to buy her own clothes shop; to have a family and maybe do some travelling to places she had never seen before, and now all she could see was a bleak future ahead of her.

When she arrived at her flat she took her coat off and went to the fridge and took out a bottle of wine. She then got a glass from the cupboard and placed them on the coffee table and went into her bedroom to put on her pyjamas. She sat on the settee and the next few hours she spent drinking one glass after another to numb the pain, crying constantly until there were no more tears and she fell into an exhausted sleep.

By 10 o'clock the next morning Bella was getting worried, as Marcie hadn't arrived at work. She had tried several times to ring her but was getting no reply. By 10.30 she had a gut feeling that something was dreadfully wrong and phoned Barry. 'Would you do me a favour, Barry? I need you to come to the shop for an hour while I go to Marcie's flat. She went to the hospital for some results yesterday and hasn't turned up for work this morning and isn't answering her phone.'

'No problem love; give me half an hour and I'll be there.'

'You're a star. I wouldn't ask, but I don't feel happy leaving Ella alone.'

'No worries; I'll see you shortly.'

Marcie was awake but had no intentions of going to work. She had the headache from hell and just lay there and didn't care about anything at that moment in time. It was 11 o'clock when Barry arrived at the shop.

'Am I pleased to see you – I'm worried sick.' Putting her coat on and grabbing her handbag she kissed Barry on the cheek, thanked him and made her way to the door. 'Ella, mop the floor at the back and sweep the front of shop, please; I won't be long,' and walked off down the road.

When she arrived at Marcie's flat she rang the doorbell and knocked on the door but got no answer. She knew she was there as all the curtains were closed. Bending down she lifted the letterbox and called out. 'Marcie, it's Bella! Open the door love; I know you're in there.'

Finally the door slowly opened and Marcie stood there in her pyjamas looking like death warmed up. Walking through to the sitting room the first thing Bella saw was an empty wine bottle and a dirty glass. 'Oh, I see! You had people round last night and you're too hung-over to come to work today. And there was me worried sick. I've had to call Barry in to look after the shop because of you!'

Marcie burst into tears.

'My dear, I'm sorry – I didn't mean to upset you. What's happened?'

Marcie picked up her bag from the floor and took the booklet out and handed it to Bella.

'So you have multiple sclerosis...'

Marcie nodded her head.

'Mary mother of God, no wonder you're upset. Sit down while I make us a cup tea.'

Bella busied herself making the tea and when she brought it back into the sitting room she sat next to Marcie and enfolded her in her arms. Gently pulling away after several minutes, she took Marcie's hand and said, 'I know you must feel it's the end of the world, but life is precious and who knows what may happen to any one of us? I've never told you this, but I had cancer ten years ago in my left breast and had to have it removed. When I was lying in that hospital bed I made the decision that I was going to fight with all my might as I had far too much to live for. Look at me, Marcie. What do you want to do? Would you like to go and stay with Malcolm – I know he has been a father figure to you? As you know pet, I have the business to run, otherwise you could stay with me, but you do need a loved one around you and I wouldn't be able to give you all the time you need to help you get through this awful experience. I don't like the idea of you being in the flat on your own - you need time to take this all in and come to terms with it, but not alone.'

Marcie began to sob again. 'I just wish Nancy was alive - she was like a mother to me.'

'I know love, but she is looking down on you I'm sure, and

would want you to be strong and not to give up. That's settled then; I will get Barry to take you to the station, and I want you to take as much time off as you want.'

Bella helped Marcie pack a few items of clothing in a suitcase and told her to have a bath and she would arrange everything for her and give her a ring later on. 'Give me Malcolm's number and I will give him a ring when I get back to the shop so he can meet you at the station when you get off the train.'

Marcie gave Bella the number and dried her tears. She couldn't wait to see Malcolm again, the one person who she loved dearly and would make sense of all this and advise her on what to do. Marcie gave Bella a kiss and thanked her.

'Don't thank me, you're a valued member of staff in my shop and when you get back I will expect a lot of overtime from you to make up for the time off,' she said winking.

Marcie smiled; she was a true friend and felt lucky to have her in her life.

Bella rang a few hours later to say that Barry was on his way round to take her to the station and that she had phoned Malcolm with the times of the trains and he would pick her up at the other end. She had taken a long bath and was now ready, her suitcase by the door.

A short while later the doorbell rang and Barry stood there. Stepping forward he gave Marcie a hug. 'Are you ready? Got everything?'

'Yes. Thank you so much, Barry,' she said handing him her case. 'I hope I haven't put you to too much trouble.'

'Don't be silly, it's my pleasure. Now hop in the car - you don't want to miss your train.'

They set off down the road and Barry felt awkward at first, not sure what to say, so he made small talk.

'Bella went to the bakery and got you some lunch for the journey – I picked it up on my way. It's in a carrier bag on the back seat along with a bottle of orange juice and some magazines.'

'Oh, how kind of her. I hate to let her down like this; I know the shop is busy at the moment.'

'Get the shop straight out of your mind, Marcie; she is very fond of you. And anyway, if push comes to shove I will give her a hand in the shop, so no worries there.'

Barry made sure she was put her on the train and waved her goodbye. When Marcie arrived at her destination Malcolm was there waiting for her.

'Aye lass, so glad to see you,' and Marcie's eyes filled with tears. 'Let's get you home, me bairn,' and they both got into the car.

On the journey home Malcolm could see Marcie was distressed. 'You'll be alright pet, you're here now and I'm so pleased you came to me. Nothing is ever as bad as it seems.'

When they arrived at the bungalow he took Marcie's coat and went into the kitchen to make a cup of tea. They both sat down and Marcie relayed her fears about her illness.

'That's a terrible blow hinny, having something thrown at you like that, but all I know is my Nancy was a fighter, bless her, and through all her pain and suffering she saw life as a challenge and never gave up. You have to do the same - who knows what's going to happen to any of us? But you must make the most of every day God gave you.'

Marcie was frustrated and before she knew it she had let loose. 'What man would ever want me knowing he had to look after me for the rest of my life when he could have it easier with someone in good health?'

'A man who truly loves you, warts and all. I nursed my Nancy all those years and remembered the person I first met - the illness hadn't changed her. I knew who she was: a caring, loving person who had a heart of gold and would do anyone a good turn. Life goes on Marcie, and I know what my Nancy would say if she was here - grab life by the balls because after all, none of us live forever, that's something we all have in common. Make the most of every day. Some people have a horrible life even though they have everything they could possibly want but are never contented and never find happiness in their lifetime. Sometimes hardship and struggling makes you appreciate life a lot more and keeps your feet firmly on the ground, making you a much stronger person.'

Marcie knew what Malcolm was trying to say, but at that precise moment she felt angry. Life wasn't fair. After her unhappy childhood she thought she had gone through enough. It was all too much to take in.

The following day Malcolm took Marcie for a stroll along the beach. 'This is what I love about living here - watching the crystal blue sea and the glorious sandy beaches. It's a beautiful sight when the boats come in at night and when you can see the sunset.'

'Do you get lonely?' Marcie asked.

'Of course I do from time to time, but I have my memories, and I was lucky I met someone like my Nancy; she gave me so much pleasure. Don't get me wrong, we had our arguments but it only lasted a few hours and the best thing was when it was bedtime we made up - she never believed couples should go to bed on an argument, and we stuck to that rule.'

'I envy you Malcolm; I don't know whether I will ever meet a couple like you two again.'

'You will meet someone one day Marcie, but you have to have faith - always hold on to your dreams. Oh, I forgot to tell you I got a phone call from Roy the other day. He phoned to say he has cancelled the wedding. Apparently he's now getting a lot of grief from his parents and was thinking of coming to stay with me at one point, but he has too much work on at the moment. It would have been good to see him. Pity he isn't here with me and you just like the old days in the B&B.'

'What did you tell him?' Marcie asked.

'I just told him he did the right thing. "When in doubt, do nought", as my Nancy used to say.'

Marcie could not believe what she was hearing. 'What do you think happened?'

'Who knows? But I think he did the right thing if he wasn't sure. Oh, and before I forget, he told me to tell you he wants you to get in touch with him; he would love to hear from you.'

'OK, not just yet, but I promise I will give him a ring sometime; I really miss him...'

Malcolm changed the subject when he saw the sadness in Marcie's eyes. 'Do you know what I fancy right now?'

'What?'

'A big ice cream with a flake in it.'

'Well, I will buy you one, my treat...and how about some fish and chips?'

'That sounds grand, my dear; I'm bloody starving.'

When it was time to head home they had both had a lovely day and when they got back to the bungalow Malcolm made some hot chocolate.

'You remembered I love that - my favourite bedtime drink.'

'I made that for my Nancy every night; I'm not too fussed myself - I prefer Horlicks,' Malcolm remarked yawning. 'I must be getting old Marcie; I get tired so easily these days. I'm off to bed now pet,' and he kissed her goodnight. 'See you in the morning.'

With all that sea air Marcie slept like a log and next morning felt thoroughly refreshed by the time she had washed and dressed. When she walked into the kitchen Malcolm was cooking the breakfast.

'Good morning!' I hope you're hungry.'

'Let me help, Malcolm; you can't be waiting on me.'

'No lass; old habits die hard. I always made breakfast every morning for my dear wife and I still get up at the same time every morning - even if I don't need to. Sit at the table and I'll dish up.' Bringing the frying pan to the table Malcolm began to put sausages on the plate in front of Marcie.

'Blimey, three's too much for me – one will do.'

'You're a growing lass.'

'But not a healthy one,' Marcie remarked with a serious face. Malcolm ignored her remarks adding bacon and egg to the plate, along with tomatoes and black pudding. 'I won't need anything else for the rest of the day after this lot. I'm going to pile the weight on at this rate.'

When Malcolm finally sat down to eat his breakfast the doorbell rang. 'Well, that's timing for you. For god's sake! My breakfast is going to get cold now.'

'You stay there and I'll answer it.' Marcie opened the door to see Shelly standing there.

'Marcie! What are you doing here? Malcolm never mentioned you were coming. It's lovely to see you - how have you been?'

Malcolm interrupted, 'Who's that Marcie? Your bloody breakfast is getting cold!'

Shelly walked into the kitchen. 'Just me; so sorry to disturb you, but I was wondering if you could do me a favour?'

'What's that?'

'Look after the bakery for a couple of hours. My daughter has a hospital appointment and I want to go with her.'

'You're a nuisance, you know that? But I know you did me a good turn helping me with the fence in the garden last week, so I can hardly refuse even if I wanted to.'

'Cheeky bugger!' Shelly replied, then turning to Marcie said, 'He can be a cantankerous old sod when he wants to be,' and they both laughed.

'What time do you want me to come?'

'Say about one o'clock?'

'Alright. Now let me eat my breakfast in peace and be off with you.'

When Shelly had gone, Marcie told Malcolm off for being rude.

'Don't be daft; she knows my banter and is used to me.'

'Can I make a quick phone call to Bella when we've had breakfast?'

'Yes of course...but don't be too long gassing hinny, the last bill cost me a fortune.'

Breakfast finished, Marcie cleared the table and went and phoned Bella.

'Marcie, good to hear from you. You OK? How's Malcolm?'

'We're both fine. I just thought I'd give you a quick ring, we're on our way out in a bit.'

'OK, love. Don't worry about the shop – everything's alright. You just look after yourself.'

'Well that's good. Give my love to Barry, and I'll speak to you at the weekend.'

'I will. You take care. Speak to you soon.'

'You too. Bye.' Marcie put the phone down and turned to Malcolm who was hovering behind her.

'I was thinking last night Marcie, what about if you come to live with me? You know I have the room... I just worry about you. What will you do when Bella sells the shop?'

'I'm not sure, Malcolm, but I feel I have to stay there till it happens, she's always been so good to me. I couldn't leave her in the lurch.'

'Fair enough, but you know there is always a home for you here...and I have a few bob in my bank account till you get yourself sorted.'

Marcie put her arms around him and gave him a kiss on the top of his head. 'I love you like a father and appreciate all that you and Nancy have done for me, but I can't run away from what's happened and I'll just have to take each day as it comes. But it's comforting to know you're here supporting me and it's my home if ever I need it. Thank you.'

Marcie washed up the breakfast things and Malcolm pottered in the garden watering the plants. The bungalow was clean and tidy as Malcolm had a cleaner come in once a week but when Marcie opened the fridge she could see he needed a big shop and went into the garden to talk to him.

'How about we go to the supermarket today? Looks like we need a few things.'

'Alright, but I like to be in and out - I hate standing in queues, it annoys me. I much prefer the small businesses on the high road, but the poor buggers are getting squeezed out by the large supermarkets and having to sell up. Just ordinary people trying to make a good honest living!'

'Have you finished, you moany old crow?'

Malcolm grinned. 'Put the kettle on me bairn, and I'll get changed. Are you coming to the bakery with me?'

'Why not? And we'll go shopping after that.'

They were sitting in the garden having their tea, nattering, when Malcolm looked at his watch and realised it was ten past one. 'Good god! Shelly will have her knickers in a twist – let's go.'

They got in the car and when they arrived Shelly was standing outside the shop all guns blazing. 'What the frigging hell time do you call this? We might miss the appointment now!'

'Sorry misses; keep your hair on,' said Malcolm giving her a hug.

Shelly and her daughter went off and Marcie put an apron on that was hanging on a peg at the back of the shop and went behind the counter with Malcolm. Twenty minutes passed and there had not been a customer in sight.

'Business must be slow. People should be rolling in, especially at lunch time.'

'I don't think Shelly cares, so long as she can make ends meet and pay her bills. She's not a greedy woman and has her regulars that she's known for years.'

Over the next couple of hours only a few customers came through the door. 'I'll tell you what...let's have two sausage rolls each and a cup of tea, I'm sure we deserve that for standing here the last few hours. It's what I call the perks of the job, and what the eye doesn't see the heart won't grieve.'

'You're a sly dog Malcolm, but I must admit, they do look tempting.'

When Shelley finally came back she couldn't thank them enough. 'Many customers?'

'Half a dozen, but I don't think you will be making your millions just yet,' Malcolm remarked.

'Just as well you're not married to me then, you skinflint,' laughed Shelly, and they all chuckled. Malcolm loved a woman with a bit of fire in her belly and in many ways that's why their friendship worked. 'I will give you a ring during the week, I can see you're itching to get off.'

Marcie gave Shelly and her daughter a hug and when she turned round Malcolm was out the door waiting on the pavement.

The supermarket was packed when they arrived and Malcolm did nothing but moan. 'I hate this bloody store...look at the prices - it blows my mind.' Marcie kept her cool; she knew not all men liked shopping and tried to be as quick as she could. An hour or so later they were loading the bags into the boot of the car.

'You look tired Malcolm; when we get home have a rest and I'll unload the car and unpack this lot and put it away.'

'Thanks lass; I do feel bushed. Old age is starting to set in and my back is killing me. I just need a few painkillers and that normally does the trick.'

When they arrived back at the bungalow Marcie insisted Malcolm go and lay down straight away, and he didn't put up an argument and went straight to bed. Marcie put the kettle on and made him a cup of tea and took it into him along with two painkillers.

'You're a good girl Marcie, but I should be looking after you, you're my guest.'

'Rubbish! You're my nearest and dearest and we should be looking after each other.'

And that's what they did for the following days, but after a fortnight Malcolm could see that Marcie was getting restless.

'I think it may be time for you to think about getting back to work,' he remarked one day when they were sitting having lunch in the kitchen. 'As much as I have loved having you here pet, life unfortunately must go on, and I can see you're getting bored.'

Marcie knew Malcolm was right but felt guilty - she loved him dearly but wanted to be independent for as long as she could be, plus she missed her friends in London.

'Come on now; let's see that lovely smile of yours. You're not to worry about me, I'm fine, and it's time to start thinking about yourself. How about we enjoy the rest of the day together and tomorrow I'll take you to get your train?'

'OK, but only if you're sure.'

'I'm sure, lass.'

The next day Malcolm took her to the station but on the way kept reminding her that there was always a home for her with him if ever things got too tough and he would never turn his back on her, as he loved her like a daughter. Marcie cried; she knew that, but had to face this problem head on and come to terms with the illness at some point, but at this moment in time she needed to keep herself busy with less time on her hands to think about the full extent of her diagnosis.

'We pass the cemetery in a moment and I'm going to stop and put some fresh flowers on Nancy's grave. There's a chap who sells them just outside.'

A few minutes later Malcolm pulled up and purchased a spray of yellow flowers and then drove slowly in through the gates of the cemetery and parked the car. They both got out and walked the short distance to the grave, Marcie desperately trying to swallow down the lump that was forming in her throat. As Malcolm replaced the wilting flowers with the fresh ones she could hold back the tears no longer and cried uncontrollably. Malcolm pulled her close and wrapped his strong arms around her, reassuring her of just how proud Nancy was of her and saying that all she would have wanted was for her to be happy, whatever choices she made in life.

Getting back into the car Malcolm's heart was filled with sadness as he knew the battle Marcie would have in the future fighting this awful disease. It was going to be an uphill struggle and would take all the strength she could muster, but he didn't want to show any sign of weakness and remained strong for her sake.

Arriving at the station, they both got out of the car and Malcolm opened the boot and handed Marcie her small suitcase. 'Don't forget to phone and let me know you've arrived home safely, will you girl?' he said smiling. Clearing his throat he added, 'And you take good care of yourself.' He loved this girl as if she was his own and was finding it hard to hold back the tears. Who knew what the future held for her with this illness? This was one problem he couldn't solve but he knew he would always be there for her no matter what; that's what his beloved wife would have wanted as Marcie had brought so much joy into their lives.

She hugged him tightly and promised to phone as soon as she got home. Waiting at the barrier he watched her go towards the station entrance and waved until she disappeared from view.

Chapter Nineteen

The train pulled into the station and Marcie got off and went to the taxi rank. On the short journey home she felt so alone, but then reminded herself that she was looking forward to getting back to work and seeing Bella. She just had to get back to normality - whatever that was.

As the taxi pulled up outside the flat she could see a man standing by her door with his back to her. Grabbing her case and paying the driver she walked up her path and he turned to face her.

'Roy! What are you doing here?'

'I've been waiting for you.'

'How did you know I was coming home?'

'Malcolm gave me a ring - he was worried about you coming back to an empty flat.'

'Roy I'm so pleased to see you...but you must have driven all night to get here.'

'Yeah, I did, but it was worth it.'

Marcie opened her door, her heart beating twenty to the dozen, hardly able to contain her feelings. She put her suitcase down, removed her coat and repeated, 'I am so pleased to see you.'

'I know, you told me already. Now, how about putting the kettle on and making me a nice cup of tea, I'm parched.'

Sitting down on the settee with their tea Roy immediately mentioned that Malcolm had told him all about her diagnosis. Marcie had mixed feelings – she was overjoyed to see Roy but she didn't need his sympathy and told him as much. 'Is that why you have come here – you're feeling sorry for me? Well, fuck you; I don't need your sympathy.'

'You're the most annoying person I have ever met, Marcie Thomas. The world doesn't revolve around you, you know. I care about you and if you don't know that by now I may as well walk out the door right this minute.'

The relief she felt was overwhelming and the floodgates opened. Wiping her eyes, she looked at Roy. 'I'm sorry. I admit I am on the defensive side but it's because I'm so scared - I haven't actually come to terms with it myself yet.'

'Well, you're not alone; we can work it out together.'

'I don't know about that Roy; we have never had a relationship. When you really get to know me it may not work...'

'You're thinking about the MS. Don't be stupid, I have loved you from the first time I met you...but if you don't feel the same way I can't do anything about that.'

'I do love you Roy, but I want you to realize what you're getting yourself into otherwise you could be making the biggest mistake of your life.'

'Let me be the judge of that,' and he put his arms around her and held her close.

'Can I ask you something? What went wrong with you and Kim?'

'What can I say? I am fond of her, I won't deny that – she's the mother of my child - but I don't think she ever really loved me, just wanted to marry me as a last resort having been through a succession of failed relationships. Better the devil you know and all that, and me owning properties made it a better deal for her at the time. I know someone would have come along eventually who she'd fall in love with and that would have been me out of her life. Let's just call it intuition.'

'Well. I think you are very special and anyone who gets you should think themselves lucky.'

'Then in that case you're a lucky girl, Marcie Thomas, because I am all yours,' he grinned and softly kissed her lips. She responded, surprised by the excitement she felt at his touch. Very slowly Roy began to remove her blouse, unbuttoning it and kissing her neck as he pushed the flimsy material gently back over her shoulders, and at the same time Marcie unbuttoned his shirt. When they were both naked Roy gently lifted her up and took her into the bedroom, laying her on the bed and easing himself on top of her. Exploring each other's bodies and kissing passionately, when he finally entered her Marcie was overcome with desire and with tears of happiness in her eyes they found their rhythm until they climaxed as one. Afterwards, relaxed and happy laying in Roy's arms, Marcie realised that she had never felt this way before and wished the last few weeks had just been a bad dream, but she knew that wasn't true and held on to him tightly and told him how much she loved him.

In the morning she woke to find she was alone. Calling his name she got no response so getting out of bed and putting her dressing gown on she went into the sitting room, but he was nowhere to be seen and when she looked out the window his car had gone. Bitterly disappointed and confused, she slumped down onto the settee – how could he do that to her? Just then she heard the key in the door and Roy came in holding a carrier bag. 'Breakfast,' he said cheerfully holding the bag aloft. Seeing the look on her face he put the bag down and went to her. Taking her in his arms he said, 'You thought I'd done a runner, didn't you?'

'Don't be daft!'

'Yes you did, ye of little faith.'

'What's in the bag?' she laughed.

'Oh, just some milk. I got up to make us a cup of tea and noticed you didn't have any. You'd left your door keys on the table so I thought I'd pop to the shops and get some.'

'I'll make some scrambled eggs on toast, I don't have much else in I'm afraid - I need to go shopping.'

'No don't worry about that, I'll take you out for lunch later on, I'm not really that hungry at the moment.'

Marcie made two mugs of tea and they relaxed on the settee.

'When are you going home?'

'Trying to get rid of me already?'

'Course not,' she laughed, 'but I know you have work commitments, that's all.'

'You're right, actually I have three blokes doing some work on one of the flats and I'll have to go back tomorrow...but what if I come and stay with you next weekend?'

'That would be great!' Then her face dropped. 'This is going to be a long distance relationship, isn't it?'

Roy wanted to reassure her but didn't know what to say. 'Look, the way I see it, if we are going to make a go of it I'll have to think about moving down here...'

'Why can't I move to Yorkshire and be with you there?'

'I was talking to Malcolm and he said London has the best hospitals...you know...if your illness gets worse...'

'Excuse me, but I can make up my own mind...and how dare you both talk about me behind my back. And anyway, how did he know we were getting together?'

'He didn't, he thought that when Bella has sold the shop you would think about maybe moving to Southend to live with him.'

'Roy, you would hate living here; I know you, you're a Yorkshire lad through and through!'

'Now who's calling the shots? I can find work anywhere - you forget, I have worked in London and Scotland and Wales, in fact anywhere the work takes me.'

'What about Molly?'

'I can commute and have her at weekends.'

'I'm a bit worried about Kim - she may give you a hard time, especially with you cancelling the wedding.'

'I'm not saying we won't have a few problems, but that's life and I can't imagine not having you in mine. I love you Marcie Thomas, and now I have you I'm not going anywhere,' and he leant over to kiss her.

Stopping him with a finger on his lips she said, 'That's not quite true, you're going back home tomorrow,' and they both laughed.

'Well in that case, Miss Thomas, I think we should make the most of our time together now,' he said taking her hand and leading her into the bedroom.

'Right, come on you, I think we should get dressed and we'll go to that greasy spoon café on the corner and have a late lunch - my stomach is starting to rumble, and later on tonight I will take you out for dinner or we can stay in with a take-away and a bottle of wine, whatever you fancy.'

'Sounds good to me - I'm such a lucky girl having you.'

Walking down the road hand in hand Marcie felt she was floating on air and was so proud to be with him, nothing was going to spoil her afternoon, until Roy asked her if she'd remembered to bring her tablets with her as she mustn't forget to take them after meals.

'You're on the ball, but do me a favour Roy, let's forget about my illness just for now and have a good time.'

'Sorry, my darling, but I will always worry about you.'

'I understand that but I don't want our relationship to be all about my illness.'

'That's why I fell in love with you; you're the most unselfish person I have ever met,' he said looking at her adoringly, 'but you must look after yourself.'

They sat down for lunch in the cafe and wished they have never entered the place, it was appalling. The tables hadn't been wiped down and the floor looked like it had never seen a mop, so on second thoughts they just ordered a cup of tea each.

'Christ,' Roy whispered, 'I can see why they call it a greasy spoon, it's disgusting,' and they quickly drank their tea, paid the bill and left.

'I'm so sorry Roy, I should have taken you somewhere else. Tell you what, let's get a fresh crusty loaf from the bakery and some cheese and take it home.'

Walking along the high street towards the bakers, Marcie said, 'Let's go and see Bella and let her know I'm back. The shop is just a bit further up the road.'

'Good idea,' said Roy, 'I'd love to meet her.'

They walked into the shop and Bella came out from behind the counter to greet them. 'Lovely to see you pet, but I didn't expect you home just yet.'

'I know but I feel fine and I want to introduce you to Roy, my boyfriend.'

Bella looked stunned but quickly put a smile on her face. 'Pleased to meet you Roy, I have heard so much about you.'

'Good things, I hope? Pleased to meet you, too Bella.'

'I must say, this is a bolt from the blue. When did this all happen?'

'He was waiting for me on the doorstep when I got home yesterday.'

Bella smiled and asked Marcie when she was coming back to work.

'Tomorrow, if that's alright with you?'

'We have missed you here, and so have our regular customers.'

'Marcie told me you're selling the shop,' Roy remarked.

'I don't really want to but there is so much I want to do in retirement before it's too late.'

'Well, I can certainly understand that. I bet it's a little goldmine right here in the middle of the high street. I can imagine business is good?'

'We get our busy periods. I have run the shop for many years and

I have to say I have no complaints.'

'Have you anyone interested in buying?'

'I did have, but he pulled out - he wanted bigger premises.'

Marcie pulled Roy's arm. 'Leave her alone, Roy, she will sell it eventually.'

'I'm just interested, that's all.'

'Would you both like a coffee? Bella asked. 'I was just about to make one. Ella's just popped to the shop for some biscuits.'

'No we're fine, thanks. We had better let you get on...and I'll see you tomorrow,' said Marcie kissing her on the cheek.

Just as they were leaving Ella came through the door. 'Marcie, good to see you, I've missed you!'

'Me, too. I hope you're behaving yourself?'

'My girlfriend has finished with me...'

'Less of that,' Bella interrupted, 'too much information. Get out the back and empty those boxes.'

'You're harsh sometimes, Bella.'

'You haven't been here having to listen to all the details of her love life – it drives me mad. She should have more sense; she's young and has her whole life in front of her.'

Marcie and Roy said their goodbyes and left the shop. Marcie was curious to know why Roy was so interested in the shop. 'I admire people in any kind of business. Bella is a tough old bird and has done well to keep it going on her own and I respect her for that.'

'You're a soft bugger, but I must admit when I have to leave the shop I will miss it; I love working there and I will miss Bella terribly...'

'What's going to happen to Ella?'

'She's a sweet little thing. I don't think she's worried – she's young enough to get a job anywhere.'

Is there a flat above the shop vacant?'

'No, Daisy lives there, she's an old lady, but Bella owns the whole building. What's going on in that head of yours Roy?'

'Nothing just wondered, that's all.'

'Come on, let's go home and we can order a takeaway, I want you all to myself.'

'Getting bossy already, Miss Thomas. I will have to keep my eye on you.'

They came to the off licence and Marcie waited outside while

Roy went in and bought two bottles of red wine and some crisps and peanuts for later. When he came out he noticed Marcie looked a little tired. 'Come on, let's get you home...and you still haven't taken your tablets.'

'Your fault chatting to Bella for too long, and we passed the bakery and forgot the crusty bread.'

'Blaming me, you little minx. Come on, let's get you home.'

They arrived back at the flat and Marcie quickly threw off her shoes - her feet were killing her. 'I don't understand that, we haven't done much walking and I feel knackered. What do you fancy to eat? An Indian, Chinese, or a pizza?'

'Spoilt for choice, but I think a pizza; what about you?'

'I'll have the same. Is margarita OK?'

'Great.'

'I'll give them a ring in a tick and you can pour me a glass of wine.'

Roy poured two glasses and relaxed on the settee. 'What are you up to Marcie?' he called.

'Just putting my pyjamas on to get comfy; I'll be out in a bit.'

Twenty minutes later the doorbell rang and Roy went and paid the pizza delivery boy. Hearing the doorbell Marcie came out of the bedroom at last. Her hair which had been up in a bun all day now fell in soft curls around her shoulders and she had applied a little make-up to freshen herself up.

'My god, you are a beauty...'

'Thank you kind sir, and you're not so bad yourself.'

They ate their pizza and chatted whilst almost finishing the two bottles of red wine between them, and after kissing passionately they made their way into the bedroom, but there was no hurry, they took things slowly and their love making went on for hours till they fell asleep in each other's arms.

When they woke the next morning they both felt hungover but happy, and Marcie got up and made a pot of strong black coffee. It was still early and she took it into the bedroom and got back into bed beside Roy.

'I can't believe you're leaving today... Drink your coffee, it'll make you feel a bit better,' she said passing him a cup.

'Thanks, I need that. I told you, I'll be back at the weekend. '

'Did you tell your mum and dad you were coming here?'

'Yes, I did. They've calmed down a bit now...once I sat down with them and explained my reasons for cancelling the wedding. I told them how I feel about you, too...and I really felt mum understood and came round in the end.'

'I don't think she likes me.'

'Rubbish, she doesn't know you! I think she just wants what any mother wants - me to be happy - but when she gets to know you she will love you like I do.'

'Oh well, I had better start getting ready for work – don't want to be late.'

'Don't worry about me – I'll have to be going myself soon, so see to yourself and I'll get breakfast at one of the motorway restaurants on the journey home.'

Once she was ready Marcie grabbed her bag, gave Roy a big hug and kiss, told him to drive carefully and phone her when he arrived home, and then rushed out of the door.

'Thank god you're here, Marcie,' said Bella who was in the shop window struggling with a mannequin, this really isn't my forte. I'll let you see to it, my joints are killing me.'

Marcie took off her coat and took over.

'He seems like a nice lad, Roy.'

'He is and he's coming to stay with me next weekend – I can't wait!'

'I thought he was getting married?'

'He called it off.'

'None of my business pet, but I hope he's a good 'un, you don't want to make another mistake.'

'I have never been so happy, Bella.'

'Good for you. He seems to be a sensible lad, but I hope you're taking precautions and he puts a condom on his John Thomas.'

Marcie blushed. 'Bella! You really are shameful!'

'You know me! I think at my age I can say what I want. I've been around the block too many times, and having a child can change your life forever.'

'We're making plans and I can't imagine my life without him now. He's the best thing that ever happened to me.' Marcie was grinning from ear to ear.

'I'm so happy for you both, but honesty is the best policy...and I assume he knows all about you having multiple sclerosis?'

'Yes, we have talked about it.'

'Good, that's all I wanted to know to put my mind at rest. Oh, I forgot to tell you, poor Daisy upstairs has been taken into hospital with pneumonia. And this time it's serious – the doctors don't think there's much hope.'

'Oh dear; what a shame. When did this happen?'

'A couple of days after you went away.'

'That's sad; she's such a character – I really liked her.'

'I've visited her in the hospital a few times, but I know death when it's staring you in the face. I've seen it once before...and I would say she has lost the will to live.'

'I would like to visit her. Do you think I'd be allowed?'

'I wouldn't bother pet, she wouldn't know who you are.'

'That makes me feel so sad...'

'That's life I'm afraid, but she has had an interesting life and done so much...and it comes to all of us in the end.'

The bell over the shop door rang and Jane came in.

'My god you *are* back. I've been phoning you but got no answer.'

'I meant to phone you but too much has been going on...'

Jane and Bella exchanged knowing looks. Bella had confided in her about Marcie's illness as she thought she could do with all the support she could get. 'It doesn't matter. Anyway, how are you?'

'I'm alright.'

'I was thinking about coming around to yours tonight and having a catch up. I phoned Zoe and she wants to come too.'

'What about Josh?'

'Don't worry; Charlie is going to baby sit.'

Marcie wasn't stupid and turned to Bella. 'You told her, didn't you?'

'I may have, but I was worried about you...and before you get on your high horse, they were annoyed you didn't let them know.'

'Too true!' Jane butted in. 'We are supposed to be good friends. How dare you shut us out?' she said, her voice softening and a sympathetic look on her face.

'What time are you coming?'

'About seven and Zoe will be there about seven-thirty, if that's OK?'

'I'll cook something.'

'No you won't; we'll get a takeaway or I'll go to the chippie and get some cod and chips.'

'Do me a favour and don't bring any booze with you, I'm still suffering from last night.'

'Who were you with?'

'Bugger off, I have work to do. I'll give you all the gossip later.'

'Alright, see you later on. Bye Bella, lovely to see you,' said Jane leaving the shop.

'To be truthful, Bella, I'm bushed. I wanted to go home and have an early night.'

'Stop moaning girl, they were worried about you, and if they stay too long just tell them to go home – I'm sure they'll understand.'

'You're right...and to be honest, I have missed our girlie chats. Where is Ella by the way?'

'God knows, but she will get a piece of my mind when I phone her.'

Towards late afternoon the shop started to get busy and an awkward customer came in complaining that her dress had shrunk in the wash.

'What setting did you have it on?' asked Bella.

'Hot, it was grubby.'

'Well that was a bit silly – look, it says a delicate wash on the label.'

'Don't you call me silly, you old bag!'

Marcie was furious. 'Who the hell do you thinking you're talking to, speaking to my nan like that?' and walked in front of her with her hands on her hips. Apologise right now!'

'Look, I'm sorry, but I wanted to wear it tonight. Can't I have another one?'

'Definitely not. Now get out of my shop!' and the woman quickly made an exit.

'Your nan, Marcie? Couldn't you have said your mum?'

'Hardly!' and they both starting laughing.

'You can be a feisty girl when you start.'

'I have my moments...and I think I deserve a cuppa and a large piece of chocolate cake for that.'

'Do you now?' Bella took some money out of the till and gave it

266

to her. 'Go on then, off to the bakery...and bring me back the change.'

A little later on Marcie's return to the shop Bella was on the phone. 'Ah, she's here now Roy, I'll pass you over.'

Hearing Roy's name mentioned Marcie hurried to the phone and took the receiver from her. 'Roy! You're home then?'

'Yes, I left just after you and the traffic wasn't bad at all.'

'You are still coming the weekend?'

'Yes, of course, I can't wait to see you.'

'Have you seen your mum and dad yet? Have you told them we're together now? How did they take it?'

'Blimey! Twenty questions!' he said laughing. 'Yes I have and everything's fine. In fact Mum's dying to meet you and even wants us to stay for a weekend with them.'

'Tell them thank you so much and that I'd love to, just as soon as I can get a Saturday off.'

'Will do. Look, I have to go. I hadn't been home five minutes and I got a call to say the fucking plasterer hasn't turned up at one of the jobs - excuse my language, but I'm bloody annoyed because I have to try and get someone else to do the job now. Love you so much, and I can't wait for the weekend to come.'

'Me too! Love you.'

Bella was standing quite close and heard every word. 'He seems to be quite keen on you, pet.'

'I feel the same way. By the way, when are you next going to visit Daisy?'

'Funny you should ask, I was just about to give the hospital a ring to see if she's up to having visitors. Watch the shop for a moment and I'll go out the back and call.'

When Bella returned Marcie could see by her face that it wasn't good news. 'What did they say?'

'She's failing fast. They said they'd be surprised if she lasts the night. They asked me if I know of any relatives they can contact, but the sad thing is I never saw any other visitors at the hospital and the nurse I just spoke to confirmed that I'm the only she's had, that's why they've told me what's happening even though I'm not related. I know she had a brother who passed away; he and the social workers were the only people who popped in upstairs to see her from time to time. I'll go to the hospital in a while to sit with her, not that she'll know I'm there, but she deserves someone with her in her last hours, bless her. What a wonderful human being she was - I was very fond of her - salt of the earth.'

'That's awful Bella; do you want me to lock up the shop?'

'No, but later on you can take some money to the bank for me and buy a mixed bunch of flowers at the florist for Daisy - something nice for her to look at; she loved her garden where she used to live. She showed me photos once and it was a fabulous house – like a mansion – and the garden was out of this world, magnificent. I think if I remember correctly, that lilies are her favourite.'

'No problem, I'll see what they have.'

The rest of the day was fairly busy and as soon as there was a lull Bella gave Marcie the takings she wanted banking and some money to get the flowers.

When Marcie returned to the shop half an hour later carrying a lovely mixed spray of flowers, including beautiful white lilies, Bella was more than happy. 'They are gorgeous, Marcie. Right, you can get off home now, love, I'm going to give Ella a ring and see where she got to today and then I'm off to the hospital.'

Marcie thanked her, and grabbed her coat and bag. 'See you tomorrow. Give my love to Daisy, won't you?'

'I will. See you tomorrow.'

Bella dialled the number. 'Ella, what the hell are you playing at? No phone call – nothing! I should sack you...'

'I'm so sorry Bella, but I was at the hospital with my mum; she had pains in her chest.'

'Oh dear. How is she now?'

'She's fine. They said it was caused by her angina; she hadn't been taking her tablets.'

'Alright, but next time young lady, you give me a ring.'

'I promise I will, it's just I was so worried about her it slipped my mind, but I'll be in tomorrow.'

'Well you will lose a day's wages; I'm not running a charity here.'

'I understand. I'll see you in the morning.'

'OK. Bye.'

Marcie got back to her flat and decided to give it a quick clean.

When she was satisfied it looked presentable she made herself a cup of tea and sat down to drink it. She was dreading her friends coming tonight - she didn't want their sympathy, just a good time like they used to have, and made up her mind there and then to tell them no doom and gloom. She was in a positive mood.

The doorbell rang and she put her cup down on the coffee table and answered the door to see Jane standing there holding two bottles of wine.

'For Christ's sake, I thought I told you no booze tonight!'

'Oh shut up! You may not fancy a drink but I do - I have been working my bollocks off at the hospital and it's my quality time.'

'Alright, alright, I get the message. Come on in...and you may as well pour me one, too. Hair of the dog, and all that...'

Jane chuckled. 'You're a pain in the arse sometimes Marcie, do you know that?'

'Well that's blown my theory on you coming round to give me the sympathy vote!'

'No chance. You're strong enough for the both of us, and in my experience, being a nurse, you have to go on no matter what. And I reckon that if anyone can cope with the MS, you can. You're still my best friend who I first met all those years ago in my mum's hotel and you haven't changed – you're still the same person.'

'That's what I love about you Jane, say it as it is, you insensitive bitch!' and they both giggled. Marcie knew Jane well enough to know she was putting on a brave face and not knowing what to say.

Zoe arrived fifteen minutes later and brought some wine as well. 'I'm not being funny girls but my stomach thinks my throats been cut – who's going to get some grub in?'

Jane offered to go down the chippie and get them all cod and chips and that left Zoe and Marcie alone to have a good gossip.

'What been happening in your life, Zoe?'

'Much the same, really. Josh is growing fast and Charlie loves working in the garden centre. I feel a bit trapped at home sometimes, but don't get me wrong, I love being a mum and Charlie is a fantastic dad but I would love to finish off my course and do something with my life.'

'You should,' Marcie said, 'don't let that stop you.'

'I'm sorry to hear about your illness Marcie, how are you coping?'

269

'It was a shock at first but maybe my childhood made me strong because I try to make every day a positive one.'

Zoe bent over and gave her a hug. 'You know I will always be here for you no matter what, don't you?'

'I know that, but at the moment I feel fine. Now, let's have another drink.'

Jane was complaining when she walked through the door with the fish and chips. 'Bloody hell! Their prices have gone up - I just had enough on me.'

'I'll pay for them,' Zoe offered, and immediately got up to get her purse from her bag.

'No you won't, my treat,' said Jane, 'but will you do me a favour and pour me a glass of wine and I'll put the food on some plates.' They all sat at the table and there was a deadly silence.

'What's wrong with you two? You don't have to walk on egg shells for me, you know. Just spit it out. What's on your mind?'

'Well, what I really want to know is how you and Roy got together. Did you get in touch with him?'

'No, Malcolm told him what I was going through and he turned up on my doorstep when I got back home.'

'Special delivery, eh?'

'Shut up, Jane, no sarcy comments! We had a great time and he is coming to stay this weekend...and before you ask, we are planning to move in together in the future.'

'What about his daughter?'

'What about her? Roy will always have contact with her and she can stay with us whenever she wants; holidays, etc.'

Zoe was more concerned about the distance between them and chose her words carefully. 'I can't see how it will work out, Marcie. I hope it does, but Roy lives in Yorkshire and you are living here...'

Marcie was getting irritated. 'We have talked about it and he is willing to move here if need be - we're not stupid!'

Jane quickly changed the subject. 'That scumbag Peppi is seeing an auxiliary nurse at the hospital. Justin doesn't have anything to do with him after what he did to you.'

'It's water under the bridge; she's welcome to him. We weren't seeing each other that long anyway.'

'Are you speaking to Amy?'

'I haven't been, but I think I might give her a ring.'

'Why?'

'I believe her when she said she never had sex with Peppi, and to be honest, having the illness has put everything into perspective. We all make mistakes and I do miss Tilly and Biba.'

'You're a fool,' Zoe piped up.

'But hopefully she might have learnt her lesson - I just feel sorry for the kids.'

'I have some news for you.'

'What's that Jane? Don't tell me you're pregnant,' Zoe said sarcastically.

'No, I'm not, but I'm getting engaged to Justin this Saturday and I'm having a party in the evening and you are both invited. I hope Charlie and Roy will come. What about Bella, Marcie? I like her; I hope she'll come.'

'I'm not sure about that but I'll ask her tomorrow and let you know. Congratulations! So pleased for you both!' and Marcie raised her glass. 'To Jane and Justin!'

Zoe hugged Jane. 'That's amazing; I am so happy for you both! Would it be alright if my mum came along as well?'

'The more the merrier...but could you all bring a bottle of wine with you?'

'Good god, Jane,' Marcie laughed, 'you do take the biscuit. Should we bring some food as well?'

'That's alright, I can manage that.'

'All I can say is you're hardly the hostess with the mostest, just a penny pinching little madam...and I feel sorry for poor Justin. I just hope he knows what he's letting himself in for!'

'Marcie Thomas, hold your tongue!' laughed Jane.

'I will have to agree with Marcie; Scrooge has got nothing on you, Jane,' added Zoe.

Jane looked at her watch. 'Oops! I've got to go, Justin's expecting me.'

'I hope it wasn't anything we said?' Marcie laughed.

'Piss off you two; that's the last time I pay for your dinner.'

'We're joking,' they said in unison.

'I know, but I have got feelings you know.'

Zoe grinned at Jane. 'Let's go - my Josh will need his night feed and Charlie will be tearing his hair out; I said I wouldn't be too long.'

'Lovely seeing you both. Thanks for coming, and I will see you Saturday at the party,' Marcie said, getting up to see them to the door. 'Take care and I'll see you both soon.' It had been an enjoyable evening and she felt lucky that she had good friends like them.

The following morning when Marcie went into work, the first thing she noticed was that Bella looked worse for wear.

'What's up Bella? You look knackered.'

'I was at the hospital till the early hours of the morning when poor Daisy took her last breath. But she looked peaceful when she passed away, bless her.'

'I'm so sorry...anything I can do?'

'Yes, you're in charge of the shop. I'm going home to get some rest - I only came in to open up. I'll be back at closing time to cash up,' she said grabbing her coat and bag and making her way to the front of the shop. 'See you later.'

Within five minutes she had returned. 'Marcie, I've just remembered something. Here's the key to Daisy's flat if the social worker comes round, but make sure you get it back,' she said putting it on the counter. 'Right, I'm off; see you later.'

Ella came hurrying into the shop five minutes later. 'You're lucky, you've just missed Bella; she's just left. She told me she gave you an earful on the phone for not turning up for work.'

'It wasn't my fault!'

'I know, but she's got a lot on her mind at the moment so if it happens again just give her a ring.'

'Don't you start, Marcie, I've had Mum on my back.'

'What have you been up to now?'

'I sneaked my girlfriend Gemma through my bedroom window and Mum caught us together in bed this morning when she brought me in a cuppa. I forgot to set the alarm clock to wake up early enough to get her out the house.'

'You want your arse kicking, Ella. Your mum must find you a handful. Well, she won't trust you now.'

'I know, but I'll cook the dinner when I get home, that will please her.'

'Are you a good cook?'

'Lousy, I just do frozen chips, frozen hamburgers and baked beans to go with it, but they seem to like it.'

'Hardly cordon bleu cooking!'

'What's that?'

'Never mind,' Marcie smiled, 'just go and put the kettle on and make us both a cup of tea.'

The shop was quiet so Marcie took full advantage and phoned Roy.

'Hello my darling, I wasn't expecting to hear from you this morning.'

'I'm in the shop with Ella on my own, Bella has gone home - Daisy passed away in the early hours of the morning.'

'That's sad, I know you were fond of her.'

'I didn't know her that well; it was Bella who kept an eye on her.'

'I was thinking of coming Friday afternoon till Sunday night - is that alright? I know you will be working all day Friday but I will let myself in, just put the key under the plant pot outside.'

'That'll be great. I miss you Roy.'

'Me too, but I'll be there before you know it. Listen, I have to go Marcie, the lads are waiting for me to give them a lift to the builder's yard. Love you, and I'll see you soon.'

Ella had put both mugs of tea on the counter and after Marcie put the phone down remarked, 'I reckon Bella will have your guts for garters, Marcie. You know she doesn't like you using her phone for personal calls – just saying...'

'You cheeky little mare! Don't push your luck with me - I'm in charge now so you can go out the back and wash the floors and clean the toilet.'

'I was just kidding! No need to get your knickers in a twist!'

'Right, now I'm really going to lose my temper,' and Marcie chased her around the shop laughing.

Marcie phoned Amy later on in the afternoon. When she answered she wasn't sure what to say.

'How are you?' enquired Marcie rather formally.

'I'm doing alright, but it's good to hear from you Marcie.'

'Look Amy, I know we have had our differences in the past - and I am still pissed off with you - but let's start again.'

'I've missed you and so have the girls and we would love to see you.'

'Do you remember my friend Jane? She's getting engaged on Saturday and if you haven't got the girls at the weekend you could drive to my flat Saturday around seven and come with me and my boyfriend, Roy.'

'That will be lovely...but are you sure?'

'Jane won't mind - just bring a bottle of wine with you.'

'That sounds great. Actually, John has the girls this weekend and I would love to come.'

'That's settled then. See you on Saturday.'

'It will be great to have a catch up; see you then.'

Marcie felt relieved when she put the phone down. She liked Amy and maybe she would finally see Biba and Tilly who she was so fond of.

There weren't many customers the rest of the day and when Bella cashed up she was disappointed with the takings. It was the worst day in a long time, but she knew running a shop had its ups and downs and always took it in her stride.

Marcie mentioned to Bella about the engagement party on the Saturday and that Jane had invited her.

'That's good of her but my days of partying after working all week are over pet. I will leave it to you youngsters. Barry and I love sitting watching TV on a Saturday night with our meals on a tray. I know we are boring old farts but when you get to our age that's all we need, but I will get her a card and a bottle of wine and you can take it to her from us and wish her all the best. I think it was very sweet of her to ask all the same.'

'No worries, I'm sure she'll understand,' said Marcie putting on her coat. She hugged Bella. 'See you tomorrow.'

'Yes, see you tomorrow, pet.'

Marcie was glad to get home. Her joints were painful and she remembered she hadn't taken her tablets at lunchtime. A hot drink and a bath would help, then she would put her feet up and watch TV. Bugger, she thought when the phone rang. She picked it up reluctantly. 'Hello? Hello, who is it?' she could barely hear as it was such a bad line.

'It's me, Doris. I'm phoning from work.'

'I'm sorry I didn't get back to you Doris; so much has been happening. How are you?'

'I'm fine. I phoned to thank you - did Bella not tell you?'

'Tell me what?'

'She got me a job working at a hostel for girls in Camden. It's only part-time but I love it.'

'That's great news, Doris! What do you do?'

'I'm the cook but I have an assistant working with me.'

'When did this happen?'

'Whilst you were away at Malcolm's in Southend.'

Marcie was puzzled. 'I wonder why Bella didn't tell me.'

'Perhaps she forgot.'

'That isn't like her; mind you, she has had a lot on her plate lately.'

'Look, don't get annoyed Marcie, but she told me about you having multiple sclerosis. I'm so sorry my darling, that's so unfair. If you need anything at all I'm here for you.'

'I know you are, you're a good friend Doris, and no, I'm not cross at all; you would have found out anyway. Actually, I've just walked in the door from work and my feet are killing me, can I phone you later or tomorrow?'

'No worries; go and put your feet up my lovely.'

Marcie had a hot bath, put her pyjamas on and made herself a coffee. She didn't feel hungry so sat relaxing on the settee watching the TV. About an hour later the doorbell rang. I don't believe it, she thought to herself, no peace for the wicked.

'It's only me!' came Bella's voice through the letterbox.

Marcie jumped up and opened the door. 'Anything wrong Bella?'

'No, I just came round to give you the keys to the shop. Something has come up so I need you to be in charge the next few days.'

'Come on in.'

'OK, but just for a few minutes. I also wanted to ask you where the keys to Daisy's flat are.'

'Sorry, I should have said - I left them in the drawer behind the counter.'

'No problem, as long as I know.'

'I've just come off the phone to Doris. She rang to say you got her the job in Camden.'

'Oh yes, I forgot to tell you – it must have slipped my mind. It was all down to her own merit. I gave her the address and she was interviewed and then I got a phone call from Mrs Heslop who runs the place to say she was satisfied with her CV and she was going to give her the position. To be honest, with her years of experience it was in the bag - she was an ideal candidate for the job. Now, I must dash but I will give you a ring tomorrow. Just don't let Ella run rings around you; she can be a little devil when she wants to be.'

Chapter Twenty

The week flew by and Friday soon came round. Marcie had butterflies in her stomach and couldn't wait to finish work knowing that Roy would be there when she got home.

Ella had just made them both a cup of tea after lunch when the phone rang. Marcie picked it up. 'Bella's Boutique. How may I help you?'

'It's me, Roy. I'm at your flat having a cold beer. What time do you finish work?'

'Not sure, but I think I'll probably get home around about 6.30.'

'Why so late?'

'I've been in charge all week. Bella hasn't rung me to say she's coming in tonight to cash up so that means I'm doing it and I finish a bit later.'

'Don't worry pet, I'll take you out tonight for a meal.'

'I don't mean to be ungrateful Roy, but that's the last thing I want. Can we just get a takeaway?'

'Of course, no problem. Can't wait to see you later. Love you.'

'You too! Must go and do some work. See you later.'

Bella did arrive at 6 o'clock and was pleased with the takings. 'I think I should be away more often, Marcie; the shop has been busy. Well done.' Bella handed her a carrier bag.

'What's this?'

'There's a card I want you to give Jane and a bottle of whisky for the two of them.'

'Thanks Bella, they will appreciate that.'

'Have a good weekend. Now off you go...and you, Ella – you *can* pull your weight when you want to. Marcie has been so pleased with your work. She said you were very good with the customers, although I think seeing is believing in your case.'

Marcie hugged Bella and walked out the shop. 'Night all.'

Ella was dragging her feet, seemingly not wanting to leave right away.

'What's on your mind, Ella?'

'I was just wondering if you could give me a pay rise...'

'You are a cheeky little monkey! When you have earned it you can have one. You haven't been working here that long!'

'I only asked.'

'And now you have your answer you can get going!' Ella hurried out the shop. Bella watched her go, a smile on her face. It was funny, but in a way she reminded her of herself when she was her age - she had a lot of spunk and was never too shy to speak her mind.

When Marcie arrived home Roy was waiting with open arms. 'I'm just running you a hot bath and there is a bottle of wine in the fridge; we can order a takeaway later. It's so good to see you; I've missed you...' he said, and kissed her gently.

'Me too. That sounds wonderful,' she said smiling, 'but I hope you will join me - it seems a shame to waste all that lovely hot water just on me.'

'Well I could do with a nice soak after driving all this way.'

'A nice soak wasn't quite what I had in mind,' she laughed, leading him towards the bedroom.

They slowly undressed each other and walked naked hand in hand into the bathroom.

'Oh Roy, this is so romantic!' The bath was surrounded by tea lights and candles and almost overflowing with scented bubbles.

Roy quickly turned off the taps.

Marcie was delighted. 'You are so thoughtful.'

Roy kissed her lips and took her hand helping her into the bath. When he had joined her he picked up the soap and gently started to wash her all over, massaging her breasts gently and kissing her neck. 'You are just perfect Marcie; so beautiful,' he whispered between kisses. Marcie then took the soap from him and began to reciprocate...the chemistry between them was electric. When they could wait no longer they slowly made love and when it was all over she was in no doubt that this was what she wanted for the rest of her life. She was truly happy and had never felt like this before with any man.

'I'm chilly Roy, are you?'

'Yes, this water's going cold. Come on, let's get you out of here.'

After they had dried each other off, Roy helped her on with her dressing gown and they went into the sitting room. He poured them a glass of chilled wine and Marcie phoned and ordered pizza before they snuggled up on the settee. Marcie became quiet.

'Are you alright?'

'I 'm scared Roy?'

'Why?'

'My illness is going to get worse; there is no cure you know.'

'I know that, but I was so lucky to come out of my coma the way I did and it taught me one thing - live each day as it comes. If you love someone, warts and all, you make the most of what you have and appreciate every minute with them. I can never imagine my life without you now.'

'Have you spoken any more with your parents about us?'

'I'm not going to lie to you, when I told them about your illness they had reservations about the future. But all parents worry about their children, it's natural.'

'Not mine,' she remarked looking sad.

'I know you didn't have the best start in life, but I'm here now Marcie, and I love you. I think you have to put the past behind you.'

'My god, your parents must hate me coming into your life.'

'Don't be silly. When I explained how I felt about you they said I must make my own decisions and they wished us every happiness. They will give us all their support if need be. I've not long sold one of my flats and the other two are on the market and have had a bit of interest shown already so I'm confident they'll sell and we'll be OK for money.'

Just then the doorbell rang and Roy got up to answer it to see a dishevelled young lad standing there looking shaken.

'So sorry mate, but I have just been knocked off my bike and your pizza has been nicked.'

'Where did this happen?'

'Just across the road.'

'Are you alright?'

'I'm OK, but do you want to order another one?'

'No, that's alright; I'll get some fish and chips instead.'

When he went back in the sitting room he put on his coat.

'What's up Roy? Where are you going?'

Bloody rough area this is. Some bugger has pushed the poor pizza lad off his bike and gone off with our pizza so I'm going down the chippie. What do you fancy?'

Oh, poor thing! Is he OK?'

'Yes, just a bit shaken. What are you having?'

'Cod and chips, please.'

'I won't be long. Be back soon.'

Marcie went into the kitchen and got a tablecloth out of the drawer and the plates out of the cupboard. She set the table and lit a candle. She chuckled to herself. If he can be romantic so can I, she thought, dimming the lights.

When Roy returned he smiled. It's only cod and chips pet; 'I'm used to eating them out of the paper - saves washing up.'

Marcie's faced dropped. 'Thanks for spoiling the surprise!'

'Don't be daft, it's lovely. I was only teasing you.' Roy sat at the table. 'Just one thing though; where are the flowers?'

Marcie threw the tea towel at him. 'I can see I have my work cut out being with you.'

After they had eaten they watched a bit of TV and then went to bed and fell asleep in each other's arms.

When they eventually got up the next day after a lie in, Marcie made some scrambled eggs on toast and a pot of coffee. Breakfast over, Roy helped her tidy the flat and they got washed and dressed. They were both looking forward to Jane's engagement party that evening and Marcie asked Roy if he would go and get a card and a couple of bottles of wine.

'You look pale today Marcie, are you alright?'

'I'm fine, I just feel a bit weak on my legs and get tired very easily.'

'How are you managing at work?'

'It's not too bad. When there's not much to do Bella lets me sit on the stool behind the counter.'

'You just sit down and relax on the settee for now. Is there anything else you need while I'm out?'

'I need loads but it's not fair sending you out to do the shopping.'

'Don't be silly, I don't mind,' and he went to get a pen and paper out of the drawer and handed it to her. 'Here; write me a list and I'll get everything.'

'Well, only if you're sure.'

'Yes, course I am.'

'Don't buy any carrier bags, there's some in the kitchen drawer, and my purse is in my bag behind the armchair.'

'You don't need it; I'll pay for this, no worries.'

'Are you sure?'

'What do you think? Now let me get going. Do you want me to make you a cup of tea before I go? You haven't taken your tablets yet.'

'No, I'll make it myself and take my tablets. Thanks so much Roy, you're a sweetheart.'

'No problem. Now you relax and I'll see you later love,' and he kissed her on the forehead.

He hadn't been gone five minutes when Jane rang. 'Are you still coming tonight?'

'Too right I am! We are both looking forward to it, Jane.'

'Great. Is Bella coming?'

'No, but she has given me a card and a bottle of whisky for you both.'

'That was good of her. When you see her, will you thank her from us?'

'I will. Have you got your ring?'

'No, not yet. Justin's taking me to the jewellers in the high street this afternoon. I'm so excited!'

'I hope he's got plenty of money, I know how high maintenance you can be,' Marcie laughed.

'Well you only get engaged once and I don't want any cheap rubbish.'

'Tell Justin congrats and that I said if he has any sense he'll leave his credit cards at home and take you to Woolworths. They're doing a deal at the moment – buy one get one free!' She loved to wind Jane up.

'All I can say is thank god you're not coming with me, jealous bitch!' Jane laughed.

'No, seriously, we're really looking forward to the party Jane. Enjoy your afternoon and we'll see you later.'

'Will do – can't wait!'

A couple of hours later Roy arrived home carrying six bags of shopping. 'Goodness me, Roy, did you buy the whole store?'

'I noticed your freezer was empty so I got you chicken, chops, steak and mince, as well as everything on the list. Hold on a minute...I've left the flowers I got you in the car.'

When Roy came back with a huge bunch of pink and white carnations she was delighted and threw her arms around his neck and kissed him. 'You are the best thing that ever happened to me Roy Clark and I love you.'

'I hope so. I do like to make good investments.'

'You cheeky sod! Now let me put the shopping away and you sit down and have a cold beer, you deserve it.'

'I won't say no; its thirsty work this shopping lark.'

Marcie put all the shopping away and carefully arranged the flowers in a vase. 'Do you want me to make you a sandwich?'

'In a minute. Come and sit down and talk to me. I was thinking, would you like to come up to West Yorkshire and meet my parents and my sister next weekend?'

'I'd love to but Bella likes me to work some Saturdays and as I'm off today the chances are she'll want me in next week, but I'll ask her. We're not staying with them are we?'

'No, as you know, two of my flats are still up for sale so we can stay in one of those.'

'I hope they like me, your mum and dad...'

'I'm sure they will love you when they get to know you, just like I do. I'd hate to live round here Marcie. If I move to London I want something better than this.'

'You're a snob Roy; beggars can't be choosers.'

'I know that, and the area's nice but the flats are on top of one another, they all look the same and there aren't many trees or gardens around.'

'I hope you aren't going to be too materialistic; I'm just a simple girl and could live anywhere as long as I have you.'

'Alright then, I'll buy you a shed. Will that do?'

'I wouldn't go that far,' she laughed. Come on, let's eat, I'm hungry.'

Later on after a relaxing afternoon chatting and listening to music, they were getting ready for the party when Amy rang.

'Marcie, I'm so sorry but I won't be able to make it tonight after all - John wants me to have the girls.'

'That's alright. How about we meet up next week?'

'I'd love that. Give me a ring after the weekend and we'll arrange it. Enjoy yourselves tonight and give my congratulations to Jane and Justin.'

'Will do. Speak to you next week. Bye...and say hello to the girls for me.'

'I will. Bye.'

Marcie put the phone down and turned to Roy. 'Amy can't come, she has the girls now.'

'That's a shame. Never mind,' he remarked, 'but I think we should get dressed now or we'll be late.'

When they were ready Marcie thought Roy looked so handsome in his grey suit and blue tie. He was equally impressed with the bright red dress she had chosen, which clung to her lovely figure, and worn with sexy black high heels he thought she looked stunning.

'Do you think I should wear my hair up or down?'

'Down.' He adored her long black, curly hair and beautiful brown eyes. 'You look amazing.'

'Thank you kind sir...and you look very handsome – I'm loving the suit. Have you got the drinks and cards? Don't forget Bella's things.'

'I've got everything. Now come on Marcie, otherwise we will be late.'

When they arrived at the flat in Highgate they could hear the music blaring before they got to the front door. They rang the bell.

'Come in, come in,' said Jane opening the door. 'Everyone is here. Zoe and Charlie arrived about an hour ago. And this must be Roy. Pleased to meet you...I've heard so much about you.'

Roy shook Jane's hand. 'All good I hope! Pleased to meet you, too.'

'Give me your coats and I'll get you both a drink.'

Marcie couldn't believe how many people there were – none of whom she had seen before. Jane took their coats and put them in the bedroom and poured them both a glass of wine. 'You look surprised Marcie.'

'I was expecting half a dozen people...'

'Blame Justin, he invited all the student doctors from the hospital and their girlfriends. Seen my ring?' she said holding out her left hand and wiggling her fingers.

'It's beautiful, Jane, really lovely,' she said pulling her hand nearer to have a closer inspection. It was a small green emerald set in diamantes. 'I'm envious – it's beautiful...and I'm so pleased for you both.'

'Yes, it is,' agreed Roy. 'Congratulations.'

'Where's Zoe?' asked Marcie.

'On the balcony, but Charlie has been knocking them back; he's a bit worse for wear by the looks of it!'

Justin came over and chatted to Roy, and Marcie went to the balcony to find Zoe.

'Caught you, you little bugger, smoking a cigarette! I thought you had stopped?'

'Don't you start! Charlie hates me smoking, he thinks I'll be like my mum, a pot head. She's still smoking hashish...'

'You don't do that now though, do you?'

'Bloody hell, no! But I love a ciggie when I'm having a drink.'

'Is your mum here?'

'No, I couldn't find a babysitter so she's at home looking after Josh.'

'Oh, right. I can't believe Jane's engaged. Do you think you'll ever marry Charlie?'

'We have talked about it, but you know me, in my opinion a ring on your finger doesn't change anything and we're happy the way we are. But who knows? One day I may change my mind.'

'What about you?'

'I would love to marry Roy but he hasn't asked me yet. It's still early days.'

"I think you have a good man there Marcie; he adores you, I can tell.'

'I hope so. I have never felt so happy.'

'Come on, we had better find Charlie before he gets too paralytic; I want to keep my eye on him. Bless him; we don't get out that often any more as he's always working.'

The party was a success and everyone enjoyed themselves. At two in the morning Roy could see Marcie was getting very tired and told her he thought it was time to leave.

'Thanks so much for coming,' said Jane hugging them both.

'Yes, thanks guys,' added Justin as they showed them to the door.

'Come up for dinner at the flat sometime or we could all go out for a meal.'

''That would be great; thanks mate,' said Roy shaking Justin's hand. 'See you both soon.'

Sunday was spent going for a walk around Hampstead Heath and they stopped to have a meal at Kenwood House with views overlooking the lake. It was a perfect finish to a lovely weekend.

When it was time to say goodbye Marcie felt downhearted, but Roy reassured her he would pick her up on the Friday evening to visit his parents, all being well with Bella, and he would ring her tomorrow to find out if she could have Saturday off work.

When he had left, the flat felt empty and quiet and Marcie was reminded just how much she hated living on her own. She hoped that one day they would get engaged but she was petrified Roy's parents would think he was taking on too much having her in his life.

It had been a hectic weekend and Marcie felt tired so she went to bed, but lay there for some time thinking about what the future held for them and hoped everything would be alright in the end. She felt so complete and happy; she even felt able to cope with her illness just so long as Roy was by her side. Why shouldn't she find happiness?

The next morning Marcie got washed and dressed for work and made herself a cup of tea but as usual she was running late and quickly hurried out the door leaving her cup of tea on the side.

Bella was at the shop on time as usual. 'Did you have a nice weekend? How did the party go?'

'It was fabulous and Roy really enjoyed himself. Jane said to thank you for the card and whisky by the way. Bella, I was wondering, do you need me to work this Saturday?'

'Why's that?'

'Roy wants me to catch the train to West Yorkshire and spend the weekend with him...and meet his parents. Only thing is, I'd need to leave a bit earlier on Friday too...'

'Well, you've got me on a good day, and I need a favour from you, too, so that's fine.'

'Oh, thanks, that's great! What's the favour?'

'I want to take a week off the following week so me and Barry can go to Brighton for a seaside break, but that means you would be solely in charge of the shop.'

'No problem, Bella. Can I leave at about 4 o'clock Friday then?'

'That will be fine, just as long as you are back to open the shop Monday morning, of course. I'll pop the keys through your letter box on the Sunday evening...and don't let me down.'

'I promise I won't Bella - you have my word.'

Thankfully, the shop was busy and the week passed quickly. Happy and excited, Marcie caught the train from Kings Cross, but as she neared her destination the butterflies in her stomach increased as she worried more and more about the possibility of Roy's parents not liking her.

Three hours after the train had first set off it pulled into the station and Marcie eagerly grabbed her small case and got off, looking up and down the platform for Roy.

'How was the journey?' Roy asked, sneaking up behind her and wrapping his arms around her waist.

'Oh, Roy! You made me jump!' she said spinning round to face him.

'Hello my darling,' he said, kissing her gently on the lips. 'Am I pleased to see you – I've missed you'

'The journey was fine. I've missed you, too,' she said kissing him back.

Taking her case he put his arm around her shoulders. 'Come on, the car park's this way. Let's go.'

Twenty minutes later they arrived at the flat. Marcie wasn't surprised to see that it was very much a bachelor pad; there were no ornaments and it was very stark, lacking a woman's touch, although bright and airy, and as it was a ground floor flat it had a small but neat garden.

'I'll put your case in the bedroom. I'm taking you out for an Indian – do you want to freshen up first? Then we had better make a move as it's getting late. You must be starving.'

'Yes, I am. I'll just go through to the bathroom and brush my hair and put on a bit of lippy – won't be long.'

Once in the restaurant they chatted about their week and when the meal was finished Marcie told Roy how worried she was about meeting his parents. 'Don't fret, it'll be fine,' he reassured her.

'Come on, let's get back, you look beat. I think we could both do with an early night.'

The next morning Roy's mum phoned just as they were getting ready.

'When are you coming over? You won't be long will you?'

'We're just getting dressed, Mum, and we'll be there shortly.'

'Don't be long son, will you?'

'Give me a break Mum, we'll be there soon.'

About an hour later they pulled up outside Roy's parent's house. Marcie couldn't believe her eyes. The entrance had double iron gates and a crazy paving pathway edged with flowerbeds leading up to the large detached house with huge bay windows. Marcie thought it was beautiful, with such character.

When she got out of the car Roy's mum greeted her with a hug. 'So lovely to meet you Marcie.'

'Thank you for inviting me Mrs Clark.'

'Just call me Susan, and this is George, my husband.'

'Lovely to meet you, Marcie,' he said kissing her on the cheek. 'Come on, let's go inside.'

Marcie was impressed by the décor - light and airy with cream walls and carpets. 'I love your home,' she remarked, 'it's beautiful, and so tastefully done.'

George grunted. 'She's a slave driver my wife. Blood, sweat and tears have gone into this place; she is never satisfied...'

'I'm sure Marcie doesn't want to know all about your moans and groans, George. Come and give me a hand in the kitchen. Marcie, take a seat...and Roy, fetch Marie a drink,' and she grabbed George's arm and whisked him away.

Just as Marcie sat down on the settee she heard the patter of feet and a little girl came running into the living room. Roy picked her up and swung her around laughing before setting her down on her feet and quickly introducing her. 'Marcie, this is my daughter, Molly.'

'Hello, Molly. I'm very pleased to meet you. I'm Marcie,' she said shaking her little hand.

'Hello. Is my daddy your boyfriend?'

'I think so. Is that alright?'

Molly shrugged her shoulders and ran off into the garden to play.

'Kim has a lot of men friends on the scene at the moment,

coming and going in her flat and Molly gets confused. Mum and Dad are looking after her this weekend while Kim's off gallivanting with one of them.'

'That's a shame; a child needs stability. She's beautiful Roy, but I know not to push it. I don't want to upset the poor child by pushing myself on her. I'm sure we'll be friends though.'

'I'm sure you will. Now, a glass of wine?'

'Yes please. That would be lovely.'

A few minutes later Susan called them through to the dining room for lunch where they enjoyed a wonderful meal of roast pork with crackling, roast potatoes and veg. They all chatted amiably and Molly was obviously on her best behaviour, quietly eating her meal and sitting still for the first time since Marcie had arrived. The butterflies had calmed down a little and by the time they were eating their pudding, delicious homemade apple pie and cream, she was feeling relaxed and happy.

'Right, I'm going to clear the table,' Susan remarked, 'I can't stand knowing it's got to be done later.'

'Let me help you,' offered Marcie, 'it'll make it quicker.'

'I'll leave you two to it then,' said Roy. 'Come on Molly, let's go out into the garden with Granddad and I'll push you on the swing.'

Susan was in the kitchen filling the sink when Marcie came in with the last of the plates. 'Thank you, dear, but you're our guest and should be taking it easy. How are you feeling? Are you coping alright with your illness?'

'I'm alright...it's early days...'

'You're such a brave girl, Marcie; I don't know how I would cope.'

'Well, I have no choice but to cope,' Marcie remarked defensively.

Susan could see the serious expression on her face. 'I do hope I haven't spoken out of turn, dear?'

'No, you haven't. I just don't like talking about it much. I have my good days and bad days - sometimes I get really tired and have painful joints, but I take each day as it comes. Touch wood I'm not too bad at the moment.'

'When my son came out of his coma I thanked God, and thought what a lucky family we were – I had never prayed so much for anything in my life. I must admit that I was unsure when Roy cancelled the wedding to Kim; I thought he wasn't thinking straight at the time. She had been by his side all through his ordeal and at first I was cross and felt sorry for her, but it wasn't long before she found someone else...in fact it was only a few weeks later...'

'It had nothing to do with me, Susan,' Marcie interrupted.

'I know dear. And I also know that I have never seen my son this happy. I brought him up to be true to himself and follow his heart and I can see now what he saw in you: you are a beautiful, intelligent girl and I can tell how much you care about him.'

'I do,' Marcie replied with tears in her eyes. 'I love him.'

Susan hugged her. 'That's all I wanted to know - I think we are going to get on just fine. I think I'll make a pot of tea before my George starts moaning,' she said, starting to fill the kettle. 'He likes his tea and biscuits after a meal.'

Tea made, Susan asked Marcie to take the tray out to the garden. 'I'll be out in a while, I'll just finish off here.'

Marcie saw Roy playing with Molly on the swings so she put the tray down on the table and sat down next to George.

'Where are the biscuits then?'

Susan came out with them. 'I heard that remark. You just be patient. Honestly Marcie, some men like to be waited on hand and foot. Start off as you mean to go on, I say, otherwise they will have you run ragged.'

'Now who's moaning?' George grunted, and winked at Marcie and she smiled.

Roy came over. 'Where is Kate, Mum?'

'Don't ask me, Roy, she stayed with her friend last night but I told her to be here for lunch as you and Marcie were coming. She could at least have phoned! I'll be having words when she gets here.'

'She's young, Mum. I was no different at her age.'

'You were, Roy. You never gave me a day's worry. Kate is so head strong and stubborn.'

'She takes after you, Susan,' George piped up.

'I have to agree, Mum; you can be as tough as old boots if you want to be.'

'Cheeky buggers. In that case you can both wash up,' and she looked at Marcie and grinned. 'That will teach them not to open their mouths.'

Molly went up to Marcie. 'Will you read me some stories?'

'I would love that. Go bring me some books,' and Molly ran up to her bedroom.

'I think she likes you,' Roy said. 'Can I leave you to entertain her while I look at the bird boxes Dad's been making in the shed?'

'Of course.'

'I won't be long, but if you get fed up call me.'

Kate walked in the door and Susan let loose. 'You're so inconsiderate! Why didn't you phone me?'

'Don't start, Mum. Me and Ann and a few other friends went to a disco and it finished late so I slept in, OK?'

'Are you hungry?'

'I'm bloody starving.'

'Then it's a good job I saved you some dinner, but next time let me know. And mind your language, young lady.'

Susan went in the kitchen to heat up the dinner and Kate went in the garden to the others. Molly ran and hugged her. 'Did you buy me any sweets?'

'Sorry, I forgot.'

Molly's face dropped. 'You promised!'

'I'll get you some later,' she said and walked towards Marcie. 'Hi, I'm Kate, Roy's sister.'

'Nice to meet you,' Marcie said shyly. 'I think your mum's on the warpath.'

'I know, but her bark's worse than her bite - she'll calm down in a minute. I love your hair!'

'Thanks,' Marcie replied.

'I'm trying to grow mine but I don't know if it will suit me.'

'I think you're so pretty it would look lovely either way.'

'Thank you. I think I can hear my mum calling me for my dinner, so I'll see you later. Molly, be a good girl and stop walking on the plants.'

Molly ran back to Marcie. 'Can we read this book now?'

'*Rupert the Bear*, of course we can,' and Molly climbed up onto her lap.

A little later Roy came back to join Marcie. 'You look tired; do you think we should leave now and go back to the flat?'

'What about Molly?'

'You won't be able to tear her away from her nanna and

granddad, they spoil her rotten. We can see her tomorrow, anyway.'

'Your sister Kate is in the dining room.'

'I'll just go and say hello before we go,' and he headed into the house.

'Hi, cheeky chops! Have you been giving Mum and Dad a load of grief?' he asked laughing and kissing her head.

'I think they forget they were young once themselves.'

'Go easy; they worry about you.'

Kate changed the subject. 'Your girlfriend's beautiful, Roy. What the hell does she see in you?'

'Bloody cheek ! Don't you think your brother's handsome then?'

'No, not really,' she laughed.

'Well you won't be wanting the £10 I was going to give you then.'

'You know I love you Roy; you're the best brother in the world.'

'I thought you would change your tune! But don't let Mum and Dad know - they think I spoil you.'

When Roy and Marcie had their coats on and were ready to leave, they all came to the door to see them off, except Molly who was too interested in playing with her Barbie dolls to take any notice.

'We'll see you both in the Huntsman tomorrow, say about one o'clock, for lunch,' said Susan kissing them goodbye.

George shook his son's hand as he had always done and said goodbye to Marcie.

'Why did your dad shake your hand?' Marcie asked on the journey home. 'Rather formal I thought.'

'That's just his way. He was in the army years ago and he has old fashioned ideas, but it doesn't bother me. He was a bit strict when I was young but my mum rules the roost, she knows how to handle him.'

'Well, I think you have a wonderful family Roy, I envy you.'

'We'll have a wonderful family of our own one day; I promise you.'

When they arrived at the flat Marcie headed for the bedroom.

'Blimey! You're keen!'

'I just feel tired Roy; you don't mind if I have a little rest, do you?'

'Don't be daft, of course not. I'll just pop out and get a bit of shopping - there's nothing in,' and he gave her a kiss and closed the bedroom door.

Marcie closed her eyes. She had enjoyed meeting Roy's family but had a few doubts in her mind about Roy coming to live in London with her. Molly and the rest of his family were here and he may one day change his mind and have reservations. After all, he had been used to living in the countryside most of his life and she worried that he would be out of his comfort zone. Malcolm had always said there was a north and south divide and living in London would be a completely different way of life for him. Her head was spinning with all these thoughts but tiredness eventually took over and she fell fast asleep.

The next thing she knew was when she heard the front door open and Roy came back with the shopping. She got out of bed and went through to the kitchen feeling guilty when she saw all the bags and his stressed face. 'Sorry Roy, I'm not much help, am I?'

'Don't be silly, it's fine; just the bloody traffic on the way back was a nightmare. I went to the meat van in the market and got some bargains though – two packs of steak for the price of one, and the same with the bacon. I saw a mate when I was there and we went and had a pint together.'

'That's nice. I prefer to go to the butchers; you can't take any chances with meat.'

'You're a fuss pot. I buy food from the market all the time. At least the money's going to local people and not the large supermarkets.'

'Yes, that's true, I suppose.'

'And it hasn't done me any harm yet,' he laughed.

He unpacked the shopping and opened a bottle of red wine. 'How are you feeling now? Did you manage to get some sleep?'

'I slept like a log. I can't understand how I get so tired so easily.'

'The main thing is that you feel better now. Do you?'

'Yes, I feel great!'

'Well that's all that matters then. Let me pour you a glass of wine.'

Roy cooked them a lovely meal of steak with jacket potato and grated cheese on the top with beetroot. 'My god Roy, that was good! I'm stuffed – we've done nothing but eat today.'

'I have a big appetite; I love my grub.'

Marcie felt so content with Roy; he was kind and caring and made her feel loved. They settled down for the evening snuggled up on the settee watching telly.

'I love your parents, Roy. They made me feel so welcome and your daughter is so cute. I don't know why I was so worried.'

'My sister can be a headache, but she's not a bad girl – a bit rebellious at times but she is just finding her feet. I was like that at her age.'

'You're yawning Roy, let's go to bed.'

'Sounds good to me.'

The following morning they got up at the same time and when Marcie came out of the bathroom Roy was busy cooking breakfast.

'Mmmm...something smells good. '

'Bacon and egg Marcie, with tomatoes and toast.'

'Lovely. What are we doing this morning?'

'I was thinking we could go for a drive in the countryside as we don't have to meet my mum and dad till one o'clock.'

'I would love that...and maybe stop at a pub for a drink?'

'Anything you say my darling, so long as you're happy.'

'Can I speak my mind Roy?'

'Of course. What's up?'

'It's just that I think it would be wrong of me to expect you to tear yourself away from your family and friends. Why don't we just live here together?'

'I have thought about that, but if I'm being honest, financially it makes more sense to move to London. I think investing my money in a property in your area will give me a better return in the long run, and if we buy a small house in a good area we can have a good lifestyle. I can live anywhere, it doesn't bother me; I've worked all over the country and can put my hand to anything, though I much prefer to be self employed. Buying old properties and renovating them is what I really want to do. I can do most of the work myself and a lot of my mates are skilled workers, plumbers and electricians who can help me out and who would be willing to travel for work.'

'Are you sure that's what you want?'

'Look Marcie, so long as we are together I don't care, but I want us to have a good life and I don't want us to struggle. It's my job to take care of you, so let me do the worrying.'

'Do you know what?'

'What?'

'I think I was one of the luckiest girls on the planet the day I met you,' she said putting her arms around his neck.

'Well in that case you can make me another cup of tea and iron me a shirt to show your gratitude woman,' he said kissing her forehead.

Roy always managed to make her feel positive and have a good outlook on life. He had seen her as a confident person before she was diagnosed with the MS, but had noticed a change in her of late and was patient and understanding when he noticed she was feeling a bit down.

Breakfast over, they got in the car and set off for their drive into the countryside.

'Roy this is a beautiful place. I must admit, I don't miss the hustle and bustle of the London traffic and all the car fumes.'

'I know what you mean, but every place has its disadvantages. People here are crying out for work. There is so much unemployment that a lot of my friends have had to find work away from home just to make ends meet, and they only see their families at weekends.'

'Roy look, there's a pub on the corner there that looks quite quaint. Can we stop?'

'Yes, why not.' Roy parked the car and they went in.

'Oh, what a lovely place. Talk about olde worlde! It has so much character – it's like something out of a Dickens novel.'

'Yes, you're right,' agreed Roy as they walked up to the bar. 'Red wine?'

'Yes, please.'

'And a pint of lager for me,' said Roy to the barman.

Roy paid and picked up the drinks leading Marcie through to the beer garden where they sat down. 'What time's your train?'

'I think its four o'clock.'

'Well we can't hang around too long with my family after lunch, you haven't packed yet.'

'That won't take me long to do.'

They sat and chatted and enjoyed their drinks in the sunshine until noon and then got back in the car.

'I hate the thought of going back home without you...and I'm working next Saturday so it's hardly worth you coming up just for one day.'

'I agree pet; it's a long journey just for a day. Let's just see what happens.'

They eventually arrived at the Huntsman half an hour late as Roy took a wrong turning. All the family were sitting in the garden at the back of the pub.

'You're bloody late Roy. I'm starving, let's go inside and eat,' said a long-faced George, a stickler for punctuality.

'Yes, sir!' said Roy, sarcastically.

There was roast pork and roast beef with all the trimmings on the menu and they were all hungry by now except for Molly who was more interested in looking through the French windows at the children playing on the swings and slide in the garden and kept leaving the table. Roy was beginning to get cross with her. 'Get back in your chair and eat your dinner otherwise no ice-cream for afters.' Molly stuck her tongue out but everyone ignored her and she slowly eased her way back onto her chair.

'I love coming here,' Susan remarked. 'The food is lovely.'

When they had finished the waiter came back to take their dessert order. 'There is apple pie with cream or custard, ice-cream...'

'Hold your horses,' George interrupted, 'there's no hurry. Come back in five minutes.'

'Sorry, sir,' the young waiter replied red-faced.

'I have something to tell you, Roy. I got a telephone call from a bloke called Mr Dunlop who said he worked for a genealogist probate researchers called Grayson and Grayson who have offices in London, and he asked me a few questions about my brother Wally.'

Roy looked intrigued but Molly was getting bored. 'Kate, take her out to play on the swings, would you?'

'Do I have to?'

'Yes,' Susan insisted, 'you do. Now go on.'

Kate took her out in the garden but turned back to give her mum a filthy look.

'Can I finish my story now?' George asked. 'Otherwise I'll forget what I want to say.'

'Yes, go on Dad. What happened after that?'

'Well, to cut a long story short, this Mr Dunlop turned up on the door step Friday morning and went into great detail about my family history...'

'I can't remember Uncle Wally,' Roy remarked, 'I was too young when you stopped speaking to him. 'What was it over anyway?'

'My mother's funeral - he didn't like the arrangements I made.'

'How old were you when your dad died?'

'I was about twelve at the time. He worked as a builder, just like you, Roy. Wally never married and continued to live with my mother. I met your mum and moved away from Enfield and after our mum Dolly got buried and we argued about the arrangements I never got in touch with him again.'

'What did Wally die of?' Roy asked.

'A heart attack, apparently. Mr Dunlop was surprised we hadn't been in touch with each other all those years but I told him we never got on as kids as he was a miserable bugger and a mean git.'

'Watch your tongue, George Clark, there are ladies present.'

'Sorry my dear,' said George, winking at Marcie. 'Anyway, it turns out Wally had thousands of pounds hidden all over the flat - under the carpets, in the wardrobe, and even in a shoe box. He obviously didn't trust banks.'

'Did he own his own property?' Roy asked.

'No, it was council. My mother scrimped and saved all her life cleaning houses and taking neighbours' washing in, but she always told me she liked living there and got on well with everyone. I know we didn't see eye to eye but I can't help feeling sad that my brother passed away and had no one there to give him a good send off. If I had been informed I would have gone to the funeral. He apparently was found slumped on the settee by a care worker...' Roy got up out of his chair and gave his dad a hug. 'That's alright son, families can drift apart. We're not the first and we won't be the last,' but he had tears in his eyes all the same.

'Did this Mr Dunlop tell you how much you will be getting?'

'He mentioned thirty thousand. I'm the sole heir, but it might take quite a while to come through. Mind you, he doesn't think there will be any problems; it's pretty cut and dried apparently.'

'Did you have to sign anything?'

'Yes, I signed the necessary paperwork.'

Susan looked at her son. 'Your dad doesn't want the money and is investing some for Molly for her education later on and giving the rest to you and Kate, but don't let on to your sister, Roy. She'll get hers when she's a bit older. You know how teenagers are, she will be badgering her dad for a new car and think we are loaded, and I want her to learn the value of money.'

'I promise I won't say a word.'

'Your dad thinks his brother would turn in his grave if he knew the money had gone to him.'

Roy looked at his dad. 'You're bonkers, you are! You should take mum on a fabulous holiday and spoil her.'

'You tell him, son. He doesn't seem to think his wife needs a break.'

'Right,' interjected George, 'I've had enough talking about it. Now, where's my apple pie and ice-cream?'

Molly and Kate came in from the garden. 'I want to go home now Nanny, and play with my Barbie dolls.'

'We're going to order your ice-cream now and when you've eaten that we'll go home, pet.'

'Roy, are you coming back to the house afterwards?'

'No Dad, Marcie has to pack and she is catching the four o'clock train, so we're going to make a move now.'

George turned to Marcie. 'Well, it's been grand meeting you and you must come and visit us again soon.'

Susan gave Marcie a hug. 'You have a safe journey home my darling, and ring me some time; it's been lovely meeting you.'

'Likewise. Thank you for making me so welcome.'

'Molly, don't be rude and say goodbye to Marcie,' said Susan.

'Bye, Marcie,' she said, giving her a kiss. 'Is Daddy coming with us, Nanny?'

'No, your mum is coming to pick you up later.'

Kate also said her farewells to her brother and Marcie. 'Can you drop me off home, Roy, I've had enough sitting here.'

'No, you don't, young lady; you can hang on for a bit and wait for us.' With that, Kate stormed off to the toilet.

Susan looked at Marcie. 'She is getting to be a handful. She thinks she's going out tonight but she's not - she has been out every night this week. A night in with me and her dad won't hurt her for a change.'

'Right, we must go, Mum. Roy went to Molly and gave her a

hug and a kiss. 'You be a good girl and I'll see you soon.'

'I will. Bye, Daddy.'

When they arrived back at the flat Marcie went to pack her things. 'I'll put the kettle on while you do that. Tea or coffee?'

'Either will do.'

When Marcie had packed they both sat down to drink their tea.

'I can't believe my dad has inherited that money. I thought it was a scam when he first told me. That sort of thing happens to other families, not ours.'

'I'm pleased for you all. I should imagine information has to be submitted to the government department – it could take months for them to release the funds.'

'Blimey! Is that the time? We'd better make a move.'

Once at the station Roy went onto the platform with Marcie and a few minutes later the train pulled in and they said their goodbyes.

'Thank you for such a lovely weekend. It was great meeting your family – they're lovely.'

'I'll miss you – I can't wait till the next time. I love you, Marcie.'

With tears in her eyes she hugged him. 'Me too, Roy.'

He watched as she boarded with her small case and when the train disappeared from sight he walked slowly back to the car.

The train was pretty packed but Marcie was lucky enough to get a window seat. Once Roy was out of sight she stuck her head in her book. She wasn't in the mood to make small talk with people she didn't know.

When the train pulled into Kings Cross Station she grabbed her case, got off of the train and made her way outside where she was lucky enough to get a taxi straight home to her flat.

She opened the door and picked up Bella's keys off the floor and put them on the sideboard. Taking her case through to the bedroom she unpacked her few things and ran a bath. Just as she was about to undress the phone rang.

'Good, you're home safely.'

'Yes, I've been in about half an hour. I'm missing you already.'

'Me, too. How was your journey?'

'It was fine. I read most of the way.'

'Darling, I have to go – Molly's crying. She wants me to tell her a bedtime story.'

'I thought her mum was picking her up?'

'She hasn't turned up yet - typical of her - she can be a selfish cow sometimes. I'm going to ring her in a few minutes to tell her not to bother coming; she can pick Molly up tomorrow morning.'

'I don't blame you getting annoyed, Roy. You had better go and see to her...and give her a kiss from me.'

'I will.'

'Love you Roy.'

'I love you too, sweetheart. I'll call you tomorrow,' and he was gone.

Marcie put the phone down and went and had her bath. It had been a long day so she went straight to bed afterwards and fell into a deep sleep.

Chapter Twenty-One

Marcie woke up bright and early and was looking forward to the day ahead in charge of the shop. With Bella away she wanted to show she could cope and do a good job and hoped it would be a busy day with plenty of customers.

When she arrived Ella was waiting outside. 'Morning, Ella. You're early for once.'

'Yes, I know. My mum is giving me grief - I couldn't wait to come to work.'

'What have you been up to now?'

'Staying out late as usual.'

'Ella, you need to show your mum a bit more respect. I expect she worries about you. If it was me I would put the bolt on the door so you couldn't get in.'

'No you wouldn't, you're a softie.'

Ignoring her remark Marcie opened the shop. 'Right, you can start by making us both a cup of tea,' she said, and busied herself putting the lights on and rearranging a couple of dress rails.

Ella came through with a mug of tea and a letter.

'What's that?'

'It was in the back – it has your name on.'

Marcie opened the envelope to find a message from Bella.

Hi Marcie,

There will be two deliveries today. One is bags and the other is T-shirts, but when you sign for them please make sure you check the contents against the invoice.

Have a good week,

Bella xxxx

'I thought she wasn't going to buy bags anymore because they take up too much space. Oh well, she's the boss, so she must know what she's doing. Ella, finish your tea then start mopping the floor out the back and clean the toilet, and when you've done that you can sweep outside the front of the shop.'

'You're a slave driver, Marcie.'

'Maybe your right, but you can be a lazy sod, and I'm in charge, so do as I say.'

Ella didn't make a fuss. She needed the job, so quickly went out the back to get started.

Later that day the first delivery arrived and Marcie signed for it making sure everything was in order first. There was a range of bags, each one as fabulous as the next: colourful clutch bags, chocolate leather backpacks, Totes, and there at the very bottom of the box were the most gorgeous quilted bags - again in a range of beautiful colours - that Marcie had ever seen. She could see why Bella had been in business for so long; she certainly had an eye for the latest trends, despite her advanced years.

Marcie started to unpack the bags and display most of them where she could around the shop, matching them up to individual garments to show them off to their full advantage. She then boxed the rest of the bags up and put them in the store room at the back of the shop.

'Bella certainly knows her stuff,' Ella remarked. 'Any chance of her giving me a discount on one of those leather backpacks, do you think? I love it, and it's my birthday Saturday.'

'I'm not sure. I'm sorry, Ella, but I'm not asking her for you, you'll have to ask her yourself when she comes back.'

The day was busy with a constant stream of customers. The best selling items were the miniskirts and the T-shirts, which were off the shoulder and had printed designs on them.

At three-thirty Marcie asked Ella to watch the shop as she had to take some cash to the bank. 'I won't be long.'

'Don't worry; you can leave me in charge.'

'Don't get above your station, I'll only be about fifteen minutes,' Marcie giggled walking out the shop.

When she returned, Ella was in a panic as there were four customers in the shop waiting to be served. Marcie quickly took off her jacket and went behind the counter to help. When everything had settled down she told Ella to go through to the back and make them both some tea. It had been a successful day but she felt exhausted, and when it came to closing time she was pleased to lock up.

'I'll see you tomorrow, Ella. Don't let me down - be here at nine o'clock sharp,' said Marcie locking the door.

301

When she arrived home she was so shattered she just took her coat off and sat on the settee for twenty minutes before getting up and putting the kettle on to make a cup of tea. Her joints were aching and her feet were killing her so she took two painkillers and sat back down with her tea. Just then the phone rang. It was Roy.

'Have you had a good day?'

'I'm blooming exhausted, but yes, it was a good day. What happened yesterday? Did Kim pick Molly up?'

'You're kidding; she was at a club with some guy and said she forgot.'

'That's terrible Roy; she's not very reliable. I wish I was there with you...'

'I know Marcie, but be patient. I have to sort things out at this end. I won't come Sunday; you're right, it's a long journey there and back.'

'I don't blame you, Roy, and anyway, we'll see each other the following weekend,' she said trying to sound upbeat although she knew how much she would miss him.

'I'm going now sweetheart; I have a pizza in the oven. I'll speak to you tomorrow.'

'OK, love you loads. Think of me in bed tonight.'

'You're never far away from my thoughts, Marcie. Speak to you tomorrow.'

As it happened, the shop was so busy that the week flew by. The new bags sold like hot cakes and the T-shirts were literally flying off the shelves – Bella would be over the moon.

Marcie had invited Amy for Sunday lunch at one o'clock, as she hadn't seen her for so long. She had just finished preparing a lovely chicken salad with new potatoes and a mayonnaise dressing when the doorbell rang. That'll be her, she thought, looking at her watch. She wiped her hands on a tea towel and hurried to open the door.

'Hello stranger! How are you?'

'Amy, come on in! Long time no see.'

'It's hot out there today I should have put my shorts on,' she said hugging Marcie.

'You certainly have the legs for them. Would you like a glass of wine?'

'Yes please, I'm parched.'

Marcie poured two glasses and they both sat down.

'So, how are you feeling Marcie?'

'What do you mean?'

'Jane told me on the phone about your multiple sclerosis.'

'What was she doing ringing you? You're more my friend than hers.'

'She just said she was sorry I couldn't come to her engagement party and we got talking.'

'News travels fast. I'm OK. It hasn't all quite sunk in yet but I'm dealing with it in a positive way - setting myself goals for the future and so on.'

'Such as?' Amy asked.

'Marrying Roy, having a couple of kids and a beautiful house with plenty of room, and maybe running my own business eventually...but you can forget about the latter, that's more a pipe dream; I could never afford that...'

'I can't wait to meet him. Jane said he's a lovely bloke.'

'He's adorable. I'll have to bring him to yours one weekend; I know you'll like him.'

'That would be great. Have you forgiven me now? I still feel very guilty going behind your back seeing Peppi.'

'So you should! Don't get me wrong, I'm still pissed off with you - good friends don't do that to one another, but I believe you when you say nothing happened, though I'm sure he would have liked it to. So, yes, you're forgiven, but if you ever do anything like that again, Amy, I will never speak to you again.'

'I deserve that. Point taken,' she replied looking sheepish.

Marcie quickly changed the subject. 'What do you want the future to hold for *you*, Amy?'

'I just want to find a guy who I can trust really.'

'Have you met anyone recently?'

'I did but...'

'Spit it out. What's with the hesitation?'

'Well OK, I'll tell you, but you must promise you won't spill the beans to anyone.'

'Of course I won't,' Marcie replied looking bemused.

'I bumped into this old friend of Joe's...'

'Is he a doctor?' Marcie interrupted.

'No, he's an administrator at the hospital. Anyway, we went out for dinner and ended up back at his flat in bed...'

'Is that it?'

'Will you let me finish, Marcie? Gosh! You're so impatient – it's getting on my nerves!'

'OK, OK, keep your hair on! I'm all ears. Carry on.'

Amy continued, 'We met up again a few times and this particular night we had a meal out and went back to my place this time.'

'I take it the girls weren't there?'

'Of course not, they were staying with their dad that weekend. Anyway, we made love and it was fantastic and when I got dressed he said he had something to tell me.'

'What was that?'

'He said he'd had a fling with one of the nurses at the hospital and caught something and advised me to go to the STD clinic.'

'How did he know?'

'This nurse had phoned him and told him.'

'Jesus Christ, Amy, what a bastard! Have you been to the clinic?'

'Of course I have, but a person in my position should have known better. I was always informing my patients to use protection. Can you imagine how embarrassed I felt?'

'What were the results?'

'He gave me Gonorrhoea.'

'Shit, Amy, that's disgusting!'

'I know, but don't tell anyone – I'm so ashamed.'

'I won't; I promise your secret is safe with me.'

'It's been treated and I'm fine now, thank God, but I've learned a lesson, believe me. I can't believe I was so stupid...'

After a lovely lunch and the remains of the bottle of wine, Amy could see Marcie was beginning to look tired, and said it was time she was going home. 'I'll give you a ring soon, Marcie, and thanks for lunch.'

'You're welcome; I'll see you soon.'

After washing up the dishes Marcie gave Malcolm a ring.

'Hi hinny! How are you?'

'I'm good, thanks. How about you?'

'I've just been pottering around in the garden and making the most of this lovely weather.'

'That's good, it keeps you active. I met Roy's parents last

weekend - they are lovely, and his daughter Molly is gorgeous. They were so welcoming; even his sister Kate is sweet.'

'That's a turn up for the books. So you are both courting?'

'That's an old fashioned word Malcolm, but yes we are, and it's partly thanks to you.'

'My Nancy will be looking down on you both smiling; you know how much she loved you two.'

'I really love him Malcolm, and I think we have a future together.'

'Well, that's fabulous news! I'm so pleased for you, but what I want to know is when you are both paying me a visit?'

'We'll come up to see you as soon as we can. I miss you so much, but Roy wants to live in London with me anyway so we will be closer to you and we can spend lots of quality time together, the three of us.'

'That sounds grand - I would love that. Oh, that's someone knocking at my door so I'd better go, but I will phone you next week. Love you pet.'

'I love you too, Malcolm; bye.'

She put the kettle on and made a cup of tea. Taking it through to the sitting room and making herself comfortable her thoughts went back to Amy. She had been brought up in a loving family home with a good education and opportunities in life, unlike herself, and still life hadn't been particularly kind to her and she'd had her fair share of problems in the past. She couldn't help but feel sorry for her and hoped that one day she would meet someone who truly loved her.

As it was now getting late Marcie had a bath and ironed some clothes and went to bed thinking how lucky she was to have Roy in her life. She was just beginning to doze off when she heard the phone ring. She reluctantly got out of bed and answered it.

'Hi, it's me, Roy. Bad news I'm afraid.'

'Oh no! What's that?'

'I've got some viewings on the two flats Friday evening so I will have to drive down Saturday morning instead.'

'That's OK. What time will you get here?'

'Hopefully about midday.'

'Don't worry I understand, Roy. I'll see you then. I'm going back to bed now; you woke me up,' she said, stifling a yawn.

305

'Sorry love. Goodnight, God bless, and I'll see you Saturday.'

'I can't wait to see you Roy; goodnight,' and she put the phone down and climbed back into bed. It wasn't too long before she fell into a contented sleep.

Marcie opened her eyes and stretched. Yawning, she sat up and looked at her clock. 8.30. 'Shit!' her alarm hadn't gone off. Panicking, she leapt out of bed, ran to the bathroom and quickly brushed her teeth before getting dressed and running a brush through her hair. Usually she never left the house before having a cup of tea but today she would just have to go without. She still had the keys to the shop and Bella would be furious if she was left waiting outside. Hurrying down the road she eventually arrived outside the shop, breathless. Bella stood there looking annoyed.

'Bella, I'm so sorry. My alarm didn't go off.'

'Well, you're here now – let's get inside, my feet are killing me standing here all this time.'

Bella had a smile on her face when she walked in the shop. It looked clean and tidy and the clothes looked fantastic the way they were displayed, and especially in the window.

'I take my hat off to you Marcie; you have an eye for fashion. I love the way you have matched the clutch bags with the outfits – that should help them to sell – that stock cost me a small fortune.'

'Well, luckily they've sold well so far.'

Bella checked the books and the takings had gone up considerably. 'Well done Marcie; I can see you having a good future running your own shop one day. You remind me of myself when I started out in business.'

'I'm not sure about that Bella, I mean the part about running my own shop, but thanks for the compliment - it means a lot to me.'

The door opened and Ella walked in. 'You're late! How many more times?'

'Sorry...'

'I just don't know what to do with you, Ella!'

Marcie spoke up for her. 'She was great last week Bella, really helpful.'

'Well, she can pull her weight right now and make us all a coffee,' she said softening and giving Ella a smile.

'Did you enjoy your break Bella?' Marcie asked.

'I thoroughly enjoyed it and Barry did, too, the only thing that spoilt it was our room was quite small - you couldn't swing a cat in it - maybe I'm getting a bit fussy in my old age...but I have to say the food was excellent. Next time we're thinking of going to France for a break; I went there years ago and loved it. Barry's been there many times.'

'I haven't been anywhere.'

'Your time will come, love, you have plenty of years ahead of you. Has Ella gone to Brazil for that coffee? Ella! I'm dying of thirst in here!'

Walking through to the back she saw the whole jar of coffee spilled all over the floor. 'You clumsy girl! Get that swept up and go to the shop and buy another one.'

'I couldn't help it; it just slipped out of my hand.'

'Have we any tea-bags in the cupboard?'

'Yes.'

'Well just make some tea - you can manage that, can't you? And you can wipe that silly grin off your face.' Bella wasn't much of a morning person and Ella was pushing her to the limit.

Marcie was busy serving a difficult customer front of shop who insisted she had handed her a £50 note and not £20. Bella came out and intervened.

'I think you're mistaken, young lady; there is no £50 note in the till. Now if I were you, I would take your £5 change and your T-shirt and leave before I call the police.' The girl picked up her carrier bag and made a quick exit from the shop.

'That girl has tried this once before,' Bella remarked, fuming. I have a good memory for faces and I distinctly remember Pat having the same problem with her, the cheeky little mare.'

Ella brought three mugs of tea out on a tray. 'Good girl. I hope you have mopped the floor?'

'I have, Bella.'

'Seeing that Marcie has been singing your praises I am going to put a little extra in your wage packet.'

'Thank you, Bella!' and she flung her arms tightly around her.

'And you can stop that nonsense – you're bloody suffocating me!' Bella was rather reserved and not used to anyone being quite so demonstrative. 'Marcie, I will be giving you a bonus too, but a kiss on the cheek will do,' she said laughing.

'Thank you so much, Bella,' and Marcie kissed her on both cheeks.

Another busy week meant that again it flew by. Late Friday afternoon when the customers had thinned out a bit and Bella and Marcie were tidying up some of the rails, Marcie asked if there had been any interest in the shop.

'I have had some interest - if he can sort out his finances and we agree on a price.'

'Oh! Who is it? Anyone I know?' she asked, pleased for Bella, though she had a sick feeling in the pit of her stomach. What would she do...? She tried to compose herself and look happy for her.

'He's called Billy Shipman and owns some shops in Golders Green. Right, I'm going to cash up now, you get off, love. Have a lovely weekend.'

'You too, Bella. Bye Ella,' and she grabbed her jacket and bag and walked home feeling excited that Roy was coming tomorrow but disappointed that he wasn't going to be there when she got home. Their time together seemed to get less and less, but she knew it was hard for him commuting back and forth and hoped there would be good news about the sale of the flats so that he could start making plans to move in with her. She stopped at the chippie and bought sausage and chips – she hadn't eaten all day and was starving.

When she arrived home she ate her tea and tidied the flat ready for tomorrow. Afterwards she watched a bit of TV and then had a long soak in a hot bath before turning the lights out and going to bed.

Next morning she woke up after a good night's sleep feeling happy and excited. She couldn't wait to see Roy. Getting out of bed she had a cup of tea and got ready to go to the shops, as she wanted to get some nice food in and make him a lovely meal when he arrived.

Walking down the high street her first stop was the butchers where she bought some sirloin steak, a leg of lamb, bacon and sausages. She then went next door to the greengrocers and bought plenty of fruit and veg.

The sun was shining and most of the cafe bars had their chairs outside on the pavement so she stopped at one and ordered a coffee.

'Alright for some,' came a familiar voice from behind her.

'Bella, hi! What are you doing here? Who's minding the shop?'

'Barry, bless him. I've just been to the bakery. Where's Roy, at home?

'No, he's arriving this afternoon. He had viewings on his flats so he couldn't come last night.'

'Well he doesn't have to be there - the estate agents can see to the perspective buyers, that's their job. Mind you, I don't blame him I suppose; a lot of them don't know what they're talking about.'

'Shall I order a coffee for you?'

'No, love, I had better get back; Barry gets panicky in the shop on his own. Give Roy my regards, and I'll see you Monday. Must dash.'

Marcie finished her coffee, paid the bill and crossed the road to the florist where she bought a lovely bunch of lilies before finally calling in at the supermarket further down the road to get the rest of her groceries.

When she eventually got home she put the four bags of shopping down on the kitchen floor and put the kettle on. She felt shattered. She looked at the clock. Eleven-thirty – plenty of time to put the shopping away and have a soak in the bath to sooth her aching joints.

Afterwards, feeling heaps better, she arranged the flowers in a vase of water and placed it on her small dining table. They looked beautiful. Everything was ready and she felt rather pleased with herself. Damn! She had forgotten wine and beers. Roy can get those later, she thought sitting down and relaxing on the settee.

Just then the doorbell rang and when she opened the door her face lit up. 'Roy! I expected you much later,' she said, flinging her arms round him.

'I was lucky, not much traffic on the roads,' he said hugging her tightly.

'It's so good to see you. I bet your starving,' she said taking his arm. 'Come on, come in.'

'I must admit, I am.'

'Sit down and I'll make you a sandwich and later on we can have steak and chips.'

'Sounds good to me.'

'Fancy a beer? I think I've got one left in the fridge, but I'll go to the off licence later on and get some more.'

'You mean I will!' he said laughing.

'Well, OK, it did cross my mind.'

'My mum and dad send their love.'

'How are they?'

'Just the same, but Molly tires them out; she can be demanding at times. Changing the subject, I have some good news.'

'What's that?'

The people who viewed the two flats are very interested and are putting in an offer.'

'That's brilliant news Roy! I'm so happy for you.'

There's no chain apparently, so it might only take about three months for completion.'

'Bloody hell! I didn't realise it would take that long!'

'Well, that's quite quick really – these things take time.'

'I'll go and make your sandwich.'

Roy sensed her disappointment. 'Are you alright? Do you need a hand?' he shouted to her.

'No, I'm fine.'

When she came out with a mug of tea and a sandwich he asked her what was wrong.

'Nothing really. It's only just dawned on me that it could even be six months or more before you move in with me.'

'Marcie you have to be patient, sweetheart. I could move in here tomorrow but that means I still have to commute up and down. You forget I still have a couple of blokes working with me when work does come up, and I'm not getting any rental money because I'm selling the flats and want them to look presentable. Loose ends have to be tied up – I can't just up and leave.'

'I understand Roy, but why can't your dad look after them?'

'Come off it Marcie, he isn't always available, and anyway, why should he? It's my problem, not his.'

Marcie sat in silence for a few minutes and it was making Roy agitated. 'I've driven all this way to see you and you're giving me a load of grief! And now the silent treatment and I haven't done anything wrong!'

'You sound like a school boy Roy. I didn't say you had!'

'Right, that's it – I've had enough! I'm going for a pint,' he said getting up and walking out.

Marcie went into the bedroom, lay on the bed and sobbed her heart out. When she could cry no more tears she replayed the argument in her head and realised how stupid she had been. She missed him when he wasn't there but he was just being sensible trying to make sure he was financially secure before he moved in with her. And then of course there was Molly. He had to get her used to the idea he was moving away. Oh god! I've been so selfish, she thought, willing him to come home soon. She looked at the clock; it was four-thirty - he had been out a long time. Looking out of the window she could see his car still parked out the front so knew he hadn't gone too far. She needed a glass of wine to calm her nerves and was annoyed with herself as she had forgotten to buy any.

The doorbell rang. She ran to answer it and it was Roy. She flung her arms around him. 'I'm so sorry Roy; I can be a bitch sometimes.'

'I'm sorry, too; I flew off the handle. I've had a lot on my plate lately,' he said hugging her.

'What's in the carrier bag?'

'A bottle of your favourite Chardonnay.'

'Where did you go?'

I had a pint at the pub and I was starving but they had stopped serving lunch so I had two Cornish pasties and a coffee at a cafe in the high street.'

'You were out a long time...'

'Alright, I confess, I popped in to say hello to Bella at the shop as I was passing and we got chatting.'

'Did you tell her we had a row?'

'Not exactly, but she guessed something was wrong and told me to go home and make up and have a lovely evening.'

'Roy, I can't tell you how sorry I am. I'm so selfish at times but I have been feeling a bit stressed lately.'

'Why? Is it your illness?'

'Bella thinks she might have a buyer for the shop. Somebody's really interested and I worry about who will employ me...having the MS. I love working there and Bella is a good boss - I can't imagine I would be happy anywhere else...'

'Don't be silly Marcie, you would be an asset to any employer. It doesn't have to be a physical job; you could maybe work in an

311

office.'

'Roy I would hate that, it would bore me to tears.'

He tried to cheer her up. 'Come on, sweetheart, let me pour you a glass of wine and make you something to eat.'

'I'm not hungry at the moment.'

'Tell you what; I'll take you out for dinner later on tonight.'

'That would make a nice change Roy; I'd like that.' Marcie cuddled up to him on the settee. 'I think we have had our first domestic.'

'You started it!'

'Hush, Roy Clark, and come to bed.'

'Now that is a proposition I can't refuse,' said Roy grinning from ear to ear.

Marcie loved making love with Roy. He was gentle, caring and considerate, and when it was all over she always felt contented and complete, just as she did now lying wrapped in his arms in silence. She didn't have to say anything, she always felt safe and secure with Roy.

'I think we should get up now sweetheart, it's going on six o'clock. I'll go and make us a coffee.'

'And I'll run a bath, but we don't have to go out this evening Roy, I have plenty of food in.'

'No, I'd like to take you out – my treat.'

When they were both ready, Roy drove them to the restaurant – a new little Italian on the high street. 'I haven't been in here before; it looks a bit posh,' said Marcie as they walked in.

'I noticed it when I passed this afternoon...and Bella recommended it.'

They both had spaghetti and meatballs followed by the most delicious tiramisu they had ever tasted.

'I'm stuffed Roy; I couldn't eat another thing.'

'Do you want another drink or maybe a coffee?'

'No, thank you; let's get the bill and go home.'

Roy paid the bill and left a generous tip and as they left the restaurant noticed a young homeless girl sitting outside on the pavement.

'I hate to see that. She can't be much older than my sister. Do you have any change on you Marcie?'

'Sorry, I haven't.' And with that, Roy took £10 out of his wallet and put it in the girl's plastic cup.

'Thank you, and God bless,' she smiled, and carried on drinking her can of beer.

As they walked home they were both deep in thought. 'Do you think she is an alcoholic, Roy?'

'Probably, but you can't judge a book by its cover. God knows what happened in her past.'

When they got home they got undressed and went straight to bed. Marcie could see Roy was looking weary and wasn't surprised after the hectic week he'd had tidying up some of the loose ends, and then of course he would have been up very early to get to London at the time he did. Tiredness had caught up with him – with them both - and they went straight to sleep in each other's arms.

It was midday before they got out of bed and Marcie made them both a mug of tea. 'What would you like to do today?' she asked, putting the mugs down on the coffee table.

'Don't bother cooking, Marcie, we'll have a pub lunch.'

'I don't mind, really; I have loads of food in.'

'I know, but it's a sunny day and I want to take you out.'

'Well, all right, but I think you spoil me too much.'

'You're worth it. Now go and get ready; I'm just wearing my shorts and t-shirt. I'll shave later on.'

An hour later they were ready and set off for the short walk to the pub. As they were walking along the high street approaching the pub, Roy pointed out the familiar figure of the homeless girl they had seen the day before, this time sitting on a blanket in a shop doorway. Roy walked over to her. Although her clothes were old and ill-fitting she looked fairly clean and tidy considering the way she lived, and she had a pretty, round face, piercing blue eyes and long blonde hair.

'Have you eaten?' asked Roy, genuinely concerned.'

'No, I haven't - I'm hungry...'

He turned to Marcie. 'She can come in the pub and have lunch with us. This girl needs a decent meal down her.'

'Christ Roy, you don't know her!' whispered Marcie.

'We'll just feed her up and she can be on her way. I feel sorry for her.'

'Alright, but on your head be it. I don't think she is as innocent as she looks - she is probably as tough as old boots living on the streets.'

Roy turned to the girl. 'What's your name?'

'Sharon.'

'Why don't you come and eat with us - my shout.'

'Great! Just give me five minutes and I'll hide my stuff in the park round the corner and I'll come in the pub to you.'

Roy went to the bar and ordered a beer and a glass of red wine while Marcie found a table. It wasn't long before Sharon came in and they all sat down.

'What can I get you to drink Sharon?' asked Roy getting up again.

'A lager, please.'

Marcie felt uncomfortable and wasn't sure what to say once they were on their own. 'Do you come from this area, Sharon?'

'Yeah, Kentish Town, but I left home at sixteen.'

'Why?'

'I hated my stepfather; we couldn't get on at all.'

'How old are you?'

'Eighteen, but everyone says I'm mature for my age.'

'Have you any brothers or sisters?'

'An older brother – he's in the army. He's 26.'

Roy came back with Sharon's drink and sat down at the table, much to Marcie's relief. She had run out of things to say to the girl and was beginning to feel awkward sitting with this stranger making small talk. Roy was a bit more confident talking to Sharon, but then he had a sister more or less her age.

'I've ordered three Sunday lunches: roast beef, Yorkshire puddings and all the trimmings.'

'Thank you. I'll have to go as soon as I've eaten though in case my stuff gets nicked.'

'Why aren't you living in a hostel? Surely social workers can help you?' Roy asked.

'I've been in one and I hated it. Too many rules and regulations.'

The waitress came with the food and Sharon couldn't eat it quickly enough. She had nearly demolished everything on her plate and Roy and Marcie had barely started theirs. Roy bent down to pick up the napkin Sharon had just dropped on the floor. 'Do you fancy a dessert, Sharon? Have a look at the menu and choose what you want.'

'Nah, I have to go, but thanks anyway.'

The couple on the next table were looking over with interest. 'Excuse me,' the chap said to Roy, 'she's just pinched your wallet from your back pocket.'

'Are you saying I'm a thief?' shouted Sharon.

'Well I know what I saw. My wife saw you, too.'

'Fuck off you old gits and get your facts straight before you start accusing people!' Sharon hollered.

With that, the waitress came over to the table. 'Is everything OK here? Please keep the noise down or I'll have to ask you to leave I'm afraid.'

Marcie apologised, glaring at Sharon.

Roy checked his back pocket. His wallet was gone. 'Hand it over Sharon; that was a really stupid thing to do.'

'I don't know what you're talking about!'

'Yes you do. Now hand it back otherwise I'll call the police.'

Sharon panicked, reached inside her jacket, threw the wallet on the table and legged it out of the pub.

'Thanks mate,' said Roy to the chap on the next table. You try to do someone a good turn and they throw it in your face.'

'You can't help some people, lad,' the elderly gentleman replied. 'I'm just glad I spotted her doing it.'

Whilst Marcie was annoyed with Roy for being so trusting, she couldn't help admiring him - he had a good heart and always looked for the best in people. He paid the bill and apologised to her. 'Sorry sweetheart, that wasn't one of my better ideas.'

'You weren't to know Roy. Come on, let's get back to the flat - you'll be going home soon.'

'I hate driving in the dark so I'll be off in ten minutes, love.'

'Do you want a coffee before you go, Roy?'

'No, but I wouldn't say no to a cuddle.'

She went to him. Enveloped in his strong arms she could feel the tears welling up in her eyes. 'I wish you didn't have to go...'

'Come on,' he said, putting a finger gently under her chin and lifting her face to look in her lovely eyes, 'don't start getting upset. I'll be back before you know it.'

Chapter Twenty-Two

The next few months passed and things were much the same, with Roy continuing to make the long journey and stay with Marcie as much as he could, but inevitably there were times when arguments erupted because of her impatience. She was beginning to think living with Roy was just a pipe dream and found it hard to stay positive. She loved the few occasions when she got time off to spend her weekends with his family in West Yorkshire and hated the times when his work had to come first and he couldn't travel down to see her.

On one such occasion when Roy phoned to say he couldn't see her as he had a big job on, the feelings of loneliness overcame her and her thoughts turned to her mum. She hadn't seen her for some time and decided to give her a ring and invite her to stay. Nellie was out of rehab and living in a ground floor one bedroom council flat with the help of social services.

It had been another busy week at the shop and Marcie was exhausted and pleased it was Friday evening so she could relax. Her mum was getting a taxi from the station and was due to arrive at about 8 o'clock.

When Marcie opened the door to Nellie she was standing there holding a bunch of flowers she had bought from a stall at the station.

'That's a turn up for the books, Mum; you've never bought me flowers before! I assume they are for me?'

'Cheeky sod! Who else would they be for? Now let me sit down, I'm knackered.'

Marcie made some tea and brought it through on a tray. Looking at her mother she couldn't help but feel pleased – she looked amazing in her smart blue dress with her hair tied back in a bun, and even had make up on, which was very unusual for her.

'You're looking great, Mum.'

'I feel great...and believe it or not, I have a job.'

'Really? What kind of job?'

'I'm working at a residential home for the elderly as a care worker. Some of the residents are bed-bound, so it's hard work and at times challenging, but it's also very satisfying – I love it.'

'Oh, Mum, I'm so proud of you – you've come on leaps and bounds!'

'Enough talk about me, Marcie, I want to know all about what's happening in your life.'

'There's no easy way to say this, but I have multiple sclerosis, Mum.'

'Dear Lord! You poor child; why didn't you let me know?'

'I was worried the news would set you back...'

'Oh Marcie...I have really let you down, haven't I? As your mother you should be able to come to me with anything...'

'I think when Jack died you should have had some kind of counselling, to be honest, Mum.'

'Yes, I think you're right. I have never truly learned to live with Jack's death...but there was no excuse for the way I treated you. I know that now. I made so many mistakes... I'm so sorry, love.' She started to cry, overcome with feelings of guilt and shame.

'Well, you're here now, Mum. Let's make a fresh start - life's too short. My illness has taught me that I have to make the most of life, and by that I mean no regrets and no looking back – and I want you to be a part of my future – there's a lot to look forward to.'

'I promise you, Marcie, I won't disappoint you. I'm here for you whenever you need me. I've been given a second chance and I have no intention of letting you down ever again. I'll prove it to you.'

'Come on, no more tears – we're meant to be making up for lost time, not dwelling on the past. Now, you must be hungry; I'll make us a sandwich.'

'Let me do that; you put your feet up and relax; I intend to spoil you this weekend. Cup of tea with your sandwich?'

The next day Nellie suggested they go to the market where she bought Marcie a new dress and two new lamps for her bedroom. They called at the supermarket on the way home and she also bought all the groceries.

'Thanks Mum.'

'You're welcome. My feet are killing me now, let's go home.'

That evening Nellie cooked them cod, chips, and peas, and when the meal was over Marcie insisted on doing the washing up and afterwards made them both a cup of tea. They sat down on the settee with the TV on in the background.

'Do you have a boyfriend?' Nellie asked.

'Your memory's terrible, Mum – I told you about Roy on the phone when I last called!'

'Oh yes, I remember now. How are things going between you two?'

'Really good; he's my soul mate. I can't wait till he moves in with me but he has things to sort out at his end. He owns two properties – he's not long sold one but he still has to sell the other.'

'Rome wasn't built in a day, pet. Just be patient; he sounds like a really nice bloke – worth waiting for.'

'He is, Mum. You'll love him. I've stayed with his family in West Yorkshire – they're wonderful, and always make me feel so welcome - they can't do enough for me. Roy has a daughter called Molly; she's adorable.'

'I can't wait to meet them all.'

'You will, Mum, one day.'

'Are you still enjoying your job at the boutique?'

'I love it, but Bella has a buyer for the shop now so I will have to start looking around for another job soon... I'm not looking forward to that.'

'That's a shame. Will you do shop work again?'

'Not sure. I have to find the rent money and pay the bills so I may have no choice but to take anything that comes along.'

'What about Roy, can't he help you out?'

'He would but I'm not asking him. I prefer to be independent and earn my own money for as long as I'm capable.'

'You'll be alright, love, I feel it in my bones. And anyway, I have a few bob put away and it's yours if you ever need it.'

'Thanks Mum; I might have to take you up on that.'

'Please do - just say the word.'

'What's your flat like?'

'Lovely. It's very spacious considering it's only a one bedroom. I bought a sofa bed last week just in case you ever want to stay.'

'That's sweet of you, Mum.'

'Well, you know my home is yours and you're welcome any time. We have so much time to make up for...'

318

'Oh Mum, you're crying again. What's wrong?'

'I wish we were this close when you were growing up. I really made a mess of things, didn't I?'

'Yes, you screwed up, I agree, but we're getting on now and that's all that matters. Now wipe your eyes and you can give me a hand to get your bedding out; I feel shattered,' she said handing her a box of tissues.

It had been a lovely weekend and it was soon time for them to say their goodbyes. Marcie was surprised at just how sad she felt when Nellie had gone but told herself to snap out of it and think positively. After all, they were both in a good place and closer than they had ever been. She finally felt that she had a mum she could rely on, not to mention a new friend. She had a lot to be thankful for.

The following day Marcie went into work but could see Bella was in a funny mood and acting a little strange.

'I need to make a phone call Marcie, go out the back and make some coffee, would you?' Strange, she thought, Bella was usually quite open and made her phone calls in front of her, even if they were personal.

When she came back out with the coffee, Bella was deep in thought.

'Penny for them?'

Sorry, love, I was miles away. She took a sip of her coffee. 'Tell me, Marcie, if you had the shop what would you call it?'

'Marcie's Modes,' she said without hesitation. 'Why?'

'Good name. This bloke that's buying the shop wants to call it Tonia's Togs. How stupid is that? Right, we need to do a stock check today, so we had better get on.'

'We only did one last week,' Marcie remarked.

'Well I want to keep on top of things. Come on, let's get cracking.'

The day was spent checking every item in the shop while Ella served the customers. At lunchtime Ella was sent to the bakers for rolls and when she came back and the shop had emptied out, Bella turned the sign on the door to 'CLOSED' and called them through to the back where she had made them all a cup of tea.

'Come and sit down and have your lunch, girls, I need to talk to you both.' They did as they were asked. 'Thank you. Now, as you know, I have a buyer for the shop. Today I've had the news that everything has gone through and the new owners will take over on the first of next month.' Marcie and Ella looked at each other. 'Don't look so worried - I'm hoping there's a chance they'll keep you on, but at this stage I can't make any promises. Ultimately it's up to the new owners and they will discuss your future employment before they take over. I would like to thank you both so much for all the support and help you have given me and intend to give you each a month's salary to show my appreciation.'

Marcie's face dropped, the realization that she could soon be out of a job hitting her hard for the first time. She had been so happy working for Bella. A tear ran down her cheek.

'Hey, come on, love, let's have none of that. We will always keep in touch Marcie; you know I'm here for you always.'

Ella on the other hand took it in her stride and didn't seem too concerned. She still lived at home with her parents and she had already enquired about a job at the new department store up the road.

At closing time Bella gave Marcie a big hug and couldn't help but feel guilty, though she knew she had a lot to look forward to in the future..

That evening Roy phoned to say he was travelling up on Friday afternoon and would arrive at about six o'clock. Marcie was pleased; as usual she had missed him and more than ever needed him to confide in after Bella's news.

On Friday Bella let Marcie leave at 5 o'clock and she rushed home filled with excitement at the coming weekend with Roy. She had a quick tidy round, ran a brush through her hair, applied some lipstick and sat and waited for him. Every time she heard a car outside she would jump up and look out of the window expecting it to be him. When Roy's car finally pulled up she rushed out to greet him, and when he got out of the car she flung her arms around him.

'My goodness Marcie, what a nice welcome! What I have I done to deserve this? Come on, let's go indoors.'

'Roy, why are you wearing a suit and tie?'

'I just thought we could go somewhere special tonight.'

'Ooh, lovely!' She went to the boot of the car to take out his small holdall as she always did.

'That's OK, sweetheart; I'll come out and get it in a while. Let's go inside, I'm parched after that journey.'

They went inside. 'Do you want a cuppa?'

'No, but I wouldn't mind a beer.'

'Well, you're in luck; I have some in the fridge.'

Roy sat down in the armchair with his drink. 'My god Roy, get changed, you must feel so uncomfortable dressed up like that. You look like you've been to a wedding,' she laughed.

'I'm alright. It's not worth getting changed; I'm taking you out in an hour or so. Go on, get your glad rags on. I'm going to take you somewhere really nice tonight.'

'Well, that's lovely, but what's the hurry?'

'I'm starving for one thing, and the sooner we eat the sooner I can bring you home and have you all to myself.'

'OK, when you put it like that... I'll just go and get ready then,' she said tossing him the TV remote. 'Help yourself to another beer if you want. I won't be too long,' she said happily.

When Marcie reappeared in the room she looked amazing in a black mini dress, which she had adorned with a colourful long beaded necklace and red high heels. She also wore a red hair band which held her fringe back and the rest of her long black curly hair tumbled down over her shoulders. She wore very little make-up, just a touch of mascara to accentuate her thick lashes and a little lipstick. She was a sight for sore eyes and Roy couldn't believe how stunning she looked.

'Marcie Thomas, you are the most beautiful girl I have ever seen.'

'Thank you, kind sir.'

'Come on, let's get going.'

It was a beautiful evening and Marcie felt so special holding Roy's hand walking down the road. As they neared Bella's Boutique it dawned on her. 'I know where we are going. To our favourite restaurant, the one near Bella's.'

'Which one's that then?' Roy asked.

'The Italian one.'

Roy didn't answer and she could see he was miles away. 'What are you thinking about?'

'Nothing sweetheart.'

She was about to question him further when her eyes were drawn across the road to Bella's and two people standing outside deep in conversation. As they got nearer she could see that it was Bella and Barry. 'Look, Roy. What would Bella and Barry be doing outside the shop at this time? It's been shut a couple of hours. I do hope nothing's happened...'

'Well, we had best cross over and find out. Come on.'

Roy took Marcie's hand and they crossed the road and walked up to them. 'Is everything alright Bella? What's happened?'

'You had better come into the shop and see, Marcie,' Bella replied, a grave look on her face.

As they all walked through the door the first thing she saw was a huge banner which read: *UNDER NEW MANAGEMENT – MARCIE'S MODES.*

Marcie stood there staring at it in astonishment. 'But I don't understand.' She turned to Roy who had a huge grin on his face. And then the penny dropped. 'Roy, you haven't?'

'Yes, I have, my darling, it's true – it's all ours. And I have one more surprise,' he said getting down on one knee and producing a small blue velvet box from out of his jacket pocket. Marcie gasped when she saw the beautiful diamond and ruby engagement ring inside. 'Marcie Thomas, will you marry me?'

'Oh Roy, of course I will! Yes!' and she broke down and cried with happiness.

'It's my grandmother's ring – Mum and Dad wanted you to have it.'

Bella's eyes were brimming with tears. 'You sly old dog – you kept that part quiet! Congratulations to you both!'

Roy put the ring on her finger and just as he did there was a chorus of 'Surprise!' and from out the back came Malcolm, Nellie, Jane and Justin, Zoe and Charlie and Amy and Doris.

Marcie was dumbfounded. 'How on earth did you arrange all this?' she asked no one in particular. Just then Barry and Bella reappeared carrying a beautiful cake with *Marcie's Modes* on it and a huge bottle of champagne, and Marcie burst into tears again. 'I don't know what to say, except thank you...and miracles do happen. I really am the luckiest girl in the world.'

Roy thanked everyone, especially Bella who had managed to keep it all a secret for the last few months.

'Thank god it's out at last,' she said smiling. I don't know how I didn't let the cat out of the bag!'

The celebrations went on long into the evening and when they had thanked everyone and the last guest had gone Marcie and Roy walked home hand in hand.

'It's ever so nice of Bella to put Malcolm and my mum up for the weekend. She's a good old stick.'

'Yes, she is,' agreed Roy. 'Tonight couldn't have happened without her. You couldn't have asked for a nicer boss.'

'I want this weekend to last forever. I hate to think of you leaving on Sunday afternoon.'

'No chance darling; I'm here to stay now. I just hope you have room for all my worldly possessions.'

'Do you mean it, Roy? Really?'

'Well, I have four suitcases in the boot of my car. I'm staying if you'll have me.'

Throwing her arms round him they held each other tightly, safe in the knowledge that nothing would ever come between them and the love they had for each other. She could finally put the past behind her and look forward to the future ahead, and she felt truly blessed to have good friends, a good relationship with her mum and most of all Roy, the man who she truly loved – her soul mate. What more could a girl ask for?

***